An Oath Sworn

Saga of the Stone King Book 1

M. T. Kadisin

KRAKEN TREE

Kraken Tree Publishing

DEDICATION

For Jemma.
My muse and favorite reading buddy, without whom this book would
never exist.

PART 1

Divided by catastrophe, cut off from each other, Pre-Unification era city-states developed unique societal quirks centered around age and genealogy. In Icemount Fastness, tracking one's age, and the accumulation of status, involved a complex system of face painting. The denizens of Rockhome practically worshiped their genealogy. This belief blighted the so-called *Clanless* into a state of perpetual servitude and poverty in the heart of a thriving mountain. There are many examples such as these. Let us learn from them.

-From *Lessons from the Past*, Alberth of Clan Seraphinite, Historian, 2798 U.E.

INK SPILLS, GREEN EYES

His foes' corpses were stacked like cords of wood as high as his waist. Grady the Invincible surveyed the quiet battlefield with a fierce smile, his thick beard's intricate and torc filled braids fluttering in the wind. Blood dripped artfully from the raised blade of his trusty ax. The impressively massive, double-bladed weapon swung over his head as he roared out his victory. The other thegen around him raised their weapons and added their cries to the din.

The goblin raiders were many, but they stood no chance against the defenders of Rockhome and their honored leader.

Emerlda stepped out of the crowd of huddling miners, safe behind the line held by the storied protectors. She removed her helmet and shook out her long blond locks, setting the shining fringe of golden hair lining her chin to wave. The small red cut on her cheek and her shining green eyes contrasted sharply against the dusting of black over the rest of her. "I knew you'd come. As soon as those things broke through the walls, I knew."

Grady's chest swelled with fear and something softer, warmer. He reached over and drew Emerlda in a couple steps. She was a tall dvergr, but she only reached his chin. Grady looked her over again in relief at finding her unharmed. "I'm just glad you're alright."

Emerlda stepped closer to Grady. The warmth radiating from her stoked his heart's furnace. Her smell, wholly her own, made him dizzy. She leaned in even closer and tilted her head up to him. "Grady," she whispered urgently. Grady closed his eyes and leaned in anticipating the taste of her lips.

A strong hand shook him at the shoulder. "Phukit's coming Grady. Wake up."

"Gah!" Ripped from his dream, Grady jumped in his seat, his knees knocking painfully into the underside of his desk. The violent upheaval upset the pot of waiting ink, spilling its contents over the nearly completed forms. It glowed a faint green in the lichen light of his office. "What? Phukit! Oh shit." He looked at the clock on his wall. Fifteen to Ten. "Shit." He took in the sight of the ink eating up the neatly numbered rows of a particularly tricky maintenance cost report. "I can fix it. I can fix it." Grady dipped at the spill with the corner of his already stained smock. "Thanks, Emerlda. I'm at the end of a triple. Phukit promised to fire me if she caught me napping again!"

"She's down the corner and should be here..."

His supervisor interrupted from the doorway, brusk and unamused. "Having some sort of gathering are you, Computer Grady?"

"No, Senior Clerk." Grady shuffled to the side, hiding the spill and the fresh ink on his sleeves behind his back.

Senior Clerk Phukit examined Emerlda over her handlebar swooped beard. She took her time to absorb the scene before her. She adjusted her brown and gold tartan jacket and lightly touched her paisley neck scarf. Phukit pivoted to face Emerlda. Grady was relieved when her tone was cool and polite. "And you are?"

"I'm Emerlda, daughter of Rubin. Miner. B-Class." She held out her hand. Her warm open smile was at such odds with Phukit's stoney expression, Grady couldn't help but grin. He did his best to hide it behind a cough.

"Pleasure." One pump and Phukit released her grip. "Pardon me." Her return smile was business sharp and polite and faded once her attention returned to Grady. "Computer Grady, have you compiled the maintenance numbers yet?"

"Yes, of course."

Phukit held out her hand. "Well?"

"Yes, of course, I had it done." Grady braced himself. He cast about for some way to soften the blow. Quickly he decided there was only one way out. Through. "There was an accident..." He stepped aside revealing the mess behind him. Grady prepared his best cringe. Done properly it would blunt the force of Phukit's incoming tirade.

Phukit scowled and pursed her lips, building up pressure to let him have it all in one go. Emerlda ducked around her and interposed herself between them. "It was my fault, Senior Clerk. Practically kicked the door in when I arrived. Forgot I was in an office for a second."

The Senior Clerk peered over Emerlda's shoulder at Grady, who shrugged apologetically. "I am easily startled, Senior Clerk."

Pinching the bridge of her nose she sighed. She took note of the time. "These things happen. Emerlda, was it? Computer I believe you are on the end of a triple?"

"Yes, Senior Clerk."

She referred to several sheets of paper on her clipboard. "According to my notes, your output was more than acceptable. Thank you for your efforts. I know triples can be rough. Once you have cleaned up this mess and repaired any ruined work you may clock out. Take a double off. Rest up."

"Yes, Senior Clerk. Thank you, Senior Clerk." He bobbed out several short bows.

"It was a pleasure to make your acquaintance, Miner B-Class."

"Yours too, Senior Clerk." One more quick shake and Phukit was out the door checking on the clerk in the next office over.

"Oh, wow, 'Merlda. You really saved my bacon. I owe you one. No, five. I owe you five." Grady wanted to run forward and give her a big hug. He didn't, but he wanted to.

"What are friends for?" She shrugged her strong, rounded shoulders. The light in the room flickered along the golden outlines of the tattoos covering her arms. Grady admired how she looked in the glow from his office lamp. She had clearly taken the time to trade in the miner's end of shift coating of grime for the artful smudging favored by those who followed the fashions from Up-Wall. Her eyes were tastefully darkened and a thumb wide streak of smoke marred the playful yellow fringe of the hair dangling from her jaw line. The way she was smiling at him, with her thumbs tucked into the belt of her pale gray coveralls, thrilled him to his toes. "What's that you're reading?"

"Huh?" Grady followed her eyes and saw his novel open, pages down. The cover sported two weapon wielding figures clothed mostly in sweat and tasteful lines of blood. Grady grabbed up the book and held it behind his back. "Oh. Ha. Nothing. Just another of my silly heroes' tales." Looking up at Emerlda's warm face encouraged a blush to bloom on his cheeks. He hoped his beard hid most of it.

"A bunch of the crew are going to get a flagon and some deep fried 'shrooms at some new tavern near the East Wall." She brushed an errant strand of hair behind her ear. There was a dare poorly hidden in her merry green eyes. "Care to come?"

"Uh." His mind worked furiously. He looked back and forth between the mess on his desk and his friend. The world, for a moment, sparkled green. "I'd love to, really, but..." He gestured vaguely behind himself.

"Yeah! Of course. Gotta keep the bosses happy." Grady was sure he only imagined the slight disappointment in her voice. She stopped half out of his office door and leaned against the jam. "We'll be there for a good chunk of the shift. If this doesn't take you a rock's age to fix up, maybe you could meet us, me, there after?"

"Uh. Yeah. For sure, yeah. Shouldn't take me more than an hour or two."

"Alright! Get to it. No shirking. The pub's a part of block 625 East. I'll be waiting. See yuh soon, Grady. Sorry again!" She waved enthusiastically.

"No need to apologize! Thank you!" Grady followed her out of the door with a half raised wave of his own waiting to see if she would look back. She didn't. Not that it mattered.

The bone deep weariness that nearly ninety straight hours at a desk engenders in a body evaporated. There was no room for exhaustion, Grady had plans! Plans to hang out, to get some drinks with, of all dvergr, Emerlda.

The glowing pond of ink on his desk mocked his newfound excitement. He grumbled at the delay created by care as he bent the paper around the ruinous liquid and poured the spilled ink into the trash. A critical examination of his handiwork revealed that not too much was ruined and all of it was legible enough. A simple copy job would not keep him.

He bounced in his chair as he grabbed some clean sheets, filled his pen from a different, upright inkwell, and took a moment to breathe and shake out his hands to settle them. He dutifully copied figures onto a clean sheet, freeing a great portion of his mind to imagine the revelry to come. His mind's eye watched himself open the pub door. With a rush, Emerlda leaps up and drags him to a seat next to her at the bar. Grady hears indistinct echoes of himself being funny, winning Emerlda's miner friends over. Their slaps on the back are hard but well meaning. The scene changes to a quiet corner where just Emerlda and he sits to drink and talk away the late hours of the shift. Then... who knows.

In the real world, the practical one with paperwork to fix and a boss to please, the clean pages filled with numbers neatly written and correctly summed and subtracted. Each column represented the cost of some vital piece of the puzzle that kept the mine functioning at peak efficiency. A flicker of satisfaction at the fresh copies flared like a spark from an anvil and was gone. He placed it in the clearly marked 'Done' tray. Grady shuttered his lamp, cutting off the lichens' glow. He sat in the darkness for a moment to steel himself for what was to come.

As he locked up his office, he realized he forgot his book. "Yup. That seems right." He chafed at even this small delay.

Once he hitched his bag onto his shoulder, one novel heavier, Grady started to wend his way to Eastern block 625. A press of dvergr bodies filled the raised walkway. Grady waited for a gap in incoming pedestrian traffic, scuttled into the opening, and began to make his way upstream against the flood of miners entering the yard ready to start their next working shift. Normally, the pathways flowed in both directions, but Grady had not left on time. Shifts wait for no one. Grady had to concentrate to successfully weave his way through the push of gray clad bodies. A misjudged angle caused a passing shoulder to slam into him. That was going to bruise. He rubbed his shoulder and hoped that the passing miner's shoulder also hurt, that their brief collision impacted the other person at least a little.

Once he reached the pedestrian gate, Grady swung out of the press and found the small open space between the wall and flow of bodies. He leaned against the wrought iron fence, waiting for the shift change traffic to end and for the walkway to grow a little quieter. His desire to join up with Emerlda urged him onward, but the traffic was against him and clearer paths would make for faster travel. Ignoring the constant rumble of the laden chain carts in the sunken avenues below, he continued to rub at his shoulder and looked up as the last reflected rays of the sun painted the Ceiling with reds and purples.

Through the coal-dark fog Grady was able to make out bits of the great stalactite palaces that housed Rockhome's elite. They hung over the Floor like all consuming teeth from Wall to Wall to Wall to Wall in every direction. Far above him, Grady could just make out the small color-filled figures of people walking along the impossibly delicate looking layers of artistically carved bridges and walkways strung between the buildings. Not for the first time Grady wondered what it would be like to work and live above the continuous pall of noxious, industrial fog that clung to the Floor.

By the time the last of the miners left the pathway, only the highest reaches of the Ceiling were colored by the fading sun. The Floor itself was deep in darkness's grip. Even during the height of a topside day, the gloom was never fully banished. The street lights flickered to life as their internal clockwork ignited pilot lights and opened up gas spouts. Patchy warning paint glowed in the dim light, lining the walkways to keep unwary pedestrians from falling into the constantly moving carts below.

After all, the cost would be too high to halt the flow of commerce for such a small, cheap thing as an individual's lost life.

After the press of the shift change the new openness of the walkway was a balm to Grady's bruised shoulder and the habitually emotional ache he felt when alone in a large crowd.

Without others around it was easier to know that he mattered.

He left the mine's entrance way and entered the lamp lit pathways of the Floor proper. Grady walked with his hands in his pockets and his eyes locked on the Ceiling as it twinkled with its own lights. Millions of bright points outlined the hanging buildings and their spiderweb of walkways. Stories about the night sky brought by surface traders spoke about the stars that twinkled in that impossible empty firmament.

As far as Grady was concerned, they could keep it. He could not imagine a sight more impressive or one with more twinkle than the Ceiling in the darkt. *I wonder if the people up there ever look down here? Does the Floor sparkle as much?* He doubted it. They probably couldn't see a thing through the fog.

Grady had not spent any time on the east side of the city during his fifty odd years of life. The orphan asylum in which he grew up was in the North West, if it still existed. Both the tenement he called home and the mine office where he spent most of his time were westerly. The sameness of every inch of the Floor and the effort it took to remain alive and comfortable stifled any desire Grady possessed to explore. Despite his lack of familiarity with the immediate area surrounding his destination, Grady's steps never faltered nor did he ever feel lost. He knew how the grid worked and which way was east. Concentrating on his path made it easier to ignore the building buzz of stomach churning anticipation about what was to come.

The sounds of raucous singing drew Grady down one of block 625 East's side streets. He stopped in front of a door underneath the same simple sign that read 'Pub' and hung over every one of the Floor's many drinking establishments. He remained still, staring up at the sign for a good few minutes.

He stood frozen by an internal war. One faction consisted of his joy at being invited by Emerlda, his hopes about what that invite meant, and his excitement about being wanted at any kind of social situation. They battled the Adversaries, a teeming horde of Grady's doubts and insecurities, supported by lumbering, monstrous cadres of fear and inadequacy.

The door flung open and two figures, linked by arms flung over shoulders, burst out into the street dragging noise and the funk of good beer in their wake. They swayed and stumbled off into the city singing the bawdy chorus of some drinking song that reddened Grady's ears and added three new words to his vocabulary. The party beyond the swiftly shutting door pinned Grady in place with awful fascination. Dvergr, jammed from wall to wall, standing and at tables, hoisted flagons, conversed with lubricated vigor, or laughed heartily in unison.

The door swung shut and Grady made some calculations. The arms he saw hauling drinks were as thick as his leg. A number of the seated revelers still topped Grady's standing height by a hand. The pub was a boozer, one of the unofficial miner only establishments spread throughout the Floor. Grady had never been to one before. He wouldn't dare.

This is too much. I can't. He'd apologize to Emerlda and say the work took longer than expected. *Next time for sure.* He'd even promise. *If there's a next time.*

The muffled cries and shouts of a good time bubbled behind the door.

"First fear, then bravery," Grady quoted and pressed against the solid rectangle of the book in his shoulder bag. He slapped his palms to his cheeks, the sharpish shock grounding him. The promise of Emerlda drew him in like a loadstone. With a gulp Grady pushed the door inward on its two way hinges and stepped into the alien world of a pub at full swing.

BELLY UP

Aside from a few gray beards, who glared over their drinks, none of the reveling miners noticed Grady's entrance. They turned away from his sheepish smile with disinterest and resumed their conversation. How they could hear each other, even sitting knee to knee as they were at the bar, was beyond Grady's understanding. The patrons' songs, conversations, cheers, and guffaws filled the stone room with a din that buffeted Grady's temples.

There's that headache.

He stood in the doorway searching in vain for a glimpse of Emerlda. Gaps between elbows and the ever shifting lines of sight created by bodies in transit provided only narrow tunnels to spy more elbows and faceless bodies. Propped up on his tiptoes proved the better vantage. Straining beyond his normal height allowed him to see over shoulders and get a sense for the undulating press of revelers.

At the opposite end of the bar he caught a glimpse of a familiar green. The sudden thumping of his heart managed to drown out the pub's forceful ambiance. He swallowed, squared his shoulders, and began to weave his way through the crowded space while trying to figure out the best way to say hello.

Hey there! Too simple. *Greetings, Emerlda.* Too formal. *Emerlda? What a surprise? You drink here too?* No, she invited him. Though, on second thought she might consider that funny. *Hail and well met!* He snorted at that one. Was he going to make a grandiose bow, like an actor playing some antique roll, as well?

His back foot caught on something, sending him tumbling forward. On his way down he crashed through a tray heavy-laden with frothing steins. He barely had time to catch himself before he slammed face first into the ground. He lay there for a moment, soggy with sticky beer, disbelief vying for supremacy against a sense of the inevitable.

"Oye!" a gruff voice shouted into the new bubble of silence surrounding the incident. "Get him up, my squadies." Two sets of hands grabbed him by his shoulders and hauled him off his feet to hover before a burley dvergr. A mean smile cut through his squared beard below hard eyes sharpened by anger and the potential of violence.

Grady hated the automatic snivel that entered his voice as he attempted to diffuse the situation. "I am terribly sorry. Just an accident. I tripped..." Square Beard cut him off by leaning in until their noses almost touched. The angry miner gave him a once over and sneered.

"You're no miner. Too puny." His rough hands grabbed Grady's wrists and turned his palms up, red from the fall. "Not a single callus. You some kind of paper pushing 'crat?" He practically spat the word out.

Grady nodded. More words bubbled up under the angry dvergr glare. "A computer. At Iron Mine Six."

"Move," Square Beard ordered one of his friends. He forced Grady's long sleeve up, revealing his bare upper arm. "Pfft. Not even related to a miner. You got some pair of stones to walk into a boozer uninvited. Think sitting around in a chair, safe as you please, earns you the right to drink here? With us?"

Grady mumbled a reply too quiet to be heard over the ambient noise.

"Eh? Got something to say?" Square Beard leaned back in, clearly enjoying himself and putting on a show for the small audience that gathered in to watch.

"I was invited," Grady said, drooping into the grip of the toughs. "By a friend."

"Invited you say?" Square Beard repeated as if it was the funniest joke under the mountain. His cronies yucked it up too. "That's all fine and good." He brushed ineffectually at the bits of sawdust stuck to Grady's tunic. "One problem though, my new clerky friend. Those drinks you knocked down were for me and mine." He gestured at a table full of dvergr. "Seems to me that you owe us a replacement round. What say you?"

Grady's mind automatically tabulated the cost of a table full of drinks. Secure in his wallet was the last of his money until the next pay-day, only enough coin for a few drinks. He'd planned to buy Emerlda a round or two as a sign of his largesse. "I don't think-" The hardening scowls of his new acquaintances stopped him short. He pulled out his money with a shaky hand and held it out to Square Beard.

"Oh how generous," he said with his chest puffed out, eliciting more laughter from his cronies. Square Beard donned a playful air, pinching the wallet and lifting it for a shake near his ear. The act dropped away at the meager tinkling of Grady's few coins. He dumped the wallet's contents onto his palm and slammed them on the table with disgust.

The table of dvergr looked from the small stack of coins to Grady. Shrinking between his shoulders, Grady wished himself away. He cursed himself for coming here. For daring. For being brave. For hoping. Anger soured his stomach.

"Seems like you're a little... short," said one of the miners holding Grady up. She mugged for the chuckling table and tightened her grip until it hurt.

The other gave Grady a little shake. "Wasting drinks! Punishable offense around here, I think, yeah?" He flicked Grady's forehead with a sausage-thick finger.

Square Beard pushed the others back a little. Grady distrusted the calm, conciliatory way he spoke. "Now, now. I'm as parched as the next dvergr, but there's a right and wrong way, right? Our little lost friend has incurred a debt and we demand repayment now." The smooth curve of his smile, at odds with his edged eyes, sent a shiver down Grady's spine. "Fetch a rod."

Shouts of "A rod! A rod!" sprung up in the immediate vicinity. A straight metal bar made its way hand to hand over from the bar to Square Beard.

The large miner leaned down so as to be eye to eye with Grady. He held the rod out to Grady. "Come on, take it." He teased and waggled it a little, while Grady stared. "Take it," Square Beard snapped.

Grady clutched the metal bar to his chest. It felt heavier than it should. Looking from face to face of the crowd surrounding him, he readied himself for the blow he knew was coming.

"Bend it and you're free to go. We'll forget what you owe and let you be about your merry way." He must have noticed Grady's incredulous looks at the thumb thick metal rod in his hands. "Think it's impossible, eh? Look."

Following his finger Grady took in the wall behind the bar. It was covered with countless metal hooks each bearing bent metal rods.

"This is a miner's bar, 'crat. You ain't strong enough to bend the rod you ain't worthy of bending your elbow," a voice sneered into his ear.

"Aye. Well said." Square Beard nodded and crossed his bulging and scared arms. "Any questions?"

Grady knew the answer, but asked anyway. "What happens when-if I can't bend the rod?"

"You don't have the metal to make up what you owe. Fail to bend it and we get to take what you owe out of your hide." Square Beard's even tone led Grady to believe that either way was fine by him. "Bend it. Bend it!" he waved his arms encouraging the crowd to take up his chant.

The onlookers crowded in, smothering Grady's fledgling plan to throw down the metal bar and make a break for it. He sighed from the bottom of his feet. He held the bar out in front of himself and tried to bend the rod, to bring his hands together and get out of this situation physically unharmed.

His every effort was met with ridicule and laughter. He strained until it felt like something inside of him would burst. Using his knee as leverage only ended up hurting his knee. Propping the bar against the ground and stomping on it did nothing. Exhausted and panting he dropped the bar.

They pummeled Grady to the ground, where he rolled up into a ball to protect his softer parts. Undeterred, they rained kicks on him, bruising his forearms and back. Next thing he knew he was flying into and through the pub's doors and tumbling against the stoney walkway. His bag followed, landing on his chest.

A minute spent soaking in the ground's chill was cut short when the aches started. Knowing from experience that the pain from a beating grew worse before it got better, Grady lurched to his feet to find his way home. He caught the eye of a pair of chainmail armored thegen patrolling the streets. One whispered to the other. They both laughed and continued on their route.

By the time Grady stood before the plain rock facade of Family Millan's Boarding House (Now with REAL running water), every inch of Grady hurt. None of the other off-shift dvergr in the common room paid him any mind as he struggled to scrape a bowl's worth of stew from one of the pots hanging over the wall-length smoldering fire. One of the perks of renting a room here. All the food you could stand.

He walked into his room, placed the bowl of stew down on his desk, and closed the door. The world shrunk to the size of his small room and Grady finally let go. Tears streaming down his face, he limped over into his bed and curled up once more. He tried to savor the dusty scent of the books piled up near his bed stand. The collection, made up of stories of ancient heroes, of adventures impossible, and of loves requited, or not, mocked him. Their richly colored and garish covers promised that things worked out and that happy endings happen.

A ball of suffering inside and out, Grady wanted to sink deep into his mattress, through the stone, and into the empty nothingness beneath all things. But his heart kept beating. His stomach rumbled. A voice in his head reminded him that rent was due soon. Another complained that food seemed to always cost more and the last of his coin was back on a table in that cursed pub. It was impossible to escape the weariness of three straight shifts of work leadening his bones.

At least the stomach I can fix.

Groaning, he hobbled out of bed and grabbed his stew. He winced as he flopped a little too hard into his chair. Forcing down spoonfuls of the ever cooling and thickening stew, Grady was full of wishes. Instead of cold stew washed down with watery ale, he wished for a plate piled high with deep fried 'shrooms and a freshly poured flagon. He wished the lonely silence of his room, punctuated by the scrapes of his spoon in the bowl were instead Emerlda's tinkling laughter. Laughter inspired by some witty joke. He wished his sigh was full of contentment and inspired by a wonderful meal and dear company.

A mean, insidious voice wished for strength, for revenge, for the chance to dish out the pain for once.

Having had enough stew, beer, and wishes for now, too tired and sore to read, Grady undressed with care. As he slipped under his covers, he hoped that next shift would be a better one.

It wasn't.

Grady, heart sick and sore, never managed to sleep. He stayed in bed in a restful enough stupor until the bells rang to indicate the start of a new shift. To say he enjoyed lying in his bed listening to the peal reverberate through his room was a stretch, but there was a calm stillness he appreciated. The humming ring washed his mind clear for a moment.

Grady sat up in his bed. He prodded at his sorest bits and debated with himself. Phukit had granted him a double, he had one more shift to spend at leisure before he returned to work. The idea of taking a shift by himself, to read and recuperate sounded lovely. An escape, even a short one, might help leach some of the sadness from his bones. Then his traitorous stomach growled again. His larder was nearly empty. More importantly, so was his wallet, wherever it was.

Costs rattled through his head. Everything cost coin and rent was due soon. Even sitting in his room doing nothing, going nowhere, and eating what was on hand cost him in the form of lost wages. Turns out the most relaxing thing he could do was go to work. Being busy made the time pass quicker as well. A glance to the small clock made of exposed gears sitting on his desk read a quarter past ten. As long as he got to the mine's office by one he could get a full shift in.

Lucky me. He bit back his groan as he stood and gathered his toiletries.

When he opened his door and saw the line for the communal washroom winding past, Grady sighed through his nose. No matter when he awoke there was always a cartful of other tenants waiting, towels and toiletry bags in hand. They chatted quietly in sibling groups of twos or threes, bathed in the lime green fluorescent light of the cheaper lichen. The line was inorganically straight, following the path worn into the floor by the hundreds of years worth of inhabitants who had come before.

The small clusters eyed Grady with disdain as he walked past them to the end of the line. Some even flexed their bare biceps to better show off the few family names tattooed there. Clanless, by definition, lacked the support and history afforded a dvergr by their clan. The dvergr, in Grady's tenement, existed as a fractured scree of small family units, scattered by accident or tragedy. Clanless only looked out for their relatives, a survival trait beaten into them by the rest of Rockhome's inhabitants.

Grady tugged at the cuffs of his long sleeved, ash-gray robe. He kept his eyes to himself as he took his place at the end of the line. A particularly deep breath sent a lance of pain down his side.

"Oh me, oh my? What have we here, brother?"

"I don't know, brother. Can't be a dvergr can it?"

Experience told Grady that ignoring the twins only made things worse. Forcing his gloom down, he plastered an integrating smile on his face. He turned around and nodded. "Good shift start, Kaluk. Kulak."

Two dvergr loomed over Grady. Identical of feature, the two brothers had taken to wearing opposite beards to ensure that everyone could tell who was who. Kaluk wore long mutton chops and a goatee that ended in long braids. Kulak sported a luscious horseshoe mustache, sporting a few shiny beads.

Kulak elbowed Kaluk. He made a show of examining Grady. "I think yer right though. Can't be a dvergr. Too small. Patchy moss for a beard. Check his arms!"

There was no point in resisting. The two miners possessed grips of iron. Last time he struggled they had placed his head in the toilets and flushed a few times. Oh, how they laughed. Together the twins pulled back his robe sleeves, only to pantomime shock and disgust at finding his arms bare of ink.

"You were right," Kaluk said to Kulak. "Can't be a dvergr, can it? But it's underground, isn't it? Must be a type of rock."

"It certainly doesn't belong here though. Just some erratic blocking our path, yeah?"

Sharing a brain, the two reveled in their cruel cleverness. Their raucous laughter filled the hall and earned them a few displeased stares from the other residents in line. One or two shot a pitying look Grady's way. He begged for help with his eyes, but he knew none was coming. He wasn't their concern. His name did not belong to them. The twins glared back until everyone returned to minding their own business.

With his gaze even lower, Grady was unsure which of the twins ordered him to "Move."

"Yes, of course. Please." Grady mumbled as he shifted around them. He was shoulder checked for his trouble as they took his spot. The fact they neither noticed or cared that his arms and face were speckled with bruises was not surprising. However, the lump forcing its way into his throat at their blindness was. They were the only two dvergr in this whole place that ever spoke with him for whatever that's worth.

The word 'erratic' echoed in his head. It was a word referring to an out of place rock. One moved by geological forces to a new location where it did not belong. The worst part was that Grady could not deny it fit. From the new back of the line, Grady watched the others talk, laugh, plan, discuss, and simply be near each other, quiet and comfortable.

The line shifted forward as each took their turns at the handful of doored stalls. Each stall was a tight bathroom all its own, complete with a pull-chain activated shower, sink, toilet, and mirror. The slight funk of astringent, cleaning supplies, and standing water was a bonus.

Grady took his turn. He pulled the chains and turned the knobs that summoned the water from wherever it came from. Though Grady had always known running water, it was a relatively recent development of the last six decades or so.

"Ancestors be praised," Grady said with a pleased groan. There was still warm water left. Truly a miracle and a bright spot in his shift worth noting. It washed away some of his ache and a bit of the shame an encounter with the twins always inspired. With sensations this good, Grady reasoned, life was not all bad. The events of his excursion last shift played out in his memory.

Just mostly.

Grady prodded at the bruising on his cheek bone, grateful he didn't have a black eye. He gingerly brushed his beard in the mirror, wishing with each stroke that he could braid it, shape it, anything. The patchy growth left him few options. There was no unguent or oil or extract under the mountain that could help. He had tried them all. Leaving him with no other options than to hope and make due.

The never diminishing line ignored him as he returned to his room. He hung up his towel and toiletries, walked over to his meager closet. For no one, he made a show of rubbing his chin. "Ah, choices choices," Grady said as he stared at his monochrome collection. He felt a little ridiculous struggling to decide between wearing his slate gray tabby spun tunic or the granite twill one or the shale one with the subtle swirled pattern. Gray on gray on gray. He pretended it mattered, that they looked different, that he wore them differently. He almost fooled himself most shifts.

Since there was no need to rush, Grady took his time as he made his sandwich from the last of his provisions. The process soothed him somewhat. Grady sawed off slabs of the good, brown bread, a luxury he never skimped on. The sound of the knife moving through the bread and the smell as more of its soft core was exposed to the air were two little pleasures he could count on. Today's filling was a thick sausage of cured pork and spices. He slathered one slice of bread with mayo and the other with mustard. He wrapped it in wax paper wrap and carefully placed it, along with his current book, in his bag.

His trudge to work lacked the beauty of the sparkling city above and the softening of oncoming darkness. The skylights that fed the sun's rays into the heart of the mountain were a newer edition to Rockhome than the plumbing. In the daylight filtering from above, the Floor's grimey and grim nature was writ large. It was the oldest part of Rockhome. The founding ancestors had started from the bottom and worked their way up, carving their city from the bones of the mountain. Each building, the walkways, the sunken tracks for the constantly moving carts, were a mass of right angles and plain surfaces. All artistry was saved for the tunnel communities of the Walls and the palaces and bridges of the Roof. The signs hanging over doors or the occasional wide shop window were the only indication that different things were going on behind the repetitive facades.

Normally, Grady admired the beauty of the Floor's design. The simplicity of its aesthetics were at odds with the complexities of its function. In thousands of years there had been no expansions or changes made to the cart tracks, walkways, or even the foundational sewers beneath it all. There was room enough to allow for the innovations of the gas lamps and the aforementioned miracle of running, warm water.

The ancestors were wise and forward-thinking.

This shift all Grady saw was the centuries of industrial grime hiding the striations, glinting with minerals and subtle variations of color, of the deep rock. Could they have guessed the place it all started would become the primary home of the Clanless outcasts of their people? Would they have cared?

Grady was consumed by the mass of dvergr. The foot traffic on the walkways was slow and hurried all at once. Everyone had somewhere to be now, not later. Everyone's business was the most important. Grady had marveled once, years ago, at the moving mass of dvergr from the top of a pedestrian bridge over the constant flow of loaded carts. From that vantage the commuters made up a gray river dotted with clumps of brown and gold- the colors of Clan Pyrite, clan of middle managers, landlords, and shopkeepers.

Even the air was full. Scents of all kinds, foul and fair, intermingled freely. Grady, overly familiar with them all, barely noticed the confusing dichotomy. Industrial waste, acids, and oils burned the back of the throat and stung at the eyes, while the smells of fresh bread, roasting meats, and frying mushrooms inspired the mouth to water. Above it all, the constant rattle of the chain-pulled carts shook Grady's teeth.

Entering his office cut him off from the Floor's sounds and smells. This place was as much his home as his room back in the tenement. Once his bag rested in its usual spot next to his chair, Grady settled in and got to work. There was a comforting, if boring, predictability about his job. No matter how empty the shift before, the in-box waiting on his desk was always full when he returned. Today was no exception.

There were documents and records to be copied, collated, digested and regurgitated. When Phukit appeared at his door, she did not question his presence or greet him. Grady only half-listened as she began to outline how he should prioritize his work today. It was always the same. Senior Clerk Phukit might as well have been reading her daily instructions to Grady from a script. Grady took a small amount of muted pleasure from her fondness for bright and clashing scarves. He assumed she had thousands and was unsure if he had ever seen the same one twice. Today's choice was a bright purple, floral affair that looked terrible atop her brown and gold suit.

The shift passed by without incident. Staring at and writing tiny rows of numbers, double checking his math, and collating everything to Phukit's exacting requirements didn't make time fly, so much as steadily ooze by. The labor only paused when he used the facilities, took ten minutes to eat his sandwich, or during one of the thousand times he looked up at his office door expectantly.

Emerlda never came.

As he worked that shift he sunk deeper into despair. Every throbbing ache, every completed form, sunk him deeper and deeper. Lost in a malaise, at some point he went home, then came back. He lived half-asleep, dreaming while awake, unaware of anything except for the smothering weight of his sadness and the hollow where his hope should be. Food tasted flat, devoid of any savor. Emerlda's absence continued, stretching into weeks.

Our shifts must be out of sync. That's all. His own reassurances wrang hollower each repetition.

Grady sank into despondency. His heart grew hard and unfeeling. In the dark of his room, his whole unfortunate future played out before him until he finally, mercifully, joined the ancestors. The terror inspired by that dusty, monochrome fate glued his eyes open and sent his mind desperately casting around for any way to escape. By the time the bells rang to signal the end of the old shift and the start of the new, he always reached the same conclusion.

There was no way out.

THE BARGAIN

The poster hadn't been there when Grady left for work two shifts ago. He was sure of it. Its garish brightness burned through the fog of his depressed disinterest in the world around him. It screamed at his eyes from its perch plastered on the side of his tenement door, impossible to ignore amidst the general drabness of the Floor. Glancing around in confusion, Grady saw that identical stamps of color were hung next to every entranceway he could see. How many had he walked past on his way home?

They were lovely to behold, no doubt some printer's mastercraft. A noble figure stood ready, straight-bearded and draped in gray with the gold crossed hammer and ax of the warrior's crest pinned to his chest. He smiled widely next to a set of words that Grady never thought to see in sequence with each other. They promised an impossibility:

Calling all Clanless!
Your City and Your People NEED YOU!
Unprecedented opportunities await for those
willing to heed the call and take the chance!
Earn your place amongst the Thegen!
Bring glory and honor to your name! Protect your homeland!

At first, Grady assumed it was just a cruel prank. Every five years, trials were held to find Clanned dvergr worthy of becoming thegen, one of the warrior caste charged with keeping the peace and defending Rockhome from the threats that rise from beneath. As with all other things, Clanless were considered unworthy and were not allowed to participate. But, there, in the corner of the poster was the official seal of the Keyrdegen, Sazlum

Aurum. No dvergr in their right mind would dare to forge that seal. Not for something as profitless as a prank aimed at the lowest of the low.

He licked his lips and wiped his suddenly clammy palms on his pants. The thumping of his heart pounded in his ears blocking out the sounds of the street. Hunger filled his eyes as he stared at the golden mark on the Clanless's chest. The quiet voice in his center marveled at the promise and power within that tiny, little pin. The poster directed those interested to inquire at a building a handful of blocks westwards.

The weariness of two hard shifts worth of sifting papers and making rows of numbers battled against a dizzying, fresh-born hope. Weariness, aided by practicality, won out in the end. He needed a rest, a shower, and a change of clothes before he dealt with the poster and its promises of opportunity. Dazed by spinning thoughts, Grady walked into the common room, but was forced to stop in the doorway. Bodies filled the room except for a small gap in the crowd through which an argument was raging.

"How could it not be real? They're all over. Saw at least forty of the posters from here to my mine at East Wall," said a dvergr with a curly fringe and bare lip. Those standing nearest to her, nodded their heads and added calls of agreement to the din. "They have the Keyrdegen's seal and everything."

"And all those colors!" Another added. "Some of those inks are not cheap." He held up his stained fingers to show he knew what he was talking about.

"Bah!" Kaluk, red in the face, shouted in response from the center of the skeptics across the room. His brother nodded along as Kaluk ranted. "Believe what you want. You watch. It will turn out to be some sort of scam. They are looking for toilet scrubbers and garbage haulers for the thegen halls. Someone to do their laundry and cook their meals. I don't know how many times I need to say it. They'd never make Clanless real thegen. You need honor and deeds on your name to be worthy, yeah? My ma, may she feast with the ancestors, was a good dvergr. Did right by us, sure as sure. Her parents did the same. But being a launderer isn't a deed and getting out stains doesn't earn one honor."

"The clans would never stand for it," added a bespectacled dvergr with a long, white beard. He coughed gently. "No precedent. The clans love their precedent. Nothing new under the mountain. That's how they like it."

"Nothing? Eh?" Curly fringe was incensed. "Always had running water, have we? Gas lamps? The light of the sun under the mountain?"

"Technological innovation is different from upending the mores and traditions that are the foundation of dvergr society," white beard responded with a snide curl to his lips. His glasses nearly fell off his nose when Kaluk slapped him on the back and added his own, "Hear, hear!"

Another voice rose above the noise to add its support to believing the posters. Another against. It all became too much for Grady. He slunk around the outside of the crowd and went to his room.

He entered in a rush, practically slamming the door closed. Grady pressed his back to the door as if trying to keep out an intruder. The argument was still dimly audible through the thick, fungal wood. It took a moment of slow breathing before Grady was able to think again.

He decided it was best to go about his down time as he had envisioned it before the poster woke him up with a gasp of false hope. He settled onto his bed with a book, the remainder of his lunch meat log, and a big mug of watery beer. His eyes slid over the words of the same three sentences in the book over and over. The bites of the cured meat were tasteless and he chewed them automatically. The beer warmed slowly on his bedside table, forgotten.

Ignored, the book dropped to the bed, one finger wedged in the pages to hold his place. He tapped the gnawed sausage idly against his chest. It stilled as his stare pierced through his ceiling to take in the stalactite buildings of the Roof hanging above him. Kaluk's and the other detractors' arguments echoed through his mind. Their view of the matter was more in sync with Grady's recent past experiences. The few spots that still ached after the miners took what they were owed were evidence enough. There was no such thing as a free drink.

And yet, what if?

That was the unshakeable thought at the core of the small discomfort in his heart. The ember of hope, recently unbanked by the garish poster's promises, was refusing to be extinguished by reason. Grady grew twitchy. Before he fully realized what he was doing, he was sneaking past the edge of the still arguing crowd and out the tenement house door.

Driven like never before, he cut through the flow of the traffic instead of allowing himself to be tossed along with the current. He earned himself a few hard stares and some discontented mutterings as he used his smaller frame to make headway. Grady surprised himself by not muttering a litany of "sorry's" and "excuse me's" as he momentarily inconvenienced those around him. When one disgruntled clanner, clothed in the white and blue of Clan Seraphinite with a complex braid in his beard signaling his importance, flipped him off, Grady swung the pick right back with both hands.

What did I just do? Grady thought as his arm lowered. He giggled like a madman for just a moment, tickled by his own audacity. He noticed an anomaly forming as he made his way. A small space was emptying around him. No one bumped his shoulders. No one forced him to side step to avoid their path. "Make way!" he said to no one and everyone around him. "I'm a brick on a mission!" While he did not yell at the top of his lungs, he knew he was audible to those in his immediate vicinity. A thrilling looseness opened up in him.

The euphoria drained from him a little when he reached his destination. It was, of course, another plain, gray, and squat building. Its sign, which hung over a plain stone door, was not neon and bright like the poster. It was newly painted and, like most things on the Floor, it was a drab combination: black letters on a mustard yellow field. Even the font was dull and straight. It read, simply, "Recruitment Office."

Grady hesitated, his hand outstretched to push through the door as the flow of people continued behind him. He savored the fading feeling that carried him through the streets for a moment longer. Behind this door was, potentially, everything Grady ever wanted. He laughed at a quick shiver of deja vu. The hesitation holding him back in this moment was the same that had stilled him right before he entered the pub.

"Well," he said to himself, "at the very least no one is going to beat you up for going in there. If this doesn't work out, you are no worse off than you were before." He heard the lie in his own words, but took heart in how often he was wrong about things.

The door swung open smoothly and lightly, good dvergr design making a stone slab into a working portal. The single room was brightly lit. He had never seen so much white lichen. Copies of the eye-burning poster were extra garish and loud in the stark lighting and were plastered along the ceiling's edge like wallpaper. A queue made of ropes hung between movable poles to guide the handful of hopefuls up towards a window containing a clerk with a polite, professional air. She handed out clipboards struggling to hold a thick stack of papers. Applicants sat in chairs sprouting little desks around the perimeter of the room.

Grady was not surprised to see so many people here. Of course, the posters were plastered all over the Floor. A few of the rougher looking hopefuls in line threw out glances at the others giving Grady the impression that this was an opportunity some Clanless would kill for.

The line was, as is the dvergr way, as quick and efficient as it could be. Grady approached the window and gulped.

"Welcome to the Recruitment Center for Clanless Individuals," said the young clerk in that bored professional way of the front-facing bureaucrat. Her gold and brown uniform was sharp, as were her beard's tight braids, fashionably slung over her ears. Her name tag identified her as "Durana."

"Uh, hi." Grady, having watched the exchange a dozen and a half times already, knew the drill and held out his hands for his clipboard and a small, metal tipped tube.

"Fill out all the questions, please. As neatly as possible. Write your address clearly. If we cannot find you, you will not be considered. More details about the position will be supplied to the lucky chosen..."

Grady marveled at the writing implement in his hand instead of listening to the clerk's spiel. The pen was a marvel! It had captured his attention as soon as he entered the room. In his time in line none of the applicants had to refill their writing implements. He did not see anyone splotch the page or smudge their lines. If he needed more proof that this was an official operation, the expense of bringing so many of these treasures made it clear.

"I said, do you have any questions?" The clerk's tone made it clear she did not like having to repeat herself, at least not to the same person twice.

"What? Oh sorry. No. Fill it out. Hand it back. Good luck to me. Right?" Grady tried out a smile he hoped was more apologetic than embarrassed.

A nod and brusque, "Next," launched Grady from the window to one of the recently vacated desk-chair combos.

Makes sense that filling out some paperwork would be my ticket out of not having to do more paperwork, Grady thought as he flipped through the packet on his clipboard.

It was thick, but a quick scan showed him that aside from the spaces for his name, address, and information about current employment, most of the questions were answerable by ticking either yes or no from the columns on the side.

What, no essay portion? Grady was hoping he would have a chance to plead his case in his own words. With a sigh, and a prayer to his unknown ancestors, he got to work.

The nature of the questions seemed aimed at reminding him of his current, lonely lot. Do you have any close family? Do you have any close friends? Are you a member of any social clubs that meet regularly? Others reminded him of how little he had achieved and accumulated. Is your name known for any major creative or industrial works? Do you own a home? Have you been promoted or received accolades at your current place of employment recently?

A few just felt mean. Do you consider yourself physically fit? Do you consider yourself of above average intelligence? In your opinion, do others consider you attractive?

The questions grew repetitive. They asked the same questions but worded in the opposite fashion. He doggedly answered every question truthfully and to the best of his ability. Trying to game the system and give the answers the Keyr(or whoever was actually evaluating these questions) wanted felt too risky. By the end, Grady's hand, one well used to writing for shifts at a time, was cramped and sore.

The last page of the form was a contract. The print was very small and he had to squint to make out the complex legalese. It all seemed pretty basic. If chosen, the undersigned gave up all rights to any property they owned, were released from all other contracts and agreements, including but not limited to employment contracts and any debt accrued from loans. The thegen and the City State of Rockhome were not liable for any injuries the undersigned may sustain when employed by said warriors and said city state. Grady reached the bottom of the page only because he began to skim about half way down.

They could melt me in magma or turn me to stone and use me as a paperweight. As long as he became thegen.

Grady signed with a flourish. He hoped handwriting counted.

His pen made a satisfying clatter when he deposited it with the others. Grady felt light headed as he handed the clerk his completed form. She wished him luck in a perfunctory manner. On his way out the queue was longer than when he entered, almost reaching the entrance. Thousands were going to reply and the odds were slim that out of all the Clanless in the city, Grady was the most deserving. He knew that.

Still, as he exited the recruitment office, Grady's steps were lighter. The gray expanse of the Floor stretching in every direction around him felt less oppressive, less final than it had in a long while. He hummed tunelessly to the staccato rhythm of the clattering carts. Emptying his wallet of his last few coins, he treated himself to a bowl of noodles in pork broth from

a kiosk run by a dvergr in Clan Feldspar's red and orange on his way back to his room.

It was wonderful. The updraft of savory steam pushed away the foul smells of the city for a time. The noodles were chewy, rich with the broth and their own goodness.

Whatever made people give way to him on his walk to the recruitment office was gone. He walked carefully in his little pocket of personal space at a pace chosen by those around him.

Over and over he told himself that his chances were slim. Every one of the Clanless were going to fill out one of those forms sooner or later. Better dvergr than he. More accomplished. Smarter, stronger, and more loved. None of his thoughts, no matter how bleak or realistic, were able to snuff out the newborn spark of hope warming his heart.

The common room was back to its normal, cozy emptiness. The argument must have fizzled out while he was gone. The line of bathroom goers ignored him as usual. He lay on his bed, which didn't feel as hard and lumpy as it had earlier, in his room, which didn't seem so small or terrible anymore. For the first time in a long time, Grady looked forward to tomorrow.

Nothing Ventured

While Grady was brushing his teeth for the next shift he realized two things.

The first was logistical. As a paper pusher himself, Grady knew that simply sorting, scoring, and evaluating every candidate was going to take a geologically long while. Considering how long Grady took to order food at a cart or to make any of the other small everyday decisions not dictated by habit, picking a person would take even longer. Patience was the only thing that would see him through the nebulous time to come.

The second was more personal. It started as a tiny notion that grew as his shift went on, taking on an unbelievable shape. The streets were full of the ever-present, ear-grinding clank of loaded carts as always. The walkways were still bursting with cliquey pedestrians. He was still alone, an erratic without an ancestor to his name. His clothes were still gray.

And yet, he bounced a little as he walked. He hummed a pleasant tune. The small spark of hope still glimmered within his heart, easing his burden and softening the sharp edges around him. Even if he wasn't chosen, *when* he wasn't chosen, Grady was determined to do everything in his power to keep the spark alive.

The pile of papers waiting for him in his office, as tall as he was and just as wide, threatened to snuff it out that very first shift. Senior Clerk Phukit pounced on him as soon as he sat down at his desk, appearing as if by magic at his office door.

"Computer Grady," Phukit said. Her brusque, dismissive, and demanding tone was at odds with the pink and purple patterned scarf adorning her neck. The wide swept fringe of her handlebar beard, shellacked in place by too much product, did not so much as wiggle. "These need to be dealt with by end of shift tomorrow. There was a delay in shipping which needs to be accounted for and we over-ordered the new Mark 3 mining helmets. A return request needs to be filled out and the costs recorded."

She's in a good mood today.

"Right-o, Boss," Grady said with a mock salute. "I'm on it." She paused as she turned to leave, giving Grady an odd look. The lack of a dejected, "Yes, Senior Clerk Phukit, right away Senior Clerk Phukit", must have caught her off guard.

A strange impulse seized Grady. "Senior Clerk? Can I have a moment of your time?" Phukit stopped at the doorway and turned back, her face screwed up with confusion and reddening with anger. She opened her mouth to begin her "Don't you waste my time with nonsense" speech. Grady swallowed and pressed on, cutting her off. "Have you heard about these new preloaded pens? I was wondering if we could order some for the offices here. I got to try one, even got to see a bunch being used at once. They worked great. Wrote with smooth, legible lines. Barely noticeable blotting. Between not seeming to need sharpening or fiddling about with ink pots, I think they would save the administrative branch lots of time." Grady's nerves got the better of him. His last words came out as a rush and he took sudden interest in his hands fiddling on his lap.

Phukit's mouth hung open for a second as she swallowed her well practiced words. The silence in the room grew heavy as the moment dragged on. "I actually have, Grady. Heard of them. Another Artificer wonder, Ancestors bless 'em. Figured they have as much chance of working right as they have of blowing up. Hadn't had a chance to try one yet." She snorted, twirling a beard-end around her finger. "If it's one thing you know, I imagine it's pens." The twirling finger tapped her chin. Grady knew a calculating look when he saw one. "I'll take your word for it. I will make the request and start it up the chain." Grady looked up, unsure of how well he was succeeding at hiding his astonishment.

"Th-thanks." Grady managed to get out as Phukit nodded and left.

A pinch to the arm assured Grady he wasn't dreaming. Phukit had listened to him, agreed with him. She was going to 'start it up the chain.' The encounter played out in his head for a minute or two. Grady was glad he was sitting. For a moment, he felt dizzied as his understanding of the world realigned ever so slightly.

The momentum of his life tumbled him along and the rest of the month passed by uneventfully. Life was just a nicer ride now that he had hope to pad him against the harder impacts and rougher moments.

Grady felt more in control of his own life. He reorganized and restacked the books in his room. The addition of a throw rug and a small desk fungi made his room homier. Insulated from their taunts and minor cruelties by his new outlook, run-ins with the Twins became minor, every-day annoyances. Though his work tasks remained as tedious and as menial as ever, for the first time in his life, Grady felt useful. His abject loneliness softened into a more comfortable and easier to bear solitariness.

One shift, Grady walked, whistling, into his office to find a small box with five pens on his desk, accompanied by a small note. It read: The higher ups liked the idea. I took all the credit, but you still get the pens. It was signed 'Senior Clerk Supervisor Phukit'. 'Supervisor' was written larger, and underlined, to ensure that Grady would not miss her minor promotion. Grady, surprised he wasn't irked at her for taking all the credit, spun one of his new pens in his fingers feeling inordinately proud.

Every shift this past month Grady had waited for word from the Floor Recruitment Office. Each shift he heard nothing his sense of certainty grew that whoever was chosen was not him. The realization did not crush him like he had feared it would.

Even worse, he had heard not one word from Emerlda since the incident at the pub. Work acquaintances for a decade and a half, friends for nearly six years, her complete and sudden absence from his life both hurt and bewildered him. Was he the butt of some long planned joke, making the invitation a trap? Their friendship had always felt as real as the stone all around. Might as well believe the world was hollow. Perhaps she had heard about his failure to bend the bar and his subsequent ass kicking.

Would associating with him somehow tarnish her standing amongst the other miners?

He turned the pen in his hands, making the desk light sparkle off the metal.

The sound of a muted steam whistle pricked at his ears. He shot up out of his chair, a mad idea forming. He swallowed dryly and wiped his suddenly soggy hands on his shirt. A rising panic fruitlessly battered against a cool clarity empowered by the necessity of the moment. Grady fixed his mustache and smoothed down his beard.

Time to swing my pick. What's the worst that can happen? His mind, always helpful, supplied an immediate myriad of possibilities.

With one last deep breath, Grady opened his door. A stream of miners, freshly showered, changed, and done up for some hours on the town, jostled and laughed their way past Grady's office. He leaned against the doorjamb, crossed one foot over the other and folded his arms against his chest. He did his best to compose his face into a semblance of nonchalance. Grady even nodded occasionally as if greeting random people he knew, despite no one even glancing in his direction.

There! Even though she was near the middle of the pack, Grady spotted Emerlda instantly. Her laugh tinkled above the general hubbub and chatter. Timid at first, Grady gave a little, ineffectual wave. He waved higher and harder to similar effect. Grady sighed.

I guess stone-cool isn't my style. Time to be more himself.

He started jumping in the air and waving his hands over his head. "Emerlda! Hey! Over here! Emeeeeerlda!"

He couldn't care less about the odd looks passing miners shot him because it worked! When she turned towards him, her big beaming smile faltered for just a moment. Was it a little brighter when it returned? She waved back. With some parting words to her friends, she pushed through the crowd. The green in her eyes danced and shone, brighter for the dark swipe of kohl across her face.

"Hiyuh, Grady." She walked up close to him to avoid being in the way of the moving people. Grady craned his head up ever so slightly to be able to look her in the face. He marveled at the push of her muscles against her shirt as she replaced a strand of hair behind her ears and fiddled with a small pearl twined into her beard. Her normal exuberance seemed muted, almost bashful. "It's been a minute. What's up?"

As Grady, mouth coppery tasting and dry, smiled his lips stuck for a moment against his teeth. "Not much. Um, would you like to, uh, c-come in for a sec?"

Emerlda pursed her lips and gave Grady an appraising look. She nodded as if pleased by something. "Sure."

Grady turned to the side with an arm outstretched to guide and welcome her in. She grabbed the extended hand and pulled him in after her. Grady thrilled at the contact. When was the last time he had touched another living person on purpose? Her hand was warm, strong, and calloused from years of mine work. His hand felt dainty and overly smooth by comparison. Grady dragged the door closed as she pulled him into his lichen lit office. When Emerlda let go, the feeling of her touch lingered and ignited a warmth in his cheeks.

Grady watched, a little dazed, as Emerlda walked over to lean against the desk. The effect as she crossed her arms under her chest made Grady swallow again. Was that the crinkle of a smile around her eyes? Grady took in the sight for a precious and fragile moment.

"Look, Grady I-"

"Emerlda, I-"

They laughed awkwardly, filling the room with an expectant tension.

Grady placed his pen on the desk and rolled it back and forth. "Mind if I go first?"

"Sure. Please," Emerlda responded quickly. She tapped out a nervous tattoo on her forearm.

Grady opened his mouth, not sure that words were soon to follow. And just like that, all of his questions disappeared. "I, uh..." *You're blowing it, brick. Get yourself together.* He dropped all pretense with a sigh. "Look,

Emerlda, I've missed you." He paused, trying to transmute his jumbled feelings into words.

"Me too," Emerlda said, filling the silence.

Grady felt his blush grow deeper and spread to the tips of his ears. Relief tinged with anger and hurt colored his words. "Where have you been?"

Emerlda looked down, unable to meet Grady's eyes. "I've been avoiding you. I-" She sniffled a little and wiped away a tear. "I heard what happened to you. I invited you along without thinking. We were in the back. By the time I could see what was going on, you were on the ground and they were kicking you."

Her next words were choked out by a wave of body-wracking sobs. She flung her arms over Grady's. Her tears doused his shoulder. "I'm so sorry. So very sorry."

Emerlda shuddered and cried, clinging to him. Grady, having very little experience with soothing or being soothed, was unsure of what to do. His arms settled around her while one hand patted her back. Each time she repeated her apology, Grady responded. "I forgive you. It's okay. I'm okay." The hug, his first since leaving childhood behind, warmed Grady to his core.

Over time the sobbing slowed. The two friends separated and Emerlda sniffed a little. "I'm sorry for carrying on like that. And... oh! Your shirt. You're wet down to your elbow." She picked at the clingy fabric of his sleeve and they laughed a little.

"It's okay. Really. They only embarrassed me and roughed me up some. I'm as good as ever." He swung his arms and twisted at the hips to show the extent of his recovery. A twinge in his back froze him in place for a moment. "Don't worry. Don't worry. This is a work injury. It's harder to sit all shift than you think." He rotated his shoulder to work at the pain.

"I thought you were mad at me for everything. I know I was." Her normal bubbly energy changed into something fiercer when she cracked her knuckles against her palm. "I want you to know that me and some of my crew gave that cropolite-for-brains and his friends as good as you got, or better."

Grady was stunned, locked up like a rusted gear. Throughout his life there had been few dvergr who treated him with basic consideration and even less that had done him a kind turn. This was the first time anyone had ever fought for him. One question gnawed at him, demanded out. "Why me? Why would you defend me?"

Incensed, Emerlda approached Grady, growing louder with each step. "That's a dumb question. Have we not known each other for a quarter century? Do you think I'm the kind of dvergr who turns her back on her friends?"

Grady took an involuntary step back. "No. Of course not. Never. But-" Grady still didn't understand, "why me?"

She pulled him closer and placed a hand on his cheek. "Do you think so low of yourself? You're one of the smartest dvergr I've ever known. It's cute how you read those books. How your eyes light up when you talk about them. I've never seen you be mean to anyone who didn't deserve it. You make me laugh and when we talk, you really listen. Plus..." Emerlda leaned in close so that her hair tickled Grady's nose, and her warm breath brushed against his ear. "I think you're cute."

Before Grady could react, she kissed his cheek. Her lips were smooth and warm. He touched the spot where the contact lingered as a pleasant tingle. A stillness grew between them that was heavy and light all at once.

The spark in his chest expanded, roaring into a bonfire. "How about a do-over?" Grady asked. "Let's meet in a neutral location, someplace without a feat of strength cover charge?"

She moved to the door, brushing past Grady despite there being plenty of room for her to go around. Grady turned as she walked. This was an experience he wanted to remember forever. "Sure. There's this Elven cuisine place near South Wall. Best food under the mountain if you ask me. Sound good?"

She could have suggested they eat charcoal for all it mattered to Grady. "Yeah that sounds great. I've never had Elven."

Emerlda stopped in the doorway and turned back to him. "How about next shift? Right after work, like now-ish? You free?"

It took actual effort to refrain from touching the warm spot on his cheek. "Barring surprise overtime and the Roof collapsing, I should be."

Her laugh thrilled him almost as much as the kiss had. "Can't wait! We'll meet here okay? That'll give us lots of time for a walk and talk on the way."

"Sounds like a plan."

"Perfect! See you then." With a wave and one final smile Emerlda was gone.

Grady's breathless "Bye" trailed behind.

Grady floated the whole way home. He played out the conversation over and over in his head. His shoulders, the palm of his hand, his cheek, and the parts of him she brushed past all still vibrated warmly. He grabbed a pocket bread stuffed with mushrooms and deep fried pork in a thick brown sauce from a vendor to celebrate on his way home. He savored every bite, wondering what sort of dishes Elven cuisine consisted of.

In the darkness of his room, he wondered if any of the dvergr who lived here in the past had ever felt this happy, been this content, or felt so hopeful. Unable to sleep, he lay in his bed reliving the conversation from before over and over with his fingers lingering on his cheek.

THE ABDUCTION

The crash of his bedroom door being kicked-in tore Grady from a deep sleep. Scattering the last wisps of a pleasant dream, indistinct hulks rattling in the darkness, surrounded his bed and grabbed his arms and legs. He screamed for help, flailing against the iron grips of his assailants.

A pair of hands gagged him with a foul tasting piece of fabric. Another shoved a rough burlap sack over his head that stank of old potatoes. They secured his hands and legs with rope. The bindings hurt. He whimpered through the gag.

"Shut it, you," said a rough voice. Grady turned in the voice's direction and an impact on his forehead filled the burlap dimness with stars. Grady froze, hoping they would ignore the fluttering of his heart and the panicked hitching caused by his snot laden, nasally breaths. He prayed hard into the darkness behind his eyes, calling out to his unnamed ancestors, begging for this all to be some all-too-real nightmare.

"Alright, lads," said an authoritative voice. "Quick and profession-al-like."

Grady was hoisted from the bed. They dragged from his room by his armpits. They were not walking long before his captors came to a sudden halt.

"For the door," the authoritative voice said again. Followed by the distinctive clinking of a purse full of coins. "A bit of extra weight for your cooperation with this matter."

"It is my honor to aid the thegen." Grady recognized the voice of the hosteler who rented him his room. "Surprised you wanted him of all dvergr. Quiet one, him. Should have known really. My ma' always warned against the quiet ones."

Whirling thoughts filled him as he was carried out into the streets. What could he have done to earn the attention of the thegen, the warriors tasked with defending Rockhome from external threats and internal disorder? It was all a big misunderstanding. They must have confused him for a different Grady. It had to be.

In the stinking darkness of the sack he quickly lost track of where in the city he was. All Grady could hear was the sucking of his own breath and the ever-present clanking of the carts below. A kind of terrified apathy set in. The pain in his head and the numbness spreading into his hands and feet pulsed in time with his slowing heart. A small detached part of Grady marveled at the novelty of the feeling and the situation he was in.

I can't wait to tell Emerlda about this. It will make for some scintillating dinner conversation.

What was Emerlda up to right now? Not knowing the time, he could only guess. In her own bed sleeping comfortably? No. Out at the pub drinking and laughing. With her friends. Yes, that is how he wanted her to be at this moment, surrounded by a riotous air pulsing with songs and sparkling droplets flung forth by flagons crashing together.

When they stopped moving for a moment, Grady was amazed at how calm he felt, calm and cold. The questions and prayers were quiet now. Even the pain in his head bothered him less. He hung loosely in the hands of his captors, letting them bear his weight. There was an ease to giving up. In time he would be free again, back in his room, and this would all be a bad memory.

Stone grated ominously and the dragging continued. His captors must have tired of carrying him completely and they let his feet trail behind as they made their way down some kind of ramp. The smell of dirty, pitch burning torches cut through the sack's tuberous funk. Grady sneezed uncomfortably hard through his nose causing snot to squirt down his beard and gag stuffed lips. The ramp twisted and turned, ever downward.

Grady knew little about the workings of the thegen and their jails. He was surprised that they were placed so deep beneath the Floor itself.

The abductors halted again. A metal-gloved fist tapped out a series of long and short raps on wood. *Trim and a cheek shave- two coins,* Grady hummed to himself with a mad little giggle. One of the warriors holding him gave him a shake.

Grady heard the lifting of a latch and the rasp of stone on stone. His captors continued forward and he knew they crossed a threshold when his feet bumped against a door jam. The door rasped in reverse as it swung shut behind them. The soft clicks of the door closing and a bolt being thrown rang with finality.

"Is this my specimen, eh? Mm?" This new voice grated on his ears. It rasped and screeched in equal measure. Grady could feel the speaker's scrutiny like spiderwebs brushing his skin.

"This is the target, Artificer," The authoritative voice from before responded. "Our orders were clear". His tone was neutral but firm.

"Of course, Sergeant, of course. Hmm. Yes. My comment was rhetorical, I assure you, and was in no way a slight to your competence or your compatriots'." The Artificer's voice circled Grady. "Hmm. Soft. Small. A low starting point will make the outcome all the more impressive. Yes. He'll do. Hm. Strip him, chain him up, and then take your place outside. *He* will be here shortly."

The ropes were cut from his wrists and ankles, but Grady did not dare move. Fear held him tighter than any physical bonds could manage. He yelped when his pajamas were similarly cut and ripped away. Grady bit down on the gag in his mouth to stifle a cry as the air coldly nipped at his sweat-dappled skin.

Grady stumbled on his numb feet as the thegen walked him a few steps deeper into the room. They raised his arms over his head and clamped tight manacles around his wrists. Grady was forced to stand on his tiptoes to avoid feeling like his hands were about to be ripped off by his own body weight.

The sound of their boots and the twin rasping of the door told Grady the others had left. He was alone with the artificer and his grating voice. A thunk filled the room with light powerful enough to glow dimly through the sack over his head. The light flared to blinding as the sack was torn away. The bright, unnatural lights caused the lump on his head to throb in sympathy.

The absolute strangeness of it all was too much for Grady. He lost his grip on the gibbering panic that had been building since he woke up. Screaming into the gag, Grady struggled awkwardly against his manacles. They quickly cut into his wrists and sent rivulets of blood flowing down his dangling arms. His thrashing slowed as he tired until his efforts crumbled into sobs and weak tugs.

"Hmmm. Maybe you are not as soft as I thought? Spirited, eh? Hmm. The true strength of our kind. Yes. Present even in the, hm, least of us. Yes. Let's get a better look at you."

Grady squinted as a blurry figure leaned into view. It was impossible to make out any details through the glare..

"Shh." A gentle touch on his cheek caused him to flinch. "Shh, shh." The touch turned into a gentle stroking, the kind used to soothe anxious animals. "You were treated so poorly, my specimen. Uh. Yes. Here, let's take away this terrible gag." Palsied hands, coated with wrinkled, paper-thin skin marked by a map of blue veins and pale scars, loosened the gag and freed the sodden mass from Grady's mouth.

Grady worked his jaw as best he could. The interior of his mouth felt, and tasted, like the inside of a three shift sock. "P-please. Don't hurt me anymore. Please? I didn't do it. Whatever it was, it wa-wasn't me. I just want to go home."

"My, my. You've done nothing wrong. They had no cause to treat you so roughly. Yes. You are bruised like an overripe, hm, white cap. Let me see here." Grady's captor leaned in to inspect the lump on his forehead, blocking out a portion of the light blinding him. The sight of the captor's visage sent a shiver of revulsion down his spine and coated his tongue with the taste of copper.

The dvergr face before him was an ancient ruin, partially collapsed and derelict. Thin translucent skin clung tightly to his bald pate, only to crease into a mass of wrinkles as it reached his mismatched eyes. One was clouded over completely. The other was covered by a bronze monocle-like apparatus of gears and whirring lenses. His mouth was stretched in a gummy smile, dotted by a few yellowed teeth. Below the mouth his beard floated down from his chin, shapeless and wispy.

Loose hairs from his mustache tickled Grady's nose as the old dvergr leaned in to inspect the various bruises on his face and the throbbing knot on his forehead. The artificer's prodding was gentle but with a practiced firmness that caused Grady to wince. A couple of clicks sounded from the old dvergr's eye. "Ah. Good. Yes. No lasting harm done. Hm. None at all! And luckily your early thrashing only scraped your wrists. They should not be a problem." He squinted, noticing something he did not like. "My, you are a bit hirsuted though. Hm, it all must go before we get to work. I am prepared though." He gently patted Grady on the shoulder. "I am prepared."

"Hir... what? All go?" Grady asked the question while fearing he knew the answer.

"First things, hm, first. Yes," The decrepit madman said to himself and pulled on a pair of gloves, tight and thin looking. Next he produced a vial filled with a white substance that gave off a burning, chemical reek. The next minutes were the most humiliating of Grady's life.

So far, a mad little voice added.

Shaking with palsy, Grady's captor began to work the stuff into Grady's hair, then beard. He smeared it all over his chest, sides, back, legs, and genitals. The touch was soft yet mechanical and workmanlike. Grady, weakened by fear and pain, was so full of shame he did not even squirm in protest.

"Yes, good. Let's clean you off now, hm?" Using a moist towel the old dvergr wiped away the cream and with it every bit of hair on Grady's body. Even his beard–tearing his soul away as it sloughed off. His chin was cold and burned slightly just like every other inch of his body. "There, yes. All ready. Hm. All prepped. This will do nicely. Yes."

With nothing left to lose, aside from his life, Grady glared at his captor. "Why are you doing this to me? What do you want?" His demanding tone quavered and failed him. Grady was unable to hold back a sob.

"Well, you lucky child, you will find out soon enough, yes? Soon enough. It is not my, hm, place to tell." The old creature chuckled and moved out of Grady's eyeline. Fully blinded by the white brightness, Grady could only listen. He heard the sounds of rattling metal, like his captor was digging through a collection of tools. Inspired by some of the darker moments in his books, his unhelpful mind supplied images of implements both sharp and crushing. Grady squeezed his eyes shut trying to block out the light and the terrible possibilities.

The old dvergr could not contain himself. "It may not seem like it, yes, but you are blessed. You see? Chosen! First!" Another chuckle. Some merry humming. More rattling. "You will advance the cause of our people forward hundreds if not thousands of years! Forward, by looking back! Hm. Who would have thought? Ah ha! Yes. Here it is."

His captor was whistling merrily when he stepped back into the circle of light. Grady's eyes were drawn to the glinting bronze contraption encasing his captor's right hand. Wires and braces connected the boney, frail fingers to multi-jointed appendages. Gripped in the elongated, bronze digits was a small, exceedingly sharp knife. Despite the shaking of the fleshy hand within, the bronze framing held steady. The captor did not miss Grady's terrified interest. "This? Ah. Designed it myself. Not as young as I used to be, you see." He cackled. "Keeps the work steady while the hand shakes. This is some delicate work and I do not want your sacrifice to go to waste. Yes."

At the word "sacrifice," Grady sobbed again. The sob wrenched some mooring loose inside his head. The absolute horror of it all was stained with a patina of ridiculousness.

"Yes. Sacrifice is painful. Hm. But I promise you, soon you will be beyond all pain. Yes. And oh, the good you'll do." The old Dvergr leaned in and placed his free hand on Grady's chest. His fingertips were smooth and dry. Like paper. If there was one sensation in the world Grady knew, it was the feel of paper. Paper to read from, to write on, to stack, and to fold. There was a neatness to the fact that at his end, his ender would feel like paper.

With a calm, jovial air the old creature brought his bronze encased hand forward, the scalpel glinting in the light. "I am so excited to get started. Hmm. Yes. I feel a century younger." A papery hand patted Grady's now-bare cheek. "Great honor is yours this shift, my specimen. It's not often one of your kind, hmm, get's to be in the presence of the Keyrdegen, himself! Yes." The knife, bronze contraption, and the withered figure pulled back and stepped through the whiteness into the unseeable space beyond.

The relief that flooded Grady at the reprieve was weak and shallow. The urge to laugh fermented uncomfortably in his belly. As time stretched out, the mundane sought to reassert itself. Smaller problems demanded his attention despite his current lack of agency. His butt and his nose itched. Terribly. The cracked part of him argued with itself about which he would scratch first if his hands were free.

Oh, and the Keyrdegen! He was going to meet the Warriors' Warrior, the living legend who for centuries had commanded the city's defenses? It was his lucky shift after all. A haircut and a hero's visit!

The caretakers at the Ground Floor Orphan Asylum for the Young and Clanless had a saying they would drill into their charges as the tally of life's petty pains piled up and the shallowness of its available joys became more evident. *It is important to take the good with the bad.*

I wonder if he'll let me try on his helm, the mad sliver thought.

He most certainly did not think of Emerlda's strong arms and kind eyes. Or the curl of her lips when she smiled. Or the words she had said that made him feel seen and valued. The taste of Elven cuisine seasoned by her laughter was beyond his imagination at this point. No, thinking all those things would only make the horror of this moment more unbearable and the upcoming finality of Grady's life all the more terrible.

THE CARVING

As Grady hung from the ceiling, the pain in his arms crescendoed briefly, then faded to numbness. His calves, to protest the effort of holding him up on tiptoe for so long, seized with vicious cramps. Between quick, hissing breaths, Grady decided that this was the most uncomfortable he had ever been.

Up until now, it was a toss up between whether hanging from his hands or spending most of a triple's ninety hours sitting in the creaky torture device that masqueraded as his office chair was more uncomfortable. The miners had every right to complain at the end of a shift, but Grady always wondered how well they could handle the muscle-locking ache from being chairbound for so long. The cramps finally tipped the scale.

Off in the white void of the lights, the door's bolt was thrown. Grady heard it slide open. "Ah, Master Keyrdegen, just on time, yes, just on time. Come in, come in. Your, hm, agents performed their task admirably." The door rasped closed. "The specimen is adequate, yes, to our needs. He is prepped and ready for your final inspection."

The veteran warrior did not deign to answer, at least not in any way Grady heard. Confident footsteps rang into the room, stopping at the illumination's edge. Grady was just able to make out the front of an expansive gut, draped in fine, burgundy velvet, peeking into view. The gem-encrusted gold of the figure's belt buckle twinkled in the light. It bobbed as he spoke.

"Not much to see, is he, Plenabus?"

Grady knew that name. There wasn't a soul in Rockhome who didn't. Plenabus was famous, the lead Artificer who was single-handedly responsible for ushering in the modernization of Rockhome. He engineered the excavations and the series of mirrors that opened up Rockhome to the surface's sun. The twinkling gas lights that Grady loved so much were also his inventions. His genius kept the water clean, warm, and flowing. Grady was glad he never knew life in Rockhome before cold boxes and flush toilets.

His time-ravaged appearance made more sense now. Plenabus was also known for his preternatural longevity. Rare was the dvergr who could push six-hundred years. At a budding forty-three, Grady wondered what the weight of all those years felt like. He hoped to find out one shift.

"No, more slight and shorter than average. Hmm. By my estimation, this one is healthy enough to withstand the rigors of the procedure. He has all his limbs. Yes. A more than adequate test subject."

The rest of The Protector, the Wall Against the Rising Darkness, Keyrdegen Sazlum Aurum, entered into Grady's tiny bright world. He dripped with jewels. Layers of fine cloth and rare furs swayed as he walked. His beard, auburn and streaked with white, hung in two arm-thick braids tossed over his shoulders to ensure they did not trail on the ground. Both braids were filled with rings of ivory and precious metals, each marking a great feat or victory. A simple metal circlet, at odds with the rest of his grand appearance, rested on his brow.

The Keyrdegen noted Grady's wide-eyed stare. "No need to bow," Salzum said with a single chuckle. His wave was both dismissive and sparkly. He carried a thick, familiar stack of paper in one beringed hand. The warlord read from the top page. He flipped through the stack and shook his head. "So, Grady of No Clan, you think yourself worthy of being a thegen?"

"Please, sir-" Grady's entreaty was cut short by a powerful backhand. Grady rocked in his chains. The rings raked his cheek and his ears rang. Tears, unbidden, rolled down his cheeks. They ran over his new cuts, salty and abrasive. There they grew pink and then dripped down his chin.

The Keyrdegen snarled, spraying Grady with spittle as he was upbraided. "Take no liberties with me, brick. Speak only when you are so bidden. I don't know where this delusional sense of worthiness comes from. Your kind are little more than the fuel this city burns in order to thrive." The warrior's vehemence vanished in a blink, replaced with syrupy condescension. "I... We," he nodded towards the Father of Modern Artifice, "are going to give your life value. Purpose. Take heart that your suffering is but a stepping stone to make our city, our people safer. Haven't you always said, Plenabus, that the best way to learn is to do?"

"Yes, yes. Practice makes, hm, perfect."

"You will be practice, Grady." The warrior spat his name out like a foul-tasting curse. "A whet stone upon which Plenabus will sharpen his skills. Perfect his methods." The oration paused so that Salzum could peer deeply into Grady's eyes. What he saw there must have pleased him because he smiled and leaned away from his captive. "This is an ancient ritual, a legacy of our ancestors when our people were whole. 'Only the willing may exchange the gifts of flesh for the gifts of stone'. Am I remembering correctly, Artificer?"

"Yes, my lord. It sounds more, hm, stirring in the original dialect, of course."

The Keyrdegen turned up the bottom page of the packet he held. "Is this your signature, Grady of No Clan?" He held the paper up for Grady's inspection. The unnatural light was so bright the ink lost its usual green glow, leaving it a glistening black. "You may speak," the Keyrdegen said gently. When the answer did not come quick enough, he bellowed, "Answer me!"

Grady's teeth ground. His jaw clenched tight. The Keyrdegen raised his hand again and wound up to deliver another slap.

"Yes!" Grady answered, desperate to not be hurt again.

The Keyrdegen struck anyway. Spots danced before Grady's eyes and the white void undulated.

"Address me properly, brick." The words were cold and full of dark promises.

"Yes, my lord."

The Keyrdegen nodded. "You are sure this will work?"

"It should, lord. Yes. The instructions were very, hm, clear. The wording on the document was crafted to specifications. Yes. The subject has acknowledged his agreement. It is, hm, binding."

"Good. Very good." The Keyrdegen's wide grin revealed gold teeth that shone warmly. He sauntered from Grady's field of vision. "You may begin whenever you are ready, my teacher. I eagerly wish to observe your work."

The ancient wreck of a dvergr, his arm wrapped in brass, reappeared. The too-long digits now held a syringe filled with a clear fluid. "First, a paralytic." The needle pierced into Grady's neck. An almost pleasant warmth rushed through his veins. The warmth faded and Grady slumped against the wrenching pull of his chains. No matter how hard he tried, Grady was unable to even wiggle a toe. He still felt every inch of his body, the communication was only working one way. He mentally shouted at his body to move, for it to wake up, be his again. It was a discomfort beyond pain. There was no fate worse than being like this forever, awake but trapped in a body unresponsive to his demands.

"Fast-acting, yes?" Plenabus nearly burst with pride. "It is derived from a specific type of mold found only-" The Keyrdegen cleared his throat loudly. "Yes. Hmm. Let's continue." Plenabus left and returned, wheeling a metal table towards Grady. He looked helplessly back and forth between Grady's hanging body and the table's smooth top. "If you would call one of the thegen back in, I am in, hm, need of some physical assistance."

"It would be my honor to assist you, Artificer Plenabus. Truly," the Keyrdegen said with an edge of frustration. "We discussed this."

"Yes, oh yes." Plenabus tapped his lips with an upturned finger. "I know how much you love to dabble, you have since you were just a welp. Yes."

Salzum was not gentle as he unbuckled Grady's wrists. Paralyzed, he was unable to soften his crumple to the stone floor. Grady marveled at how easily the Keyrdegen lifted his inert body over his shoulder. He flopped Grady face up onto the table with a loud bang, leaving his hands and feet to dangle lifelessly.

"Marvelous, yes, marvelous." Plenabus circled Grady, repositioning his limbs so that they rested on the table. The adjustments were gentle, but the touches left itching in their wake. "It was recommended to start at the, hm, legs and work your way up." This was said over his shoulder to the Keyrdegen.

With his body immobilized, Grady was unable to follow Plenabus's walk toward his feet. He heard the whir of some gears and a cold metallic pressure encased his foot. Then the pain began. Lines of hot fire igniting in precise locations on the top of his foot and along each toe. Characters in books were always being flayed and Grady imagined this sensation was similar. Maybe, before this was all over, he would get to make the comparison.

The Keyrdegen's voice reached him through the pain, hushed with awed excitement. "Does that say, 'stand'?"

"Close, yes close! 'Rooted' actually, hm."

The fire spent a time at his ankle then scorched him up his shin, carving into the bone. A short pause to raise his leg and then his calf ignited.

Is this what paper feels when written on? The small, detached voice in his mind asked.

"Bend?"

"Close, hm, again. Flex. The ancients were poetic, yes? I will make that mark three hundred and fifty times. One for each, hm, joint. Of course, yes, for later subjects we may limit the number. Best to be, hm, thorough for our first attempt."

Grady tried to scream as the knife began to carve on the surface of his knee. He managed a weak mewling. Grady begged the ancestors to make him unconscious, for nothingness to swallow him up and help him escape the pain and the terror. It did not come as his thigh was marked, front and back. As his hip received a similar treatment. Each cut was as sharp and fresh as the last.

"Must you be so liberal with the powder?"

"I understand your concern, yes, but I assure you I am using the bare minimum required. As stated in the supplied outline of the procedure, without a decent powdering of the styptic blend of alum and mythril dust the excessive bleeding would weaken the subject and threaten the viability of the final product. Yes. The ancients were clear on that. The mithril must fill the wounds to make it all possible. Yes."

Mithril. The word reached Grady deep in his suffering. Every dvergr who delved into the earth dreamed of uncovering even the smallest seam. Such a feat guaranteed those responsible remembrance amongst the most honored of ancestors. Legends say that ancient dvergr were made out of the stuff by the first gods, long since forgotten.

And here Grady was, being sprinkled with it.

By the time his torturer, the wondrous Plenabus, moved on to his other leg the pain from the first dulled to a throbbing ache. Though the second leg hurt as much as the first, Grady was too weak to even attempt more of the mewling screams. He bore the pain silently, unable to even wince. Every sensation was trapped inside him, with no possible release. He burned from the waist down.

Plenabus entered Grady's peripheral vision. The scalpel hovered for a moment over his chest. He was interrupted by the Keyrdegen. "I've seen the mockups you sent us. Why are you skipping the line work in the middle?"

"This runic mechanism will be responsible for moving energy through the body." Plenabus answered calmly and with an academic air. "I found a footnote that mentioned a better outcome when letting the heart rune settle a bit before connecting the whole sequence." Grady's breath hitched at the first touch of the scalpel. The rune was intricate and complex and took as long to do as both legs had in their entirety. The left section of his chest ached from a thousand little cuts "Yes. There. Care to, hm, try again?"

The Keyrdegen took his time. Bending into the light he peered down at the freshly carved rune. He 'hm'd' and scratched at his chin. "'Unbreakable'?"

"Again, so close. Hm, '*infrangible*'. The ancients and their, yes, lofty notions." Plenabus spoke some words that scraped the back of his throat and were filled with the hard sounds of consonants. "From Klazkitzen. 'The horrors may break a mind, but the true heart of a dvergr is infrangible'. He is one of my favorite philosophers. Hm. Pre-diaspora. Yes."

"Enough with ancient philosophy." The Keyrdegen's patience was wearing thin. "Get on with it. You've been at this for hours already."

"And hours, hm, more to go. Haste makes waste. Yes. One wrong mark and all this is ruined. Patience, Salzum. Patience. You'll get your new, hm, toy soon enough."

Grady felt the scalpel carving into his gut. It was another intricate rune mechanism possessing lots of sharp angles. His insides undulated in protest. The Keyrdegen hazarded no guess this time.

Tired of being wrong, I suspect.

The fire spread out along his torso. Plenabus begged for the Keyrdegen's assistance once more. He tilted Grady up and held him there while Plenabus marked his back.

Grady was awash in a sea of pain. While the release of unconsciousness was refused to him, existence blurred and time passed without Grady having to pay attention. The line of runes from his tailbone to the nape of his neck burned particularly bright.

"Place the, hm, cushion beneath his back and we can, yes, lay him down, my lord. We don't want his weight to mar any of the marks." The cushion was softer than the table, but it gave him no comfort. Raw as it was, his back did not care for the heavy fabric's rough feel.

The cold metal of Plenabus's mechanical claw braced one hand and the carving began again, meticulous and precise. He worked from the hand upwards to the shoulder. Each major muscle group and every joint received their individual attention. At his shoulder new carvings met older ones. Then the other arm, fingers to shoulder.

Plenabus broke the tense silence of the room. "Do you spot the, hm, new rune?"

"On the hand?" The Keyrdegen answered begrudgingly. Plenabus nodded as he worked. "'Smart'? No. Wait! 'Cleverness'?"

"Well done, hm, well done. Rooted for the feet, cleverness for the hands, yes." Plenabus sighed in awed admiration. "We are, hm, descended from true poets."

Plenabus finished a last line on the top of Grady's shoulder. He paused, his hands stained red with Grady's blood. "Do you want, hm, it to be able to speak? The ancients gave their creations a voice. I do not believe we will, or have any need to, for future subjects."

"Proceed."

Plenabus etched pain into his throat and moved onto his jaw. Grady willed the knife to slip, dig too deeply into his throat, and end it all. It listened no better than his body. "The next bit is delicate, yes." Using his gloved fingers the artificer closed Grady's eyes. At first the darkness was a relief. The peripheral glimpses of the knife at work made it all harder to bear.

Pain drew upon his eyelids, carving brighter red lines in the warm darkness of his closed eyes. The work on his temples was brief. "One 'thought' on either temple will allow the subject to retain the, yes, ability to reason. Small but important." His voice was hoarser than normal, strained by exhaustion.

Salzum noted the wear. His words played at being tender with concern. "Teacher, old friend, perhaps you should rest. This- You are too important to risk."

"I appreciate your, hm, concern, but I must press on. This last rune is the, yes, key stone to the whole project."

The knife worked away at Grady's forehead. These new carvings failed to increase his suffering. It was like adding darkness to a deep hole. It could only be so dark. Plenabus spent an eternity writing the largest and most intricate rune above his brow. There was a strangeness in this rune. A diminishing beyond the pain. Each new line pulled him away. The voices grew distant.

"I know this rune. It's engraved in the coronet you gifted me." The Keyrdegen laughed warmly. "You sly mole. No wonder you insisted I wear it today."

The edges of the conversation between his captors sounded like it came from behind a wall. "The most important, hm, rune. Dominance. We will not need a paralytic now." The bronze contraption hummed as Plenabus continued to cut.

A stumbling rattle filled the little room, so far away. "Plenabus!"

"I am alright, my lord, hm, this was a taxing exercise indeed, yes. A few more lines and it will be done."

Grady did not hear the Keyrdegen's response, if there was one. Two more knife lines on his forehead. The pain began to fade. The still quiet Grady beyond it all, the one who was lucky enough to get to watch and observe as his body was marred and his old life eradicated, sighed. He felt a void growing as the feeling in his limbs faded. His consciousness constricted, pooling behind his eyes. Regrets for things undone and chances taken too late guttered out and left behind a peace Grady never felt before.

At least it's over.

The darkness took him.

TRAPPED IN STONE

The darkness sucked inward and pulled a world in behind it. The new world was a round, open space encrusted with crystalline structures like the inside of a giant uncracked geode. A perspective floated in the center of the cavern, formless, nameless. Spires of crystal surrounded, shimmering with rainbows from a sourceless light. The scene was beautiful–serene.

The peace of a moment stretched on for either an eternity or a second. Time meant little here. *Wherever here is?* First came the thought and then the rest coalesced after. The perspective took on a shape, gained a name, grew dense with memories and associations. Layer upon layer, Grady of No Clan came back together. The last bit that returned to him was the memory of the carving. Of being cut by a scalpel by the city's greatest mind while the Keyrdegen watched on.

Oh, and I spoke with the Keyrdegen myself. Truly, I am fortunate. The thought echoed in the enclosed space, causing a ripple of rainbows throughout the interior of the geode.

The hand he raised to check his forehead and the forehead itself were smooth, untouched by the artificer's scrawls. More importantly, his beard, miracle of miracles, was back in all its patchy glory. Grady's floating body was full of hair again and entirely free of both clothes and cuts. His twisting inspections sent him spinning in space.

As far as dreams go, *What else could this be?*, this one was fine. Grady preferred the ones where he got to play at being the hero in a story. They were more exciting. Plus, Emerlda played a role in most of them. Emerlda. Grady was not sure how much time had passed since their conversation in his office, since he asked her out, since she kissed his cheek and said she liked him. He remembered her smell, the solid softness of her shoulders. *One order of that, please,* he asked the dreamscape around him.

A tug at his foot stopped Grady's spinning. A red and jagged current sizzled through the crystal spire in front of him. The energy coruscated out until the whole geode buzzed, red and angry. A red mote leaped from the crystal, nipping at the same foot that was tugged. It tingled more than hurt.

Plenabus's grating voice filled the empty space. It sounded like the artificer was right next to him in a small room. "It tickles me, yes, the simplicity at the heart of science. To think these ley lines function the same as the wire that brings the energy to the lights here. Their connections to the runes allow for better-"

The Keyrdegen cut him off with a barked, "Enough. Carry on."

The voices, the hated voices, were flat and mundane in the geode's heart. They didn't echo or cause ripples in the crystals like Grady's thought had. They sounded as normal as two people chatting while performing profane surgery on an unwilling victim could sound.

Grady spat curses at his captors, the vilest he knew and some he made up on the spot. His words pulsed out through the crystals as a prismatic rippling. It was hard to make out beneath the mass of red energy, but Grady felt them reverberate until they grew still.

Chastened, Plenabus's explanation of the procedure diminished to a personal mutter while he went about his all-important work. The 'Hm's' and 'Yes's' were plentiful enough to choke a boar. The Keyrdegen only spoke in response to a direct request from Plenabus for help moving around Grady's body.

Must be mine. I'm still in it. He looked around at the geode. *I think.*

The pain was distant. It clawed at the edges of his being, informative but not demanding. This experience was worse, somehow, than being present for the initial cutting.

The red energy spread up Grady's legs as he floated in the geode. The courses were perfectly straight and right-angled. Where they met, runes flared to life, made of the same red wire-thin energy. The grid of tingling sparks grew to coat him up to his neck. Arcs of red lightning leaped from his feet and hands back to the crystal spires closest to them. The tingling rose to his jaw, tickled his nose, and vibrated his eyes.

The buzzing intensified to a fevered pitch and exploded into a whoop of sound. In its wake, the geode world disappeared, and Grady was back in his cell, bathed in the unnatural white lights. His eyes refused to glance in any direction or to even blink. On the far edges of his peripheral vision, the geode's crystals sparked.

"Plenabus... his eyes." Salzum leaned in over Grady. His face was flush with excitement and his eyes were wide with wonder. A wave of joy surged over Grady. It felt foreign and deserved. It was the Keyrdegen's! The bastard was enjoying himself and Grady *felt* it.

That's odd. Can't say I care for it one bit.

"What? Hm. Purely involuntary, my lord. Yes." Plenabus's ruin of a face entered Grady's field of view opposite the Keyr's. "See the pupils. Wide. Unfocused. Hm. He most likely sees nothing."

Fat lot you know. I see you. For whatever it's worth, I see you.

The artificer and warrior swung back out of view and the procedure continued. The tingling spread to the very top of Grady's head. When the last lines connected back again to the complex rune on his forehead, the red energy's dance doubled its tempo. Flashes of feeling rocked him. Physical memories flooded his mind, each one tinged in red. He ran and dodged through a busy crowd in a desperate rush to not be late. Again. He yawned and stretched, only to tweak a muscle in his back he never knew he had. He patted his stomach after gorging himself so much that his options were either get up and walk or be immediately sick. Of holding a pen. Of laying down after a long shift. A kiss on the cheek. Taunting words. A cold shower.

"That is some fine line work, Plenabus. You are a genius and a craftsman unparalleled in this age." Grady's understanding of the Keyrdegen's words ran deeper than before. The tone was one of praise and admiration. Beneath it hid a sinkhole of condescension and mild contempt.

A war leader and an actor. So talented, my lord.

"You flatter me, yes. But please, hold your praise until the procedure is, hm, finished."

"Results are not all that matters. Each step of an experiment well executed is worth celebrating." Now the Keyrdegen was pleased at his own craftwork, the easy flattery and the lie of care aimed at manipulating the artificer for the fun of it.

A grating warble of a screech filled the room. *What an infectious laugh*, Grady though. It sawed at him and made him wish for the ability to cover his ears. "You do love quoting me to myself, yes."

"I merely honor my great teacher." The warmth and love in his voice was hollow. The Keyrdegen radiated a calculating coldness. Why was Grady able to see beneath Salzum's masks?

Why? Why can I feel him?

"Always the flatterer, yes, my lord. It is time I show you the water wheel's true, hm, purpose. Yes. Its true purpose."

"It does more than power these marvelous lights of yours? They alone are worth the weight of copper wire and loadstone you demanded. A practical fortune." There. The praise was hollow inside, but that grumble at the end. That was true. The begrudging anger was real.

There he is.

"You always, yes, loved our little experiments. Reminds me of old, hm, times. Yes. Please do the honors. Clamp these wires to the meat of his palms between his thumb and forefinger, and these to the big toes on each foot." Plenabus leaned in and Grady felt something clamp over the runes above his heart and gut. The artificer muttered in thought as he worked. "Perhaps a sort of, hm, prefabricated brace to help place them on the assembly line..." More connections were made to his hips, elbows, and the meat of his shoulders. It tickled a little.

The lights were blocked out temporarily by the wispy beard and blood-stained labcoat of the artificer. He attached a disc at the end of a wire to the intricate rune on Grady's forehead.

"Yes. Everything is secure. All that's left is to throw the switch and apply the, hm, current. The change should be immediate. If you would be so kind as to operate the switch?"

"Of course." Grady felt the Keyrdegen walk across the room. "On your mark," Salzum said. He roiled with a mix of emotions Grady wasn't sure he had ever felt before. It was a volatile compound made up of three parts ambition, two parts confidence, and just a dash of impending triumph.

"Now."

The lights flickered and dimmed, their brightness stolen to dance across Grady's vision and shake the world. The geometric tingling in his carvings intensified. Grady felt his mind, *My soul?*, being pulled strongly in all directions. The force was attempting to quarter him! Nothing hurt, but it was far from pleasant.

The cell shook away and the world within the geode returned. Energy burst out of Grady, connecting him to surrounding crystals with jagged red bolts. Unable to move once more, Grady watched helplessly from the corner of his eyes as crystal grew along the paths of red lightning until his hands and feet were trapped. It spread up to his hips and down his shoulders, engulfing Grady. The crystals pushed against his head. Grady closed what he knew now were not really his eyes. He had no desire to watch the crystal finish devouring him. The energy spread deeper into his body until his very bones shook.

The geode grew still. The hum of the red energy faded. The light inside the geode was white and bright again. His head remained free. Grady counted that as a small win and sighed with relief. It was important to take the good with the bad, after all. The world of the cell and his tortured body slid up into place, reasserting itself until the geode world was gone. The white light filled his vision until it shrank to a line and then winked out. No matter how he tried, Grady could not will his eyes to open again. Nothing he tried brought back the crystalline world of the geode.

All was black.

Am I back? Checking in with his body was fruitless. He felt only a cold and stoney numbness. Every impulse he sent was ignored by every part of his body he sent it to. All was nothing and a complete lack of sensation. *No. This is the worst yet,* Grady decided. He frantically searched for any of the small background sensations he habitually ignored. No heartbeat pulsed in his neck. No rush of air entered his lungs. Come to think of it, there wasn't even a desire for air. He felt no thirst and, when he thought about it, no hunger. A horror settled into his soul, chilling his being.

What did they do to me?

AWAKE AND SERVE

"Remarkable." The Keyrdegen's wonder was tangible and edged with a hunger Grady did not fully understand.

"Too kind. Too kind." At the sound of Plenabus's ear-scraping voice, red sparks of frustration burst to life within Grady's void.

Is this death then? Was he going to remain in his body until it rotted away and became earth? Grady did not often imagine death, but to think and feel inside of his own corpse? *That's a bit of a let down.* It just didn't seem fair, which made a sad kind of sense. *If life was never fair, I don't know why I thought what came after would be.*

"Amazing." Salzum whispered this time. A soft touch ran up Grady's leg. "It's stone." A ripple of disappointment soured the Keyrdegen's growing wonder. "It is a bit of a shame. Without a proper beard it looks like the statue of an impossibly old baby." His excitement returned in full force, accompanied by that strange hunger. "Is it done? Is it ready?" Impatience roiled off the warrior and tugged at Grady, whispering unintelligible commands.

What was that?

"Yes, all is in order. It is ready. The ancients made no mention of a need to, hm, wait. And they were meticulous, yes, to say the least." A fumbling rattle came from Grady's left. "Now, the coronet you wear. My gift, yes. The rune etched in the center matches the one on the subject's, hm, forehead. Simply speak a command and it will attempt any task you set to the best of its current knowledge and abilities. Yes. The command to turn it on is 'awake'. 'Sleep' is, logically, the command to turn it off, to put it in a, hm, resting state."

"Awake."

The word thrummed through Grady, flinging his eyes open. The familiar room was unchanged. The white lights still shone, but he could now see past them. Every inch of the room was clearly visible. His eyes refused to dart around. He commanded them to glance, scan, blink, anything. They ignored him completely. They only stared straight ahead at the smooth rock of the ceiling. He wanted to scream, but his jaw and the various parts of his body needed for a good yell were as mutinous as his eyes.

"Look at me, golem." This command his eyes obeyed with alacrity. With a scrape of stone on metal, Grady's head and eyes snapped to face the Keyrdegen. The Keyrdegen smiled and stroked at his beard, fingering the valuable rings woven amongst the intricate plaiting. His every move radiated deep satisfaction. "Excellent! Most excellent." The Keyrdegen moved toward Grady and peered into his eyes. "Does anything remain? Of who it was?"

"Only, hm, echoes, my lord. The texts were clear. The brain maintains all its pathways and capabilities to learn, yes, but the process purges the animus, the, hm, will." The ancient artificer stepped up next to Salzum. His palsied fingers tented and tapping in front of him. "Yes. Its processing power remains. Problem solving and, hm, the like. It should be able to complete complex tasks and not need constant commands for every single step. It can learn, if taught. It is only, hm, limited by what it knows how to do. Aren't we all though, yes?" He laughed lightly and Grady was reminded of a fork scraping at a plate. Plenabus smiled with soft loving eyes down at Grady, who fumed at his inability to properly glare back. Or to pull away from the gentle caress on his cheek.

"What is your name?" The Keyrdegen asked, one hand absently touched the simple coronet above his brow. When nothing happened immediately, he frowned into Grady's immobile face. His nostrils flared with impatience.

Energy swept through Grady's mind. A tension built, pressure burgeoning on pain, that demanded he answer the Keyrdegen's question. When he spoke, the sound Grady made was more the rumble of an avalanche than a voice. "Grady of No Clan." Pure relief flooded him as soon as he fulfilled the request

"Plenabus!" The artificer shrunk back from the warrior's ire. Was that an undercurrent of fear beneath the anger? "What is the meaning of this?"

"Just an echo, sire," Plenabus assured his lord. Though he sounded less confident than before. "A fossilized, hm, remnant of the dvergr that once was. Yes. Command the name away, and you will never hear it uttered again."

"Can't have it running around blaring that about. Grady of No Clan is no more, thing. You have no name." Grady felt the power of the command try to rip his name away, to tear away the memories serving as his foundation. He struggled to hold on to it, to himself. When the storm of power passed, Grady felt scoured, but he remembered. "Let us try that again, shall we? What is your name?"

"I have no name," the avalanche voice answered. Grady felt his body speak the words and felt the truth of the answer. The small part of Grady, observing everything from behind the stone eyes, still remembered. Grady felt the distance between himself and his body widen.

"Wonderful, wonderful." Pensively the Keyrdegen stared at Grady. Grady never liked prolonged eye contact. Paralyzed, Grady's eyes and head remained still until the Keyrdegen began to pace, dragging Grady's eyes back and forth. When the pacing took him a bit further than the eyes alone could follow, Grady's head moved to compensate.

"That's disconcerting," Salzum said with a laugh. "At ease, thing." At the command, Grady's head snapped back to neutral. Staring at the ceiling again was more comfortable for Grady and far less awkward. "Marvelous. The thing should have a name though. Calling it, well, *thing* lacks a bit of artistry, I think."

"When there are more of them, it will be, hm, imperative, that each possess a unique cognomen. I have a few labeling systems in mind. Yes. This unit, though, is singular, anything will do."

Slimy condescension oozed within the Keyrdegen's friendly words. "What would I do without you, brilliant Plenabus? Anything will do. Sit up and look at me." Grady hinged upwards from his waist and sat impossibly straight. Before him Keyrdegen Salzum stood looking resplendent. He was large enough to bear all the trappings of his station while easily containing the near-constant duality between his outer actions and his inner thoughts. Gravity-like, he tugged at Grady. Plenabus was a wasted wreck in comparison. Frail and shaking slightly, pride had to be the only thing holding him up without assistance. His one good eye looked on lovingly at Grady.

"Pardon my need for theatrics and metaphor at this moment. You more than anyone else, Plenabus, understand how great a shift we have set into motion. Sitting before us is the first golem created in thousands of years. Can you feel it? Change comes and we stand at its epicenter. Rockhome. Our people," Grady heard the unspoken 'my power', "will grow and change. Golem, hear me. From now on, you are designated as Radix." The Keyrdegen primped for a moment, brushing the large gems of his rings through his beard. Again he commanded. "Tell me your name."

"Radix." *Grady,* the voice inside insisted. The distance between Grady and his body now had a name. The barrier thickened. The space Grady occupied felt more cramped. Would Radix grow large enough to crush him? Was Grady just some ghost in the stone that, like all echoes, would fade in time?

He ordered me to forget, yet I remain. I resisted.

The lord of the thegen was not done playing with his new toy. Its ambitious core was the only thing keeping Grady from describing the Keyrdegen's joy as childlike. "Raise your right hand." Radix complied with the command the instant it was said. "Now, your left." Grady could only watch. The sensation of moving his body without willing it to action felt like a livelier version of the paralysis brought on by Plenabus's special cocktail. "Interesting. It did not alternate its hands like I expected."

"Yes. Fascinating. Actions without a, hm, grander design or purpose might require more specific instructions, yes."

"And it will just stay like that until I release it?"

"Until time wears it away to, hm, nothing. Yes. That is my under-standing." Salzum's joy redoubled at the idea of nigh-eternal obedience.

I think the Keyrdegen has control issues.

It was nothing, holding his hands up. They stood ramrod straight above his head. His stone muscles bunched and held with no burn, no shake, no discernible effort at all.

Salzum was giddy with the possibilities before him. He command-ed Grady's arms to be lowered and directed him to get down from the table on which he was reborn. This brought out more 'ooo's' and 'ah's' as Grady took his first steps since before his abduction. Stone on stone, his feet clattered loudly in the small room with each step. His gait was off because his knees were refusing to bend completely. Even standing felt all wrong. He felt heavier. Far heavier.

"Marvelous." Even though Salzum was staring at Grady, he got the distinct impression the Keyrdegen was looking through him, past him, to visions inspired by a steel-scented ambition. "His movements are rather stiff though."

"Hm, Fascinating. I found vague mentions of an adjustment pe-riod, yes, after the change." Plenabus hobbled to a desk to scribble down some observations. "Give it time, yes. Time."

Grady didn't like the way the Keyrdegen was looking at him, chuckling, and brimming with cruel mirth. "Radix, raise your right leg."

Obedient Grady's right foot shot up at an incredible speed. His knee locked in a perfect right angle and his foot was flat. Grady internally braced himself for the inevitable crash when he fell over. Balance was never his strong suit. He didn't even wobble.

That's new. Curious, Grady focused his attention on his legs. The sensations he received were dulled by the distance between himself and his body. There was a vague awareness of the muscles working, but nothing more.

Plenabus clapped limply with delight. "I wonder..." The old dvergr squared up in front of Grady and tried to shove him over. His muscles resisted easily. The artificer grunted as he pushed with all his might, huffing and puffing the entire time. "Remarkable. Like it's, hm, rooted to the floor."

"Stand back, stand back." The Keyrdegen was feeling clever again.

Here it comes.

"Lift your left leg."

His left leg flashed up, same as the right. The rest of Grady fell. He clattered to the floor, tailbone first. The world bounced around. When he came to rest on his back, his legs were still at perfect ninety degree angles, his feet were still flat. Uncommanded, his arms remained steady at his side. Internally, Grady was overwhelmed by an instinctual flash of fear of what comes at the end of a fall. Without the familiar twisting of his guts and the taste of copper on his tongue, the fear was clawless. Grady felt the impacts as the different parts of himself hit the floor. There was a distinct lack of pain. Mind clear, the fear receded.

Well, that was interesting.

"March in place," Salzum ordered after he made Grady stand back up. Grady did as ordered. His legs pistoned up and down in place. "Why is he doing that with his arms?" It took a little effort for Grady to notice his arms had joined in. They went down and up in opposition to the legs.

"It is following your command to the best of its, hm, knowledge. Yes. That must be how the subject believed marching works."

"Ridiculous. Stop that flailing about." Grady froze with one foot just off the floor and his arms nearly akimbo. Grady didn't need his new intimate empathy with the Keyrdegen to know he was irritated. "No. No. Stupid thing. Just stand there. Normally." Grady's body twitched and shifted as he pondered what it meant to stand normally. He settled and the watching Keyrdegen swelled with triumph. "Let's have some real fun. Radix, dance the hopak."

Nothing happened for a brief moment. "I do not know how to dance the hopak," Grady said. The raucous, squatting dance was for show-offs all around Rockhome. He'd seen the dance done, there wasn't a dvergr alive who hadn't. He tried to do it once. Back then his body was less resistant to falls and bruised very easily. The pain in his knees had persisted for a week.

Was that giggle from Plenabus? The artificer rapidly clapped. "You see! It must know or be, hm, taught."

"What do you know how to do, Radix?" The Keyrdegen demanded, the grumpiness Grady felt in him was at odds with Salzum's stately overbearance.

Grady listened with interest as his body listed all he knew how to do. "I am a capable computer. I can record, tabulate, do sums, and make basic recommendations regarding the procurement of materials for basic mine operation. I can write with a neat hand. I can sharpen quills. I can-"

"Enough! Stop. Ha. We certainly picked a winner." The Keyrdegen laughed right into Grady's face.

Laugh all you want. Grady doubted the Keyrdegen could make sense of even the most basic usage report that crossed Grady's desk.

The warrior's thick finger wagged in Grady's face. "I would actually like to see that. Might as well try it out, right Plenabus? Create a... what would you say... a baseline. See what one of these things can do with the skills it came with?"

"Hm, excellent idea, my lord. Yes."

Grady got a good look at the Keyrdegen's leg-thick, gold laden braids as his majesty turned his back and opened the door. He barked orders to the guards outside. Despite the highly unusual nature of the demand, one of the guards saluted with a fist to his chest and darted off back up the ramp and into the rest of the world.

"Hm, sir?" Plenabus fussed around Grady who felt the strong urge to swat him away like a fly.

"Yes?"

"It's still on. Yes. It will be a while until what we need is, hm, gathered and brought. It is best to reserve its energy. Yes."

"Of course, of course. A wise recommendation." The last vestiges of his pleasant smile faded as the Keyrdegen turned away from his artificer. "You know best. Radix, sleep."

The world went out and was replaced by the inside of the geode. His whirling mind was soothed by the dim light. Still encased in crystal, he was no more capable of moving under his own will here, than he was back under the mountain in his new body of stone. It was all so much, so very much. There were no eyes for him to close, not really, but the world of the geode lost focus and dimmed. His mind fluttered like a closing eye-lid. Fiercely, the dvergr encased in the crystal repeated one thought over and over again as a peaceful oblivion asserted itself.

I am Grady of No Clan. I am Grady. I am.

PART 2

The silvery glint at the bottom of the hole promised Betina everything she ever dreamed of. Each swing of her pick pierced deeper into the stone, creating cracks and revealing more of the mithril beneath her feet. With a triumphant cry she drove the pick down with all her might. The earth beneath her crumbled away. She reached to touch the thick silver seam of metal as she tumbled past it into the darkness.

-Excerpt from a dvergr folk tale "Betina Who Dug Downwards"

THE MORE THINGS CHANGE

"**A**wake, Radix!"

At Salzum's command, a low hum filled the void. It grew in pitch and intensity until it whistled. A quick glimpse of the geode world peeled back to reveal the hated face of Keyrdegen Salzum and the tiny, unnaturally lit laboratory-prison. The equally despised Plenabus leered over the warrior's shoulder like a decaying gargoyle. Overall, Grady preferred oblivion.

"Fast start up time, yes?" Plenabus scribbled a note onto his clipboard. "Please, hm, proceed, sir."

Taking in all of Grady, Plenabus was enraptured. His expression was a twisted perversion of the joy upon the faces of new parents as they showed off their latest child. The mad artificer missed the disgusted look Salzum shot at him and was blind to the smothered anger radiating from the Keyrdegen. He needed no one's permission.

"Are you hungry?" The Keyrdegen held out a fine looking basket filled with shiny black rocks.

Is that...? Hungry? Do they...? No. No. No, no, no, no.

A tendril of Grady's mind reached down towards his stomach. Grady was surprised to find a hunger-like hole there. It did not gnaw at him, demanding to be filled like he was used to. It was just a lack to be noted and filled at the earliest convenience. "Yes. My fuel reserves are a quarter full."

Oh, goody. My natural optimism persists. And that voice is awful.

Awkwardly, Salzum held forth the basket of coal. It brimmed with shiny anthracite, the good stuff, and, apparently, Grady's breakfast. Salzum looked back and forth between the basket and Grady a few times.

"Hm, Sir? A command-"

"Yes! Fine. Understood. I thought the damned thing would at least have the sense to eat when it needs to."

"Technically, it does not eat..."

"Shut it!" Salzum took a deep, slow breath. Grady would not have been surprised to see steam coming from any of the holes in the Keyrdegen's head. "Eat."

Grady could only watch as his stone hands, tattooed with deep carved, silver runes and flecked with minerals, reached into the basket and brought the shiny lumps of coal to his waiting mouth. It was Grady's first glimpse of any part of his real body. His captors' descriptions of his new stone exterior were one thing and seeing it for himself was another. The shock of the sight was dulled by the lack of any physical response.

They had made him gray, all over and to the bone.

His body chomped and chewed and swallowed. The sensations were familiar. The biting into and the grinding chew of the coal reminded him, not unpleasantly, of munching rock candy. He was able to follow the bits swallowed down his throat, but only so far. While he would not call the messages sent from his tongue 'taste', the sensation told him this was good fuel he was shoveling into himself. His captors watched Grady eat, Plenabus with an adoring smile and Salzum with a hunger all his own. The artificer mimed chewing motions and nodded encouragingly. Fullness in his stomach stilled his hands. While it was the weirdest meal Grady ever ate, it was not the worst.

"Are you done?" The Keyrdegen asked, rattling the few remaining coals under his nose.

"I am filled to capacity," Grady answered with his avalanche of a voice. The feeling of his stomach being full was surprisingly comforting and familiar.

"My lord? Should we set it to today's, hm, task? I have a lot of data to collect and am excited to observe. Yes. Sir, remember. Try to give an order aimed at the completion of the, hm, whole, not just a single step. Let us see how our golem does, yes."

"Radix," Salzum said after taking a moment to gather his thoughts, "find the inefficiencies within the Zegrumrin Chalcocite mine." The Keyrdegen stepped aside, revealing a small clerk's desk with a metal chair. Stacks, higher than the desk itself, ringed the workstation like an easy to topple mountain range. It was a heavy triple shift's worth of documents by Grady's estimation. One of the unnaturally bright lights was moved so that it hung over the desk. One of the new pens glinted in too bright light.

A surprised '*Huh?*' was the last thought Grady was sure came from himself. Driven by Salzum's command, he walked over to the desk, sat down, and began to work. The lab and his torturers faded away. Even though the papers came from a different mine, this was the same work Grady had done his entire adult life. The familiar nature of the task soothed him. There was a greater sense of ease to it all. He felt no need to shift in his chair to get comfortable, or pause for a drink, or to eat, or to sneeze, or to merely stare off into space for a while to rest his mind and his eyes.

He read, copied, collated, tabulated, annotated, and organized the papers in a blur. His movements were so exact that, no matter how precarious the pile, not one stack toppled while he worked. Beneath the all consuming concentration forced on him by the Keyrdegen's command, Grady marveled at the speed, precision, and neatness of his hand writing. His numbers were never so small and clear. Not a single smudge or blot marred the pages of his summaries.

The report he wrote was concise and pointed to two issues as the cause of the inefficiency. First, an issue with supply of carbon disulfide was limiting output, and, second, there was an odd shortfall in the odd shift's output that personnel should look into. He ended it with a note saying there was not sufficient information here to suggest a solution to either problem.

Grady felt the command's grip on his mind release as he placed his finished report on the corner of the desk where his Out box used to be. His thoughts were his own to control again. His body remained sitting in the metal chair, with his stone hands folded neatly on the top of the desk.

What a rush! Nothing like some good paperwork to take your mind off of being turned into a stone monstrosity. He was only half kidding. The familiarity of it all left him feeling a bit refreshed.

"In life you must have been a very good computer, yes," Plenabus said, beaming with pride. He patted Grady gently on the shoulder. "That was remarkably fast, hm, work. By all accounts that was a multi-shift task, two to three by our estimates. Yes. You managed to complete it in a few hours. The speed. Remarkable. Your hands were a, hm, blur!"

Plenabus leaned his ruin of face too close to Grady's. His smile was small, almost melancholic. "I wish you were still in there, Grady of No Clan, so you could see the value of your, hm, sacrifice. It beggars the imagination, yes, to think what Rockhome could be with an army of golems like you." The madman sounded wistful. "Salzum has great plans for you and yours, my golem. My creation."

Yes, Grady was sure, there was actual love in his voice. *Looney, old dvergr.*

"His, hm, august self is out attending to matters of state. We were unsure how long you would take to complete your task and you certainly, hm, surprised us all. Yes. Sitting there should not drain your power reserves, hm, heavily at all. Though I wish I could calculate how much all that brain power used up. Yes."

He puttered in and out of Grady's field of vision while he tidied up. Plenabus took up the completed report, smiled at it, and hugged it to his chest. "And don't you, hm, worry. I will make sure that your report reaches eyes that will benefit from it. Yes." He limped out of sight again. The door slid open. The lights extinguished with the chunk of a thrown lever. "We will be back, my masterpiece."

Immobile, Grady stared off into the absolute darkness that was the real home of the dvergr. The gas lamps, the mirrored-in sunlight, and the new eye burning lights were aberrations underground. They were, ultimately, ineffectual and only held the darkness back temporarily. As a child, Grady never feared the dark. At his lowest times he wrapped the darkness around himself like a comforter, knowing it kept his misery private and him in the gentleness of solitude. During his higher moments, few though they were, the dark served as the canvas on which he painted his dreams. It was in the dark that the tiny spark kindled by hope was brightest and easiest to see.

The blackness of his room, his cell, his re-birthplace, peeled back as he stared into it. The geode returned and Grady was trapped once more in his personal crystal prison. Layered behind the glowing crystals, Grady could still make out the darkness waiting beyond.

"Oh. This is new," Grady said in his own voice. He watched the crystals ripple in response.

Despite the circumstance, he felt a warming ember of pride at the work he had done. A multishift task and he completed it in hours. That was something.

But did I want to do it?

But did he ever really want to? Work wasn't optional before, even if he was responsible for dragging himself out of bed and to his office each shift. Want was nothing. He needed a place to sleep and food in his mouth. He chose none of his circumstances. Those needs did far more of the choosing for him. The more Grady thought about it, the more he realized exactly how little actual agency and choice factored into his old life.

What about Emerlda? What about her? Was she a choice he made or one made by convenience? Her path out of work just happened to take her past his office. Convenience and chance nurtured their friendship. By treating him like a person instead of a useless brick in a rock-carved city, had she made the choice for him, for his heart? Maybe. Of course she would seem like his choice, when in reality she was his only option. Grady knew these thoughts were unkind and unfair.

But are they untrue?

If he was being honest with himself, there was an ease in being unable to exert his own will. During his assigned task his mind was quiet. There was no constant weedling and whining for things he wanted or felt he needed. No thirst or hunger clamored to be appeased. The spaces in between his thoughts were empty. His body and his heart, the physical and metaphorical ones, were still.

Is this peace?

Trapped in crystal in an impossible geode, it was clear. Grady, the old Grady, was dead. His life was irrevocably over. His new stone hands and the lingering 'taste' of the coal dust on his tongue were only the latest evidence.

Trapped in crystal, with the darkness of his cell just beyond, Grady spoke. "I am Grady of No Clan." The words echoed within the crystal lined space. They felt untrue. Grady spoke again. "I am Radix, the Keyrdegen's Golem." Again, the words echoed in the geode's heart. They, too, felt untrue. "I am... lost." Finally, there was the truth.

Unmoored from identity and unable to move, Grady retreated into that quiet space between his thoughts. He stared ahead without seeing the nothing of the physical world or the bright sharpness of the world within. In that place that was nowhere, in an unending moment stretched thin, he simply was.

TO BEND

Huffing exertion was soon followed by the clatter of a heavy, wooden crate on the floor. Salzum's voice, imperious with the expectation of instant obedience, dismissed the crate bearers. The darkness popped like a bubble. Despite the flooding in of experience, Grady (or whoever he was) maintained his position between thoughts. There was no point in being curious. He would know what he needed to know when it needed to be known.

Grady recognized the footsteps and wheezing breath of his creator. "Ah, Salzum, you are, hm, earlier than expected. Feeling eager, are we? Yes?"

"As Keyrdegen I keep my own hours and go where I please, when it pleases me to do so." The Keyrdegen's strong sense of effrontery marred Grady's newfound sense of peace.

"Hm. Of course, sir." Plenabus must have bowed because it sounded like he spoke into the floor.

"Get up. Roisten Zegrumrin sought me out. He had high praise for the accounting and recommendations that were returned to him. He marveled at the speed. Assumed we had a team of clerks working on it through the shift. His thanks were voluble."

"Yes, it was most remarkable. It pleases me to hear that the accuracy of my creation's work was, hm, validated." His words nearly stumbled over each other in an excited rush. "The potential for an army of clerks with this capability at the ready... Yes, we could change the world. I was thinking, my lord, of pausing at this stage for a while to focus on the golem's mental capabilities. Try to see if a golem can learn the basics of a, hm, trade, yes, or maybe even the basics of artifice. With that sort of computational potential our technologies would–"

"No." Plenabus, interrupted midstream, continued to dribble out his thoughts unintelligibly. Grady was able to hear Salzum's smirk in his voice and feel his cruel joy at the artificer's fumblings. "We continue as originally planned."

"I must protest. Listen to reason! This could change how we think, how we create and reshape, hm, everything that is to come after! Do not treat this golem as some tin soldier for you to play with. We mu–gah!" Plenabus squawked. Choked whimpers from the left preceded the entrance of the Keyrdegen and his artificer into Grady's field of vision. The former clutched the latter beneath his chin, bunching up the collar of Plenabus's white jacket. Salzum's beringed hands fully enveloped the elder's scrawny neck.

The warrior lord leaned in until his nose nearly touched the artificer's. His voice, low and intense, smoldered like a banked smith's fire. Rage radiated from the Keyrdegen so strongly that Grady experienced it as a warmth on his face. "I 'must' nothing. Do you forget to whom you are speaking?"

Salzum shook Plenabus when he attempted to answer. "The future you have planned is neat, orderly, and unbeset by outside dangers. Secluded in your tower, dreaming your dreams, your vision is clouded. Trust that my high position grants me a better vantage point from which to gauge what Rockhome needs. War wracks the world above. You know what lies in wait below." The Keyrdegen's glare promised more than a wrung neck. "We proceed as originally planned. Yes?"

Plenabus nodded as much as he was able to with the meaty, powerful mitts wrapped around his throat.

"Excellent." Grady marveled at how fast the Keyrdegen was able to hide his ire. A heartbeat was all he needed to put on the jovial air of a kind and friendly leader, full of respect and love for an old teacher. Except in Salzum's eyes. They burned coldly and were untouched by the gentle smile now gracing his face. "Radix, stand and offer Artificer Plenabus your seat."

In a smooth motion, Grady rose and swung the chair around to place it behind the artificer. He even offered a hand to gently help the old dvergr lower himself into the chair. At Plenabus's touch, a personal fury burst up through Grady's purposeless apathy. The fury urged Grady to act. He strained against his internal, crystal confines.

Crush, he commanded his hands, *Mash. Tear. Hurt. Nudge. Flick? Dammit.* Nothing. His body simply straightened up and stood patiently. Grady sank down through his disappointment and sought to return to the peace he found in pure observation.

The Keyrdegen stood before Grady and Plenabus for a bit, creating space to ensure his lesson sunk in. "Are you ready to begin, Artificer? There is much for me to do today. Heavy is the head, and all that."

"Yes, hm, sire." Plenabus's usual squeak was roughened by his handling. He cleared his throat to little effect. "If my, yes, specifications were followed, the bars in the crate should give us a general idea of the golem's physical strength. It should start with the thinnest and end with the thickest. Yes. Naturally."

"Radix, do you understand what is expected of you?"

"Yes."

"Are you ready to observe, Plenabus?" Plenabus acquiesced in a way Grady could not see, but which clearly pleased Salzum. "Fetch the crate, bring it back here, and begin."

Once more, Grady's mind was hijacked. He moved his body and reasoned as much as he needed to, but controlled none of it. He walked to the door, opened it and, for the first time, saw the world outside his cell. Well, he saw the dark, angled tunnel that led from the door to the rest of the world. Stiff-limbed, Grady hoisted the crate up easily and carried it to the empty place where the small desk had been. The Keyrdegen must have moved it himself.

The crate's top was hinged and easy to open. A series of rounded metal bars, made of unremarkable iron, were piled inside. While each was one Grady's shoulder width long, they ranged widely in thickness. The

smallest, and the first Grady grabbed, was no thicker than his pinky. It was
the same kind of rod that had foiled him that shift at the pub.

The memory of the incident at the boozer occupied the little bit
of Grady's mind not focused on the task at hand. It felt like a lifetime ago.
His recollection of the whole event, made sharp by the trauma of it all,
was splintered into sharded sensations. The heat from the gathered crowd
pressing in to see his trial by rod incongruously mixed with the cool of the
stone footpaths against his burgeoning bruises. The pain in his hands as
he struggled against the metal's rigidity overlapped the pain his heart felt
at being denied his high hopes for that outing.

While Grady was lost in his memories, his body took up the smallest rod, an end in either hand, held it out straight, and brought his hands
together. The metal squeaked in protest, but folded in half smoothly with
little discernible effort.

The sight of the twisted metal in his hands brought Grady back to
the present. *Oh. That's something.*

"Why do you waste my time? I could have bent that one."

"Indeed, many strong dvergrs are able to, hm, bend that thickness.
Yes. It was included as a control. Our little ex-clerk was certainly not
capable of such a feat prior to his, hm, transformation. The fact that it
so easily lifted the crate, yes, hints at a vast increase in physical prowess.
Patience, my lord. Patience."

Grady's body neatly folded the second metal rod, this one was
as thick as his thumb, adding a tiny twist at the bottom, with one end
wrapping a bit around the other. *Just like the ones on the wall.* Grady felt a
little thrill of wonder. How strong was he now?

Plenabus spoke to himself as he wrote on his clipboard. "That one
is at the far edge of what a flesh and, hm, blood dvergr can do purely by
hand. Beyond that, each bar requires industrial efforts to be shaped."

The bars were as unable to resist Grady's efforts as he was the
Keyrdegen's commands. Each grew in diameter, two fingers thick, then
three, then as thick as his wrist. Plenabus, awed by his creation's power,
grew silent. The Keyrdegen giggled and licked his lips a few times as he

watched the spectacle. Grady, observing from the safety of his stone head, enjoyed every moment.

The bar as thick as his forearm protested until Grady applied the bar to his knee. Salzum's command drove him on. He felt his body exert energy, struggle, and finally force the ends together.

The last cylinder in the crate was as thick as Grady's thigh. It was a bit longer to account for the extra girth. Grady lifted it out with little effort. He finagled the small beam, calling it a rod felt wrong, until he held each end with an outstretched arm.

The strain was intense. Every rocky ounce of Grady was focused on bending the beam's two ends together. The wedge of his knee was ineffectual. "Come on, Radix, push. Bend it." Salzum commanded and so it must be. Pain sizzled through Grady's consciousness, tearing into his very being, demanding that the Keyrdegen's will be done.

Like a piston, Grady brought the solid, metal beam down on his knee, filling the room with thunder. Grady raised the cylinder and slammed it down again. And again. And again. Sparks flew. Plenabus and the Keyrdegen yelled into the din. Again and the metal bent slightly. Again and it folded. Again and it screamed, snapping in two. The pain evaporated. The job was done. Grady placed the pieces down on the floor and returned to waiting.

Would you look at that, Grady thought. *With the right motivation, anything is possible.* Tender and bruised from the command's onslaught, he wanted to cheer and cry at the same time.

In his peripheral vision, Grady saw the Keyrdegen stroking his beard up onto his shoulder, a pleased gesture if Grady ever saw one. Strong hunger filled his eyes, and he smiled like Grady was a meal long waited for. Plenabus fretted in and out of Grady's line of sight, checking his creation for damage. His muttering was worried, incoherent, and to himself.

"Extraordinary. Yes. The golem is undamaged. His efforts managed to drive his footprint into the, hm, floor. The strength, the fortitude, yes, is beyond the pale." He stooped out of sight. "There are finger indents in the metal..." He sounded like he was going to swoon.

Yay! They're proud of me.

There was too much truth in that thought. Most of his life had enforced his worthlessness, time and again proving him incapable of doing anything noteworthy. The bent and broken metal was scattered at his feet. He had not chosen to do it, but he had done it. He bent metal with his own bare hands. *Stone hands,* he corrected. Such power would make short work of Square Beard and his cronies.

Gravity increased its pull on him, and it now took effort to hold himself up. The odd, detached hunger in his gut made itself known. He felt his posture slacken as his body came to rest.

"Wonderful, wonderful. Your creation performed admirably, Plenabus. You should feel proud." Plenabus muttered a few thank yous and bowed. "Golem, clean this mess up."

The command surged through Grady's mind, but was grounded by his body's inability to move. "Energy reserves are too low for gross movement," Grady reported in his avalanche of a voice. It sounded softer than before. Instead of pain, Grady's inability to comply summoned only minor discomfort, a feeling akin to pins and needles.

Salzum grunted with displeasure. He sighed out of his nose while rubbing the bridge between his eyes. "Have someone fetch more coal for…" the Keyrdegen waved his hand vaguely in Grady's direction. "Plenabus, be sure to put the bucket within its reach. I will be back later for the next test. Golem, when there is a bucket of coal in front of you, eat until you are full." The new order washed over the old and took with it the weakening pins and needles sticking at his being.

His relief was distant and hazy.

A bucket brimming with that good, good shiny black rock roused Grady from his stupor. Utilizing the last of its current reserves, his body launched (*Lunched,* Grady amended) into action. He was ready for the new and satisfying sensation of eating literal rocks. It was almost pleasurable this time. Deliciousness was just out of reach, akin to searching for taste when drinking heavily watered down beer. Aside from a smattering of coal dust, the bucket was completely empty by the time Grady was full.

"Interesting, yes. That was more than you ate last time, hm. I wonder if there was residual energy carried over from its biological state..." Plenabus continued to annotate on his small clipboard and mutter to himself. Grady understood little of what Plenabus said when he started to get technical. Plenabus ended his notes with a flourish. "After your stunt with the last rod, I have a feeling you will pass the, hm, endurance tests with flying colors."

Oh my, 'endurance trials'? I can't say I care for the implication. Plenabus was too close again, running his hand down Grady's cheek once more. Everything in him wanted to recoil from the feathery touch. *I don't care for this either.* One little hope occurred to Grady as he suffered the foul petting. *Maybe I'll get lucky, and they will just smash me to bits.*

A Smashing Good Time

T he two thegen were encased in metal, head to toe. Intricate filigree filled every plate of their armor, depicting the wearers' greatest deeds. Their helmets were identical, each with a visor sculpted into a perfect rendition of an emotionless Salzum. Their armor marked them as members of the Throng, the elite sect of warriors sworn in service to the Keyrdegen. The beards sticking out from under their helmets, heavy with honor tokens for valor and battle prowess, marked them as long-serving veterans.

"We call it Radix." Grady watched the warrior's eyes widen when Salzum revealed his new pet project to them. Their reaction to him was surprising. A number of their honors came from fighting actual monsters. Grady couldn't remember the last time he scared anyone.

I must be a sight.

"It is a construct created by the honored elder, Artificer Plenabus." Plenabus nodded at the acknowledgment with a sour expression on his face. "I appreciate that you took my odd order so seriously."

Each of the warriors was weighed down by an excess amount of chopping, slicing, and crushing implements. This gave Grady a clear picture of how this shift's round of tests was going to go. Was that a crossbow?

All that for little, old me? I'm honored.

The one on Grady's left clanked when he shrugged. "You ordered us to empty out the armory and bring it with us."

"Aye," added the other, "so rarely are our orders so clear. Or easy."

Salzum's laugh was warm and, to Grady's surprise, genuine. "Don't get used to it. However, I do think you will enjoy today's experiments." The Keyrdegen explained what they were going to do rather

quickly. It wasn't complicated. While the visors made it impossible
to tell what the warriors thought about it, Salzum's excitement was
written large by his wide grin.

The thegen nodded when asked if they understood their instructions. Both started to flex and twist in preparation to ensure
they performed at their best. "It must be said: Everything you do,
see, and hear today must be kept in the strictest of confidence. This
cannot be spoken of, even to other members of the Throng. Not even
the Captain. Not yet." They saluted with mechanical precision, their
gauntlets hitting their breastplates above their hearts in unison.

Salzum met each of their eyes and nodded in thanks. Grady felt
the Keyrdegen's attention on him. "Radix, extend out your right arm.
Do not move."

His right arm flew out to the side. Grady bent his knees slightly
to make his stance more secure and braced himself to better rest the
weight of his body on his legs. It was only as the first warrior approached that Grady remembered he was naked.

So many people have seen my pick and potatoes lately.

They started with the sword first. After some discussion, the
two settled on a classic straight blade, the kind made in factories and
shipped out to the human lands by the hundreds. Grady admired the
simple craftsmanship as one of the warriors swung the blade around
to get a feel for its balance. The steel-clad figure stepped forward and
brought the blade up high. He brought it down with a cry. Grady, face
forward, only saw the blur of the swing from the corner of his eye. It
clanged off his arm with an uncomfortably loud report.

Grady felt the impact and the obvious strength behind it. His
arm did not budge, and there was no pain. The blow failed to shift him
in the slightest.

Well, that's something.

The Keyrdegen was giddy. "Bring the blade here. Quickly now.
Ha. Outstanding. Look at the blade, Plenabus."

"Hm. Chipped, sire. The subject's arm is..." Plenabus's fingers traced the runes and lines on his forearm. "Unmarked. Yes." Plenabus's normal squeak was subdued and lacked his normal exuberance. The artificer's deflation pleased Grady in a petty way.

"Excellent. Give it a few more whacks, if you would, Karl."

"My lord."

The burly dvergr took the sword in two hands and brought it down three times onto Grady's arm. The first merely clanged as before. The second impact sent out a shower of sparks. As the sword connected for the third time, it shrieked in protest and splintered in two at the point of contact. The end of the blade clattered off into the corner. Again, all Grady felt was the force of an impact, no pain. The Keyrdegen clapped his hands with ample, bone-deep enthusiasm.

Plenabus worried about his arm again. "Still, hm, mark free. Yes." He scratched at his clipboard in a lethargic, spared manner.

"Wonderful! Just wonderful. Let's try the crossbow next, shall we? Plenabus, come join me. This time, aim for the chest and head." The Keyrdegen moved into view behind the warrior readying his crossbow. In a practiced motion, Salzum hoisted up a dvergr shield, that was really a small wall made of planks of fungal wood banded with iron, and took cover behind it. Plenabus limped over to join him. They stared out through a windowed slot in the shield.

Oh well, no lucky ricochets today. Grady let go of the already fading image of the Keyrdegen and artificer pierced through, say in the chest and head respectively, by the same errant bolt.

"Sir, I fail to see why this test is, hm, necessary. The sword made sense, yes. Taking that kind of a hit proves that golems would be impervious in most industrial settings. The chances of a factory worker being shot by a crossbow are, hm, slim."

The Keyrdegen's anger, like molten metal shining through slag, glowed underneath the tiny cracks in his kind and patient demeanor. "As I have explained, many times now, Plenabus, many times, it would be irresponsible to not learn all we can about your creation's capabilities. 'All knowledge is good knowledge'. Isn't that another one of yours?"

The artificer's response was lost to Grady as the air was filled with the twanging of three bolts being fired in quick succession. At this range, it was impossible for the seasoned soldier to miss. The first two impacted on his chest to no effect, at least to Grady. The bolts were less resilient. They shattered on impact, their heads blunted into uselessness. The last bolt left the crossbow and slowed. Its tip spun as it flew, straight and true, towards his eye. Grady tried with all his might to close his eyes and block out the inexorable approach of the chisel shaped head. The Keyrdegen's command was clear: Do not move. Grady watched with perfect clarity, as the bolt head blunted against his eye. The shaft shattered, freeing its pieces to flutter around his head.

Time returned to normal as Plenabus scuttled out behind the shield. He was not pleased. "The eye! No! A terrible shot, good dvergr. Hm, terrible... I..." He trailed off as he examined the impacted eye. Having Plenabus so close made Grady more uncomfortable than any of the bolt strikes. "Astounding. Simply astounding. Yes. Not a mark, sir, not a, hm, mark. Ah, my creation." Another loving, papery caress on his cheek. With one last, "Remarkable," he sidled back to stand next to the Keyr.

Salzum's ambitious hunger spiked as he twirled one side of his mustache around a ringed finger. The bottomless well of want deep within the Keyrdegen tugged at Grady, thick with unvoiced commands that hinted at his future role in plans already set in motion. "The ax next. Harder."

The long-hafted ax that the other warrior produced was nothing more than a simple, murderous wedge of metal. It lacked any sense of artistry in its design. Its purpose was singular and clear. The soldier looked over his shoulder for his cue to begin.

"First a chop to the arm, I am curious. Then chop the torso. Until failure." *It's nice to see Salzum having such a good time. Someone should be.* If it wasn't for the constant existential dread, Grady would have been bored.

The warrior hefted the ax onto his shoulder with a grunt, steadied his stance, and swung down on Grady's outstretched arm with his whole body. Sparks and a clang. There was more pressure this time, sure, but still no pain. The soldier took a second to shake out his hands before chopping at Grady's abdomen. The first impact almost rocked Grady back on his heels. He dug his toes into the flagstone. He did not move, would not move, as ordered. The rest of the swings were of little further consequence to Grady. The ax felt them. Its blade chipped each time it came into contact with Grady's stone exterior. On the tenth blow, the Throng member's stamina was impressive, the haft finally gave way and snapped, midway between the grip and the head. The mangled ax blade clanged to the floor in defeat.

Tools of War, zero. Imprisoned Stone Dvergr, three. Grady was filled with pride at his resilience. *Nothing like an unearned sense of accomplishment to improve your mood.*

Plenabus's post-test examination revealed not even so much as a dent in Grady. The Keyrdegen bounced from foot to foot, all sense of decorum lost in his giddiness. Grady didn't like it, not one bit. "The hammers!" Salzum applauded. "Both of you at once. Golem, raise your left hand and do not lower it."

Grady extended his other arm. If he could swallow, he would have. Bolts and blades were one thing. He was now made of stone. But hammers, they were made for crushing.

They're probably leaving the picks and explosives for later.

To say he was afraid as the armored pair raised their blunt instruments was not completely accurate, but it was the closest word Grady had for what he was feeling. He was used to a fear that included a need to run or fight and turned his bowels to water. Robbed of that instinctual gut response, Grady was unsure of what this variant feeling was. Apprehension?

Karl 1, Grady had long since lost track of which one was which, wielded a small but weighty warhammer. Its head was the size of a flat fist and a long spike stuck out from the back.

Ah! There's the pick. Wonderful. Thorough.

Karl 2 wielded a massive, two-handed hammer. Its head was a rectangular block of solid metal. Karl 2 had no trouble bringing the heavy weapon up over his shoulder. If anything could still hurt Grady, he imagined these were the weapons.

The hammer blows rattled Grady's teeth. The cacophonous impacts were all he could hear. The sensation of the blows was uncomfortable and just shy of painful. He felt his shoulders working overtime to keep his arms steady in the face of the onslaught. An unheard order from the Keyrdegen spread the blows to the rest of his body. They worked their way down his chest and midsection, to no effect. Then they reached his legs. The large hammer caught the inside of one knee, and the small hammer's spike came around and tugged at the back of the other.

The combined force was too much and Grady toppled onto his back, his arms still outstretched. *Good for them-* pain came and obliterated his ability to think. It coursed over his body, following the channels that Plenabus carved into him. The Keyrdegen's words echoed. "Do not move. Do. Not. Move." For a flash, Grady was back in the geode and his crystal prison. Every glittering surface crackled with the red lightning which bored into him, essence and soul.

The pain faded as quickly as it came. The cell returned. Grady was upright again, his feet comfortably nestled in the imprints they had pressed into the ground. He was following the Keyrdegen's command again. Plenabus tutted around Grady, looking for damage, muttering quietly about brutes abusing his creation to please a spoiled brat's curiosity.

Salzum brought his fists down hard on the thegens' shoulders in thanks. "Excellent work, as always. Wait for me outside." They saluted crisply to their chests, gathered up their broken arsenal, and left. "How about that! It took the coordinated efforts of two of my best to even budge the thing."

"Yes, most, hm, edifying, my lord."

"Stop whinging. You're over six-hundred years old, by the ancestors. Are you ready for the last test?" From the sheath at his waist, the Keyrdegen drew forth a silver dagger. Faint blue swirls spun and bounced across the flat of the blade. The master-level workmanship of the heirloom was obvious, despite its simple design. Deep within himself, Grady's soul resonated with the sight. Every dvergr in the mountain knew the dagger's name. Mountain's Tear, the blade of Thikarum, founder of Rockhome and the first Keyrdegen. It was the most, and only, mithril Grady had ever seen in person.

Plenabus bowed to acknowledge his chastisement. "The scroll's warnings were, hm, direct. Have the golem place his hand on the table, and then, yes, the rest is up to you." Grady found no crack in the artificer's renewed professional demeanor.

"Radix, lower your arms. You look ridiculous. Place one hand on the table. Your choice."

A choice! The potential of it set his mind working in a way it had not since the controlling rune was carved into his forehead. He reasoned with himself, weighing pros and cons. He made a real meal out of deciding. Grady settled on his left. After-all, he wrote with his right hand. Grady leaned forward slightly and pressed his left palm onto the proffered table.

The Keyrdegen brought the dagger close to Grady's mineral-flecked skin, licked his lips, and drew the tip closer with the greatest of care. "Mind the carvings!" The artificer lunged forward, startling the focused dvergr and causing Salzum to jump. The blade slid along the inside of Grady's middle finger. With ease, it carved a short, shallow, and bloodless line. The wound burned, the pain growing worse with each passing moment.

"You idiot!" Salzum roared. He pushed the old dvergr to the ground. He berated the supine artificer who raised his shaking hands as if to ward off any incoming blows. The Keyrdegen's tirade was muted by the roar of suffering emanating from his sliced finger.

Grady rode the pain for he had no other choice. One would think that since his whole body resembled a piece of scrimshaw, that a little scratch on a finger would be more bearable. Especially when you consider that he was now made of stone. The pain did not care for logic. Through the scorching ache, Grady watched Plenabus rise, with no help from the angry Keyrdegen, and lean in to examine the marred digit.

"The stone parted like, hm, flesh. As expected. Yes."

Staring lovingly at the dagger, Salzum kissed the flat of the blade and slid it into its sheath. "Is the damage severe?"

"No. The placement was fortunate. No runes or ley lines reside on the inside of the finger. Its ability to function should not be, hm, permanently impaired."

The Keyrdegen leaned in close to examine his handiwork. "Will it heal? Repair itself?"

Plenabus only shrugged. "Theoretically, yes. But the documents were,hm, incomplete. We will have to see."

OUT OF THE FRYING PAN

The shifts following the first round of tests were dull. The Keyrde-gen's last command, after using an ancient relic to slice his finger, was for Grady to stand with said finger out at the perfect height for Plenabus to examine the wound. Time was slippery in his cell, hours and shifts were much the same. The pain in his finger dulled. When its last embers died out, the lack itself was deeply pleasurable. Joy welled up in him, had nowhere to overflow to, and subsided just as he felt fit to burst.

Gotta take the good with the bad. Not like he had any other choice.

Grady spent a chunk of time marveling over the fact that he had seen, and technically touched, the Mountain's Tear. Here he was living his own horror-filled adventure, where legends were real and where a mad artificer conspired with the city's protector to turn him into a mindless, stone slave. At times, Grady still felt the swirling of an energy, similar to the blue glimmering of the blade's surface, spiraling through his being. It was not a wholly pleasant sensation.

He yearned for just a little bit of an escape. Anything from his old life to help occupy his stone trapped mind and distract it from his unbe-lievable reality. He missed his books and making half decent sandwiches.

The rest of the time Grady got to watch Plenabus watch his finger heal. The artificer muttered while he examined, measured, and observed. Little was inteligible. Most of what Plenabus said was artificer jargon that Grady was completely unable to parse. The bits he could hear and un-derstand were bothersome. Apparently the mithril blade parted his stone skin "like, hm, flesh" and that to be fully understood this phenomenon required "further testing, yes."

Being so close, of course, Plenabus needed to touch him. They were feathery light caresses that tickled, but without the deep rooted need to escape or itch the sensation away. Plenabus clearly loved him or, more accurately, loved his creation. Had the prototypes for his inventions all received this kind of treatment or was Grady special? It was a struggle to quiet the need for the latter to be true.

Every now and then Plenabus met Grady's unmoving eyes. The first few times, Grady screamed in his mind trying to alert the madman to the person remaining beneath the stone. Trapped in crystal. Suffering. His cries went unheard. Plenabus was an artificer, not a mind reader. Grady doubted greatly that Plenabus would care. Through all his mutterings the word 'sacrifice', often preceded by 'noble', rang loud and clear.

Keyrdegen Salzum only returned to the cell once Grady's finger was completely healed. He entered the room smiling and carrying a bundle of ratty, gray clothing with a scuffed pair of boots standing on top. "The preparations are ready." He carelessly tossed the clothes at Grady's feet. "Radix, get dressed. I'm tired of seeing your-" he waved his hand in a circular motion, "everything."

After being naked for so long, the feel of the rough spun garments was an experience all its own. His new body felt every warp and weft, every flyaway fiber. They picked and scratched at him ineffectually. The boots were snug, but the leather quickly yielded to the stone of his feet. He donned the hat, a floppy brimmed affair with a drooping neck cover hanging down the sides and back.

"You are to follow me from a few paces back. Keep your brim down and your face hidden. Come, Plenabus. We don't have all shift."

Grady's excitement would have been hard to contain if it had anywhere to go. They were headed outside! Where were they going? What was this next test? Would he like it?

Probably not.

A small portion of his mind was compelled to keep his body walking, his distance from the Keyrdegen steady, and his head down. As they walked through the cell door, two thegen in unassuming brown leathers and chain mail joined the procession. One took point and the other hung back as a rear guard. Grady assumed they were members of the Throng. There was a chance that they were even his friends from the first round of testing.

After so long in the cell, the smells and sounds of the city bemused Grady's senses. Familiar scents were made strange through the lack of a physical response. He noted the savory aroma of a shaved pork stand and the acrid waft of piss from a gutter with equal indifference. The ever constant clatter of the transport carts and the various whistles, thuds, crunches, and booms of industry were familiar enough. Grady tried to sink into the sounds, get lost in them for a moment. Perhaps he could pretend this all a daydream, fanciful and mad, created by a bored and under-stimulated mind as he walked to work.

He almost succeeded, until Plenabus began to wheeze and broke the illusion. "May we pause for a, hm, moment? Our pace is, yes, a bit brisk for me." He gasped for breath between every word. If he wasn't the one who carved his skin and petrified his very body, Grady would have felt bad for the old dvergr.

"We rest when we get there. Taking this thing out into the city is risky enough without us idling about in the open." Salzum's tone brooked no argument. If anything, his pace quickened. Grady felt a spike of cruel pleasure from him. "We are nearly there."

The Keyrdegen's boots, very fine with gold thread accents stitched right into the leather, stepped from the uniform gray stone of the pedestrian walkways onto a metal decking that rattled under them. Industrial sounds, the origin of which Grady could only guess, grew louder and more specific as they walked. A rolling door rattled up, releasing the roar of a furnace to shake the air. The party stepped over the threshold and onto a floor illuminated by an angry red glow.

They were expected. "This way, my lord Keyrdegen, this way. We got the workshop all cleared out for yuh. Everything is all set up, like you asked. An honor, truly." Their liaison yelled over the din in a way that spoke of long hours barking orders in similar conditions. Grady was able to make out a tartan of gold and brown underneath his protective leather apron. It made him miss Phukit.

"The honor is ours. We are grateful for your service." Grady, standing close to Salzum, heard the distinctive clink of a bag filled with gems landing in an open palm. Whether it was a bribe or a fair payment didn't really matter to Grady.

The foreman led them past things that hissed, steamed, and radiated heat. Bored shouts accompanied the percussion of work. Then they were through another door that, when closed behind them, blocked out some of the noise. The Keyrdegen barely had to raise his voice. "And the workers who saw us enter?"

The foreman tucked thumbs into his belt. He spoke with pride. "Told 'em to expect an inspection. Shouldn't be a matter to concern yourself with, my lord. They know it's best to keep their minds on their work and leave the thegen to theirs."

"Excellent. You may go. We will leave as we came in, once our business is completed." Salzum smiled warmly and shook the foreman's hand, his contempt clear only to Grady with his window into the Keyrdegen's soul.

"Aye, sire. An honor to meet you, truly." The foreman bowed over one arm.

"Clan Pyrite is the backbone of Rockhome's industry, and you are clearly one of their best. Dismissed."

A short blast of noise signaled his departure. Salzum turned towards his guards who had taken up positions on either side of Grady. The tug of Grady's commands, namely "stay behind" and be "a few paces back" threw him into the guard waiting to his left. Instinct turned the Keyrdegen further to see the source of the curse and clatter. That, in turn, swung Grady into the other guard. There was a brief minute of Salzum spinning in order to face Grady and Grady moving as quickly as he could to remain behind him.

The Keyrdegen threw up his arms, stopped, and yelled. "You stupid thing. Radix, stand still!" Grady's body straightened up and locked in place. The whole spectacle left Grady giggling wildly in his own head.

Good one, me. Good one. I never would have thought of that.

Was that the ghost of mirth haunting Plenabus's exhausted wheezing? "I suggest, sir, we start with the, hm, acid. Yes?"

"You two, guard the door from this side. No one comes in." Salutes and a pair of simultaneous, sharp 'Yes, sir's' were the thegens' wise responses. "Seems your 'thinking automaton' is not that smart, Plenabus." The artificer could only nod as he caught his breath. "As for you," the Keyrdegen aimed the whole of his disheveled ire at Grady, "I am going to enjoy today's round of tests. Radix, stand over by that table there, the one with the vials. And take off your clothes, we will need them intact later."

Grady politely requested that his body ignore the command to go stand by the table and its three glass jars filled with, he assumed, the aforementioned acid. To his body, Salzum's command was all that mattered. Grady folded the clothes into a neat pile that he placed next to the last beaker. Naked again, Grady took his position next to the table and turned towards the dvergr controlling him. Never having seen acid before, Grady was disappointed. He expected them to be noxious colors with thick steam rising from the top. The liquids in the jars were clear and still.

"Golem, dip the pointer finger from the hand of your choice into each solution for a count of 5."

Left. Again.

Salzum admired the back of his hand, wiggled his fingers. "Go up to the first knuckle. Just the tip. Just in case." Plenabus cleared his throat and caught the Keyrdegen's eye. "And if the artificer tells you to hold, do so."

The acid in the first vial bubbled a bit as his finger soaked. It tingled. Grady counted to five and removed his finger. Halfway to the next vial, Plenabus's creaking voice froze him. "Hold, hm." The artificer's words, empowered by the Keyrdegen's command, froze Grady. Memories overran his mind. The world was white. He rested on a metal table as the mad artificer used his bronze hand to mark his flesh and take away his everything. "No, hm, pitting from sample 1. Next, yes."

His body moved on to the next vial before the vision ended. The liquid in the second jar reacted like the first. "Hold." Grady's stone finger dripped as Plenabus noted some tiny, structurally insignificant, pitting. The empowered order from Plenabus trapped Grady into the memories of his transformation.

The third jar was the most active. It fizzed and popped around Grady's finger. Plenabus ordered he remove it from the jar by the count of three. "Hold, hm." He scribbled on his clipboard. This time it was flashes of Plenabus's sweet moments, his vile loving caresses, that came and went. They left Grady feeling sick and weak. "Oh my, yes. Subject is most reactive to, hm, hydrofluoric acid. Short exposure caused no lasting damage."

As soon as the last jar was tested, Grady felt Plenabus's control of him break. The memories associated with the artificer lost their potency. Plenabus muttered to himself as he scribbled down some notes. "It appears that the Golem's makeup is mostly, hm, inert. Yes. There was little reaction with the acids. It shouldn't bathe in any of them, but the effect of small exposures would be, hm, negligible."

"Wonderful. Shall we?" Salzum walked past Grady who still held his finger out. "Radix, come here. Pump these bellows."

A small stone forge was built into the corner of the room, hot coals shining through its closed grate. The bellows sticking from the side were large. The longer, top handle sported two places wrapped in sweat stained leather. Despite it being Grady's first time seeing a bellows this large, its use was clear enough. His body knew what to do.

"Radix, faster."

Look at me go!

Grady, ignoring what was coming next, decided to be impressed with himself instead. With some concentration he was able to feel his body at work. Even though his muscles and tendons were now stone, there was goodness in experiencing their movement. Grady felt the forge's heat building and felt the satisfaction of effort spent to successfully complete a goal. He basked in both for a moment, the heat and the satisfaction. The heat's shine on his skin penetrated bone deep. It was the first time Grady had felt warm since the change. For a brief instant Grady felt whole.

"Enough. Step in front of the forge. Open it."

The temporary unity of Grady's mind and body was shattered by the new command. His body stepped in front of the forge and swung the grate open. The impact of the freed heat managed to do what the warriors failed to accomplish during the first test. It forced Grady back on his heels. He stared, unblinking, into the white hot inferno fed by his pumping. The glow's beauty, the roil of the energy inside the forge, filled his heart.

Wow. Between the intensity of the heat and light pouring out of the open grate, Grady wondered if he was the first dvergr to see this sight with his bare eyes.

"Radix, place your arm in, up to the elbow."

Plenabus scurried up, wrapped in thick fire-proof gear. He struggled to lower the welder's mask. "I must, hm, observe! I must. Yes!"

Hesitation free, Grady's body drove its arm into the forge's raging heart. Predictably, pain was hiding among the flames and metal liquifying heat. It pounced and devoured his arm. "See how it, hm, glows. Remove it. Yes. Let's assess the damage." Plenabus scurried back.

"Remove your arm. Close the forge door. Present your heated arm for inspection."

His body did as commanded. Grady's mind was occupied by his struggle to come to terms with the, literally, searing pain consuming his ability to think. The carved marks glowed silver in contrast to the dull red of the rest of his arm.

"I see no, hm, permanent damage. Yes. Have it flex the hand, roll the wrist."

Salzum so ordered, basking in the heat radiating from Grady's arm. His pleasure lessened each moment the arm refused to close. Grady felt the pain of the unfollowed order, but it did little to increase his suffering.

"Extreme heat must lock up the, hm, joints. I see no damage to any of the markings. They look rather pretty glowing like that. Yes. Only thing to do now is wait for it to cool and see if function returns to, hm, normal."

"We should just have it quench the arm. They provided an oil barrel." Salzum practically radiated impatience.

"It is not made of metal. We don't, hm, know enough about his composition to risk it, my lord."

Reason prevailed. The burning in Grady's arm diminished slowly until the punishing pain from the unfollowed command gained supremacy. His fingers closed with an audible crunch. The punishment's sting eased, leaving behind a hot ache.

Let's not do that again.

"An hour, my lord, yes."

"Remarkable. I'd suggest we place the golem under a few steam-powered forge hammers, but that seems overkill." Plenabus's adamant agreement was a sight. His withered head bobbed enthusiastically, wobbling weakly above the dwarfing bulk of the fireproof suit.

"I believe we have its measure now. It is time we tried to teach it a useful skill. One that will make the most of its unique qualities and strengths." Grady's stomach would have sunk if it wasn't petrified in place.

Cooking? Probably not cooking, right? Shame. I always wanted to learn.

Plenabus retrieved his clipboard and flipped up a few pages. "Excellent, yes. I will inquire about finding a seasoned bricklayer and mason, hm, and..."

"No." Salzum snapped. He repeated himself, but softer this time. "No. Allow me to arrange for a suitable teacher. Perhaps someone that can swing a hammer."

Yes, definitely not cooking.

THE LATEST THING

T he only indication that the thegen standing before Grady was special, and not just any member of the Throng, was the small shimmer of silver in the center of the Salzum mask's forehead. A short cut beard, white with ebony streaks that made it resemble marble, hung beneath the mask's chin.

Salzum could totally pull that look off. Grady imagined sticking his tongue out. They controlled his body but his mind was still his own. He did his best not to add 'for now.'

"I have come." The warrior held his arms out wide. Every inch of his armor, not embossed with hammers, axes, and other classic dvergr warrior symbols, was packed with runes proclaiming his deeds to anyone close enough to read them. The reader would have to be very close because the writing was impressively tiny and precise. "Your missive was vague to say the least. I know you love dramatic pauses, but we are both very busy dvergr." He made a show of eyeing Grady. "Did you sculpt this, um, interesting statue? Am I to be your art critic once more?"

"I should beat you about the head and neck for thinking this is my work." Based on the warrior's less than respectful tone and the Keyrdegen's sharp retort, Grady expected to feel a rising ire in the Keyrdegen's heart. Shockingly, he found a deep fount of brotherly affection instead. Submerged in the love, too deep for Grady to get a solid sense of it, was a faint melancholy. "It is Artificer Plenabus's latest creation. It's a type of self-driving machine."

The thronger cocked his head with interest. "An automaton? Really? He did it? I thought they were just theoretical." He traced a gloved finger along a ley line and traced the runes at his joints and the ones placed over the larger muscle groups. "I don't see any seams. I don't hear any clockwork or internal mechanisms. It's not hot to the touch, so no internal furnace. Why is it covered with ancient runes?"

"That is a question best saved for Plenabus. He tried to explain how it functions to me, but you know I can only stand his voice for so long." They chuckled together at some shared inside joke. Salzum watched his friend fuss and coo over Grady for a minute. "He tells me it can think." *I can. Mostly awful stuff about you.* "Learn."

The Throng captain looked away from Grady with reluctance. "Amazing if true. An invention like that could change everything. Why are you showing this to me?"

"Because I trust you and I need your thoughts on this project. Plenabus tells me that he will be able to make more soon. Their construction is costly and not without risk. You always understood the craft of artifice better than I. We have already established how well these golems can function as laborers and even as clerks, if you can believe it. I want to see how well it can swing a hammer. Hold a shield. Follow simple commands. Well within your bailiwick, wouldn't you agree, Dulane?"

Dulane? Grady reeled. He was in the presence of one of Rockhome's most storied living warriors and Grady's personal favorite. He had idolized the dvergr since his youth. Reports of Dulane's actions in the field read like one of Grady's precious books. He was the epitome of dvergrness.

Everything Grady was not.

"You want me to teach a machine how to be thegen?" Dulane recoiled back from Grady as if he were suddenly something vile.

"Is a thegen the hammer swung or the shield raised up to protect another? This golem is just a weapon, a tool. I wish to see how effective a tool it is. Imagine with me for a moment, old friend." He held out an arm, and waved. "Come, imagine." Dulane leaned in and let the Keyrdegen take him by the shoulder.

Salzum pointed into the middle distance. "Picture a squad of thegen sweeping some newly discovered tunnels. They're ambushed by a scouting party of giant ants! They will win because they are thegen. But there is often a cost. Give that squad one of these golems. Think of the advantage a nigh indestructible stone warrior brings to the battlefield."

Dulane shifted his scrutiny to his warleader. "That is some vision to realize. You want me to- what? Teach it to swing a hammer? How to participate in a shield wall? Wrestling holds?"

"Beyond swinging a hammer properly, I leave the rest of the curriculum planning to you. Just keep our ultimate goal in mind. Create a tool to aid our warriors. We lose too many. The number of names on the wall of remembrance grows by the year. May it never fill." Dulane repeated the refrain. The two mourned together for a moment, heads bowed. The sadness popped when the Keyrdegen slapped Dulane's pauldron. He leaned in conspiratorially. "Watch this," he whispered. In a loud commanding tone, Salzum addressed Grady. "Radix, attend."

Despite Grady not knowing what specifically the Keyrdegen meant by 'attend',the command was full of intention. His vision jerked as his head shifted towards Salzum. A gasp of shock and surprise escaped from under Dulane's mask. "Radix, you will learn all you can from the Captain. Follow Dulane's orders and instructions as precisely as you would mine. Until I tell you otherwise. Do you understand?"

Not really, no. "Yes."

"Ancestors, what a horrid sound! Was that it speaking?" Dulane asked. He leaned in again to examine Grady's neck and jaws. "Plenabus is a genius. Not a joint. Not a spring. How did he hide it all?"

Salzum smiled fondly at Dulane. "Its voice does take some getting used to. I think you'll manage."

The Captain saluted, fist to chest, and gave a slight bow. "Of course, my lord. Thank you for this opportunity. It is an honor to be included."

"You honor me with your service, my First. Any questions?"

"Why does it look like that and why is it naked?" The pointing wasn't nice and Grady found his tone insulting.

"The lines and runes are functional. The rest was the whim of the artist. There's a pile of clothes over there. Just tell it to get dressed."

"But I-"

The Keyrdegen wagged his finger. "I'm not going to say one more word. Discovery is half the fun. Good luck, Captain Dulane." Salzum turned and left the room with a wink and a twinkling wave.

Once they were alone, the captain just stared at Grady with one hand stroking his beard in thought.

The metal bed and most of the lab equipment were pushed to the side of the room. This was apparently to clear a space for Grady to train in. The electric lights, free of their metal stands, were mounted in the corners of the room. A newly installed wooden rack loaded with weapons and shields took up space on the wall next to the door.

After an awkward amount of time, which Grady spent counting the rivets in the Captain's armor and wishing he could fidget, the warrior visibly steeled himself. He removed his helmet revealing a scarred face, creased with smile lines around his mouth and at the corner of his eyes.

That's a clear improvement, Grady thought. The warrior circled him.

On his second circuit he nudged Grady as he passed, on the sides, back, and chest. "Like pushing a wall," he said to himself. "An internal gyroscope for balance?" On his third, he stopped and searched Grady's eyes.

Grady desperately wanted to shout boo. Maybe pinch his cheek.

Dulane shrugged and went to stand next to the weapon rack. "Uh. Get dressed?" Grady was swept up by the order. The commanding force was less severe coming from Dulane than from Salzum directly, but Grady remained powerless to disobey. He walked over and began to dress himself in the same gray and tattered garments from the trip to the foundry. Dulane wore a stunned expression and whispered, "Impossible." He watched Grady with intent, as if he'd never seen anyone get dressed before. Grady smoothed his shirt into place and grew still once more.

"Ok, uh, back to your starting position." Grady walked back over to fill the footprints pressed into the flagstone from the earlier impact tests. "This is too weird." Dulane scratched his head and shrugged. He came to a decision and barked an order. "Stand to!"

Grady's body straightened audibly. He stamped his feet closer together, locked his knees, and slapped his arms to his side.

"No, no. You look like a child playing thegen. Chin up, chest out, shoulders back, stomach in. Your thumbs should follow the seam of your pants." He snapped to attention to demonstrate. Grady adjusted to match. "Good. Every time I call you to attention, return to this pose. For my own sanity I can't just refer to you as golem or thing. Salzum called you Radix. Is your name Radix?"

"Yes." *No.*

"Well shit. Doesn't get any better the second time does it?"

"No." *Try hearing it rumble around in your head.*

"Or the third." The captain did another circuit around Grady. "Scrawny arms and legs. Sunken chest and a pot belly. Barely as wide as it is tall. You look like you were designed to sit behind a desk."

You're not much of a looker either. And his arms and legs weren't scrawny, thank you very much. Grady preferred the term wiry.

The Captain pinched the bridge of his nose and sighed. "I am talking to a statue. Oh, Salzum, what lunacy have you dragged me into?"

You have no idea.

He looked off, set his jaw, and nodded. "The only way out is through." Grady had never seen anyone doff a full suit of plate armor before. The books never mentioned how many straps were involved. Dulane lined the pieces up against the wall on either side of the weapon rack. More high ridged scars dotted his arms and hands.

With care he pulled a well used warhammer down from the weapon wrack. He held it out to Grady. "This is a practice weapon. It's heavier than the standard and has a blunted spike on the end. Learning how to swing one of these right is as good a place to start as any. Take it and do as I do. If you can manage that, then we will really have something to show the Keyrdegen."

The Keyrdegen can jump in a hole, Grady thought quietly, careful not to ruin the solemnity of the moment as he accepted the hammer from Dulane.

The warhammer looked a bit oversized in Grady's grip, but it felt as light as a quill. Grady's excitement mounted. A hammer was in his hand. Dulane, Captain of the Throng, was to train him in its use. Under different circumstances, those facts would amount to a dream coming true. One Grady never dared to entertain because of the sheer impossibility of it.

"Watch me." The Captain squared his feet and retrieved his weapon from his belt. It was slimmer than Grady's, with a larger strike plate and a needle-sharp spike coming out the back. It shimmered in the room's artificial light. Grady knew nothing of weapons but it was, clearly, well-loved.

The Captain brought the warhammer over his shoulder. He stomped forward and brought it straight down with a loud, "Ha!" His wrist rolled at the bottom end of the hammer's arc, twerking the trajectory and flinging it up across his body. "Hwah." With a twist, he brought the hammer back down along the same arc, spike first to gauge or catch anything in the way. He pulled his arm in forcefully with a loud, "Hurgh."

"Do the same thing I just did. A thousand times."

The body went to work, leaving Grady just enough of himself to keep track of the number of times it swung. *Yay. Counting.* "Ha! Hwah. Hurgh!" He reached five repetitions before the Captain stopped him.

"Your weight is too much on your back foot. Even spread. Press your feet down. Harder you push, stronger you are." Dulane bounced on his knees and demonstrated a pair of precise and slow swings.

Grady felt his weight shift and settle as he adjusted his stance. He swung through the form from beneath his feet, crunching the flagstones under his toes. The hammer whistled softly as it swung through the air.

"There. A mostly correct swing." He sounded surprised. He appraised Grady with a squint. "Something's off. Swing again."

Grady moved and swung again. "Ha! Hwah. Hurgh!"

"Almost perfect." It was nice to hear some praise. When was the last time Grady had heard a kind word said his way? *Oh, yeah. Emerlda.* "You need to get your core more involved. Can-? I can't believe I'm asking this. Can you breathe?"

What a novel question. "I don't know." *I never thought of trying.* "Try."

It took a moment to remember where he expanded from and contracted to. What was once automatic and easy, became an effort of will. His stone diaphragm pulled downward, drawing in the air through his nose. The rush of air opened up space in his chest. As the process reversed and the air was pushed out of his petrified lungs, Grady rushed outward to fill his whole body. He rippled down to the very tips of his fingers and of his toes, where he rebounded to the confines of his head.

For that brief instant, while he filled the statue that was once his body, he was whole. The unity he had felt while pumping the bellows had been similar, but less complete. As his body stood in stasis, waiting for the next command, the feeling faded.

Tell me to breathe more. Please. It felt right to want to breathe, to need to breathe, to feel whole. The desire made Grady feel almost normal.

The Captain nodded. He got close to Grady's face for a moment, eyebrow quirked like he had seen something unexpected. He shook his head in dismissal. "That was a breath, alright. Odd that you were built to do that, but who am I to question the great artificer? Start over at one. If you were actually counting in there. Power downwards, then speed up. And really twist your hips at the end, you have to feel it. Remember to push through the ground. Breathe." He pantomimed the motion again, slower and with emphasis, breathing as he went. "Thousand times. Go."

Grady went "Ha! Hwah. Hurgh!" one thousand times in his nightmarish, avalanche of a voice, breathing the entire time. He filled his body as he moved. It was slowly improving. No. He was slowly improving. By increments, he increased the speed and the precision of his swing.

Dulane's focus remained on Grady until his four-hundred and thirty-first swing before he found a chair and sat with a sigh.

Around swing seven-hundred and fifty-six (and his two-thousand, two-hundred and twenty-seventh, eighth, and ninth breaths) Grady was sure that if he suddenly found himself made of soft flesh again the swing would remain identical. Weaker and slower, for sure. But the form would have been top-notch.

Grady enjoyed himself.

Dulane pulled a book out of a pouch at his waist.

Forge of the Heart! I love that one. A well-worn copy rested back in Grady's old apartment. It was the seventh book in the Saga of Kreth the Bulwark. Set after Kreth's return home from a long stint in the Wilds Below, it was a romance heavy novel, with lots of sighs, caresses, and regrets of time irrevocably lost. *At least he has good taste in literature. Good villain in that one, too.* The little laughs the captain let out as he read were endearing. Dulane glanced up occasionally to check Grady's form. Apparently, he saw nothing worth commenting on.

The last "Hurgh!" faded, leaving silence to reign. Dulane turned a few more pages before smiling at the pages and replacing his bookmark with care. He regarded Grady and scratched at his chin. "I have to hand it to you, and your maker, Radix. There's not been, nor ever will be, a dvergr that could rattle out a thousand perfect strikes in one go with no break or rest." The book disappeared back into its pouch as he stood and circled Grady again. "Bodies tire. The mind wanders. People get sloppy. Not you though. That's a machine for you. Salzum will be pleased." He stretched and yawned in a very un-captain-like way. "Tomorrow, we will add the shield."

Dulane reached out to take the warhammer from Grady's grip and paused. His forehead creased in thought, and he nodded to himself. "Why not? Radix, can you keep practicing?"

"Yes." *And breathing.* His wholeness was fading quickly. Grady thirsted for more.

"At will then. Keep practicing. I will see you early tomorrow." An aborted goodbye left him with his mouth half open and his hand extended for a shake. Dulane laughed at himself, "Next I'll be petting gargoyles. Ridiculous." The door closed and Grady was alone again with the hum of the lights as his only company.

He counted slowly to twenty. Standing there, warhammer in hand, he breathed in and found his body receptive, waiting, and filled with the potential for movement.

The standing order controlling him was simple. 'Feel free to keep practicing.' He raised the hammer high and let out another loud, "Ha! Hwah. Hurgh!" The delight he felt at having self-agency again, even one so limited, did not translate well into the gravel crunch of his new voice. He still could not turn his head, blink, wiggle his toes, or move himself in any way that wasn't a part of the simple sequence he had learned. He raised the arm, swung the hammer, flicked his wrist. He controlled the tempo, the speed, the strength he put behind each strike.

The hollowness of hunger grew in his gut. He refused to stop. There was nothing to be done about it, and the familiar sensation was a comfort in the face of all the unique strangeness filling his life. After countless repetitions, Grady felt himself slowing. The wholeness gained from breathing was everything to him now. A growing lethargy slowed his movements. The forced deceleration gifted him with a greater depth of physical feeling. Not one for sport or physical exertion in general, Grady could not remember the last time he moved until he was too depleted to continue doing so.

It happened suddenly. It was like blinking. One moment he was pushing his body through a final set and breathing one final breath, then the cell was gone and he was encased again in the geode's crystal prism.

Must have completely drained the tank. That thought didn't so much appear as ooze across his consciousness. Damn. His caretakers at the Ground Floor Orphan Asylum for the Young and Clanless were right again. *Move the body and tire the-* And then there was nothing. No eternal moment. No suffering. Just a pure, gentle nothing.

"Eat!" The command shattered the nothing and behind its shards was, of course, his cell. In the foreground, a very angry looking Salzum shook a bucket full of shiny coal right under Grady's nose. Grady reached out and brought one of the rocks to his lips. The Keyrdegen rattled the bucket in an attempt to hurry the low-powered golem.

It would be a shame to rush such an elegant meal. Even his thoughts felt slow.

"Why did I have to command it twice, Plenabus?"

"I do not know for sure. It was frozen in this strange, hm, posture when I entered, sir. I theorize the captain must have left it on and, yes, running unsupervised." Plenabus shuffled through the papers on his clipboard as if a more satisfactory answer would be found among the tedium of his copious notes.

Energy coursed through Grady's body as soon as the first bite reached his gut. Spurred on by the urgency implied in the Keyrdegen's last command, he ate faster. He was double-fisting pieces of coal into his mouth awkwardly because one hand was still mostly full of warhammer.

It didn't take long before Salzum decided he no longer wanted to serve Grady his meal. "Take the damn bucket."

The warhammer clattered to the ground as he took it. Shoveling coal into his mouth with one hand, Grady was shocked to realize he liked it. His tongue still registered the coal as good fuel. There was more to it now though. The coal gave off a salty sting coupled with a savory warm taste he could not name. Grady sucked his fingers clean before the Keyrdegen's command to eat was spent, and his body grew inert once more.

"Is it supposed to do that?" The confusion on Salzum's face was priceless.

"There was no mention of finger licking in my, hm, research. Just another echo of the dvergr that was. Yes. I am sure of it." Plenabus scribbled in his notes while furtively glancing at Grady.

Salzum stroked his beard with the back of his hand, running the large gems of his rings through the loose weaves. He took a decent step back. "Radix, show me what the Captain taught you yesterday."

With gusto, Grady reached down to retrieve the warhammer and flung himself into the swing of it. The command held him so tight he could not breathe. Salzum winced at each of the punctuating yells. "Horrible. Every time. Its voice, can something be done?"

"I am unsure. I'll make a, hm, note. Yes."

The Keyrdegen took his turn to walk around Grady in appraisal. "What do you think, Plenabus?"

"Of its martial prowess? I am no expert but its hammer seems well, hm, swung."

"Yes." The Keyrdegen luxuriated in more beard stroking. "Well swung, is an accurate way to describe it." Grady did not like the feel of Salzums's current smile or the fanged satisfaction growing in his breast.

"Now that this experiment is complete, sir, I have winnowed down a selection of, hm, master builders for your approval."

"Complete? No. No, Plenabus. This is only the beginning. Swinging a hammer is a small part of what it takes to be a true warrior. You claimed that these golems can learn. Well," he tapped a calloused finger to Grady's forehead, "In here is where a warrior's true strength lies. There is much more to do before I am satisfied."

Plenabus sputtered. "This is already too much. The warnings were clear." Plenabus's squeak was sharper than normal, his tone admonishing. "When I agreed to undertake this, hm, project, you promised-" The Keyrdegen's cold regard caused the artificer's words to freeze in his throat, choking him.

Salzum seethed as he waited for the coughing to stop. His voice was quiet, chilled. "Do you presume to call me liar, Artificer?"

Oh! Now you've done it. He's mad.

"No, my lord. Hm. Never!" Plenabus shrunk into his lab coat.

"His martial training continues. If you are so worried about the outcome, you should observe and record. You know how much I value your feedback. Have you begun the next phase of your work?"

The artificer bobbed his head. "Construction of the device is almost complete. We can start testing soon."

The Keyrdegen shifted his weight. The chill lifted, and he was all energy and business again. "I will get you more subjects soon. Orders have been issued. We should have the room stocked with coal. I'll give it a standing command to eat whenever it needs more fuel. That should avoid any more incidents like this. Don't you agree?"

Plenabus scribbled down a note, presumably about the coal. Grady wondered how many sheets of paper the old thing filled in a shift. "Most, hm, wise. Yes."

"I must be about my buisness. Plenabus, stay here and wait for the captain. He should be here shortly. Observe the lesson. Advise the captain on how to word his orders more judiciously. I do not like the idea of this thing being about any sort of business unattended. Radix, eat when you are hungry." He glanced at Plenabus. "I expect a detailed report." With a sweep of his cape, and the large braids of torc-bearing beard hanging over his shoulders, the Keyrdegen left.

TRUST YOUR GUT

"A thousand swings is nothing," Dulane said as he entered Grady's room, unarmored and dressed for training. "True mastery takes a thousand hours. I-" He froze when he spied the other dvergr in the room. He stood too sharply, saluted to his chest, and bowed over his fist. "To what do I owe the honor of your presence, Artificer Plenabus?"

"Honor, hm. The Keyrdegen sent me to observe the golem's martial training. He also asked me to instruct you on the proper way to manage the golem. You left it on and working all downshift. Yes. I found it inert when I came in."

"You trained the whole time?" The captain studied Grady's face, searching for something.

"Yes." *And I loved it. And I think I'm getting pretty good. And I can't wait to do more!* The desire to breathe more, to move and be one, energized the Grady within.

"I wish the newest batch of recruits were half as dedicated. Well done."

"Though it is capable of thought, it is just a, hm, machine, Captain. It possesses no emotions, no soul. It needs no praise. Yes." Grady felt the urge to squeeze Plenabus's body very hard until he possessed no emotions or soul.

Dulane casually turned away from Plenabus. He regarded Grady as he spoke, his face soft and troubled. "That's a shame. Dedication like that tends to be a sign of a dvergr full of grit and determination. One ready to walk their own Way."

Plenabus snorted at the general idea and cut in between the captain and the golem. He wagged a big knuckled finger in Dulane's face. "It needs no motivation to follow your instructions. The Keyrdegen's word is all it, hm, requires. It is an automaton, a tool. Yes No more aware than your hammer. Just far more capable."

I'll hammer you.

A scowl twisted the old dvergr's face into a mass of furrows and creases. "Also, I want to be, hm, clear with you, Captain... Dulane? Is that right?"

"Aye. Dulane, Captain of the Throng. I've been captain for over a century now. We've met before. Many times."

Plenabus waved the fact away. "Hm. I have severe reservations about your involvement. Not you, personally, but your kind. Thegen. Warriors. Yes. I would never deny the necessity of your, hm, work. Order must be kept. The threats from Below scrabble at our ankles. But my golem, my creation, is destined for more. Yes. It must be." Dulane's height forced his glare upwards.

"Understood, Artificer. Now I must be clear, it really is my honor to be in your presence. I'm a big fan. While I value your insight and your instruction, my orders come from the Keyrdegen. He has tasked me with training your golem to the best of my ability. I will do my utmost to please my lord and complete my assignment as honor demands." Dulane went to the weapon rack and returned with the same hammer from yesterday and a shield made of plain and dented wooden planks. "Step back a bit, please. Radix, listen up. This next form builds directly on top of the sequence you learned last time." He held out the hammer to Grady, who was surprised to find he was able to reach out and take it without a direct order.

The storied warrior shouted through the form. Now each swing of the hammer was offset by a movement of the shield. As the hammer swung down the shield swung to the side. The follow up swing across the body brought the shield down and in line to protect the torso. The spike's downward arc saw the shield slamming forward.

"Now you. One set." Dulane spared a quick look over to Plenabus, who scowled at the proceedings from his chair, feverishly writing notes.

Grady set himself and moved through the new maneuvers slowly. Despite wanting nothing more than to breathe and feel whole again, Grady held back. Some deep instinct warned him against revealing that ability to the artificer.

The captain nodded as Grady practiced. "Well done. Remember to keep the shield angled so that blows are deflected away from you. A thousand times at speed, Radix. Go."

This time the captain sat himself on the floor and took out his book immediately. He pointedly ignored Plenabus's presence in the room and Plenabus returned the favor. They managed to ignore each other for an hour. Plenabus, full up on notes apparently, got up out of his seat and loomed over the reclined reader.

Plenabus had to shout over the sounds of Grady practicing. "I will not waste my time, hm, further. I have seen all I need to see for today. Yes. My report to the Keyrdegen will be detailed." A hoarse bite roughed the artificer's voice. "You cannot give it leave to operate when it is, hm, unobserved." Dulane licked a finger and turned a page in his book. "Keyrdegen's orders." With a last disapproving look at his creation's budding military prowess, Plenabus pouted his way out the door.

The instant the door closed, Grady resumed breathing. Grady reveled in the feeling of each movement, lost in the euphoria of being whole. It almost felt like dancing. Captain Dulane continued to sit and read his book with only an occasional peek to check in on his pupil. Grady's count reached a thousand and he slid out of his stance and into his normal, slightly slouched posture.

Dulane finished the paragraph he was reading, placed his bookmark, and stood. "That was an impressive display. Again. Tomorrow, we will try out two hammers. It is a complicated style, but you have the speed to make the most of it." There was that look again, the inquisitive one that tried to pierce Grady's stone exterior and see the true workings beneath. "You are free to continue practicing as much as you want. However, do not let Plenabus or the Keyrdegen know about your extra training time. It will be our little secret." This time he waved as he left.

If the breath-powered connection to his body wasn't enough, in the shifts that followed Grady was cheered by the return of a recognizable routine. During his on-shifts he trained with Captain Dulane. Plenabus only watched for the first hour or so of each session, only to admonish the captain over some small slight and leave. Then, free from the artificer's judging glare, Grady allowed himself to feel whole again. Wasn't that the dream that drove him to sign his name on the dotted line, to train under a master warrior just like this one shift? *Not exactly like this. No.*

Being able to eat when he was hungry further normalized the passage of time. He started to notice some of the coal tasted different. Perhaps they were mined from different seams? It was strange, having regular meals again, without needing bathroom breaks.

What would I shit out if I had to?

Off shift, he trained alone in the confines of his cell. Grady cut out the yells just in case guards were positioned outside. Grady was fond of his trainer and didn't want him to get in trouble or the training to end. The ordered secrecy empowered his sneakiness. He switched between the stances and styles as his mood took him. With all the breathing, choosing, and eating, Grady felt almost normal.

The Keyrdegen's lack of presence was a sizable bonus.

Another glorious shift start in the cell found Grady breathlessly working through the swings the captain said would work wonders against taller opponents, like humans or elves. A lot of it involved swinging for their knees in an attempt to ground them while keeping the shield up. Grady enjoyed the low swooping movements. He waited impatiently for Plenabus to reach his limit and leave. He wanted to breathe again.

Someone must have spit in the artificer's breakfast bear. He spent the whole time shooting glares back and forth between the captain and Grady. As he took notes, Grady heard Plenabus's pen rip the paper, a truly amateur mistake. Enough was enough and Plenabus stormed out of the cell without acknowledging anyone.

No. Stop. Come back.

"At ease, Radix."

Grady stilled, sad as the first breath of the shift was interrupted. Dulane stood and walked over to Grady, tapping his book into his palm. "You don't breathe in front of Plenabus. Why?"

Am I in trouble? As the pressure to answer grew, Grady concocted a myriad of innocent half-lies. Instead, the power of the command chose to answer with unaltered truth. "A feeling. I don't want to, not in front of him."

"A feeling? Want?" He looked all around the room, then at Grady. "Damn, shit and double damn. He lied to me. But why?" The captain ground his teeth and grimaced as a myriad of emotions played across his face. His features settled into an angry scowl. The hand not holding the book clenched into a tight fist. He closed his eyes and took a moment to gather himself. As the rage cooled, Dulane's face sank, heavy with sadness. "I have a theory, Radix, about how you came to be, who you really are. Can I share it with you?"

"Please." The casual ease drained from the captain's stance. A tension thickened in the air. *This is the kind of situation where my heart would buzz and my mouth would dry out.* Grady didn't miss the flop sweat either.

"Over a month ago, a squad of throngers was sent out on a mission. The command came directly from Keyrdegen Salzum. They were charged with capturing a dissident, a Clanless agitator responsible for sowing unrest on the Floor." Dulane watched Grady's face as if expecting a reaction.

"According to the report, the operation was a simple smash and grab. It went off without a hitch. On paper, the target wasn't much. A low level functionary in some middling mine's administrative branch. No known affiliations with any of the groups or persons of interest on any of the city's watch lists. And at the bottom of the order of incarceration and interrogation was the Keyrdegen's signature." Dulane reached into his book pouch and presented a corded sheaf of papers to Grady.

"Have a look."

Grady placed his hammer and shield on the ground and took the papers gently with both hands. The sad thegen continued his story as Grady looked through the file. "I began to look for the dissident, this Grady of No Clan, everywhere. He rots in no cell that I have access to. There is no record of his interrogation. No further arrests were made. No plots foiled." Grady turned the pages seeing his earlier existence summed up in a paragraph or two. The part that mentioned he had 'no close acquaintances or affiliations with any type of recreational group' stung, truth notwithstanding. The sketch artist's rendition of him was pretty good. The Keyrdegen's signature filled the bottom of one page, grandiose and precise just like the one at the bottom of the damned poster.

The captain leaned over the page and pointed to the drawing of Grady. "Is this you?"

"Yes." *Sort of.* Grady noted Dulane's hands shaking a bit when he took back the papers.

The sadness in the captain's eyes ran deep. Grady recognized the loss at its core. Dulane, took the papers back "Fuck. Grady, what did they do to you?"

The question freed his tongue. "I signed away my name for the chance to become a thegen. They took me from my bed. Dragged me here. Then they carved me. I felt it all." He touched the complex geometry on his forehead, remembering. The dreadfulness of the facts fit perfectly with the grind of his new voice. He pointed to the lights in the corner. "Then they ran energy through me. Turned me to stone. Took away my will. Trapped me here. Here." He tapped his forehead again.

It was the most Grady had spoken since the change. It felt good to vocalize his experience, to let some of it out and share it with another. Grady wanted to say more, he just lacked the agency to do so. After he finished his tale, silence dominated the room, challenged only by the ear-tickling hum of the lights.

Dulane sighed as he sat down with his head in his hands. "I hoped I was wrong. For my sake as much as yours. A line has been crossed." He stood, unable to look directly at Grady. "I need to go. To think. This, confirming this, changes things."

He hesitated as he slipped his helmet on. Salzum's neutral visage swallowed his broken expression. "I'll be back tomorrow. Keep practicing, if it makes you happy. You were right not to breathe in front of Plenabus. The Keyrdegen, too. Trust your gut." His hand hovered over the door's latch. He left without looking back.

Grady returned to his forms. He practiced in silence, ready to freeze the moment someone approached. Yes. He was still in a cell deep under the city, and surrounded by stones soaked in his screams. Did he possess a will of his own? Only slightly.

But he didn't hurt at the moment. The stone of his body felt less foreign and lighter as he moved. Dulane knew of him. Him, not Radix. He was no longer alone. And there in his heart, the spark of hope that Grady believed long since extinguished, grew a little brighter, fanned by his own breath.

BATTLE BOOK CLUB

The next training session started off normally. Captain Dulane acted as if nothing of note had happened the shift before. The new forms built off of last session's kneecapping exercises. The modifications were to accommodate facing multiple tall enemies at once. The captain demonstrated how to keep your footing while you spun to face threats from various angles.

Plenabus, deflated, scowled and took notes. Disappointment and shame were writ large on his face. He got up after only a few minutes, creaking the whole way, and left without ceremony.

The captain stopped Grady mid swing. He shed his nonchalance to reveal the deadly serious mien beneath. "I can't imagine being stuck in a small stone room, shift in and shift out, a prisoner of your own body." Dulane shuddered. He searched the air, looking for the words he wanted to say. "Is there anything I can do for you? Is there anything you want?"

Want? That was a good question. The loss of his will and his fleshy body had drained his old desires of their gravity.

Vanity's main drive must be biological. The need to look a certain way was as gone as his beard. Given everything else he was dealing with, he did not miss the struggle to decide what to wear each shift. He hadn't really given his exterior aesthetic too much thought since the transformation, despite all the negative reactions lately regarding his appearance.

The satisfying lack of pain he enjoyed was an adequate replacement for the constant pleasure seeking of his old life. Once he dreamed of gourmet, multi-course meals. Granted, his enjoyment of coal was growing bite by bite, but that feeding lacked the quality of insatiable need that din-ing once possessed. The unfillable hole was gone. Once his tank was full, the desire to eat stopped. How many times had Grady eaten his feelings to the point of pain?

Dulane's question showed more care and concern for Grady than any other dvergr from his life that he could remember. Save one. Emerlda. The kindness and the validation he felt in the moment she kissed his cheek remained a treasure he handled sparingly, lest it be tarnished. The memory of the actual contact failed to light the same fire it once did.

All he really wanted now was to escape. Since that was impossible, any escape would have to do. "I'd like to read. Please."

"What?"

Grady pointed at the copy of *Trust Your Heart.* "The Saga of Kreth the Bulwark. He's my favorite. I've read most of them at least once."

"You've read these?" Dulane looked from the book in his hand and back to Grady.

Grady nodded with enthusiasm. "Adventure stories are my favorite."

"Yes. Stories." Dulane harrumphed in thought and shook his head. "I can't just leave a book here. You're just a machine, remember? How about I read to you while you practice, after Plenabus leaves?"

"Yes, please." His soul's deep gratitude was impossible to express with his earthslide of a voice. His mind hungered, desperate for anything other than his existence to think about, if only for a moment.

"Sure, aye! Yes. Let's do this. I was never the best at reading out loud, but any rope in a hole. Keep your 'ha's' on the quiet end so I don't have to yell."

◆

For the next five training sessions, Grady was happy. Plenabus stopped coming altogether. While Grady swung and stepped, battling imaginary enemies, the captain read to him. The story was a familiar comfort from his old life. The captain was a better narrator than he let on. He imbued the story's bouncy action scenes and poetic observations with gravitas. Lines Grady hadn't noticed before ran through his head while he continued to train in solitude.

When he grew bored of training, he took advantage of the loose wording in the captain's commands to simply stand and breathe. There was joy in being still and breathing. Focused in a breath, the cell dropped away. His body felt lighter and more familiar.

The latch rattled one shift start and Grady expelled the air he was holding. He did his best statue impression.

"It is time for the next phase." Salzum entered the cell, as large and regal as ever. Despite himself, Grady cowered in awe of the Keyrdegen's terrible presence. Captain Dulane followed on his heels. "Based on Plenabus's notes, I think it is ready to train against another warrior. Proper forms and swinging at the air will only take it so far."

"Yes, sir." Dulane was not as good an actor as Salzum, but he managed to keep his voice steady. His salute was professional and enthusiastic.

"I want a demonstration of its skills in three shift rotations. Is that enough time?" His tone indicated that it had better be. Grady heard the raspy sound of impatience gnawing away at the Keyrdegen behind the words.

"Of course, my lord. The golem learns quickly. Three rotations will be plenty."

Salzum's impatience gave way to exultation. He erupted in bubbling, friendly excitement. "Wonderful! Wonderful. I knew you were the one to trust with this." He leaned in to the captain like they were fellow conspirators. "What are your initial feelings, eh? Should I commission more golems?"

It was impossible to tell what the captain was feeling underneath his Salzum mask. "I don't know yet. I will be more confident in making a recommendation after this next phase of its training."

"A very politic answer, Captain. Very politic." Salzum's robe shook with a deep belly laugh. "You missed your calling, I think. I could use a level headed dvergr like you up in the Hall."

"Thank you, sir. I'd rather not."

"Can't say I blame you. I miss having a hammer in my hand, with my squad, surrounded only by those I trust most. I will leave you to it. I expect great things from you two, great things!" The Keyrdegen's jocularity sounded hollow to Grady. A discordant note rang within the joy Salzum presented. One more, "Great things!" and he was gone.

Grady started breathing again.

The captain removed his helmet. He nodded as he spoke. "Ok. That's fine. I kind of expected that. Storytime is over for now, I'm afraid. We have real work to do." Dulane armed himself, and rapped his hammer against his shield. "The only way out is through," he quoted. It was one of Kreth's sayings, almost a catchphrase.

Grady never liked confrontation. Raised voices made his stomach uneasy. His angry outbursts and wise mouth earned him a beating a time or two when he was younger and had taught him an important lesson. He was small and slight in a world full of dvergr larger and wider. Meekness was his only reliable defense.

He watched Captain Dulane, bearing arms and hopping from foot to foot, warming up to attack. Grady breathed in deep, settling into his body and down into the ground. Dulane readied his shield and braced himself. "Alright, you can swing first. Get a feel for striking at an opponent. Swipe at me horizontally. Go right for the shield."

Grady swung his hammer like he was taught, wide and powered by a twist from the hips. Dulane angled his shield to deflect the force of the impact. The head of Grady's hammer met the middle of the shield's boss and kept going. Dulane flew to the side and landed with a clattering crash. "Ow."

Whoa. Did I just do that? The impact was significant. Impacting the shield hardly slowed Grady's follow-through in the slightest. He reset his stance. The metronome steadiness of his breathing soothed his shock. He wanted to check on the captain to make sure he was not hurt, but his body refused to move.

"It's good form to help your opponent up if you knock them down." Dulane's voice was flattened by the mask he wore. The order implied, Grady hustled over and offered Dulane a hand. "Careful," the captain said with wide eyes as Grady's hand closed around his. Armor and all, Grady hoisted Dulane to his feet easily. The warrior dropped his shield and shook out his arm. "I think you bruised me through the bracer too. Ow. Your swing was sloppy, but fine enough for your first offensive attack. That strength though. I've been hit gentler by trolls. And Plenabus can make others like you. Salzum will be thrilled." He shivered at the thought.

Dulane removed his helmet and looked at the mask, complex emotions playing over his face. "I became a member of the Throng because I believed in Salzum. I was First among the First. At the moot where he was elected, I spoke loudest in his favor. He became Keyrdegen and changed the Oath. I swore freely. I believed in the Rockhome he promised. I trusted him to lead us forward, to a brighter future. I am—" he sighed, "*was* willing to lay down my life for his vision."

He held his bruised shield arm to his stomach and gestured towards Grady and the walls of the room. "You. This. None of it is right. There is no honor in this. What are you doing, Salzum?" Dulane stared out past the walls of the cell. He returned with a shake of his head. When he looked back at Grady, Dulane's real feelings hid behind a wry smile. "Nothing we can do about that now. We have to have something to show him. Progress is our only path forward. Thoughts?"

The captain's hurt arm claimed all of Grady's attention. Grady did not want to swing on his new friend again. Being the cause of another's pain tainted his breathing with sour guilt.

The bullies always seemed to enjoy hurting me. What was their damage?

If he couldn't swing on the captain safely, that left them with only one choice. A lifetime of taking it on the chin might finally pay off. He rapped his hammer against his shield. "Your turn. You will not be able to topple me."

A QUESTION OF HONOR

Hammer blows fell like rain. Shields thundered together. The combatants shifted around the small arena that used to be Grady's cell. Each did their best to stay within the white rope marking the field of combat. The captain was all offense. He danced through the forms and pulled every dirty trick he had learned during his long and much vaunted career. Opposite him, the Golem, Radix– Grady– fended off every blow. He moved with speed and his footing was sure. The holes in his guard were temporary. He didn't tire, didn't slow.

"Wonderful, wonderful." Salzum was spectating from a richly upholstered chair brought in for his viewing pleasure. Plenabus was not here, having declined the invitation to witness this sparring match. The Keyrdegen's applause clacked and chimed as his rings banged together. "That's enough. I've seen plenty."

The duelists stopped. The captain huffed beneath his mask, his shield and warhammer dropping. Grady stood completely still, dressed in thegen armor. The gear, an assortment of leather and chain mail, was nothing too fancy. A bucket helm with thin eye slits rattled loosely on his head. The outfit covered him completely, ensuring no one could tell that the dvergr beneath was made of stone.

Grady, deep within the golem's crystalline brain, yearned to keep going. Fighting was freeing. The complicated nature of footing, balance, and forethought made fighting the only time Grady felt full, physical agency.

"Well?" Salzum took a deep swallow of a honey yellow liquid from his fluted wine glass.

"It's good, sir. Especially once you consider that it's only been a couple of weeks. Its progress in so short a time is miraculous." The swell of pride Grady felt at the praise overrode the now familiar sting of being referred to as an object. Knowing that Dulane knew the truth made 'it' easier to ignore. "But its strength more than makes up for any minor deficiencies. I feel like I've been slamming myself against a literal wall."

The Keyrdegen swirled the glass and watched the pale golden liquid slide down the sides. "Do you still need time to make your recommendation?"

"Yes. I have taught it the basics of melee combat, but I have not been able to gauge its offensive capabilities. How well it thinks and reasons in a combat situation."

"And why is that?" The question sounded innocent. Salzum ran an unconcerned finger along the ring of the glass, making it hum. His patience waited like a trap, toothed and ready to snap.

"It took one practice swing at me and nearly broke my arm. Through a shield. I have not figured out a way to test what it can do and live." Dulane's response was baited with levity.

"Through your shield? That sounds like a ringing endorsement to me." Appraising Grady over his glass, the Keyrdegen's smile grew a sharp, predatory edge.

"It felt like being hit by a cart. But you already knew how strong it was. You asked me to train it, to create a tool designed to save dvergr lives. I've taught it enough for it to be a useful spectacle. Send it naked to fight a squad of fully armored dvergr and sell tickets." Dulane shrugged. "I think it's capable of more. As you taught me, my lord, fighting is more than just swinging a hammer. Until we know what it is truly capable of, I cannot make any sort of recommendation."

"Hm, interesting. That is a problem." In no rush, the Keyrdegen sniffed and sipped at his drink. "Your hesitation is wise." He stared into the amber liquid as if the answer he needed floated within. "I wonder. This glass is delicate. I could shatter it easily with a pinch of my fingers. Yet, I can hold it and drink from it without issue." He demonstrated by draining the glass and placing it with a faint tink on the side table. "Radix, how precisely can you control your strength?"

I hope someone poisoned that wine. His body answered the question with only a hint of the petulance Grady felt inside. "Haven't tried." He shrugged for good measure.

"The good captain has been smashing hammer and shield against you for a while now. Would you be able to, let's say, match his strength to make your blows land with an equal amount of force?" His kind tone set Grady on edge. Salzum was only nice when getting what he wanted.

After parrying and blocking hundreds of Dulane's attacks, Grady knew exactly how much force the veteran could muster. Weak as Grady was before, he knew how to be gentle. Images of scores of carefully handled eggs, tapped ever so gently on a bowl's rim, flashed before his mind's eye. The truth was pulled from him by the compulsion to obey. "Yes."

"Excellent! Shall we try? Of course by we, I mean you, Captain Dulane."

"Sir, I-" Dulane's reluctance was more than half feigned. He looked at Grady, hidden underneath his armor, and then at Salzum, reclined in expectant leisure. The only way out was through. Dulane bowed to the Keyrdegen. He readied his shield and hammer and bounced from foot to foot a bit. "You ready?" Grady nodded, and mirrored the captain's stance. "At your pleasure, my lord."

"Radix, when you swing at the captain, match his strength. Swing on my mark." He raised his hand over his head and held it there to let the drama of the moment grow. He watched the captain intently. The hand swung down to slap the arm of his chair. "Go!"

Grady's arm snapped out into the sideways swing that had floored his friend last time. Dulane braced himself and angled his shield to deflect the blow. The impact was strong and loud, but Grady's hammer bounced off and the captain remained standing. Relief flooded Grady. His friend was unhurt.

"Well?" Salzum asked, knowing the answer and oozing self-satisfaction.

"My shield isn't dented this time and I was able to keep my feet, sir."

"Clearly. Given this revelation, what next step do you intend, Captain?"

"More sparring to get a sense of its tactical abilities, if any. Then, if it performs well, exercises with a squad of handpicked thegen. See how well it works with others. If all goes well, perhaps a test out in the field. A patrol through the edge of the Wild Below." Grady shuddered at the idea of patrolling the deep border between Rockhome's safety and the terrors of the deep.

With his fingers tented and elbows on his knees, the Keyrdegen leaned forward. "Would you be willing to indulge me in a quick exhibition? A short bout between the two of you? I am too curious to wait." Dulane opened his mouth to beg off. "Please. I insist." Salzum was a master at masking iron orders behind soft words. A bow was the only acceptable response. "Wonderful. Radix, you will duel the captain until one of you is driven from the ring. Limit your strength to match Captain Dulane's until I say otherwise. Do your best to win. Start the bout on the captain's mark. I wish I had brought more wine."

The two friends squared off near the center of the white rope circle. Dulane beat his shield once and bowed to his opponent. Grady repeated the gesture.

"Always so proper! You are teaching it to be a real thegen. A golem with honor. Charming."

Bite me and chip a tooth, you condescending, fart-filled bellows.

"Go!" The captain shouted. He launched himself at Grady and the world slowed. Dulane raised his hammer for an overhead strike.

Grady whipped his hammer out, building momentum for a wide swipe. As Grady hoped he would, Dulane brought his shield to the side to block the strike, foiling his own swing. The captain's possible reactions were now limited.

You shouldn't have taught me everything you know! Grady surged with a newfound exaltation.

He was not expecting it when the captain lashed out with his shield. The next handful of exchanges threw Grady out of balance, as Dulane used his shield offensively.

Okay, mostly everything you know.

Unable to bring his whole strength to bear, the ferocity of the captain's onslaught pushed Grady backwards. Perhaps if he lost, Salzum would lose interest in him, in this whole project. He tried to topple himself, to mistime his swings. But with each attempt, the Keyrdegen's command lashed his being with pain to keep him competitive.

Mimicking the captain, he struck out with his shield as much as his warhammer. Grady attempted to pull Dulane off balance with a sharp tug on the captain's shield using the spiked end of his warhammer. Dulane followed the tug, transferring the energy into a powerful strike of his own. Grady blocked the swing with his shield and felt the vibration of the impact up to his shoulder. He flung the shield wide, knocking the hammer out of alignment, temporarily fouling the captain's footing.

Seeing an opening and driven to win, Grady improvised. He bent his knees and, shield first, launched himself at the captain. Off balance, Dulane took the shield to the torso. Grady's great stone weight pushed the captain further off balance. Driven by the pumping of Grady's legs, Dulane was bodily launched from the ring. The thegen clanged to the floor.

As soon as the captain left the ring, Grady's body went inert. The match was done, his latest set of orders complete. Grady wanted to reach a hand out towards his fallen friend. He wanted to congratulate him on a good fight and blame beginner's luck for his victory. It was good form for a warrior to help up a fallen opponent. But he wasn't a warrior, was he? *Just a tool. Just a weapon.*

Salzum whistled through his teeth as he honored the combatants with a standing ovation.

Dulane got up with a small groan, rubbing at his backside. He took his helmet off and dabbed at the sweat pouring down his face. Dulane quoted Kreth the Bulwark with a chuckle and a self-deprecating shake of his head. "It's always the blow you didn't see." To Grady, the line read like overdramatics, a tension breaking moment when the hero winks at the reader for laughs. From Dulane's mouth, the words carried the weight of a principle repeated often enough to become part of the truth. "I didn't teach him that, by the way. The shield offensive neither. It was a risky move that would not have worked if it didn't weigh as much as a full mine cart." The last part was clearly directed at Grady, who was unable to shrug sheepishly in response.

"And? You've now crossed hammers with it, traded blows. You clearly aren't dead. And it won!" Salzum hummed and stared into the middle distance, remembering. His nostalgia, soothing and fuzzy, brushed against Grady's mind. "You taught a machine to fight and so quickly too. To think, I was so proud the first time you bested me. Took you considerably longer."

"In my defense, I was a child for many of those years."

"Excuses, excuses." The teasing came out comfortable and rehearsed.

"Half a week of sparring, a week tops, and he'll be ready."

Salzum nodded, happy with what he heard. "Look at how much you accomplished with only three shifts. You have three more. Pressure creates diamonds, after all."

"Wisdom to live by, sir."

"Once again you impress me with your dedication and effort, my first. Show me what it can do." The Keyrdegen hit the 'it' with a little extra force. He met Grady's gaze for a meaningful moment, a smile hidden in his eyes.

Salzum really enjoys punching down.

He left without another word, ignoring Dulane's salute and bow. As he passed Grady, the plain coronet on the Keyrdegen's brow tugged at his essence.

Dulane regarded the closed door. His whispered words filled the cramped room. "Salzum. My master. You are treading a dark Way." He deflated with a disappointed sigh. Perking up a bit, he walked back to

Grady and put a hand on his shoulder. "Take the helmet off, let me look you in the face."

Grady took the helm from his head and let it clatter to the floor.

"Feel free to breathe, if you want."

Grady obliged. The stone of his body softened ever so slightly.

Dulane smiled. "There you are. Did you know when you breathe, your features soften? Your face relaxes and your stand eases into something more natural. When you breathed that first time, you shifted. I thought it was a trick of the light at first." Dulane reached down and picked up his hammer and slipped its handle into the loop at his belt. "You fought well. Given time, you have the potential to be the most dangerous dvergr I have ever met."

Grady wanted to protest. His old life was synonymous with weakness. Yes, he was now able to withstand a beating administered by two veteran warriors and the heat in the center of an industrial forge's burning heart. Yes, the metal bars bent easily in his hands and with a single blow he sent a fully armored dvergr across the room. But the power did not belong to Grady. It belonged to his body, altered by Plenabus's knife, guided by ancient secrets.

Dulane paced to the center of the roped-out circle. He stood with strength, his hands clasped behind his back. He radiated confidence and inspired trust. Grady imagined this is what the captain sounded like when training real warriors. "The Keyrdegen has given me three shifts to turn your amateurish flailings into the sharp and precise movements of a true warrior. Your body can learn the footwork. Your mind can memorize the stances and strategize. But a true warrior's strength comes from within." He tapped his breastplate above his heart. "You did not choose to be here, not like this. But you are here. I can't claim to have lived through anything similar, but I know what it feels like to be trapped, facing Ancestors only know what. In those times, I remember why I fight, why I took up the hammer to begin with. To me, a true thegen is needed where it is darkest in order to protect the light of the hearth and forge at home. I draw my strength from that simple, personal truth.

"'He who fights without heart has already lost'. The Bulwark knew his business. Find your reason to fight and keep fighting. No matter how impossible the situation, the only way out is through." Dulane stepped in and extended his hand. "Either way, we have some work to do. Are you with me, Grady?"

Based on the ever-present, ravenous ambition Grady felt radiating from Salzum, it was clear that he would never be content. The first steps of his plan included mass fraud, violent abduction, torture, and magically robbing an individual of their personal will. Worse was to come. He saw little choice in the matter. The Keyrdegen's commands were going to march him into the darkness, whether he was prepared or not.

The only way out-

The Keyrdegen and his artificer had already taken everything from him. What did he have left to fight for?

Green twinkled through his memory.

Ancestors help him, Grady trusted Dulane. If the captain said this was the way forward, then Grady would follow his lead. He grasped Dulane by the forearm. "I'm with you." Grady thought he heard a faint echo of his old voice tumbling amongst the rocks.

THE BEARDLESS

Dulane entered the room full of purpose, carrying a bulging backpack with a bedroll bundled on top. His tension was obvious in the bunched up way he walked and the tightness around his eyes. Without a word to Grady, he tossed down his bag and began to clatter the weapons and shields around, with an occasional glance at the door.

Grady thought Dulane's caution was reasonable since the Keyrdegen and the artificer both had the habit of showing up when they were least wanted.

Plenabus walked through the door as if summoned by Grady's thoughts. Dulane only spared him a nod before launching into a very loud practice duel with Grady. Following Dulane's lead, they filled their sparring with unnecessary percussion. Hammers beat on shields. Shields crashed together like cymbals. The bout went on and on.

The violent cacophony finally drove the old dvergr from the cell. He left quickly, pale as paper and mumbling to himself.

Dulane called a halt with an upraised hand. Grady's hammer froze mid swing inches from the captain's helmet. "Let's reset and have a little chat now that we're alone." He pushed the hammer away gingerly. "The Keyrdegen has high expectations for us both. They are your first true enemy. We need you in fighting shape nowish. I'll be bunking in here with you until the job's done."

Grady felt the mad need to clap his hands and shout, "Sleepover!" His body refused to oblige.

They fought the rest of that shift. With Grady's strength limited, Dulane's experience and skill made the matches even. Grady tried a few times to catch Dulane with the same trick that won him their first bout, but the captain was no fool. Each time Grady charged, Dulane twisted, forcing Grady out of the ring using his own momentum. Possessing a stone's weight and mass came with its own challenges.

That shift Grady lost every bout except the last one, which ended up a draw. When they stopped for food, Dulane slumped against the wall, worn and tired. He removed his gauntlets and swore. The calloused palms of his hands were red. "Like hitting a damn wall." He rummaged through his bag, removing a wax paper wrapped square and a large brown bottle triumphantly. He unwrapped the sandwich, took a bite, and talked as he chewed. "You're doing better, Grady. You need to watch your balance and figure out a way to turn all that stone more effectively."

Being stripped of its epicurean luster, the aroma of cured meat, spicy brown mustard, and red cabbage did nothing more than inform Grady of the sandwich's contents. The wafting smell of the bread struck deeper. It called to mind the memory of every sandwich from his past. Multitudes of crusts, crumbs light or dark and spongy or dense, flittered by. The barrage ended as suddenly as it began, leaving Grady with the impression that he might have eaten too many sandwiches.

He checked his fuel reserves and found himself half empty. *Full*, he corrected. *Best to stay positive.*

Grady filled his bucket from the coal hopper in the corner of the cell. He sat across from Dulane, legs crossed, and munched away. This batch's taste reminded him of a very hard cheese. It was almost nutty.

As they ate, Dulane chatted away. The fighting advice gave way to amusing stories about the captain's childhood. A member of Clan Feldspar, he grew up midway up the lichen and moss coated North Wall. He told Grady stories of the hijinks he and his young mates got up to among the fungus fields.

Lost in his memories, Dulane did not notice Grady stop breathing to avoid broadcasting his sadness to his friend. The last thing Grady wanted was for Dulane to misinterpret his gloomy countenance and cease his stories.Grady treasured this glimpse of life from up-wall. The life of the

Clanned sounded idyllic, and he was happy for his friend. While they ate and Grady listened, the bone-deep stone of his body felt more like a thin outer shell.

"Then my ma broke a wooden spoon over my head for good measure. Taught me a lesson, sure as sure. Don't get caught with your hand in the cookie jar!" Dulane slapped his knee and wiped away a laughter born tear. "She cried when I volunteered for thegen training and again when I took my oath. Proud though she was, I know in her heart she wanted me to follow in her family's footsteps. Become a brewer." Dulane closed his eyes and took a deep swig from his bottle. He smacked his lips and sighed. "They make damn fine beer," he added wistfully.

The captain's stories of home described the kind of life dreamed of by a much younger Grady. The wards of the Ground Floor Orphan Asylum for the Young and Clanless were too busy ensuring their own survival to be friends. The beatings, freely given for terrible infractions such as sneezing disrespectfully and being 'a useless brick', were not laughing matters. It wasn't the place for hijinks of any kind.

He must have noticed Grady's stillness because his laughter petered off, and he rubbed the back of his head embarrassed. "Ah, look at me. Prattling on and on. That's not a conversation. Your turn. What were your parents like?"

When his golem voice whispered, it sounded like two rocks rasping against each other. "I don't remember."

Dulane nearly dropped the last half of his sandwich. "What?"

"They died in the Incursion of 2139. And any other family I had."

"You grew up in the South East?"

Grady nodded.

"I'm sorry. That was a nasty business. Largest pack of kobolds ever recorded." Dulane focused on something in the distance past Grady's head. "They came out of nowhere. The thegen did all we could. We were forced to patrol the floor for months after. Sneaky shits, the lot of them. Lost a lot of fine warriors clearing them out for good." Returning to the present, Dulane gave Grady a weighing look. "Tell me about your life."

Grady told his story simply. He spoke briefly of the stark comforts of the orphan asylum. Dulane quirked an incredulous eyebrow when Grady described his individualistic struggle to survive his early childhood. "My fondest memories involve books and the quiet times I got to spend learning. A job meant I could have a place of my own, get out from under the proctor's thumbs. Luckily, I was good at sums and learned to write in a neat hand. My rare luck struck again when I was granted my old position at Iron Mine Six. Then I lived my life." He wanted to stop there, but the command in Dulane's question dragged one more sentence out of him. "And now I find myself here."

Through it all, Dulane listened behind a mask of empathic concern. Given the life he lived, Grady doubted that the warrior captain could really understand what the life of a Clanless orphan was like. It was touching that the attempt was made.

"I never-" Dulane cleared his throat and tried again. "You've walked a hard road, Grady. A hard road." The captain nodded. Then he resumed eating his sandwich and thinking his own private thoughts.

Grady, a little lighter sharing his difficult past with his friend, returned to his bucket. An amiable silence, marred only by the sounds of chewing, filled the cell turned training room.

When the last traces of mustard were gone from Dulane's fingers and any and all crumbs were brushed onto the ground, they went again. A string of hard fought victories in Dulane's favor gave way to a slew of draws. "Alright, that's enough for now. I've hit my useful limit for this shift. I need some shut eye." The veteran warrior huffed and puffed while he mopped at his face and neck with a towel. He rummaged in his pack and brought out a book.

It can't be! He took in the gold lettering on the red leather cover once more to be sure. *An Oath Sworn, Book 1 of the Saga of Kreth the Bulwark.* Grady had searched for a copy of that book for the last decade. His broker claimed there were no copies to be had anywhere under the mountain. The supple leather and gilded paper edges put this particular volume far out of Grady's price range.

Dulane handed the book to Grady, who held it with gentle reverence. "I figured while I'm here, there'd be no harm," he said between yawns. "Hope you don't mind that it's a bit marked up. I like to take notes. I'm gonna hit the sack. You did good today." Then he laid down on his bed roll and put an arm across his eyes to block out the light. His snoring started not long after.

Grady sat cross-legged and, for the first time in too long, began to read. Dulane's notes filled the margins on every page. The neatness and legibility of the handwriting impressed Grady, especially since it was all written in pencil. The cell's unnatural lighting bleached the pages and robbed the ink of its lichen inspired glimmer.

The book opened with Kreth as a child, long before he swore his oaths and earned his name. The hero stood up to some bullies picking on a smaller friend. They beat him to a bloody pulp for his efforts, but his friend escaped unharmed. Dark underlines emphasized the paragraph describing the beating and Kreth's sense of victory as he watched his friend run away to safety.

A drawn line ran from the paragraph to one of Dulane's notes, surrounded by scribbled stars. Grady read it aloud. "The desire to protect others at all costs is the first step along his Way."

The light fiction, enriched by Dulane's insights, touched Grady deeply. The notes exposed truths about the dvergr condition hidden amongst the overdramatics and bloody action. The truths were painful and hard to process. And yet, they seemed self-evident when stated so plainly. The notes made this story vastly different from the ones contained in the treasured volumes of Grady's lost collection.

Dulane snorted himself awake far too soon. He hopped to his feet and shook the sleep from his limbs. "Let's get started," he said with a stretch.

Grady was loath to stop reading. The answers he sought had to be deeper in the book, on the next page or one after. Despite what Grady wanted, his body returned the book, took up arms, and readied itself.

Since Grady was otherwise occupied, his body fought on without any direct input. Dulane won the first few contests in short order.

After his fourth victory, Dulane was irate. "What is going on, Grady? Plant your damn feet. There is no way that combo should have worked. Get your head out of your ass and get it back in the ring. You're not breathing, are you even paying attention?"

Grady snapped from his reverie and felt a flush of shame, happy to not have it show up on his face. He gathered his thoughts for a moment. "He never wins. He keeps fighting and never wins. All Kref's done is suffer." The opening thrashing turned out to be the least of the young dvergr's troubles. Despite his up wall origin, Kreth's early life consisted of a string of struggles, different from anything Grady faced but still recognizable. The loneliness and need for acceptance at the center of it all was far too familiar.

"Oh." Dulane sighed behind his helm's mask. He shrugged with one shoulder. "I felt the same way on my first readthrough." He removed his helmet and held it in the crook of his arm. "You're familiar with Kreth during the later installments of the saga. Triumphant. Bold. The first volume is different and is the foundation that makes what follows possible. Loss is a Truth we must all face. Perseverance, the refusal to give up and the need to keep trying, is what makes him the Bulwark. What makes his Way worth following. It turns suffering into strength." Dulane tapped on Grady's helmet. "You can do this. Ready?"

In response, Grady rapped his shield with his hammer. *The only way out is through.*

The scale began to tip once Grady's mind fully engaged in the duels. Grady's mass, speed, strength, and limitless stamina forced Dulane to fight more defensively this time. A string of draws ended with a surprising Grady victory. He managed to push Dulane back to the edge of the ring. Boxed in, the wily captain was unable to keep circling. A rain of powerful blows to his shield pushed Dulane off balance and onto his backside outside the white rope.

"Ha! About time. That was well fought, Grady." The captain got up gradually, ineffectually rubbing at his backside through his armor. "I think that's all I can take for now. I need a drink."

They spent the rest of the shift in relative ease. The captain added another large bottle of beer to his repast. Dulane popped the cork, freeing the smell of malted hops and the funk of fermented mushrooms to fill the small cell. The dvergr swigged the bottle between bites of a similar sandwich from the shift before.

They ate, and Grady listened to more of Dulane's stories. This time he told tales of his life as a thegen. "Salzum was captain then, and I was his lowly second." He took a long pull from the bottle and shivered. "We were patrolling a newer excavation, down south west, when a pack of mole lizards ripped through the raw stone. I nearly wet my trousers, but Salzum... he was a marvel, striking out in a blurring whir. Gave me and the squad enough time to get ourselves together. We had them dead before the horns needed to be sounded." He pointed to a trio of scars stripping his bicep. "But not before one of them gave me this." He burped and smacked his lips in appreciation. Then, the bottle half empty, Dulane began to sing.

Grady did not know many drinking songs and this one was completely new to him. On the surface, the song was about the love of two young dvergr from feuding clans. The melody whined, plaintive and somber. It tugged at Grady's heart. The song's beauty felt out of place in his cell. The tempo grew upbeat as the bottle grew emptier. By the time Dulane shook the last few drops into his open mouth, the lament had transformed into a bawdy, bouncing song. The lyrics began again from the start, their meaning corrupted and made suggestive by the new tempo.

Grady sang along in his head. *I really should have gone out more.*

The captain's snores were emboldened by his drinking. Grady watched his friend noisily sleep for a bit before he took up the book to pass the rest of the downtime reading. He caught himself reading the same paragraph for the fifth time. The words refused to stick. Intrusive and unhelpful thoughts, about how his present was slouching ever forward towards an unknowable future, refused to let him focus. To distract himself, he analyzed his matches from earlier and tried to strategize for the ones to come. That, and playing with his breath, helped to pass the time.

Despite his earlier indulgence, the captain woke up early on their last allotted shift. Restless, Grady had started working on his forms silently hours ago. His practice continued through Dulane's quick breakfast of jerky washed down with the first half of another bottle from his family's brewery.

The two friends squared off in the round ring. The cell's door opened.

A Throng member in full armor held the door open as Keyrdegen Salzum entered the room. Plenabus, a withered shadow, followed close behind. A second thronger followed on the artificer's heels bearing the Keyrdegen's travel throne. "Ah! So good to see you hard at work, Captain Dulane. My heart is warmed by such dedication." He gestured for his chair to be placed down opposite the door. He lowered his ample backside onto the purple cushion. "Come Plenabus."

The artificer was pale and drawn, even for him. The inner vitality that kept the withered dvergr going seemed to be waning. He looked around the cell, lost. He winced every time Salzum moved his hand. Since he gesticulated grandly as he spoke, the artificer appeared to be having a fit. Grady almost felt bad for him.

"You may sit this match out, Captain. I have brought two others to try their hand against our latest recruit." His wink was large enough to read from a stage. "They are both eager to cross steel with the newcomer. I told them all about how he made his way through the Wilds Below on his own. They insisted on the honor of testing his mettle before he joined the ranks of Rockhome's thegen." The two throngers stood silently behind Salzum, still as statues. "Please, Captain Dulane, join me."

Dulane gave Grady a furtive glance. "You are earlier than expected, my lord. As we agreed, I need one more shift to evaluate the newcomer," the captain responded, rolling with Salzum's fiction.

"Nonsense. Look at him! Standing tall, armed and armored. Looks like the true figure of a thegen. He survived a solo passage Below to come here. A rare feat worthy of an epitaph once all is said and done. This is nothing but a formality." Over his smile Salzum's eyes hardened to steel. "Join me, Captain." Dulane was powerless before his lord's clearly stated order. Uncertainty flashed on Dulane's face before it disappeared behind his Salzum shaped faceplate. He saluted his warlord and stood at rigid attention next to the throne.

Salzum waved the throngers forward. They walked into the ring opposite Grady. "Radix, ready yourself."

Grady shifted to face the thegen and raised his weapon. That he had to prove himself in a duel was not a surprise. According to Dulane, it was the done thing. Two at once, both seasoned warriors with more years wielding the hammer than Grady had under the mountain, seemed a bit much. The presence of the Keyrdegen and the artificer further unsettled Grady. The desire to fall into his breath and block them out strengthened. But he had to wait.

Not yet. I must do this. I can do this. I think.

"Defeat them, Radix, two on one, and end your roving. You will gain a Name, a place among our thegen, and a home. Do well enough and I will raise you up, place you amongst my Throng." The pomposity drained away as Salzum settled into the role of referee, looking between the throngers and Grady from his chair. "I want no lives lost. A combatant is out when they fall from their feet or step outside the ring. Do all in attendance agree?"

"Aye," said the pair of warriors in unison. They each took a step to the side, separating slightly.

"Aye," Grady echoed. His opponents shared a quick look at the sound of his voice.

"Begin."

At the word, the two warriors charged. Their beards, one a long auburn braid, the other a black fringe, and both patched with gray, fluttered as they ran. The two were veterans who knew their business well. They angled themselves to come at Grady from both sides at once. Never having fought two people simultaneously, Grady decided to avoid doing so at all costs.

They don't know me or what I am.

Grady began a glacially slow inhale as he pumped his legs and met Fringe's charge. The warrior braced herself, but was unprepared for the force a moving Grady brought to bear. She let out a cry as their shields connected and her footing faltered. Grady swung down and yanked her anchor foot up and away with a "Hwagh!". Unable to recover, she landed with a thud.

Salzum cheered.

There was no time to celebrate or watch the defeated opponent leave the ring. Braid closed on him with a roar. Grady deflected his enemy's first strike, angling his shield to create an opening to allow him to move away from the ring's edge and towards a more favorable, central position. Braid must have anticipated the move. He parried Grady's hammer with his own and attempted to shove against Grady's shield. His attack faltered when he encountered more resistance than he expected.

In the lull after the impact, Grady twisted his hammer's spike to grab at Braid's. He pushed against Braid's shield, forcing it out of place. With a stony roar, Grady shoved with his shield and pulled with his hammer. Braid spun into the forced twist and managed to back up, rebalancing in time to counter Grady's next attacks.

The two traded an extended series of blows. Braid was a better fighter than Grady. Much better. *He's been at this for at least a hundred years. Has it even been a month? All I have to do is drag this out. He can't outlast me.* Grady disengaged and made distance. Braid didn't immediately follow. He sucked air from behind his mask, heaving in his armor. Grady had yet to finish his initial inhale.

Dulane and Grady had discussed what to do about his breathing when they were before witnesses once more. They both agreed the secret must be kept. But Grady fought noticeably better while breathing. The deep connection to his body shrunk his reaction times and improved the precision of his movements. They reached no clear solution and shelved the discussion for this shift. They thought they had more time.

As Dulane had snored away, Grady, wanting something more concrete to occupy his mind, pondered and played with his breath, looking for a solution to the problem. He had stopped breathing for a moment and let himself recede. From deep in his own head, Grady initiated a slow and meager inhale. The tiniest trickle of air entered his lungs. His chest rose slowly, imperceptible under the layers of leather and chainmail he wore.

Despite the meager volume and geologic time frame of his breath, Grady was pulled out into his body's extremities. Dulane's snoring cycled a hundred times before Grady's lungs filled to capacity. Another hundred snores and his lungs were empty again. Grady had been about to excitedly show Dulane his new trick when Salzum and his entourage burst in.

From his side of the white rope ring, Grady waited long enough to convince his opponent that he was also taking a breather. The moment Braid relaxed, Grady charged, his warhammer held high and his shield out to the side. Caught off guard, Braid scrambled to set his stance and meet the charge.

He was too slow. Triumphant, Grady rained blows down on his opponent. Most hit the shield or were deflected at the last minute by the opposing hammer. A few slipped through Braid's guard to impact on a shoulder, a hip, a shin. The low blow rocked Braid's balance. On the follow-up swing, Grady's hammer glanced off his opponent's helmet, denting the metallic visage of Salzum.

The blow to the head staggered Braid. He stepped back over the white rope, and it was over. Incensed by his victory, Grady wanted to push on, punish this warrior, then the other, then Plenabus, and then Salzum. For the first time in his life, Grady felt unstoppable, powerful.

The fight was over and his orders were done. His body grew still. His exhale was slow and invisible.

"Radix, face me."

Grady turned towards the travel throne and the commanding mass sitting on top of it. "That was a fine spectacle."

Dulane nodded. "Yes, sir. Radix is a fine warrior. His tribulations have taught him much."

"Radix, traveler, you have proven yourself worthy. Strength of body and spirit carried you through the winding ways of Below. I offer you residence within my city and name you 'The Beardless.' Soon all will know it." Salzum smirked at his own cleverness.

The Beardless? Really?

"Captain Dulane, would you do the honors? Orvid and Shamas, you will act as witnesses. You will swear the oath, Radix." The power of Salzum's command thrummed through Grady. Next to the Keyrdegen, large tears flowed freely down Plenabus's face. His beard wagged side to side in mute and powerless denial of the proceedings.

Dulane stepped in front of Grady as the other two warriors limped into place at his sides. The captain's pride in his student was obvious even through the eye holes of his mask. "Radix the Beardless, kneel."

Grady dropped to a knee, one arm at his side and the other resting on his upturned leg. Dulane rested a hand on Grady's helmet. When he spoke again, his voice resonated with the authority of tradition. "Know that an oath coerced is no oath. If you take up this obligation freely, speak the words."

Every child under the mountain dreamed of becoming a thegen one shift. Grady was no exception. Pretending to be a warrior, armored in honor and free of fear, helped young Grady endure the bleakest parts of his early life. Now, he knelt in the Keyrdegen's presence before the captain of the Keyrdegen's Throng and two veteran warriors.

It was a dream come true, twisted into a nightmare.

As his body spoke, Grady couldn't help but laugh. "Bear witness, oh Ancestors! Sever all ties of craft and clan. Bind me in violent duty. Carve this oath on my soul. Shatter it if I fail. Let the fragments be lost and my name forgotten. I will walk the Thegen Way. I will speak only Truth. I will sculpt a better future with my might. I will heed the horn's call. My will and the Keyrdegen's are one." Grady had to admit that his new horror of a voice enhanced the drama of the moment.

Dulane struck Grady's shoulders three times. "It is done. This oath is binding. To break it is to die. To honor it is to live forever. Rise, thegen. Rise, Radix the Beardless."

Grady stood, unsure how to feel. Neither he nor Dulane saw this one coming. A duel to test his mettle? Sure. But to be sworn into service before witnesses was a different barrel of beer entirely.

"At ease, Captain. Well done, well done. No matter how many times I see the oath administered, it still gives me the chills." Salzum gestured at his throne and Shamas retrieved it. "You have impressed me greatly, Radix the Beardless, newest thegen of Rockhome. I raise you into place among my Throng. Based on what I witnessed, I expect great things from you. Radix is yours to command, Captain. The Throng surely misses your guidance. See that our new warrior is given lodging in the Hold. Come, Plenabus." The artificer fell in behind Salzum, silently weeping and droopier than ever. The procession left.

Dulane, shocked, and Grady, made of stone, stared motionless at the closed door.

A Room of One's Own

Once the reality of what transpired settled in, Dulane whooped and leapt around the room. Grady had never seen his friend carry on like that. "You did it, you pretty gargoyle! When he said you were going to fight those two, I swore we were finished. I've never seen Shamas lose since she was a hopeful. Orvid always gives better than he gets."

The captain scrambled around gathering up his gear and stowing it away. His obvious joy was infectious and smothered Grady's mounting uncertainty. "You did me proud. You used your mass and weight to your advantage, but your technique was on point. We'll have to see about getting you a set of Throng armor. The story of that duel will fill a bracer nicely. Maybe, a short poem." Dulane looked up from his quickly filling pack. "Plenabus didn't seem overly happy. Any idea why?"

Grady remembered the bits of conversation the Keyrdegen and his artificer had while in his presence. Then there was Plenabus's overenthusiastic reaction to the paperwork experiment. Grady raised his warhammer. "He's mad because the Keyrdegen reneged on some kind of promise. Seems like Plenabus created the golems to be a tool, not a weapon."

"Huh?" Dulane looked up from his bag, surprised. He had not expected an answer. "Another promise broken, eh?" he muttered to himself. He looked sad for a moment, shook his head, and snorted. "Plenabus has been plying his trade long enough, he shouldn't be surprised. Axes and hammers were tools first. That explains his sour disposition. Regret wears on a body. You can't unrust the iron," he added, quoting Kreth once again. All packed, he hoisted his gear onto his shoulder. "Leave your hammer and shield here. You'll have better where we're going. Stay close. Keep your head on a swivel."

Grady followed behind Dulane as they left the cell. The ramp out was shorter than Grady remembered from his trip to the foundry. The buildings were shadowless, lit evenly by the sun's diffused light radiating through the thick fog cover. Dvergr going about their normal mid-shift business hurried along the avenues.

The captain wound their way towards the West Wall. Pedestrians parted like water around the two fully armored thegen. People leaned away from them and looked anywhere else to avoid their attention in a way Grady found familiar.

Grady thought, *Tremble, peons before the might of us thegen!* And immediately felt like a jerk. He expected some kind of satisfaction from finally being an intimidating presence. It never came.

Dulane's command to keep his head on a swivel forced him to be aware of everything. The sights of the Floor were overwhelming after so long in his tiny cell. The writing on every sign and posted advertisement for goods and services demanded to be read. Copies of the damned poster that had led to all of Grady's recent suffering mocked him from nearly every corner. Deposits from the sooty air darkened them and their edges were ragged. A few were torn with only a corner still attached to the wall.

And the graffiti! Before his abduction, Grady paid little attention to the rebellious scribblings and doodles. Teams of Clanless patrolled the streets and regularly removed any out of place paint. Immediately after the graffiti's removal was the only time a wall looked clean.

Illegible names written large with garish slashes of bright paint, recreations of rude gestures, and various genitalia covered the walls. One symbol, clearly painted on the walls by slapping a thick coating of red paint over a stencil, was repeated everywhere. It was the city in reverse. A flat line representing the Floor hung above spiky contours instantly recognizable as the buildings of the Ceiling. They were surrounded by hand painted slogans. Things like: "Clans are shit!" and "Pay the Gray!" and, Grady's personal favorite, "Fuck the Keyrdegen!"

The pair followed the sunken flow of full carts towards the Wall, their rattle tangible through the soles of Grady's boots. The carts disappeared into the Wall to be hauled off to their next destination. A bank of five elevators provided a similar service to the people of Rockhome. Thick chains lifted and lowered the boxes of people powered by an ingenious system of hidden counterweights. A large, freestanding sign proclaimed this place to be the "North-West Hoist Station." The dvergr in line waited with varying degrees of patience. Each elevator had its own attendant and roped-off queue.

Instead of stopping at the back of a line, Dulane marched past the waiting Clansfolk towards the elevator marked with a gold two. Despite a few unhappy glares, there was not one grumble about their cutting in line.

The elevator was just touching down as they reached the attendant. Her boredom evaporated as the two armored thegen approached. She smiled at them and tugged at the burgundy uniform she wore, trying to smooth out the creases. Its gold epaulets and buttons were dull with age. She swallowed nervously as she glanced from Dulane to Grady and back. Her gilded name tag read 'Justa.' "Welcome, Captain. Always a pleasure. It will be a minute, while the cart empties. Thank you for your patience and your service."

Dulane's nod was perfunctory.

The elevator touched the ground softly and silently. Its metal-wrought accordion doors pulled back and twenty or so dvergr poured out. As soon as the last body left the elevator, Justa unclipped the rope and motioned for Grady and Dulane to step forward. "Have a nice shift." Once the two warriors were past the rope, Justa began checking passes and allowing other dvergr onto the elevator.

Grady had seen the elevators before, of course. He'd walked past most of the hoist stations at least once in his life. He liked to watch the smooth up and down movement of the elevators. Never, even in his wildest dreams, did he believe he would ever ride in one. He followed Dulane past the doors, genuinely excited. Instead of moving to the back to make room for the passengers boarding behind them, Dulane led Grady into a position next to the door and opposite another attendant dressed in the same burgundy and gold uniform as Justa.

"All the way?" The attendant asked with deference. Dulane answered with another nod. The attendant pressed a nodule on the very top of the metal plate he held in his hands. Each passenger told the attendant a number as they entered. The corresponding nodule was pressed down for each new number. When the last passenger boarded, the attendant inserted the metal plate into a bracket on the wall. He closed the accordion doors by pulling a large handled lever. "Brace."

The elevator rose and everyone rocked a bit, except for Grady. Its ascent was smooth enough until it shuddered to a halt. The attendant shouted, "Five!", and pulled another of the levers near his post. The accordion doors at the back of the elevator opened to reveal the interior of the West Wall, domain of Rockhome's merchants, Clan Pyrite. It was Grady's first glimpse into any Wall's interior.

A handful of dvergr dressed in the same tartan of blue and white excused their way out that door and into a wide grand hallway. An endless line of shops extended as far as Grady could see. It was impeccably clean. The Wall burst with colors. Hanging tapestries, complex mosaics, and the people themselves vibrantly shimmered.

The elevator kept rising and stopping. At each stop Grady marveled at the Wall's contents. As it elevated, Grady watched the buildings of the Floor recede, gradually losing their definition until they were nothing more than blocky elements of a too simple maze. The elevator passed through the fog layer and foul grayness swallowed the only world Grady knew.

The sight beyond the fog would have dropped Grady's jaw if it weren't made of stone. The great stalactite palaces of the Roof hung, majestic and timeless before him. The sunlight, alien and bright, added its own dreamlike sheen to the vista. The beauty of the roofline stilled his breath.

Dulane nudged him. "What do you think?"

"I have no words." Grady's voice drew a few odd looks, but their armor kept anyone from looking too long or too closely.

"I hear you. I forget to look sometimes, but when I do," Dulane whistled his appreciation.

The elevator slid into Rockhome's ceiling empty except for Dulane, Grady, and the attendant. "Top floor. Commons," the attendant cried. He pulled the first lever and the front doors accordioned open. His "Have a nice shift" was hurried.

Dulane walked past him without a word and Grady followed. The atrium's ceiling was a tangle of massive, stone-carved chains. The room itself, walls and floors, were constructed from one hunk of marble. The marble shimmered in the soft blue lichen light. Dulane led Grady towards the room's one exit. Guarding the double wide egress, were two Throng members made identical looking by their armor. The space beyond them glowed, warm and yellow.

They parted as the pair approached, swinging to the side and saluting with clockwork precision. How much practice did it take to achieve those results? Grady thought back to his hours and hours of weapons training and felt a bit of empathy for the pair. Then they stepped past the guards and into the yellow light. Grady held his breath again.

"Welcome to the Commons," Dulane said with an inviting sweep of his arm.

The space beyond was airy and bright, as high as the stalactites of the Roof hung low. Sunlight glowed through smoky banks of glass high on the tapered ceiling. A rug of short-clipped, green shag covered the ground crisscrossed by a network of marble pathways. Wherever pathways met, single-story buildings of alabaster stood and, at the very center of the stone network, a steepled, gold-tipped structure towered over the scene.

Grady knew about the Commons. One of the first things he remembered learning from his classes at the Ground Floor Orphan Asylum for the Young and Clanless was basic geography. The highest part of Rockhome, the Commons, was built inside the mountain's peak. Those buildings were the entrances to the various stalactites of the Roof and the largest one in the center, the one Dulane was leading him towards, was the entrance to the Hold itself.

Knowing about the Commons and seeing it were vastly different things. A faint breeze rustled the shag of the green rug, slipped underneath Grady's helm, and brushed against his cheeks and neck. He wanted nothing more than to sit on the path and take the place in. Instead, his body doggedly followed Dulane.

A dvergr in drab overalls with his beard braided tight to the chin, caught Grady's attention. He worked the pump of the cask strapped to his back. A tube led from the cask to the nozzle he held in his hands and water sprayed forth wetting a section of the rug. *What is he doing?* Grady lacked any frame of reference to even hazard a guess.

The two guards stationed where the walkway met the Hold entrance let Dulane and Grady through unmolested. Dvergr dressed in the communal tartans of the civil services elite, a panoply of crosshatched purples with little ribbons in their clan colors pinned to their chests, scurried in and out through the grand entrance. Most carried bundles of scrolls and stacks of folders bristling with pages.

This sight made sense. *Ah, the lifeblood of bureaucracy. Papers carried from important person to important person.*

The entrance's alabaster walls glowed in the diffused sunlight. The illumination gave the various statues mounted around the exterior a sense of inner life. The artistry of it all filled Grady with a sense of pride in his people's capacity to create beauty.

A picket line of throngers guarded the palace's entrance, spaced to not impede the constant flow of workers. Dulane marched right up the middle of the short set of stairs that led up to the entrance's landing. The thegen might as well have been statues themselves for all the reaction they gave. Then they were in and making their way down the stairs.

The wonders inside the Hold, along the walls and ceilings encasing the stairwell, plucked at Grady's ancestral roots. The statuary was painted to a lifelike finish. Ancestors, whose names Grady could not begin to guess, watched from their posts as he and Dulane made their way in.

Grady paid as little attention to the stairs as he could while not falling, overwhelmed by the beauty of it all. He retreated into wide-eyed numbness. There was only so much grandeur a brick like him could handle. Riots of rich colors filled every hallway. Carvings, statues, heirloom weapons and armor filled every inch of wall space.

Dulane walked with confidence and Grady followed as ordered.The crowded nature of the halls filled with the constant bustle of workers, reminded Grady of the pedestrian paths on the Floor. The pedestrians up here were just dressed nicer.

They descended twice more, before Dulane led them to the plainest looking door Grady had seen since their elevator ride. The clean lines and simple decorations of the curved hallway beyond soothed Grady like a balm. A single geometrically patterned carpet ran down the center. Sconces, plain bowls filled with glowing lichen, hung on one side of the hall and lit the space in a cool blue. The circular hallway's outer wall was dotted with evenly spaced doors. On each door glowed a number.

"Twenty-six should be free. Come on." Dulane walked to his left. The door numbers counted up.

The door to twenty-three opened and a Throng member with two long braids hanging below his Salzum mask walked out. He snapped a salute to the captain. "New recruit, sir?"

I am getting real sick of seeing Salzum's face everywhere.

"Yeah, Conov. The Keyrdegen found him personally. Traversed the wilds Below solo. Took down Shamas and Orvid together to earn his way in."

Behind his mask, Conov's eyes went wide. The thronger whistled through his teeth. "Impressive. Nice to meet you, neighbor. Second Conov. You need anything or have any questions, let me know." Conov held out his gauntleted hand.

The three dvergr stood in silence as the offered hand hovered in space. Dulane shifted, remembering Grady's limitations a moment too late. "Say hello, Radix the Beardless."

"Pleasure," Grady said. His rock tumble voice made Conov flinch. Grady gripped his forearm and shook it once. The tug downward pulled Conov slightly off balance. *Oops.*

"Uh, sure. Pleasure." He nodded politely at Grady. He went stiff and looked both ways, leaning back to see further along the hall's curvature. "Captain, can I speak with you?"

After regarding the second for a moment, Dulane nodded his ascent. "Wait here, Radix. I'll only be a moment. Then we can get you settled in." Grady nodded in response.

The pair of thegen walked a few paces away from Grady and checked the hall once more for anyone coming. They both took off their helmets and leaned in to each other. Their whispered exchange was impossible for Grady to make out. Dulane slipped a piece of paper out of his belt pouch into Conov's while they spoke. Conov went pale, replaced his helmet, and saluted.

When Conov walked past, he gave Grady a wide berth. Grady watched him go long enough to catch Conov's parting glance over his shoulder.

Room twenty-six was remarkably similar to Grady's old room back at the flop house. It was just nicer. It lacked the lingering industrial smell, the fungus stalk furniture bore fewer scuffs, and the linens on the bed looked smoother. Opposite the door hung a tapestry depicting an ancient warrior slaying a troll in single combat.

Dulane shuffled them both inside. "Well, that wasn't awkward. We'll have to figure out some orders that will allow you to interact normally with your fellow thegen. Jakes and showers are down the hall, not that you need to know." He scanned the room quickly. "Oh. I think you'll like this."

Dulane walked over to the tapestry and pulled it aside. Yellow light filled the room. "Come look. You have a great view of the North West corner." Grady wanted to run to the window, but had to settle for his body's determined plod. A corner of Rockhome sprawled before him. The Walls buzzed with activity. He could see all of the corner's ten elevators in their constant locomotion, rising and falling. Clan banners fluttered next to large advertisements for everything under the mountain. The fog, thinned to a haze, revealed the Floor's grid far below. The only detail Grady was able to make out from so far away was the constant flow of carts.

"I need to go wash up and catch some sleep in a real bed. Make yourself comfortable here, if you can." Dulane rummaged in his pouch for a moment. He held out his copy of *An Oath Sworn*. Grady could hear his smile beneath the mask. "Something to do while you wait. I'm sure the Keyrdegen will not let you linger here over long. I'd stay in your armor just in case." And then Grady was alone.

As he must, Grady followed the captain's order to make himself comfortable. The bed and chair groaned under his weight but held up. *No plopping down,* Grady noted. He wanted to run his bare hands over the sheets, maybe even lie under them, close his eyes, and pretend to sleep.

Instead, he placed the chair by the window and carefully lowered himself down. He took up *An Oath Sworn* and found the part where he had left off. The sunlight filtering through the window made the ink on the pages black. It was softer than the light in his cell, warmer and more pleasant. He turned a page and a flash of light from the direction of the door caught his attention.

Hanging on the back of the door was a small, square mirror. Grady placed the book open, face down, on the chair. He approached the mirror with careful and cautious steps. It was strange to see a visored helmet looking back at him. The lack of beard hanging beneath made him want to cry. It was one of the first things taken from him. His hand disappeared behind the visor to rub at his chin.

Like I'm touching one of those statues out there.

He looked closer. Beyond the faceless mask, in depths of the shadows, were his eyes. Grady never thought his eyes particularly noteworthy. If pushed to describe them, he would have used words like 'tired looking' and 'shit brown'. The beauty of the ones staring back at him from the mirror rivaled a number of the pieces he passed on his walk here. The orbs were pale dolomite, threaded through with fine red veins. His irises sparkled with swirls of marcasite and baryte. They were as lovely as their surroundings were horrible. The mineral-streaked grayness of the skin on his eyelids, each marked with its own ancient rune, was impossible to ignore.

Grady turned from the mirror with a deep, long sigh. *At least I can't take off my helm. I don't need that right now.* He returned to his chair by the window and watched the city as the sunlight faded and the gas lights flared on.

Far below, the Floor sparkled.

PART 3

F rom the 'Dug Too Deep' theory to the more fantastical 'Dooms-
day Weapon' theory, every hypothesis about what really caused the
Diaspora, no matter how different, blames the same central flaw. The
perpetrators, who worked tirelessly to bring about said doom, believed that
their ends were justifiable by any means. They forgot the intrinsic value of
a dvergr life.

-From *Lessons from the Past*, Alberth of Clan Seraphinite, Historian, 2798 U.E.

MARCHING ORDERS

At some point during his vigil at the window, Grady stopped breathing. He sat on the bed and wondered at the lack of comfort in the softness there. He watched time progress from deep inside his stone head. The lights of the Floor flickered and were consumed as banks of the factory-made clouds scudded over them. He knew it was mid-shift by the thick layer of airborne soot blocking the Floor from view.

Buried in stone, relatively safe and as comfortable as it was possible for him to be, Grady waited. There was no room to train here and the thrill of his victory over Shamas and Orvid dulled with each remembering. He avoided thinking about his forced oath. The words weighed heavily on him, ancient and binding. *An Oath Sworn* sat on his desk, chock full of the captain's thought-provoking notes.

The unknown of what comes next buzzed behind his eyes. What deeds would be demanded of him? Would his secret stay just that? Was he really still Grady? Or, divested of his flesh, was he something else now with delusions of personhood? How was Emerlda? Did she miss him? Would he ever see her again? Questions upon questions piled up, tumbling and repeating in the dark.

Grady missed sleep.

Captain Dulane found him, still sitting, still looking through the window without seeing. The shift changed an hour ago and the captured light of the sun colorlessly illuminated Rockhome's vastness. Grady did not bother to turn around as Dulane entered, walked over, and tapped him on the shoulder.

"You've been summoned. He may be a bit pompous, but you can't fault his work ethic." The pack he carried clanked as he lowered it to the ground. "Suit up. Radix the Beardless is a member of a Throng."

Grady opened the bag and removed the pieces of armor. He set the Salzum faced helmet aside. The plates of Grady's armor shone in the lichen light, smooth and bare of ornament. Except for one bracer. Etched in precise calligraphy Grady read a short recounting of his duel with Shamas and Orvid. Despite watching Dulane doff and don his armor a few times, Grady found the process slow and cumbersome.

Dulane made a frustrated noise and sped up the process by helping. He tugged one of the breastplate's straps until it could go no further. Grady knew something troubled his friend because of Dulane's silence. The dvergr enjoyed a chat.

Dulane strapped the etched bracer onto Grady's forearm with a sigh then spoke, his cadence laden and careful. "Speaking the words is a powerful thing. Life altering and binding. When I made my oath I renounced family and clan to become something else, to live a life of purpose and sacrifice. A noble pursuit, I thought. I was the first to swear the Keyrdegen's new oath when the time came. Gladly gave away my will to the dvergr who trained me, who taught me about finding my own Way, about what the words of the oath really meant. I was proud to do so, to wear his face." He mimed spitting on the floor. Dulane stood tall, he took Grady's helmeted head in his hands. "One's honor and value are not forged from dead words, but from living deeds." Kreth's words, spoken in Dulane's reverent whisper, quieted the buzzing in Grady's thoughts. His worries still hummed away, but Grady could hear himself think again.

Dulane gave Grady's armor a onceover. "Not bad for a rush job. Sorry about this." The captain scooped up the masked helmet and, removing the old bucket helm, placed it on Grady's head. "Throng to the core, is Radix." He turned to leave, Grady felt the smile in his words. "For what it's worth, I'd proudly fight alongside you, Grady of No Clan. Had the Keyrdegen kept his word and put you forth for real training, I have no doubts that you would have done well for yourself. In better times, you would have been a good and noble thegen."

Grady wanted to blush. That was easily the second nicest thing anyone had ever said to him.

"Come on, let us go see our Keyrdegen."

His order tugged Grady after him into the hallway. The captain kept glancing back as they walked. "You need to breathe, at least a little. The armor hides much, but if I noticed, others will too."

Grady lacked the will to protest and explain. He breathed, sending his consciousness out to fill his stone body again. Being a passenger, inert and disconnected, felt easier to bear. In his cell, training and fighting, breathing made him feel whole and powerful. To be present, here and now, following the captain through the heart of Rockhome, the lack of personal agency invited in a clawing panic.

They walked through endless miles of corridor and down an inexhaustible number of steps. Every floor of the Hold looked generally similar, filled with opulent comfort, a multitude of statues, and friezes from floor to ceiling. The importance of the subjects depicted in the decor grew as they descended. In his current mood the wonders of his people failed to reach him. The Keyrdegen's private apartments hung at the tip of it all, in the very center of his protectorate.

They stopped before a giant door made of surface wood, stained a deep brown and streaked by an irregular grain. The four throngers on guard saluted. Precise as clockwork, the two center warriors walked forward and used large brass pulls to open the door, giving the impression that Grady was entering the guts of a very large clock.

A forest's worth of wood filled the room. The walls were stained pale and paneled with gilt from which serpentine vines sprung, each punctuated by alternating gold leaves. On the ceiling, great beams of dark wood held up rows and rows of various tan boards. Herringbone angles striated the floor. And, oh, the furniture. Upholstered chairs, dotted with coppery buttons sat around a carpet depicting a delicate forest scene. A great wooden desk stood at the far end of the room framed by a large bay window looking over the city beyond. A rolling bar, slight and airy and wooden, was filled with exotic looking bottles.

The only visible stone in the whole room was the fireplace's mantel, fancifully carved into the shape of a dragon's open maw.

As a computer, Grady was used to seeing vast sums of money written in small containable numbers. He was intimately familiar with the costs of running a reasonably sized mine that employed hundreds of Clanless miners, Clanned engineers, hundreds more Clanless clerks and janitors, and the managers to oversee them all. He estimated the money spent on the Keyrdegen's study was enough to keep his old mine running for decades.

"Finally, finally!" Salzum rose from one of the chairs in front of the fireplace, a chemical green liquid sloshing in the tumbler he held. Instead of his normal regalia, the Keyrdegen wore a silken blue robe and fuzzy slippers. The mass of his beard trailed behind him in a single braid as thick as Grady's leg and twice as long. The simple metal coronet perched on his brow. Salzum's pleasure at seeing Grady in the armor of the Throng radiated from the coronet. It made Grady uncomfortable.

Salzum's wide grin mirrored the mantle's frozen roar. "And how is our newest recruit settling in?"

"He has been assigned-" The Keyrdegen cut off Dulane with an impatient wave of his hand.

"No, no. Not you, Captain. Radix, come here. How are you settling in? Do you like your new room?"

The order distilled all of Grady's thoughts and feelings since riding the elevator up to the Commons. An efficiently worded answer for both of the Keyrdegen's questions was found. "Well enough." If the hate boiling behind Grady's eyes was actual fire, Salzum and all his smugness would have been nothing but ash in moments.

The Keyrdegen hee-hee'd with delight at Grady's answer. "And are you fitting in with your new compatriots? Have you made any new friends?"

The awkward hand shake with Conov played out before Grady's mind's eye. "No."

More shaking laughter tumbled into a throaty cough. Salzum sipped his drink and collected himself. "No, I'm sure you haven't. Machines don't make friends. Take off your helm." Grady complied. "Ugh. I'd forgotten. I must talk to Plenabus about what can be done for the next ones. Aesthetics is just as important as utility in a machine's design. Don't you agree, Captain?"

Dulane's simple reply of, "Yes, sir." came out flat from behind the silver mask.

How many copies of his own face does Salzum have running around Rockhome? That design choice and the wooden opulence of the study raised serious concerns about Salzum's sense of aesthetics.

"It is a marvelous machine though, despite its flawed exterior. Answers questions like a real dvergr, though one of few words." His glass empty, Salzum sauntered over to the bar. He raised an empty glass towards the captain. "Drink?"

"I'm on duty, sir."

"And if I ordered you to take one?" He poured a good measure of a brown liquor, with a smell so strong Grady was surprised it wasn't visible, into the offered glass. There was steel under the jocularity of the Keyrdegen's tone. His smile, hardened by the gold teeth, was a challenge.

"Your will is mine, my Keyrdegen." The captain tried his best to sound in on the joke. He went so far as to reach for the glass in the Keyrdegen's hand.

"No, no. You were right. Duty first." Salzum bolted the liquor back and smacked his lips. "Their brains may not work too well, given their height and short lives, but humans know how to brew. Come." The Keyrdegen walked over and sat behind the imposing wooden desk. He rolled the chair back, swiveled it out, and sat down. It squeaked a little as it took on Salzum's weight. The captain and Grady stood before the desk, the former at attention while the latter simply stood, helmet in hand. "The humans are one of the reasons I summoned you. Diplomats from above are coming for a visit, one couterie from the Joined Kingdoms and another from Venthenialthin."

"Elves, my lord? Under the mountain? That hasn't happened since my father was young. The War?"

Grady knew about the War the same way he knew about the Commons. The world above was one of constant warfare. The humans encroached on Elven lands, Elves killed humans to defend their sacred spaces, the humans fought back. The conflict has existed, in one form or another, since before the founding of Rockhome. These shifts most of the fighting involved more than a few dvergr-made armaments.

"Astute as ever, Captain. To humans the conflict has spanned generations beyond number. The Elves are dwindling. Seems enough is enough. Both parties have reached out requesting an end to Rockhome's neutrality and our direct aid." For a moment, Salzum basked, like a child, in the afterglow of doing a naughty thing. "Emissaries from both parties are set to arrive in a week's time. Neither is aware the other will be present. I want the city prepared."

"Sir!" Dulane saluted. The metal on metal thunk of his fist to his chest sounded dulled by all the wood and carpeting.

"As for our manufactured friend here, I want the sight of the latest member of my Throng, the soon to be famed wanderer, Radix the Beardless, to be a common one in the Hold and the halls of the mighty. You are now my personal bodyguard, Radix. You will stay by my side and protect me from all harm."

Grady walked around the desk and up to the Keyrdegen. He approached Salzum until his leg armor bumped into the arm of his chair. The Keyrdegen rolled sideways to create some space only for Grady to shuffle forward and close the distance.

Salzum waved him back, hilariously frustrated. "Fool thing! There, stand there. A half-pace behind." Grady stepped back to the exact spot where the Keyrdegen pointed. "Oh and none of this spinning and following me around nonsense this time. For now, just stand there. Guard me from there." Salzum kept half an eye on Grady as he swung back to face the captain and rolled back to the center of the desk.

He really just ruins all my fun. Scenes of the Keyrdegen smacking him, of lording the signed contract over him, of Salzum personally handling Grady's body as Plenabus carved him flashed to the forefront.

He ruins everything.

In living memory there had not been an attack on the Keyrdegen. Safety holds back the assassin's blade better than any guard. The only dvergr who weren't truly safe had as much chance of reaching Salzum as they did the molten center of the world.

Grady, who had never really thought of the Keyrdegen at all in his previous life, wanted nothing more than to pop his head from his neck. A rage burned inside of him like a forgefire, made hotter by its containment and the lack of an outlet. It told him that killing those responsible, Salzum and Plenabus, would make all of his suffering worth it.

Salzum rattled off some particulars he wanted Captain Dulane to be aware of for the diplomatic envoys: how they would enter, where they would be lodged, how many compatriots they were bringing with them. Grady heard none of it. His attention was turned inward. He screamed at his hands to move. To strike. To throttle. He roared, voiceless, as the Keyrdegen drank in absolute comfort in the heart of his authority.

"Dismissed, Captain."

Another crisp salute and Dulane left the room. He did not acknowledge Grady in the slightest. A surge of loneliness quenched the rage-filled forge within him. Having his friend nearby seemed to ease the burden of Salzum's presence and the soul tugging of the plain coronet on his brow.

Without turning, the Keyrdegen knocked back a large swallow from his drink. He wiped his mouth with his sleeve, leaving a wet smear behind to stain the fine fabric. "Alone at last, Radix. Come, stand before me." Grady walked over and stood in front of the desk right where Dulane had stood. Salzum made a show of examining Grady, meeting his eyes for a moment. He leaned back in his chair, which canted smoothly. "I will say, you do look dashing in the Throng's regalia. You fought well and earned it. It was an impressive show. Dulane clearly put in a great deal of effort to ensure you learned what he had to teach. You absorbed it all like a sponge."

Like I had any choice.

It was true, Grady had enjoyed the training. In a way it had given him back a piece of himself, teaching him to breathe and find his place in his body once more. The suffering that started it all, inspired by some unknown plan of Salzum's, tainted the experience. Grady would never be able to touch the memory of his time under Dulane's tutelage without passing through an oily film of horror.

The world stuttered.

One moment Salzum was seated at his desk, his mouth forming words. The next, he stood in front of his desk dressed in his formal attire with his beard braided properly and tossed over his shoulders.

A dizzying wash of vertigo swirled Grady's mind. *What did-? How did-? Huh?* The vertigo faded leaving behind a feeling of unease. He must not have been paying attention. Salzum did so like to hear the sound of his own voice.

The sly smile that creased the Keyrdegen's face did little to make Grady feel better. When had it ever? "Come, Radix. I have business to attend to. Behave like a bodyguard. No speaking, unless I command it. And be sure to salute me when I give you an order, I am your Keyrdegen after all." Grady's body complied instantly. The ring of metal on metal caused Salzum to jump. "Be easy about it, don't dent the armor. How about, when I give you a command, salute just like Captain Dulane?" This time the salute's thud was sharp and quick. "Much better. Come."

A HOUSE DIVIDED

The most powerful dvergr in the city filed into the Heart's Chamber, the rectangular forum where the business of ruling Rockhome was conducted. The family elders made their way up to the bleachers, a handful of levels tall, that lined the long walls. Grady had never seen so much white hair in one place before. There were elders among the Clanless of the Floor, but they were few and far between. Life at the bottom was rough on a body.

Every august personage present was draped in expensive fabrics and ornamented with precious gems and metals. The value represented in just a single outfit could keep a denizen of the Floor living comfortably for a hundred years.

From his position near the Keyrdegen's elbow, Grady watched the elders find their seats. Each clan claimed a quadrant of the room. A thin line of empty bench space separated the clans from each other. The artificial divide forced the members of each clan to sit knee to knee. The attendees, generally wide and well-fed, looked a bit squished.

Once the rest were seated, four dvergr entered abreast through the large stone doors of the chamber, which swung silently closed behind them. The doors were a wondrous feat of artistry and mechanics. Grady marveled, cluelessly, at how the enormous stone doors moved so quietly and with so little applied effort. The clan heads ignored their peers while walking in lockstep. The dvergr in the benches cheered for their leader, and only their leader, by name. The four stopped in the middle of the room, bowed as one to the Keyrdegen, and separated to take their seats on stone chairs in front of their clan's designated bleachers.

Salzum, on his raised platform opposite the doors, stood with his hands raised in welcome. His portion of the room had no bleachers, no extra seats for the veteran thegen to voice their wisdom. At the assembly, the thegen spoke with one voice, Salzum's. "Welcome, one and all. I appreciate that you were all able to put your flagons down and do some governing." The room rumbled with polite chuckles. "I have a surprise in store for you all, but first, old business! Maulcom!"

A dvergr, wearing thick glasses and the motley of a civil servant, stepped forward carrying a book almost as large as himself. He bowed to the gathered assemblage and then to Salzum. The clerk hoisted the giant tome onto the lectern in the center of the open space with an audible grunt. The book creaked open, and the dvergr began to read.

Grady listened with half an ear. The recap of the last meeting bored him, consisting mainly of discussions about tariffs on imports, trade agreements, reports of crop yields and mine outputs, and proposals for expanding living spaces on the Walls and the plumbing to go along with them. All of it was well beyond his ken.

Rockhome's leaders completely ignored the minutes. Most chatted quietly amongst themselves. A few bobbed their heads up and down, fighting sleep. One particularly old looking dvergr whistled as she softly snored.

Grady felt vindication for his political uninvolvement. *Am I the only one listening?*

There was no doubt in his mind now that the only reason Rockhome managed to function was because of all the people currently not at this meeting.

Grady's standing order was to, well, stand and be ready in case of unlikely trouble. Luckily, the Keyrdegen had ordered Grady and the other members of the Throng to keep their heads on a bearing, granting Grady the freedom to look around. Wondrous carvings covered every surface. On the walls, stylized runes recounted the legends of their people. The saga of the dvergrs' flight from their lost homeland and the founding of Rockhome took up most of the space. Reliefs depicting important moments, intricate and precise, accompanied the runes. It managed to remind him of his people's true soul underneath all the pomp, ego, and self-interest. The artistry told of the power of enduring. At this moment, Grady wasn't sure how he felt about that lesson.

There was nothing like this on the Floor. The sight of it all nourished him. Grady let the meeting fade away and lost himself in the history of his people.

"Thrilling as always." Salzum's voice pulled Grady back. It was starting. "Since everyone waited patiently and listened with such care to the recounting of old business," Salzum paused for more polite laughter, "it is time to reveal my big surprise."

He held out a hand. One of his Throng presented two pieces of paper. Salzum held them high, one in each hand. "These are letters from our nearest neighbors above."

"Oh? Have the Joined Kingdoms upped their orders?" The Chief of Clan Pyrite was the roundest dvergr Grady had ever seen. Each of her sausage fingers bore two rings, all of them topped with precious stones the size of her thumbnail. She brushed aside an errant curl and patted her belly. The brass of her tartan flashed as she moved. "Have the tree lovers changed their tune? Do they want more than kitchenware and needles at long last? Strange we were not informed first."

Salzum took the interruption in stride. He smiled and wagged the letters in her direction. "And if that was all they requested, rest assured that your desk would have been their second stop. No. Unfortunately their requests fall directly into my purview." He paused, letting the implication hang. Every dvergr in the room leaned forward, holding their breath. After hundreds of years as their warchief, Salzum knew how best to play to this crowd. "Both wrote to request our direct involvement in the ongoing conflict. I have invited them here to discuss that possibility. Unbeknownst to either party, they are both set to arrive at the same time."

Smug satisfaction radiated from Salzum in waves while he watched the uproar inspired by his announcement. One of the clan heads commanded the podium. His richly dyed and immaculately clean blue and white clothes were precisely tailored. Given the amount of rings, pendants, chains, and brooches on display in the rest of the room, Grady found his lack of jewelry a little pretentious.

He cleared his throat and let his displeasure be known. "You have invited war into our mountain. It has ever been Rockhome's policy to remain neutral in all surface-based conflicts since the Founding. You are risking our lucrative trade with both parties. Worst of all, you did not seek this body's insight or permission beforehand." Voices from every quadrant called out their agreement. The other three clan heads clapped their support from their thrones.

The Keyrdegen rapped a small hammer made out of a shining silver metal on the arm of his throne. It rang out like a gong. The sound resonated with the voices filling the chamber, reverberating until it was all that could be heard. It faded gradually and left behind only silence. "Need I remind the assemblage of the expected behavior of its members?" No one dared to speak or even meet Salzum's eyes. "Chief Svesborg of Clan Seraphinite, am I not Keyrdegen under the mountain?"

Svesborg bowed. "Of course, Keyrdegen Salzum. The authority vested in you by our noble thegen protectors remains unquestioned." He swept his arms wide to take in the rest of the room. "If only the respect went both ways. There is to be no diplomatic outreach to a foreign power, Above or Below, without our direct involvement."

Salzum put on a contrite frown. While his acting skills surely fooled the crowd, Grady saw right through him. "I have overstepped, but I assure you, Svesborg, and the rest of you, that though the path we walk is perilous, prosperity awaits at the end. This opportunity is time sensitive. The die is cast. Our guests will arrive in five shifts time and it will take every dvergr working together to ensure that everything is prepared. There is no room for debate or equivocation. Are you satisfied, Chief Svesborg?"

"Yes. Though I want it recorded that I do not like how you are forcing our hand." He bowed graciously and left the podium for his seat nearby.

"Unacceptable! Wholly unacceptable." When the chief of Clan Feldspar rose from her chair, her translucent and wispy beard tumbled from her lap to hang by her ankles. Her knees shook with the effort. She certainly hadn't skimped on her jewelry. Two massive rubies pulled on the lobes of her ears and Grady was surprised she was able to stand under the weight of the many necklaces she wore. The silver of her jewelry sparkled dramatically against the red and orange of her clan's tartan. Her bow of apology to the Keyrdegen came up just shy of an insult. "I'm sorry, but without knowing more about this mysterious opportunity I refuse to offer Clan Feldspar's support."

The chief's declaration set off another round of excited conversations on the bleachers. Feldspar controlled the production of food, from the pens and fields to the dinner table. More importantly, they were responsible for every keg of beer brewed and the distillation of every drop of alcohol. Her words carried the weight of every libation and comestible under the mountain.

"It is within your right, Chief Ludmil, to put such a heavy price on your cooperation." The Keyrdegen's tone was perfectly neutral and wholly manufactured. Under the surface, Saulzum boiled at the denial. "However, the information you seek is a military secret. To reveal it too soon risks the security of our home and the ruination of years of hard work. All I can safely say is that Master Artificer Plenabus toils tirelessly at the center of it all. I swear on the lost names of the first ancestors that all I have done was necessary and serves our home above all else. Do you doubt my word?"

The rattling of hammers on shields tumbled from the recessed balcony above the Keyrdegen's throne. Grady craned his neck to see. A band of armored thegen stepped forward, ensuring that they were visible to the attendees below. The Throng guards around the throne added to the growing din. More than mere tradition backed the Keyrdegen's authority.

Ludmil paled but refused to look down. "Of course not. My lord."

Grady admired the chief's bravery in the face of the warriors' cacophonous support for their Keyrdegen. Ludmil waited until all was quiet again before she bowed, as deeply as she could while sitting back down.

Salzum put on a show of looking pensive. He tapped his chin and ran a hand along his whiskers. Grady thought the hemming and hawing a bit much. "Chief Ludmil, you've been a great ally and a strong voice in favor of the modernization of Rockhome. I have much appreciated your council and support when my efforts go beyond the scope of my direct responsibilities. Your experience enriches Rockhome. Know that I hear you." Ludmil nodded, but her expression was dire. Though not politically savvy, Grady knew a brush off when he heard one.

The Keyrdegen rose from his throne. The thegen loomed above. "I did not make this decision lightly. I have gone against protocol as old as the clans. I shake the bedrock of our prosperity and you are scared. Rightly so. But there is no reward without risk." Every eye was on Salzum. A sense of history being made filled the room. "We must be ready to greet our guests. They will see only our best and leave in awe at what we have accomplished beneath their feet. The clans know their work. I want spectacle. Marvelous gifts. A feast to end all feasts. Clerks are on their way with the specifics. Go and be about it. We will reconvene next shift."

Footsteps, the swishing of cloth, and the tinkling of jewelry were the only sounds as the leaders of Rockhome filed out of the room in two orderly lines. The four chiefs were the last to leave. They kept apace until they reached the door, only to scatter as they passed the threshold.

Once the magnificent doors were closed again, Salzum flopped back onto his throne and threw a leg over one arm. "Sergeant?" One of the Throng leaned in. "Gather up your squad and go find me Captain Dulane please."

"Yes, sir." The sergeant's voice was incongruously reedy coming from behind the silver version of Salzum's face. The other warriors filed out, their footsteps echoing in the now empty space.

Once they were alone, Salzum turned to Grady, who felt the urge to spit right into his face. "Well? What did you think, Radix? Of the august body of dvergr tasked with leading Rockhome?"

The complex bundle of thoughts and feelings Grady had on the matter was too much. He stepped back and let his body answer with a simple truth. "They are rich."

"Ugh. You sound even worse with an echo." One beringed hand dipped into his robe and pulled out a plain metal flask. After a long draft, Salzum smacked his lips and sighed. "No foreign brew this. Truffle brandy. Aged fifty years. What did you think of the chiefs' concerns?"

Grady did not want to play the Keyrdegen's game. The command pulled the answer from his body. "They come too late."

His answer delighted Salzum. Confident laughter echoed, punctuated by a few slaps onto the arm of his chair. "For you, surely." The Keyrdegen wiped away a mirthful tear. "They mean well. I truly believe they act in Rockhome's best interest. Well, their clan's interest first, then Rockhome's." The hunger was back in Salzum's eyes. "Only I see the full picture. Only I see the path that Rockhome must walk in order to ascend from a mere trade post into a true power. To free us from the dangers Below and win us our share of the bounties available Above. Your creation was the first step on that path." Another draft from the flask led to further sighing and smacking of lips. The Keyrdegen stared at the ceiling, losing himself in thought.

Unnerved by Salzum's confidences, Grady was more than happy to wait in silence and take in the beauty of the Heart's Chamber undisturbed. How could a people, capable of creating such lasting and wondrous art, also be responsible for the millions of cruelties that made up life on the Floor? In the face of the beauty of the Walls and the Roof, the grime and plain stone work of his home took on a punitive aspect.

As if being born alone and disconnected wasn't punishment enough.

The throngers returned, led by Captain Dulane. They walked up to the Keyrdegen's platform in lockstep, stamped as they came to a halt, and saluted in perfect unison. "Captain, your dear friend and our newest warrior, confided in me that he is not sure he can find his way back to his room unaided. I know it is beneath your station, but would you be willing to be his guide one more time?"

Did Grady know the way? Directions were never his strong suit. He tried to picture the halls of the palace, all the routes he walked so far. Grady was shocked to discover not only did he know every turn he made with crystal clarity, but he could recount the decorations present in each hallway. The memories, so clear and sharp, didn't feel like they were coming from Grady himself, but the cold, silicate pathways of his body's brain.

Dulane saluted sharply.

"Excellent!" Salzum's voice was filled with relief, as if Dulane was really doing him a favor rather than merely following orders. "Sergeant Grendly, you and your squad will act as my personal guard this shift."

"Our honor, sir." The squad saluted, in unison, and moved to take up their place behind the Keyr.

"Radix, you are relieved of duty for now. And thank you for your insight. I found our conversation most enlightening. Dismissed." Salzum sent Dulane and Grady off with a negligent hand wave.

Dulane muttered a quiet, "Follow me," that tugged Grady along behind him.

TEA FOR TWO

N ot long after they left the Heart, Grady realized that Dulane was not leading him back to the barracks. The hallways bustled with increased activity, the various servants and functionaries all driven to greater speed by the Keyrdegen's surprise announcement. No matter how busy they were, they parted and flowed around the captain and the golem. The pair continued up the stairs and out into the Commons. Grady marveled at how the pathways glowed whitely in the wan light beaming in through the skylights above.

Dulane led Grady to the North Wall's elevator banks, offering no explanation for their detour. Grady buzzed with trapped curiosity in the face of Dulane's purposeful silence. The captain broke it briefly to direct the elevator operator to take them to level eighteen. He spared Grady a glance and a quick, baffling wink as the accordion doors closed.

The elevator ceased its short descent, the doors opened, and Grady stopped breathing. The order to follow Dulane dragged him along, but the world around him claimed Grady's full attention. In the bright blue light shining from the lichen-coated ceiling, Grady saw not one pebble's worth of stone. Thick, springy moss cushioned their steps. Flowering plants of some kind he'd never seen before covered the walls in bright patterns. A sweet and light bouquet of new smells tickled his nose. The marvel of it all rivaled anything present in the Hold.

They walked next to a display of wide white swirls in a field of dark blue petals down one hallway. Dulane turned left, and the soothing design gave way to mosaics constructed of small flowers. Their images, clear and sharp as if made from actual tiles, depicted stooped dvergr tending mushrooms and then harvesting them. Next the mushrooms were boiled and casked. Then, at the end of the hall, a barkeep pulled a tap, filling a clear glass with a frothy amber and green liquid. Golden runes along the top, their constituent petals glinting like true metal, declared "Coal powers the forge, Beer powers the blacksmith."

Grady nearly collided with Dulane when the captain stopped short in front of a small shop. Wafts of strong-smelling steam flowed from the windows and doorway, presided over by a middle-aged dvergr with streaks of silver in his thick black hair. Dulane removed his helmet and smiled at the proprietor. "Hail and well met, cousin."

"Dulane!" The dvergr leaped from his stool and embraced the captain. He slapped his back heartily despite Dulane's armor. He held the captain at arms length and inspected him. "Why, I haven't laid eyes on you for a year of fifth shifts." He rapped a fist on Dulane's pauldron. "Been following your career of course. Big captain of the Keyrdegen's own Throng. I try not to mention it too often, don't want to brag of course. But none can blame me for being proud of my little cousin."

Dulane bore the jovial torrent of praise with a bemused smile and cut in when his relative paused to take in more air. "It is my honor to serve Rockhome, but look at you! Running Leaf Soup at long last. Never thought your mother'd retire. Assumed the mountain would collapse first."

His cousin's chuckle was long suffering. "Took having great-great-grandkids to fuss over. Still, you would think we were walling her up in a tomb alive the way she carried on. Still comes by from time to time to make sure I'm not ruining her legacy. Says those exact words as well. Each time. Your ma still-"

Dulane cut his cousin off by throwing an arm over Grady. "This is my latest protege. Radix, this is my cousin Uji. Uji, Radix."

Uji blanched slightly at hearing Grady's anonym. Then he grew excited and extended a hand which Grady took and shook gently. "Radix eh? The Beardless? Pleasure to meet you, my good dvergr, pleasure. Your name is echoing through the Walls these shifts. Must have been a feat traveling the Wilds by yourself. Looking forward to hearing the tale told proper some time."

The captain came to Grady's rescue. "He's shy, cuz. The traversal was hard on him and he's not quite used to being with proper dvergr company just yet. A private room for the two of us and a pot of your best fermented black would do us just fine."

"Of course! Of course. My pleasure truly. This way," Uji said. As they entered the establishment proper, he stood stiffer and raised his chin up a little higher. He beckoned them inside with professional grace.

Framed by the abundance of growth decorating every surface, patrons sipped at small steaming cups and chatted. Grady picked up snippets of their conversations as he passed. The drinkers talked of work troubles, family drama, the last play they saw. To a dvergr they wore orange and red outfits that clashed daringly with the verdant decor. But, as far as Grady could tell, their clothing was made of ordinary, if quality, fabric.

The patrons lived in far nicer environs and were surrounded by much finer things than could be found on the Floor. These people lived recognizable lives. The kind of lives that all dvergr should possess. Not perfect, no, never that. But kinder. Grady envied the sense of contentment evident from the way the people in the tea house just sat and drank and chatted. He couldn't begrudge them their comforts.

The host said a word in passing to a server in a white apron, her whiskers tied up to her ears to keep them away from the tray of sweet and savory baked goods. She bobbed and went off in the direction of the kitchen. Uji led them past the other diners, swung open a warmly polished 'shroomwood door and gestured for them to lead the way.

"Our finest private room, for our most esteemed guests," Uji said officiously. He winked at Dulane and the corners of his mouth twitched up in a brief smile. The room was not large, with only enough space for a table and four chairs to fit comfortably. Simple colored lichens and the ever-present moss carpet served as the room's only decorations. "The server will be by with your tea, and a selection of our finest pastries, momentarily.

The room is yours for however long it is needed. It is our honor to serve the thegen who protect us so well. Food and drinks are on the house."

Uji bowed to leave but Dulane stopped him and gave him another hug, tight enough to make the tea purveyor grunt in surprise. "Your generosity does our-" Dulane coughed and corrected himself, "your clan proud. Thank you, cousin." Straightening his clothes, Uji bowed again and backed out of the door, closing it softly behind him.

Dulane took off his helmet, placed it on the table, and ran a hand through his hair. "Always a kind one was Uji. I know you are curious about the where and why of all of this, but let's wait for the tea and things to arrive. Perhaps you'd like to take in the view while we wait."

Obediently, Grady walked over to the edge of the balcony and looked out over the city. The fog clouds hung thick far below them obscuring the Floor completely. Small figures scurried about on the pathways linking the grand buildings of the Roof.

How can anyone ever be accustomed to the sight of it all? He wondered. He was overwhelmed once more by the grandeur of what his people had built here in the bones of the mountain, of what they were capable of. He touched a hand to his helmet above where Domination was carved into his forehead.

The door to the room opened, things clattered gently as they were placed down, Dulane muttered a polite thank you, and the door closed once more.

"Come. Sit with me, please." Dulane set out the cups and pastries each on a small plate on the room's lone table. "Please take off your helm and speak freely. These walls are too overgrown to have ears." Dulane sipped the tea as Grady sat. He sighed with delight. "Not a better tea house under the mountain." The relaxed quality of his smile seemed forced.

Placing his helmet next to his cup and sweet treat, Grady politely raised the tea to his nose and sniffed. It smelled of boiled leaves, gently spiced with something warming. Grady tried to take a sip but just as it wet his lips he stopped. The idea of putting it in his mouth revolted him. This liquid was not fuel. He held onto the cup with a sigh. At least the warmth seeping through the ceramic and into his hands felt nice. He met Dulane's weighing gaze.

Grady looked around the room and out the balcony, questions swarming his mind. They wrestled and squirmed together, vying to be the first one asked. The resulting "Why?" sounded bewildered even through the rock tumble of Grady's voice.

Dulane snorted and sipped his tea. "One thing the sagas fail to mention about the life of a thegen is how the job wears on the heart." He thumped his fist against his armored chest. "Warriors who believe they are iron inside and out break the soonest."

Grady recognized the quote. "Kreth the Bulwark. Volume... 4, I think?"

"Aye. You've a good mind for words and the Bulwark's are some of the wisest." Dulane leaned back in his chair with an amused air. He stroked his salt and pepper beard. "It is my tradition to bring my tyro here after an incursion or a particularly rough mission Below. The greenery, the tea, the view. I find them soothing to the soul after a trying time."

Shock silenced the chorus of questions clamoring within Grady. The sagas were full of tyros, the apprentice warriors training at the feet of battle-tested veterans. Those worthy of mention often went on to forge their own volumes and bear their own names. "You think of me as your tyro?" he asked in a grinding whisper.

Dulane waved the question away with a casual flick of his hand. "Of course! I taught you how to hold a hammer and shield. How to ground your stance. We read the sagas together." The lightness evaporated from the captain's demeanor. His words grew solemn and his gaze intensified. "We are bound, you and I. Word and deed."

Grady did his best to nod in a measured and stoic way. An upwelling of emotion crashed against the back of his eyes, failing to manifest the burn of soon to be shed tears. Grady felt grateful for his stony makeup at that moment. While most dvergr were free to express their emotions, thegen followed different rules.

The emotionally charged moment hung in the air until it grew oppressive and stifling. Dulane dispelled it by clearing his throat and taking a bite of the flaky pastry in front of him. "After times of pain and stress it is important to remember what real life is like. To take some time and soak in some normalcy. Warriors who fail to do that become riddled with fatigue, lose their Way, and break. After all you've been through, consider this a little break from... well, all of it." Dulane smiled and saluted Grady with his half-eaten pastry before taking another large bite.

Normal? He rolled the idea around for a bit. Normal was an unceasing string of shifts filled with numbers and cramped digits. Normal was an opaque and constant boredom made tolerable by quiet dreaming.

"None of this is normal," Grady said in a rocky monotone. He spoke hesitantly, weaving thought into words as he went. Life returned to his voice gradually. "My life before was gray. Low. Scarce and cheap. A never-ending monotonous progress heading nowhere. And now I'm here in a Wall surrounded by beauty beyond my wildest imaginings. The effort and care of generations are evident in even the smallest scale of lichen. Among all this living splendor you acknowledged me, an erratic paper pusher from the Floor, as your tyro. It is my proudest accomplishment in all my fifty-odd years. But deep down, I wonder if it is really my doing at all. Am I even really me? I've wondered that ever since-" The open space out past the balcony drew Grady's gaze while echoes of pain and the soft rasp of a knife over his skin grew until they drowned out his thoughts.

A weight on Grady's shoulder banished the shadows of his old cell and brought him back into the private tea room. He looked up to find Dulane standing next to him, a heavy hand resting on Grady's pauldron. "If you doubt yourself, then trust me. We have spent hours talking and sparring. I have your measure. I did not know you before. I cannot say you haven't changed. But you are more than stone. You are dvergr. I can't undo what has been done to you. I don't know that anyone can. You can't uncarve stone. When the tunnel collapses behind you, forward is the only direction left."

Grady nodded and, unable to bear his friend and master's reassuring smile, looked back out at the spires and walkways that hung from the Roof.

Dulane crouched down and adjusted Grady to face him again. "Listen. I am going to help you escape." Hope flared brightly within Grady at the words. Then it flickered, as if it was being assaulted by an invisible, doubting breeze from some unseen and dark place.

"Having both the elves and humans here at the same time is going to be a shit show. I assume this all has something to do with you and the potential for more golems like you." The captain's face soured. "Salzum's plans include a private meeting between himself and the ambassadors." Dulane rose and took his seat across from Grady, stiff as a board. "The specifics are a bit murky past that point. The long and short of it is that I will find you, dress you like a servant, walk right up to the Commons and out to the Floor, where there are places even the Keyrdegen cannot reach." Across the table his features hardened. "Any questions?"

The light angling in from the balcony played across the etchings and intricacies of Dulane's armor. Armor earned over decades and decades of service to the Keyrdegen and to Rockhome.

A thegen's oaths were simple and binding. The cost for breaking them was everything. Your life became forfeit and your honor expunged. Your very name was struck from the city's annals. Everyone connected to you was tarnished. And what was he breaking his oath for? Some worthless, computing brick from down Floor. "You risk everything for me. Why?"

Dulane's brow creased into a deep furrow as he took in the marks on Grady's face. His frown was soft, grieving. "You are my tyro, my friend," he said simply.

Not satisfied with Dulane's incomplete answer, Grady pushed harder. He rose from his chair and stood before Dulane. He spoke with a harsher edge than he meant to. "Wasn't Salzum once your friend? Weren't you his tyro once? Didn't you swear to him?"

"He was, I was, and I did. The principle at the heart of my Way, the Way taught to me by Salzum and inspired by the Bulwark's great deeds, is a simple and clear one. Every dvergr's life has value. There is room for sacrifice, to weigh the needs of many against the lives of a few when necessary, of course, but the situation must be dire, immediate. I see the same reports Salzum gets from our patrols. The Wild Below remains dangerous and our defenses are tested weekly, but that is normal. That Salzum was willing to turn people into machines does not surprise me. If it meant saving Rockhome, I believe, used to believe, that he would selflessly sacrifice everything if it meant protecting this mountain and its people.

"For a long time, I have watched my Keyrdegen grow more vain and ambitious. I turned a blind eye to many questionable behaviors, attributed them to some wisdom I lacked and that he possessed. Then he set this golem project into motion. He chose to lie to the very people he was meant to protect, to torture one of his charges, to rob him of his will, his life." Dulane rose as he answered until he towered over Grady. He spoke with certainty. "Such a choice unbinds me from any oaths I made. No one capable of perpetuating such rank evil is worth my loyalty or to lead the thegen. A great wrong was done to you. As your friend I cannot let it stand. As a thegen, word sworn and honor bound, I cannot let it happen again."

The hug caught Grady by surprise. It didn't feel like much through two suits of armor, but he felt the brush of Dulane's hair and the warmth of his exposed cheek. Apparently, there was an unspoken order in a hug, one to reciprocate if you feel the need. Grady hugged the captain back, carefully so as not to crush the life from his friend.

THE HAND THAT FEEDS

For three shifts, Grady had trailed after Salzum as he met with various family heads, guild masters, chefs, smiths, and any dvergr with an important role to play in the diplomatic proceedings to come. Surprisingly, he did not micromanage their efforts and seemed to actually listen to the concerns presented to him. Salzum suggested, but never ordered. Grady hardly believed it the first time Salzum acknowledged an individual, other than himself, might know better. As evil and manipulative as Salzum was, there was no denying his ability to lead and inspire.

The constant act took its toll.

Salzum left his final meeting of the shift, with Grady in tow, and went straight back to his personal study. The door closed behind him. Salzum leaned back against the door, looked upward, and took a deep breath. A torrent of every mean, snarky, or derisive comment the Keyrdegen left unsaid spewed forth at the top of his lungs. Lungs used to shouting orders over the din of battle. Spit flew and his face reddened. The vitriolic spray slowed to a trickle before sputtering into inaudible mumbling.

The Keyrdegen sighed. Salzum rubbed his temples in little circles, slouched over to his rolling bar, and poured himself a deep drink.

Heavy glass in hand, he moved to the window overlooking his protectorate, his weariness and frustration buzzing at Grady through their intrusive bond. He scratched absently at one arm. "I am the only thing keeping the very mountain from falling down on our heads, Radix. These dvergr, these chiefs and master craftsmen, pfah. Idiots and children, all of them. No matter how white their beards or deep their wrinkles. It's as if they have forgotten how and need me to wipe their asses." Salzum tipped his glass up and swallowed twice.

Grady tried to remember and count the number of times today the Keyrdegen nipped at his flask. He'd seen it refilled at least three times. It could have been more. Grady did his best to pay as little attention as possible. Salzum leaned his forehead against the window. His monologue fogged the pane.

He's just lucky his breath doesn't eat right through the glass.

"They only know darkness. The light to come will blind them. I will drag them if I must. Let them kick and scream. I've seen prisoners weep when set free. It is not joy that overflows their eyes. No. Their cell was safe, a home with predictable comforts and familiar troubles. Our people are like this. Trapped in this cavern with death beneath their feet. Such death."

Salzum drained the rest of his drink. His hand dropped, releasing the glass to thump harmlessly to the carpeted floor. "The world above mocks us. All we hold sacred. They call us 'dwarves' and 'mole people'. We are the butt of their jokes. Well, let them laugh while they can. Let them laugh." The Keyrdegen barked a single mirthless laugh. He turned to Grady, eyes wide with a frightening intensity. "You are the first. There will be more. They will invite their doom, thinking it a victory. Our people will rule above unchallenged. Unchallenged." He turned back to the window, his palms pressed against it.

"Go away, Radix. Be back here by oh-five hundred." Salzum did not look away from the window when Grady left.

❖

Helmet off and secure in his solitude, Grady discovered a modicum of peace looking out his window and chewing his coal. He sat there and remembered. His new life was more than passing strange and Grady worried that if he didn't at least thumb through his old memories occasionally, they would be lost. He stuck to remembering specific iterations of daily mundane tasks, like his walk to work or brushing his teeth. He avoided the sweeter moments. A kernel of overwhelming bitterness hid within them that he preferred to do without.

Grady arrived early to the Keyrdegen's study at oh-four nine-ty-nine to avoid the soul-burning pain of a flubbed command. The Keyrdegen burst through the door just as Grady arrived. Salzum gathered him up with a gesture and sped off down corridors Grady did not recognize. They turned a corner and approached an open archway that led out onto one of the latticed bridges linking the various buildings of the Roof.

No. Please, no.

Across the bridge, The Artificers' Spire hung in a flowing stillness. Its surface was the untouched, glossy finish of a stalactite. Windows, arches, and the flicker of gas lamps were the only modifications made to the outside of the stone edifice. As soon as they crossed the bridge and entered the archway, smells began a siege on Grady's senses. Chemical fumes, the stink of burnt matter, and the bite of astringent battled for olfactory supremacy. Even Salzum grimaced at the reek.

The minimalist nature of the inside of the Spire reminded Grady of a cleaner and better maintained version of the Floor. Its whitewashed walls, smooth and plain, proclaimed this a place where ornamentation was not welcome. Long stretches of flat rubber filled the center of the hallways instead of plush rugs. Grates ran along the bottom of the walls. Strange, muffled lights and sounds escaped from behind the distantly spaced metal doors. A countless tangle of pipes filled the ceiling, two of which disappeared into the walls above each door.

They went down another level. They stopped in front of the only door in the corridor. Two throngers kept watch outside. One opened the door while the other saluted.

They are really good at opening doors.

The rattle and whirring of a machine moving at speed shook Grady's teeth. A great mass of metal limbs and gears hung from the ceiling. Some of the limbs ended in glinting knives while others sported small applicators puffing powder. The limbs swung and inched over the body of a dvergr lying on a cold metal table. The tear rolling down her cheek and the shallow hitches of her chest were the only signs she was still alive. Bloody runes covered one leg.

Grady held his breath and tried to actively pull back further into his head.

"Ah, hm, my lord! Thank you for coming." Plenabus tapped forward, leaning on a brass cane topped with a gear. "See!" He waved the cane about, pointing at his mechanical monstrosity and the poor dvergr being tortured beneath. "Progress, yes."

Salzum pointedly ignored the artificer and marched forward to inspect the work being done. Grady, unable to resist, followed. Knowing to listen for it, Grady heard the dvergr's breathy, paralyzed screams.

Salzum scowled at the table and the dvergr. "This was not the subject you showed me before."

"No, sir. That one did not survive the initial cutting. A limiter on a limb was set incorrectly and it cut into an, hm, artery. The problem was corrected and we have made progress." Plenabus, unconcerned, watched the arms work with a gummy smile.

Salzum leaned forward to better watch the machine carve up the dvergr's left leg. "Say this actually works this time, by some miracle. How long will it take you to make a golem?"

"The original carving took me, hm, three shifts to complete in total. About thirty hours by hand. Fully automated, at its current pace, my apparatus should be able to finish one in three-quarters of a shift."

Salzum spun around and rushed the artificer quicker than he was able to scramble away. Plenabus squawked in protest as the warrior lord crushed him in a hug. "You did it, you mad old fossil!" He planted a loud smooch onto the artificer's sallow cheek. "And you can build more of these automated carvers?"

Plenabus sounded squeezed. "Of course."

The machinery above shuddered and sparked. The sound of a knife on bone skittered amongst the bangs and whines from inside the machine. Salzum and Plenabus turned in horror as the arm carving a rune into the dvergr's hip drilled down, tore the flesh, and cleaved her leg off.

Helpless, Grady watched as blood gushed from her mangled stump. He caught the moment the light left her eyes.

She escaped.

"No! No!" Plenabus hobbled over to a control station in the back of the room. He slammed his fist onto a red button. The carver shuddered to a halt. Blood dripped from the blades and rivulets of sparkling powder gathered on the floor. "My lord! Wait, I-"

Salzum slammed Plenabus against the wall, gripping the front of his lab coat. A deluge of spittle dampened the artificer's face. "You old fool! Fix this. You have two more shifts to get this working. Everything depends on your success. You told me you could do this. Were you lying?"

Plenabus shook his head so hard he vibrated. It took effort for him to speak past the Keyrdegen's angry grip. "No, sir. No. I swear."

"How many more test subjects do you have?"

Plenabus pawed uselessly at Salzum's fingers. "A dozen or so, yes. Plenty."

"Pah!" Salzum dropped the artificer with a disgusted snarl. "Do not fail me."

Plenabus, a pile of bones and rags, wept and wheezed quietly on the floor where he was dropped. Salzum did not look back as he turned and left. Grady followed, happy to be leaving this place. The blood dripped from the table onto the floor with asynchronous plops.

Grady's mind raced within its stone confines. *Did he say a dozen?* A dozen Clanless held, waiting for their turns to be torn up by machines.

Or turned into him.

As he and the Keyrdegen crossed the bridge back to the Hold, Grady made promises with the weight of oaths.

To the captured: *I will save you.*

To Plenabus and the Keyrdegen: *I will kill you.*

To himself: *I will escape.*

He did his best to ignore the echoing whispers of his old voice underneath it all.

If I can. If I can. If I can.

A Mountain's Welcome

Grady stood just inside the door of the warlord's study and watched Salzum drink. He'd been grumpy and preoccupied since the scouts brought news about their guests' arrival. There was no smacking of lips or snuffling of vapors. Gulps and swallows, punctuated by angry mumbling, were the current fashion. The only word Grady could make out was 'Plenabus'. They had not visited the damned artificer's foul lab again, but things must not have progressed to Salzum's liking.

A knock at the door signaled the arrival of another messenger. Salzum waved his hand and Grady opened the door with the clock-like precision the Keyrdegen demanded. The dvergr was young with the soft, first sprouts of a beard on his chin. It wouldn't surprise Grady if he bruised himself with the sharp salute he threw. *More zeal than sense, that one.* "Keyrdegen."

The Salzum who nodded was transformed. A splendid display of energy and confidence replaced the desolate funk of just seconds before. "Report." The complete lack of slurring in the Keyrdegen's speech was impressive.

Salzum is a true professional.

The young dvergr spoke with precise diction. He sped through his report as if afraid he would forget it halfway through. "Preparations at the main gate are ready. The thegen have blockaded off the envoys' route. The people of Rockhome have come out in droves to see the procession."

The jingling as Salzum rose from his desk verged on oppressive. Grady had watched him dress and the only thing stopping Salzum from emptying his jewelry case was a lack of space to wear it all. Every finger was beringed. The chest of his finery was lost beneath a tangle of necklaces and pendants. He wore a golden helm socketed with a large number of ponderous gems. The messenger's eyes widened in awe at his lord protector's majesty.

Grady thought it a bit overdone.

"And the Commons?"

The messenger licked his lips nervously. "Uh, I don't know my lord. I was only told about the gates, the route, and the blockades."

"You have eyes, yes?" *Uh oh.* Salzum's tone was quiet and patient, a clear sign of troubles ahead.

"Sir?"

Salzum grew quieter, his words deceptively soft. "Do you have eyes?"

A quick and wasted glance at Grady did not give the messenger the answer he was looking for. "Um, yes?"

"And I assume," Salzum walked around his desk, hands clasped behind his back, "that in order to get here your path must have gone through the Commons?" Now he was smiling. Grady wondered how he managed to keep his smile from touching his eyes.

"Y-yes, sir."

The Keyrdegen leaned into the messenger, looming with authority. "Then I ask again, are the Commons ready?"

The young messenger showed some steel when he resisted the urge to step back. His loud swallow belied his desire to be anywhere else right now. "As far as I could tell, sir."

"Splendid!" The mood in the room flipped. Salzum was all outward smiles and jovial bounce once more. "Thank you for your service. Head back to your post. On your way back down, find Captain Dulane and inform him I am on my way. Can you do that?"

The messenger gave another bruising salute. His "Keyrdegen" was filled with as much reverence as relief. He rushed out the door, dignity lost in his need to escape.

Salzum deflated a bit and leaned against the front of his desk. He groped behind him, searching for his unfinished drink. When he went to take a sip and discovered the glass empty, he hurled it across the room where it shattered against a wooden panel. There was no roar or declamation. Salzum simply stared into the far distance in front of him. He hoisted himself upright and sighed. Taking a moment to straighten his robes and adjust a few choice pieces of jewelry, his energy returned.

"Come, Radix. We have work to do."

The halls of the palace were emptier than usual, yet Grady felt crowded by the Keyrdegen. This wasn't the Salzum who conspired in a dark, forgotten cellar. While certainly august, this also wasn't the bully administrator presiding over an assembly in the Heart's Chamber. Here was a dvergr warrior lord, in his seat of power, draped in the trappings of his station, and ready to meet and deal with important envoys.

Through the simple diadem hidden beneath the more ostentatious helm, Grady felt Salzum's struggle against the gravity of ages. Salzum was there, but so were the legends of Rockhome's history. The past and the future of his people rested on him.

Salzum's mood was infectious. The specters of the ancients haunted Grady. Salzum wore Mountain's Tear at his waist. The artifact served as proof of a time beyond memory. The same people responsible for forging the masterwork dagger had left instructions on how to make things like Grady. Once Grady, like most dvergr, had thought them paragons, creators of naught but wonder and legends. Then came the knives, the dark, and the geode to change his mind.

Do the wonders they wrought make up for the horrors they left behind? Trapped in a small space within his own petrified head, Grady had his doubts.

Normal underground darkness still held sway in the Commons as the Keyrdegen and Grady arrived. It was even more lovely in the dark. Gleaming blue lines of bright lichen, twisted into fanciful designs, outlined the skylights and illuminated the tall walls. More glowed along the pathways and on each of the entrance buildings, placed in such a way as to accentuate the statuary and clarify the architectural lines. The green of the carpet was changed to a uniform blue-black that, in Grady's opinion, fit the space better.

Dulane and a Throng squad waited at the palace's entrance. They saluted as one. The dvergr filling the paths cheered at the sight of their protector. Each of the four clans was represented in the crowd closest to the palace. The chiefs stood beneath luminescent banners bearing their clan's symbols. The path kept clear for the Keyrdegen, a direct line from the elevators to the Hold, was the same one Grady walked his first time in the Commons.

Salzum pitched his voice to carry over the crowd. "Report, Captain."

Dulane's response was only for Salzum to hear. "We just received news from the outside. The situation is tense, sir. I was about to send a runner to fetch you. While they have not come to blows, they remain battle ready despite our assurances of guest rights." The lichen light glinted off Dulane's mask and armor. He and the other Throng members practically shined, darkened only by the deeds scrawled across their armor. Grady pushed down a surge of self-consciousness. His armor was the plainest of those present.

I'm new, he protested to no one while trying to ignore the shame of caring at all.

"Excellent. Just as I hoped." Salzum stroked one of the massive braids hanging over his shoulder. "Have my horse readied." Even his pleasure in a plan coming together could not hide the Keyrdegen's clear disdain for the surface animal. Grady, who had never seen a horse, was curious. Dvergr merchants preferred ponies for their size and hooved animals tended to struggle to thrive within the Mountain.

Orders were given and a runner sent off ahead to prepare the Keyrdegen's mount. Salzum ensured his voice was audible to the crowd once again. "Captain? Lead the way." Dulane and the warriors saluted.

The dvergr gathered in the Commons cheered as they watched the thegen and their lord proceed to the elevators. Salzum swirled his hand at the wrist in a ridiculous wave. The crowd loved it, apparently, and the cheering doubled. Despite the large crowd and Grady's position close to Salzum, he had not felt so invisible since his last commute. It was kind of nice, after all the apprehensive stares recently aimed at the Keyrdegen's newest, mostly silent, and completely beardless bodyguard.

An elevator was waiting for them, of course. The attendant was a very old dvergr with a snow white beard braided loosely to his belt. His uniform was immaculate and sported numerous gold buttons and badges. When he nodded to Salzum, Grady was surprised to see the Keyrdegen nod back.

"Germander of Clan Hematite, the Floor please."

"Aye, sir. My pleasure, sir." His cheeks puffed with pride at being addressed so respectfully by such a grand personage. "Brace."

It took two full shifts of debate to decide which Wall would receive the honor of the Keyrdegen's descent. In the end the West Wall won out. At each floor, crowds of gathered dvergr bore the banners of clan Pyrite. They cheered wildly as the elevator passed. Grady thought them mad. At least the dvergr in the Commons got a good view of the procession. The Wall's residents barely got a fleeting glimpse through the accordion doors.

Any excuse for a holiday, I guess. And who doesn't enjoy a bit of cheering.

The elevator operator showed his deft hand as he guided their descent to a gentle stop. The doors opened and the warriors, led by Dulane, stepped out first. Salzum stopped a moment before leaving. "Please keep the doors open, Germander. I'll be back soon. And with company." Then he winked.

The old man laughed and winked back. "Of course, sir. Of course. Wide open and waiting." This time he bowed low.

Clanned dvergr, from across the city, lined the walkways behind a cordon of saw horses and plainly armored thegen. There was much made over the lottery to pick who of the Walls' denizens would get to stand where. Listening to the endless bickering had bored Grady to stone.

More to stone.

It was one of the rare cases where he had witnessed Salzum putting his foot down during the preparations. He was very particular about how the lots were distributed.

The buildings lining the procession path were newly scrubbed and free of grime. Of course, not a single gray clad body dotted the crowd. They were all still working or just plain forbidden from attending. Grady thought of the Artificers' Spire and the dozen or so souls trapped there.

The negation of his people clarified the hollow and fictitious nature of the pomp around him.

No one else noticed. Everyone cheered.

The parade's path hooked towards the Windward Gate, a wide opening in the Eastern Wall surrounded by wooden docks. The rumble of the chained carts was louder as they climbed out of their trenches and reached the terminus. Here, at last, were some gray-clad Clanless. The stevedores rushed about, uncoupling and recoupling carts, and manipulating great cranes to shift loads onto outgoing wagons. It was decided to keep the flow of commerce going during this unprecedented political visit. Salzum declared it a necessary show of economic strength. When he waxed poetic about the envoys arriving amidst the comings and goings of dvergr prosperity, the chamber erupted with countless 'hear, hear's. A few already loaded wagons, pulled by lowing oxen and guided by handpicked merchants, disappeared out of sight up the ramp as the Keyrdegen's party reached the tunnel mouth.

A dvergr wearing brown leather stood holding the reins of the biggest, and only, horse Grady ever saw. The chestnut beast, a solid mass of twitching muscle, was half a dvergr taller than its handler. A second leather-clad dvergr placed a small set of stairs next to the animal.

The Keyrdegen hesitated briefly. It remained unclear whether it was the eyes of all the witnesses or Salzum's own sense of pride that drove him up the steps and into the saddle. Once seated, Salzum waved again to soak in the renewed adulation of his people. With a kick of his heels and a snap of the reins, Salzum sent his steed forward. The rest of his party, Grady included, followed on foot.

The tunnel, known as the Merchant's Way on the Walls and the Roof and the Mountain's Colon on the Floor, was a gentle incline. The road was carved into the naked bones of the mountain and made smooth by the founders of Rockhome. Spike-like stalactites hung above, but they were too regular and pointed to be natural. The creak of wagons, the tromp of feet, and the clomping of hooves echoed in a muddled clamor. Great sconces of glowing lichen filled the space with their cool, blue glow. Underneath the mélange of manure, animal bodies, and the cool tang of metal, Grady detected the growing hints of a wild, green smell. Thegen stood at attention in groups of five at each of the tunnel's guard stations. They stomped and saluted as the Keyrdegen passed.

At the ramp's plateau, yellow and sharp light shone from around the bend and transposed the exiting carts into stretched shadows on the far wall. A few of the Throng raised a hand to block the light from their eyes. Squinting hard enough to pinch his whole face, Salzum called a brief halt. The brightness did nothing to Grady. His stone eyes dealt with the unfiltered brightness of the sun as easily as they had the unnatural lights of his cell.

This gift keeps on giving.

The sight around the corner would have stopped Grady in his tracks if he had control of himself. He barely noticed the great, raised portcullis and metal doors, all linked by large chains to quick release mechanisms or the large cadre of thegen stationed nearby.

The outside world demanded his full attention.

A space larger than any Grady imagined extended to vanishing points in all directions. From the gate's mouth, roads, dotted by carts, wound their way over rolling hills. Green, waving like the Common's rug, covered everything on the ground, aside from a few boulders and graveled areas. Bright flowers dotted the sea of green. The taller plants, with brown trunks and green tops, must be trees. They didn't perfectly match the picture he was shown as a child, but all the important bits were there. The air was clean and clear like well-made glass. The unprecedented smell of growing life, underpinned by the rich scent of soil, overwhelmed Grady.

Above it all was the sky. The infinite blue dome was streaked by scant clouds, scudding away from the mountain. The sun was not the ball of fire depicted in his school books either. Instead, it was the bright, blinding eye of some watchful god. The lack of a solidity above his head disconcerted him. Grady felt certain that if he wasn't made of stone, his feet would lose their grip on the earth and away he would tumble.

The cell was better than this. Grady receded deeper into himself, overawed and frightened.

"Let's give our eyes a chance to acclimate. Captain, honor guard to the front." At the Keyrdegen's command, Dulane and the other members of the Throng took up a wedged position in front of the column. Salzum looked towards the light, eyes wide open in an attempt to force his vision to improve through sheer force of will. Each time it proved too much and the intensity forced him to look away, he cursed a little louder. "Damn it!"

"Blinking helps, sir." Dulane commented from in front without looking back.

"Blinking helps, sir." Salzum mocked quietly from his saddle. Grady was the only one close enough to hear. Despite his petulance, Salzum blinked rapidly and was soon more comfortable in the light. He cleared his throat. "Forward. Let's go meet these envoys."

Salzum called a halt again once the whole party was out in the open. He surveyed the land as if the open world was his natural habitat and part of his dominion. Grady hated that it made him admire Salzum a little. He rolled his eyes and pointed. "Ha. Look at them, lined up and facing off with each other. Seems we arrived just in time. We will go there. The open space between the two camps. Lead on, Captain."

The wedge of warriors left the road, guiding the mounted Keyrdegen to the top of a short hill in between the two enemies' positions.

To the dvergers' left, a great wheeled coach stood. Its red and black lacquered exterior shined in the light and prominently displayed the seven sigils of the Joined Kingdoms on its doors. Two humans sat in the coach box, with large, loaded crossbows on their knees. Eight other guards sat atop sleek-looking mounts, spears and shields at the ready. The horses shifted nervously underneath.

Grady noted that every bit of metal they wore or carried, their kettle helmets, long mail hauberks, greaves, and weapons, were Rock-home exports. One of the guards seated in the coach box rapped on the top of the vehicle and said something in Human. The coach's curtain twitched aside.

To the dvergr party's right, a dozen elves stood or crouched. They rode no mounts. They wore no helmets, leaving their long hair, adorned with flowers, feathers, and other trinkets, to blow in the chilly wind driving down the mountain. Grady found their attire confusing. Their pants were clearly leather, but he could not identify the scaly and wrinkled armor bits they wore strapped to their chests, wrists, and shins. Each elf carried two slim swords, naked at their waists, a bow, and a quiver full of brightly fletched arrows. A few held their bows nocked but not drawn. Two of the elves whispered to each other. Their disagreement grew heated until the taller one threw up their hands and shouted something in Elvish. The anger did little to sour the musicality of their words. It was beautiful, in an alien and disconcerting way.

Atop his horse, glinting in the sunlight, Salzum made a show of inspecting the two parties. "First, you threaten violence on my Mountain, and now you insult me by making me come to you." Despite his volume, Salzum's admonishment of the gathered envoys lacked teeth. He perfectly played the role of a patient parent reaching their limit. "Your enmity is old, but I will not have bloodshed on the feet of my home. This standoff will not do. This demesne is neutral territory. I called you here. Both of you. I have a compromise to propose."

The shorter elf, who won the earlier argument, did not hesitate. Their long limbs ate up ground and they crested the hill with startling speed. A squawk of surprise reached Grady from the human's coach. The door flung open and the largest person Grady ever saw leaped down, eschewing the steps. They brushed off the hand of a guard with a plume on their helmet as he tried to stop them. The human's ambassador was slower than their elven counterpart, but good luck trying to stop them before they wanted to.

The thegen cordon tightened for a moment as the enemy representatives drew close. Salzum waved them off from atop his horse. "Captain, draw the Throng back please."

"Sir, I don't think-"

"No. You do not. You follow orders. Draw them back." When Dulane hesitated, his obstinacy rooted in his sense of duty, Salzum capitulated. "If you are worried for my safety, leave me with Radix. He should be more than enough protection. Don't you agree?" Instead of responding, Dulane barked an order and the warriors formed around him. They retreated, but did not go far.

Clearly, the representatives were people. Any child could identify every part of their bodies. Their faces were faces. They walked upright on two legs while swinging two arms. He counted twenty fingers evenly distributed between the pair. Their uncanny familiarity scared him.

The human's shape was like a dvergr written large. As wide as Salzum, the figure towered over Grady. Their features were rounder than any dvergr's could be and they sported no beard or facial hair of any kind. The human was solid, richly dressed, unarmed, and unamused.

The elf was a pulled-taffy approximation of the dvergr form. The elf's wiry frame, willowy limbs, dagger-like ears, and pointed features repulsed Grady. The green cast to their skin didn't help. The elf was dressed in the oddly textured armor and pale leathers worn by their compatriots.

Wisely, neither approached the Keyrdegen armed.

A flash of insight clarified why Salzum chose to ride out on a horse, rather than the usual dvergr pony. Mounted, Salzum looked down on both representatives. Grady foresaw a number of platforms and raised seats in the diplomatic future.

Salzum held the silence of the meeting tightly, daring either to speak first and further impinge on his authority. The wind gusted into a howl for a moment, flapping Salzum's beard over his shoulder and flinging the ambassadors' hair about.

"Here's how we shall proceed." Salzum addressed the open space in front of him. "We will all enter the Mountain together. Humans in a column on one side, my dvergr in the middle, and the elves on the other side. Violence of any kind will not be tolerated. The instigating party will be ejected from here and earn their sovereign state a full trade embargo." He glanced at the two enemies to check for understanding. Each grimly nodded in turn, pointedly not looking at the other. "Excellent. Line up your people, on foot. We will make our official introductions once we have some proper stone over our heads."

The Keyrdegen turned his horse with an expert pull at the reins and a click of his tongue. Grady trotted after. They rejoined Dulane and the others just as they finished lining up in the middle of the stone-paved road. Salzum took his place at the front, tugging Grady along.

The humans and elves took their time getting into place. The humans balked at having to dismount for the walk into the mountain proper. The ambassador's words, though incomprehensible, were spoken with calm authority that brooked no further argument. The elves spent a great deal of time deciding the order in which they would line the road. The discussions never grew heated as far as Grady could tell. Where Grady could make out individual words in the human tongue, the swirl and flow of Elvish remained inscrutable.

The enmity-filled glances that shot over the heads of the silver line of dvergr warriors stopped as the three parties entered the great gates of Rockhome and began down the Merchant's Way. In the stone-bred darkness, the elves and humans shrank into themselves. Both parties continued to walk tall and straight, but their shoulders sank and their steps became rigid and small. More than one hand hovered near a weapon or tightly clutched a shield. Wide eyes noted the great metal portcullis, the arrow slits and fully bastioned firing platforms.

Grady heard more than one gasp as the parties breached the Windward Gate proper. The city spread out from the docks. The jagged Roof loomed above, bedecked with banners made bright by the imported light of day. The crowds of dvergr remained. They roared their greetings to the visitors and praises to their Keyrdegen. Salzum spread his arms out wide. With pride adding vibrato to his voice he said, "Welcome to Rockhome."

AFFAIRS OF STATE

The large banquet hall was filled to capacity. In the upper recesses of the vaulted ceiling, a few of Plenabus's electric lights showered the room with their unnatural white illumination. Neither of the ambassadors asked about them, and Salzum volunteered nothing. The human ambassador squinted at them periodically, while the elven representative pointedly looked anywhere else. Grady heard their crawling buzz beneath the hum of a room full of energetic conversation. It vibrated through his whole self and created a stomachless sense of nausea.

Salzum sat at the head table with an ambassador on either side. The rest of the envoys were sequestered to tables on opposite sides of the hall, separated by distance and the mass of partying dvergr. Salzum stood with his hands raised, and the good-natured murmur of side conversations cut off. "I welcome our honored guests." The Keyrdegen inclined his head towards the human ambassador and then to their elven counterpart. He said a single word to each in their respective languages. "You have entered a Rockhome far different from the one last seen by anyone from Above. Since your peoples' last visits, we have invited the sun into the heart of the mountain. Progress has made life under the mountain easier and more comfortable. Our city, our Rockhome, thrives."

Passion empowered Salzum's rhetoric, capturing the complete attention of every dvergr in the hall. The human ambassador's poorly contained awe ever so slightly widened her eyes. The elf regarded the Keyregen's vigor with polite aloofness. "Visitors, I invite you to see my home as I do. Before me, I see the past, alive and glorious, rising into the future. Building upon everything that came before us, we reach heights beyond our ancestors' imaginings." Salzum basked in those imagined heights. Eyes from all over the hall followed Salzum's upward gaze, seeking through the too-bright lights for the distant peak far above their heads.

"Friends, your peoples have warred far too long. Your enmity is old, carved into the bones of your dead and the souls of your young. It stifles you. We love you both. Equally. It pains us to see our friends at odds, stagnating in pain and unceasing war. I have invited you here to find a way past this bloody stalemate at last, and build a peace out of enduring, sturdy stone. In peace, we shall all prosper. My city, my family, please join me in celebrating our most honored guests." Salzum drank deeply from his ornate flagon. The room erupted into a cheer. The human ambassador clapped with enthusiasm, while the elven ambassador patted the table gently.

Servers wearing the bureaucratic livery appeared and deposited plates heaped with food in front of the notables. Freed to act, an army of servers appeared ladened with platters of food for the rest of the room. Giant roasted haunches steamed next to bowls of buttery mashed roots and potatoes. Bowls of mushrooms in a brown gravy shared table space with baskets piled high with knotted rolls. Grady marveled at the efficiency of the servers and the state's largesse.

The aroma of the food, no matter how rich or fresh or fatty, failed to move Grady. It smelled good, wonderful even, but none of it was fuel. He missed the flood of saliva brought about by the taste of a good smell on his tongue. Instead, the growing lack in his gut demanded fuel, and he found himself hoping for a nice bucket of sulfite-rich coal. The sulfurous tang reminded Grady of eggs.

"Now," Salzum said past a hunk of roast, "this is a proper feast. Wouldn't you agree, Lady Marfa?"

The human ambassador smiled while she chewed a dainty cut from her meat. The dvergr utensils were childlike in her large hands. She had traded her traveling clothes for a smart-looking suit of soft, plain fabrics. "Majesty, yes. Generous are you. Great is your peoples' cuisine. Say I must, though, that the elves' presence, a surprise is." The ambassador's accent was rough and her words out of place, but Grady found her understandable enough. He appreciated her efforts.

"I find myself in agreement with the ambassador," the elven leader said, sneering slightly as if she tasted something unpleasant. She poked idly with her fork at the plate in front of her, heaped high with stewed greens and mushrooms. Elves would not eat or drink anything that involved animals. "With all this talk of peace, it is less a surprise, and more a trap, I fear." Despite the elven ambassador's technical mastery of Dvergr, the singsong lilt of her accent muddled her words. Grady found her as hard to understand as her human counterpart. The diaphanous robe she wore billowed in a gentle, nonexistent breeze. The effect filled Grady with trepidation.

Salzum shrugged and took a drink. "Trust that I would not waste your time with a lie. This idea does not originate from the goodness of my heart. 'To trust in altruism is to be blind to hidden knives', as Vahvrah the Scepter said. Peace Above would be good for my people. We grow tired of being war merchants and fortification engineers. We are capable of so much more." Salzum dipped a roll into some gravy and took an overlarge bite. He made a show of chewing, of savoring the flavors, of swallowing. "Next shift is when the real fun will begin. There is a demonstration planned that will make everything clear."

The Keyrdegen leapt to his feet, arms wide. "Time for gifts!" Salzum proclaimed. The raucous hubbub forced Salzum to repeat himself and clap his hands a few times before the room quieted. Instead of frustration, Grady felt an unassailable joy shining from the Keyrdegen. "Honored guests, in preparation for your arrival, I commissioned our greatest artisans to create gifts to mark this historic gathering. Not since Rockhome's first founding have the dvergr hosted both human and elven representatives.

"First, Lady Marfa Franic of The Joined Kingdoms. I know your days of warring are behind you, but tales of your early exploits reached even us, so far from the conflict in our Mountain fastness." On cue, an armorer's dummy was wheeled out decked in a helmet, chain hauberk, and intricately gilded greaves.

The hauberk's links were tiny, and the mail swayed like cloth. The helm was wrought in the guise of some animal Grady didn't recognize. A fat wolf, perhaps? A jeweled handle and crossguard stuck out of an equally ornate and gem-encrusted scabbard. A small round shield bearing the seven sigils of the Joined Kingdoms hung opposite. The whole thing was built to the ambassador's scale.

Two dvergr stacked on top of one another, wearing the armor and making human-like sounds, marched involuntarily through Grady's imagination. He giggled in his head.

Lady Marfa expanded up from her seat. She made a show of admiring the gifts by walking all around the dummy and touching each piece. She spoke a litany of complimentary sounding human words and wiped away a grateful tear. "Much thanks, Keyrdegen Salzum, to the artisans great. Never, I have seen such craftsmanship. Honored am I and my line." She placed a hand over her heart and bowed deeply. Grady was shocked when she leaned down to embrace Salzum and kiss him on either cheek. Salzum did not hesitate, embracing and kissing in equal measure.

"Now, Elmantharala dee'Arabosandray of Venthenialthin, my old friend. I see that look," Salzum tutted and waggled his eyebrows. "Do not think your gift is a drapery of 'dead metal'. I know you better than that." A dress form wheeled out from the hidden alcove draped in a robe of a similar style to the one already worn by the elven ambassador. Rainbows shimmered and danced across it as it moved. Grady was no lover of fashion even before his change, but clearly this was no ordinary garment. An amber broach was pinned near the collar with an eight-pointed leaf sealed in its heart. The ambassador's eyes lit up. A genuine smile softened her sharp features when she leaned in and inspected the amber.

"Is that-?" Elmantharala's words failed her as she stroked the gem.

"Of course! Ansaril. Amber and leaf. Not a local find, I'm afraid. It was brought to us by one of our many merchants. But our finest jewelers polished it and mounted it. The backing is petrified wood." Salzum puffed up with pride, inspired by either his own cleverness or the skills of his people. Grady knew which he would lay his money on.

"You honor me, Salzumishty." The elf placed her hands over her eyes and bowed from the waist. Her bow became an impossible fold until her forehead touched her shins. She unfolded back to her full height, lowered her hands from her eyes, and sat back in her seat. The amber drew her gaze like a magnet.

Salzum accepted the elf's gratitude with a simple nod. "Each envoy will also receive a crate of cast iron cookware, steel needles, copper thimbles, and various other domestic products made right here in Rockhome." Both ambassadors nodded in thanks and recognition of Salzum's generosity. "Now that the business is done, let the feast continue!"

Cheers filled the hall and the general hubbub of alcohol-inspired merriment resumed.

The two enemies never directly spoke to each other. Salzum kept the balance easily by having two conversations at once. The humans enjoyed the rooms they were assigned, and the ambassador adamantly praised the view. Marfa recounted some stories of Rockhome that her grandfather told her when she was young. Apparently, being an ambassador was a family trade back in the human lands.

Elmanthrala praised the grass growing in the Commons and the Keyrdegen's forbearance in allowing them to camp there. The elven ambassador reminisced about her last visit to Rockhome a couple centuries or so in the past. Back then, Salzum, a newly risen thegen, served well as the ambassador's honor guard. Elmanthrala expressed her sadness at the passing of Salzum's father.

Watching Salzum make small talk was boring. Time needed to pass somehow. First, Grady calculated the cost of the gifts given. Every tenant of his old flophouse could have spoiled themselves for years. Then he remembered the infinite expanse of the sky and the rolling hills outside of the mountain. Safe in his memory, the fear of falling off into the sky and the limitless threat and promise of the land above took on a thrilling aspect.

For a while, he watched the others party. The stylized retellings of lavish banquets from plays or books were only part right. Those of rank supped and ate with dignity, undoubtedly using this time to shore up alliances and conspire in the open. Clusters of recognized faces from the assembly dotted the room. The clans mingled freely. Unity in the face of guests was, of course, in the interest of all.

The rest of the attendees' behavior reminded Grady of his few trips to a pub. They quaffed and chugged. Bawdy songs competed with each other as different stretches of table swayed steins to their personal tempos. Good-natured arguments flared only to subside into hugs and laughter.

The younger, unattached set flirted brazenly. Arms and beards were stroked freely. Leaning in to converse through the noise turned to nuzzling. Grady's sharp stone eyes caught a few kisses and an under the table grope or two.

Emerlda. How would he describe all he saw and felt to Emerlda? Would it thrill her and widen her green eyes to hear about the world Above? Would she punch his arm in disbelief as he described the wonders present in their very own city? Did she still think about him? Was he still the Grady she thought about? This was why he avoided thinking of her lately. It was all too complicated. Grady allowed himself a small sigh out through his nose.

Rockhome partied. And where was Grady? Same place as ever, on the fringes of it all, watching and separated. Now more than ever. He stopped his geologically slow breathing and retreated back into the relative quiet and safety of his own head.

As dictated by custom, Salzum was the first to leave the banquet. He said something to each ambassador in their own language before standing. He signaled the official end of the event by raising a full mug of heady dark beer in a toast to all in attendance. The room, warned by servers that the moment was coming, grew quiet instantly. In the hush, Salzum chugged down the mug's contents and slammed it back onto the table. The whole room erupted into cheering. The party would continue until the food was gone and the drink was drunk, but now that the Keyrdegen was leaving, no one needed to stay.

It took a long time for Salzum to actually leave the feast with Grady trailing behind him. He paused and chatted with each of the four clan heads, strategically placed along the main aisle for just this moment.

Salzum took the time to congratulate various artisans and minor dvergr on their contributions. Grady watched as each dvergr was left with the impression that they were the cornerstone of the whole operation's success and that their efforts were the ones to guarantee Rockhome's future prosperity. Salzum's praise was specific, included family members' names, and painted over thickly with self-modesty.

Grady hated Salzum. That fact was as true as steel was hard. However, with the way the dvergr he spoke with glowed at his praise and partied all the more heartily as he left, Grady had to admit that Salzum was, on the surface, a good Keyrdegen.

In the face of stagnating tradition and glacial bureaucracy, Salzum pulled Rockhome forward through sheer force of will. Grady's clear picture of the Keyrdegen as a self-serving, greed-driven tyrant fuzzed. The positive emotions Salzum transmitted as he spoke with his people lacked the duplicity Grady noted when he spoke with Dulane or Plenabus.

Was it possible for a person to be self-serving and work for the betterment of all? Back in his cell, Plenabus and Salzum spoke of the value of Grady's sacrifice, of the good it would do for the mountain's denizens. Were Grady's pain and continued degradation necessary for Rockhome's advancement? What was one life in the face of the needs of the whole city?

I don't see him volunteering.

Once the Keyrdegen and his stone bodyguard were free from the hall, the generous gladness faded from Salzum. He rubbed his hands together. "Yes," he said, talking to himself as they walked. "After the next shift. Change comes." He let out a few round and quiet laughs, his mind clearly elsewhere.

They reached the Keyrdegen's study and apartments, seeing no one. Salzum held up a hand to stop Grady as he went to follow. Gone was the master host and kind leader. Hard and hungry, this was the Salzum

Grady knew best. "Radix, you are to return to your room. Be back at the start of the next shift. Be ready to put on a show. Now go."

That was ominous. Grady rode himself through the halls, as his body took him back to his room, enjoying the solitude and the beauty filling the Hold's corridors.

Grady looked forward to some downtime, away from other people and his lordly oppressor, to simply stare out of his window. His internal shock at finding an armored thronger in his room waiting for him did not stop him in the doorway. The Keyrdegen had commanded him to return to his room, so return he did.

The light from the lichen lamp glinted off of a small star of silvery, bright metal in the forehead of the Salzum mask. Beneath hung the familiar salt and pepper-streaked beard. "Finally." Dulane removed his helmet and set it down on Grady's unused desk next to the welly-thumbed book. "Word has reached me about Salzum's planned demonstration for the ambassadors tomorrow. Only that it's happening, not what it entails. He means to sequester himself and the ambassadors into whatever negotiations he has planned. This is the opportunity we have been waiting for. I have contacted my allies. They are ready." The captain placed his gauntlet onto Grady's pauldron. "By this time next shift, you should be free, my tyro." His smile was warm, hopeful. "I should go." He put back on his helmet, nodded, and walked past Grady into the hall.

Grady was unsure how to feel. He waited for and dreamed of being freed since the moment Dulane had promised to help in the tea shop an eternity ago. Now here it was. Freedom at last?

But was he *free* before? For years Grady had suffered through a half-life of paperwork, cheap meals, and fleeting glimpses of joy. But he did his job. Played his part. His thanks were the knives and the lights and Salzum's casual cruelty.

And then, outside of Plenabus's nightmare of a laboratory, he had spoken words and made promises.

What was freedom, really?

The city sparkled outside of his window. His mind swirled and battled against the whims of his heart. A disembodied ache joined the internal maelstrom. Grady wasn't sure where the hurt came from.

A 'Live' Demonstration

G rady arrived at Salzum's study to find the Keyrdegen, dressed in his familiar purple robes, already drinking and scowling at a parchment on his desk. He didn't bother to look up as Grady entered and, free of any order, stopped just inside the doorway. Salzum's scowl took over the rest of his face as he read. Roaring in frustration, he swept his desk clear, and finished the motion with an overhead, double-fisted slam down on the desktop.

Red-rimmed, furious eyes regarded Grady from across the room. "Come closer, Radix." The alacrity with which Grady complied teased a small smile from the fuming warlord. "You remain one of a kind. Your creator continues to fail me. I must say, golem, that I did not expect much from you at first. Do you remember when we first met?"

The degradation, the flash of pain on his cheek, and the taste of coppery fear on his tongue played out again. "Yes."

"Remove your helmet. Ugh. I always forget just how ugly you are." Salzum walked over to his well-stocked and worldly bar. He chose a bottle of clear liquid and uncorked it. As he poured the room filled with the smell of licorice and berries. Salzum drank deeply as he examined Grady's face. "Do you remember your old name?"

His mind thought, *Yes,* at the same time his body answered out loud, "No." The Keyrdegen's first order tried to banish his name. The stone of his body may have forgotten, but it was indelibly printed on his soul or mind or whatever Grady was now.

Salzum nodded, soothed by the depth of obedience on display. "You have yet to fail me, Radix. I command a thing and it is done. You never complain to me or demand from me. Today will be your moment. Do as you are told and you will truly be the adit through which Rockhome will excavate its greatness." Love pulsed through Salzum, warm and bright. He looked past Grady into his imagined, great future.

Salzum took a long drink and, as he swallowed, the gentle love rehardened back to Salzum's usual mien. "In my youth, I so envied my parents. Their artistry was second to none. Their work was much sought after. Then the horns. Then I saw. My parents' work was precious because it was fragile. It is nothing without strength to protect it from thieves and destroyers." He laughed, hollow and mirthless, and scratched at his arm. "This shift I truly start to wend my Way. But first there are some loose ends to deal with."

Everything stuttered.

One second the berobed Keyrdegen and Grady were alone, the next Salzum was dressed in his full finery and a handful of the Throng were in the room as well. A familiar, dizzying wash of vertigo set the world to waving. "You have your orders. Be ready." They saluted, turned towards the door as one, and marched out in an orderly line. "Excellent, excellent. Come Radix. The ambassadors are waiting for us."

Grady followed the Keyrdegen through the Hold and up onto the Commons. As they walked, Grady prodded the hole in his memory like a cold sore on his cheek. At first, he blamed inattentiveness, but the space in his memory was too blank to be the result of a wandering mind.

It was worrying. *But what isn't these shifts?*

The skylights' dim glow cast a gray pall over the Commons. Slow smoke curled from the peaks of a long, patchwork tent off in the grass near the palace. Its organic shape and temporary nature were at odds with the sharp permanence of the stone angles surrounding it. There were no visible sentries or obvious signs of movement. The dvergr going about their normal business cast furtive glances at the tent. They went out of their way to avoid walking on the nearest walkways.

The Keyrdegen and Grady passed the two Salzum masked warriors stationed to block random traffic from heading towards the westernmost elevators. At the wide, rectangular entranceway the two visiting parties stood opposite each other, as far away as the platform allowed. Each ambassador was accompanied by two unarmed compatriots. Both parties made a show of paying the other no mind at all.

"Hello, friends!" Salzum's voice boomed. "Thank you for joining me. I trust you are all well rested?" He paused only for the barest signs of agreement from his guests before barreling past them and into the entrance corridor. Salzum didn't look back, he merely walked and talked, pulling the tall visitors behind him as surely as he did Grady. "I know you saw a good deal of our wondrous city on your way in. Today, however, is no holiday! You will have the opportunity to see my people hard at work. Come, come."

The elevator was open and waiting for them. The attendant was the wizened Germander of Clan Hematite. The Keyrdegen greeted him kindly. "Level 1, please, Germander." Grady wondered why Salzum was so polite to the elevator operator, of all people. Not that the old dvergr didn't deserve respect. He was an elder and, judging from his uniform, highly ranked in his clan. Salzum doled out politeness like it was mithril. Yet, here was a please with a thank you to follow.

As the elevator descended, Salzum talked. "I always enjoyed riding the elevators up and down. When I was younger, and freer, I'd ride them all shift." He gestured in Wall. "I loved to see the different levels in the Walls. Each a community of neighbors, families, and friends who have shared that space for hundreds of years. There is a wonder to seeing the city from above, watching the Floor grow as you descend." Salzum looked out onto the city through the iron accordion doors. He sighed like he saw the love of his life. "Helped me develop a sense for my city and people as a whole. Lady Marfa, this is your first time in Rockhome. What are your first impressions of our great city?"

The hill-sized human looked pensive as she gathered her thoughts and translated them. "Bigger is it than I thought. Feeling of old everywhere. Great craftsmanship. People welcoming. Believed I grandfather's stories were exaggerations at best, worst lies. Undersold it all to us he did." Her dvergr was improving.

A sharp edge hid in Salzum's warm smile. He spoke some words in human, 'thanks' most likely. Maybe a story about her grandfather. Grady did not understand a word, but there was no doubt the Keyrdegen's Human was impeccable. "We are heading to a newly excavated space, built just for this occasion," he added in Dvergr. "It took our engineers and artisans only two shifts from start to finish."

Elmantharala and the other elves paid no mind to the conversation. They did their best to seem unaffected by it all. The pallor invading their green skin and their quickened breathing gave away their discomfort.

The elevator came to a smooth halt. "First level, sir." The old dvergr's voice was raspy and his words clipped and professional.

"Thank you, Germander. Wait here, please. We will only be a moment."

"Of course, sir."

"This way, please." Salzum led his guests out of the elevator and into the Wall proper. This level was not a living level. It was too close to the Floor for any proper dvergr to call it home. They passed cavernous warehouses filled with crates of raw materials and manufactured goods waiting to be sent off with a caravan or be reloaded onto the cart system and sent to another part of the city. Teams of dvergr worked with large, hydraulic machines to move the massive crates. A group of gray-clad dvergr worked at bellows pumps connected to the loaders. The elves walked by the marvels of dvergr engineering with poorly concealed sneers. The humans buzzed amongst each other, pointing and gesticulating. One furiously sketched with a coal pencil on a scrap of parchment.

The Keyrdegen turned away from the bustle of the warehouses down a freshly-hewn corridor of plain stone. The only embellishments were an unusually high number of lichen lights lining the walls. "Have you ever seen a cleave so straight?" Salzum ran his hand along the perfectly smooth walls. "The corners are impeccable. All done by hand. Our destination is just ahead." Salzum's pace quickened. His obvious excitement energized his guests, whose long legs barely noticed the increase in pace.

The two visiting parties mumbled in confusion amongst themselves when the corridor ended. The wall in front of them was as smooth and unblemished as the rest of the corridor. Salzum stood with his back to the blank wall with the bearing of a showman. "Honored guests, welcome to my arena." He extended both arms behind himself and simultaneously tapped on the wall with an outstretched finger from each hand. The wall folded soundlessly, revealing a concealed door. The tall people gasped, eyes wide and wary.

The space beyond was octagonal. The theme of smooth, plain walls dotted with an unusually high number of lichen lights continued inside. The room was replicated in miniature by the eight-sided pit in its center. A mini-portcullis covered the tunnel entrance that delved into one of the pit's eight sides. From the tunnel a waft of air carried the smell of stagnant water and rot.

That isn't going to be good. Grady expected the worst. Whenever Salzum was this excited, things never worked out well for him.

"Please, have a seat." Salzum waved everyone over to a viewing box made of pale 'shroomwood at the lip of the pit. Cushions, brightly embroidered, topped each of the seven chairs. Three bore the sigils of the Joined Kingdoms, three the golden tree of Venthenialthin, and the last was plain, but upholstered in the rich purple material Salzum loved so much.

Once his guests were seated, Salzum stood before the box. "In my welcome speech I promised you a solution to your unending conflict, built of enduring stone. Recent developments in dvergr engineering have found a solution, a way to end the loss and pain of war." The visitors from Above shared urgent whispers with their compatriots.

"Radix here- Come here Radix." Grady shuffled over next to his master. "Radix the Beardless here is my silent and stoic bodyguard. Maybe you noticed? He never sneezes. Never shuffles his feet or twitches uncomfortably. Scratches an itch. Picks his nose." Salzum enjoyed his own silliness. He rapped on Grady's helmet. The hard bang echoed around the empty room. "Take off your helmet."

The sight of Grady's mineral lined face and marble eyes struck the audience dumb. Every jaw hung low enough that Grady was able to count their teeth. Salzum smiled his false, warm smile and patted Grady on the head. The many jeweled rings clinked against his pate. "This is Artificer Plenabus's latest invention. An automaton that is almost indistinguishable from a living, thinking being. Say hello, Radix!"

"Hello." The grinding of his voice caused the audience to flinch backward.

"Radix is just a prototype. More are in production and will be ready to roll out soon." Salzum walked forward and leaned on the edge of the box. "I can practically read the thoughts going through your heads now. How can a dvergr automaton end your war once and for all?" The Keyrdegen vaulted over the side of the box in an uncharacteristic display of nimbleness. He took his seat in the middle of the bewildered envoys and clapped his hands. "Let me show you. Radix, jump into the pit."

Yup, about what I expected, Grady thought as his body complied.

Salzum made no attempt to hide his glee. "Oh, I almost forgot. Radix, throw your hammer and shield out of the pit."

Grady complied.

From beyond the gate, something watched. The stagnant-rot smell ebbed and flowed like large, slow breaths. At this point, Grady was beyond dread. He doubted that whatever was behind that metal gate could really hurt him physically.

The constant dull torture of being trapped within his own body wore at him. Breathing was a respite, but the ache remained in the stillness between. Orderless and still, Grady stared into the deep darkness past the metal bars. How many more indignities and horrors was his mind going to be able to bear before it broke?

Would madness be worse than this?

"Begin!" Salzum shouted loudly. There was a click and the portcullis sank down into the floor. The foul smell thickened as faint thumping sounds echoed from the dark space, growing closer and closer. At the edge of darkness, the thing stopped. It snuffled the air, each snort burbling thick with mucus. It must have smelled something it liked, because the thing pulled itself into the light.

Well, shit. The spectators above yelled in disgust and surprise.

The lichen light played over the mass of bulbous, slug-pale hide covered in oozing tumors and taller than Lady Marfa and twice as wide. Red eyes glared with hunger from within the melted wax flesh of its monstrous face. Bone-colored claws, hanging from its too large hands and feet, scraped along the stone floor with each step.

It spotted Grady and roared in a voice like wobbly metal shaking in a deep hole. A few tattered shreds of rotting flesh stuck amongst the bristling yellow needles of its pincushion of a maw, fluttered in the foulness of its breath.

"Radix, kill it."

Vestigial fear pulled Grady back deeper into his head. In this instance he was more than content to let the power of the Keyrdegen's command drive. Watching the deep troll grow larger as he charged felt oddly familiar.

I've had this nightmare before.

The thing cocked its head to the side looking confused that the tiny morsel chose to charge instead of flee. Grady almost felt sorry for it. Grady's body took advantage of its hesitation, quickly closing with it to deliver a solid punch to the thing's shin.

Instead of cracking into solid bone with a thud, his fist punched through the leg's meaty exterior in a fountain of green blood. The troll let out a high pitched warble. If Grady still had a bladder that sound would have emptied it. His body went to pull the hand free and found it stuck fast.

The troll shook the wounded leg in an attempt to dislodge the offending fist, but the thing struggled to shift its weight. His body placed his feet on either side of the puncture in the troll's shin, bent into a deep squat, and pulled. The hand came free with a squelching pop just as the troll's dvergr-sized hand swung around and swatted him to the ground. Grady's body slammed down with a complex clamor of stone being hit by metal being hit by stone. The troll seized the opportunity and stood over its fallen foe. Each time Grady tried to rise a giant fist slammed into his back, knocking him flat again. The troll's strength was immense.

How did they catch this thing to begin with?

He hoped that Salzum felt foolish in his seat between his honored guests. There was no chance the troll would break him, but Grady felt his fuel reserves lowering with each attempt to rise. Hopefully his energy would last long enough to see Salzum's plan fail just as he believed his triumph was nigh.

A small spark of pain flared to life in the middle of his forehead. It rode the mithril lines there, scraping 'Dominance' on his soul. With each slamming attack from the troll, with every dip in his energy reserve, the pain grew. The dvergr killing blows raining down on his back were finally harming him. His body, dumb and unguided, just kept trying to rise to his hands and knees. For the pain to stop, the Keyrdegen's command must be fulfilled.

Grady needed to get involved.

Instead of rising, Grady shoved the pain aside and took a long slow breath that stuttered in time to the troll's drumming on his back. He pulled the air deeper, expanding his chest to its fullest. His battered armor screeched in protest. The troll's assault had bent his armor tightly around his body, hampering his movement.

Seeing its opponent unmoving on the ground, the troll screeched in victory.

Expelling every ounce of air within him in one rock grinding shout, Grady powered a full body effort to twist to his knees. "Hwah!"

The troll cocked its head, in shock and wonder.

The only way out is through.

Grady's fingers punched through the metal of his breastplate. With gritted teeth he pulled, but the stubborn metal resisted. Time slowed as the pain in his forehead grew. It spread along the ley lines carved into his skin, flaying his senses.

The only way out is through.

Overcoming the shock of seeing a should-have-been-pulped opponent rise, the troll cocked back its fist. Grady ripped his breastplate in two with another roar fueled burst of strength. He turned his momentum into a roll narrowly dodging the troll's next series of attacks. The two halves of his breastplate clanged loudly against opposite sides of the octagonal pit.

Grady smiled wildly and darted at the troll, fumbling its attempt to grab him. Dulane said there was only one thing to remember when facing a taller opponent, a lesson drilled into Grady over hours of training. "Go for the knees." Clasping the fingers of his gauntleted hands Grady dipped between the troll's wide set legs, planted his feet into the floor, and swung with all of his golem granted might.

His clasped fists punched through the beast's knee with a tearing splorch. The troll howled in pain and toppled. A few straining strands of muscle and sinew were all that held the beast's leg together. It looked from its demolished knee to the darkness from whence it came. Whimpering, it dragged itself away from Grady, smearing a line of green blood along the floor. The burning lines of pain drove Grady on.

Grady gave a full-throated voice to his pain. He leaped onto the retreating creature's back. When it tried to shake him off, Grady dug his fingers into the beast's flesh. Panicked, the troll flopped over onto its back to try and squash the tenacious and tiny attacker. It roared in pain as it slammed Grady against itself. It staggered up on its good foot and scraped Grady against the pit walls.

Despite the troll's best efforts, Grady climbed higher, handful by bloody handful. The troll flopped around in circles, arms flailing up and down in an attempt to get its claws on him. Grady's fuel reserves were dangerously low.

Minimally present, Grady corrected. *Stay positive.*

The pain in his soul surged to near maddening intensity. This needed to end. With a final roar of effort Grady wrapped his arms around the beast's waddled throat. He clasped his forearms and began to squeeze.

The troll flailed at Grady. It took large chunks out of its own flesh as its talons scraped uselessly off Grady's armor and stone skin.

Mechanically Grady worked his hands up his arms, tightening his grip. His pain mounted. Choking was taking too long. He braced his feet against the troll's back and tugged. It bowed back, its cries of agony diminishing into gurgling squawks. Its flailing grew more frantic. Grady pulled with every petrified fiber of his being.

A wet tearing sent Grady into the air, the troll's head and a good portion of its neck in his arms. Great gouts of viscous green blood pumped from the stump. The arms continued to flail weakly, then the mass of flesh slumped over, twitched once, and grew still.

On his back, hugging the severed head of the troll, Grady sighed with relief.

The pain was gone.

Toothy whistles and the sound of meaty hands clamored down from above. Salzum was pleased. From his vantage at the bottom of the pit, on his back with the severed troll's head in his face, Grady could not see the ambassador's reactions to the spectacle. Their silence spoke volumes. Salzum's point was made.

Salzum was a beacon of joy. His victory was at hand. "Normally, it takes at least a dozen well equipped and fully prepared dvergr to take down one of those things. Radix managed it on its own. Weaponless. Imagine the impact a mere five of these golems would have on your battlefields." Salzum paused to let them do just that. Grady did and it made his soul shudder. "Mass production is slated to begin shortly. Radix, to me." Grady stood and bounded out of the pit and landed on its edge.

I didn't know I could do that.

The spectators blanched as one. Grady must be a sight to see. How would he react to seeing a topless stone dvergr, in ragged greaves and gauntlets, covered in the stinking green blood of the troll whose head it carried like a ball?

"The task before you now is simple. Return to your homes and impress upon your leadership the importance of what you witnessed. There is no set price. That would not be fair practice. Each of your homes is rich in such different ways. I will wait to see what is offered, see what value your people set on dvergr aid for winning your unwinnable conflict." Salzum patted his stomach with both hands, smiled, and rocked back and forth on his feet.

Elmantharala stood, the color rising back into her cheeks. "You use dangerous toys to play your game, Salzum. My peoples' memories are long, longer apparently than your own. The last time the dvergr unleashed these foul abominations on the world, it shattered your home, turned your people into a diaspora. Would you see them destroyed completely?"

"Feel free to pass on my offer or not as you see fit. Your people may refuse to seek our aid, but the Joined Kingdoms wear our steel proudly. What is this golem but the latest in military technologies?" He gave Lady Marfa a pointed look. She stared at Grady with a deep knitted brow. One of her companions whispered furiously in her ear.

Salzum shrugged. The offer was made. The matter was out of his hands. "Any questions?"

Elmantharala sat down, her ears dropping a bit in defeat. The other elves were still, paralyzed by the confusion and terror playing across their faces.

Salzum the arms dealer gave way to Salzum the consummate host with a shift of his weight. "You are invited to remain our guests as long as you like. We have all greatly enjoyed your company." Salzum's gold tooth glinted out from his predator's smile. "I would hurry home though. This offer is only good while supplies last. First come, first served."

BEST LAID PLANS

The Keyrdegen led the subdued ambassadors from the octagonal room. He made a grand meal out of his victory lap. Salzum's stately pace forced the long-legged visitors to mince forward, lest they insult their host by walking in front of him. A wise precaution, considering Salzum's quick temper and recent ultimatum.

Secure in his power, Salzum took a celebratory swig from his flask. "Isn't it fascinating that each of our cultures developed their own spirits? And from such different materials! Given enough time and a good enough reason, a thinking person can ferment anything!" His voice faded to an echo as the procession continued down the tunnel.

Watching Salzum walk away was a strange experience after so long at his heels. Grady's current standing order was to stay here, wait to be cleaned up, and properly dressed. The sight of him, out and about in the open, would raise questions that Salzum did not want or need right now. The funk of the troll's blood thickened the air. Its potency made Grady thankful for his altered relationship to his sense of smell.

Besides, Grady's reserves, on the brink of exhaustion, would not be enough to carry him back to the elevator.

It was unclear how long Grady waited, alone with only the sounds and smells of the troll's body settling into death down in the pit. His consciousness faded in and out. The world blinked, and a hooded figure was in front of Grady, holding out an open sack. A nourishing smell, with clear sulfuric notes, called to him from the bag.

"Eat up, Grady."

The surge of command freed him to do what his body demanded. He shoved fistfuls of coal into his cheeks until they bulged. The
crunch was oh, so satisfying, but not nearly as much as the sensation
of the masticated coal depositing itself in his belly.

Dulane lowered his hood. "I came as soon as I was sure you were
alone. Mother below, you are a mess. Is that-?" Dulane walked past
Grady, still chewing away happily, and peered into the pit. "Gah. He
had you kill a troll?" Dulane gave Grady an appraising look. "Salzum
always did love a spectacle. When you're done, uh, eating, take off your
pants and use them to wipe yourself clean as best you can. I brought a
change of clothes. Hurry."

At Dulane's order, his body sped up and wolfed down coal in a
blur. Grady held the bag over his mouth and shook out the last few
pebbles at the bottom onto his tongue. He licked his lips, then his
fingers. The dust was the best part.

Grady stripped and scraped himself clean as best he could. The
gunk sloughed off easily from his smooth exterior. Being hairless had
its advantages, apparently. Bits of the troll's humors remained, dried
into the runnels of the ley lines and the runes carved into his upper
body, and the troll caked under his nails required water and time to
fully remove.

"Alright," Dulane said, glancing from Grady to the tunnel and
back over and over. "I think that's the cleanest you'll be for a while.
Get dressed. We have to go."

Dulane slung off his rucksack and began placing clothing at
Grady's feet. The boots and thick workman's gloves were plain brown
affairs, cheap and used. Grady marveled at the coveralls as his body
mechanically pulled them on. They were the same hooded variety worn
by Dulane and commonly throughout the city. Instead of a uniform
and bland gray, they were striped in the colors of Clan Feldspar, a
dashing tartan of red and orange. Grady reveled in the impropriety of
it all as he buttoned the last button just below his neck.

"Alright, let me get a look at you." Dulane tugged at Grady's coveralls to try and get them to drape differently. "They're a little big, but they'll do. Hood up and follow me. Keep your face down."

They left the octagonal room and the dead troll behind at a jog and reached the main avenue of Level One. Dulane struck a measured pace and Grady followed, as ordered. Every moment Grady waited for one of the many stevedores and machine operators to challenge them or call for the guards. Everyone worked at a manic pace, spurred on by managers in gold and brown shouting about missed quotas. The captain and the golem were as good as invisible.

Dulane took an unexpected turn away from the elevators. The captain stopped outside of an empty doorway, holding up his hand in a silent order for Grady to stop. He leaned his head in to look around, motioned with his head for Grady to follow, and disappeared into the space beyond. After a few more quiet corridors, the pair stepped out into the Floor proper.

The rattle of the chain carts and general dvergr hubbub enveloped Grady. The scents of street foods and spilled beer washed the last traces of troll from his nostrils. He walked again on solidly deep stone. A strange feeling bloomed amidst the blowing torrent of his emotions. Underneath the hum of tension from his flight, the fading terror of his encounter with the troll, and the burgeoning well of hope that his delivery was at hand, Grady felt an invisible knot in his heart loosen.

He was home.

Dulane turned and turned. Grady's only view was the walkway beneath his feet and the legs and shoes of those around him, making it hard for Grady to guess at their destination. The walkways were not fully packed, and the traffic was light.

Must be mid-shift. Grady cradled the once mundane thought, cherishing it.

When politeness dictated, Dulane guided them out of the way of another pedestrian, but most of the feet went around them. The red and orange of Clan Feldspar, provenders of food and drink, flashed on his legs with each step. It paid to show respect to the hands that feed you.

They stopped in front of a building that, from Grady's downward vantage, looked the same as every other building they'd passed. "We're here. You go in first. Wait for me inside. Head on a bearing." Dulane leaned against the wall and adjusted his boot. He scanned the dvergr walking past with a bored expression on his face.

Grady walked past Dulane into a small lobby. In the middle of the room sat an unmanned, neatly organized reception desk. Its lichen lamp was uncovered, bathing the room in a cool glow. There was no signage or markings that hinted at the building's purpose or clarified why they were here. A single door of pale 'shroomwood stood directly opposite Grady on the other side of the desk.

"I think we're clear." Dulane pulled back his hood. The large beads of sweat prickling his brow were at odds with his confident smile. "Come on. We're expected." He walked past the desk and knocked a pattern on the door. When a different pattern responded, Dulane sighed in relief. He opened the door and waved for Grady to follow.

A dvergr in Clan Feldspar colors shared a forearm shake with Dulane. She went to greet Grady. Her approach gave her a glimpse under his hood, which brought her up short. Clearing her throat, she straightened. "The Chief is waiting for you. Back here." They walked past a handful of empty cubicles, each desk as neat and orderly as the receptionist's in the lobby.

It must be a front. Grady knew some dvergr with obsessively neat and organized desks, but an entire office full? That beggared belief.

Their guide pulled open one of the large double doors that normally led to the file room where copies would be kept. Instead of cabinets filled with file folders, a party of dvergr watched Dulane and Grady enter. The guide nodded to the familiar face in the center of it all, and left to return to her post. Chief Ludmil stroked her long, ghost of a beard. Her auger eyes drilled into Grady. "Well, Dulane. Let's see him."

"Please remove your hood, Grady."

The sight creased Ludmil's face with sadness. "Fool boy. He really did it." She shuffled forward to peer closely at Grady's exposed face. She shook her head as if she wished to deny what her eyes saw. "My grandmother told me stories. About why our people were scattered, of what drove us from our ancestral halls. How First Home was lost. She claimed we were driven out by stone monstrosities that were once people. I thought her mad and addled by age." She cackled. "She was forty years younger than I am now. Why does the wisdom of age ring so falsely in the ears of youth?"

"We should hurry, Chief." Dulane bowed as he approached her. "He needs to be taken somewhere safe and out of the Keyrdegen's reach."

"Yes, we will take him to the West Wall, hide him. There, deep in our hall, are places that-" A crash from upstairs cut the Chief off. Her eyes grew wide. "Did anyone follow you?"

"No!" Dulane pulled a hammer from his bag and turned to face the door. "There was no tail. I was careful. No one knew." His eyes flicked towards Grady and back to the door. "Grady! You're our only hope now. Defend-" Before he could finish the command, the doors to the fake storage room crashed in. A bolt slammed into Dulane's shoulder and he dropped his hammer to clutch at the wound. A Throng squad bearing loaded crossbows poured into the room, clanking as they surrounded Dulane, Grady, Ludmil, and her handful of attendants.

The light in Grady's heart flickered and went out.Keyrdegen Salzum entered the room with the same swagger he used to lead the ambassadors away from the demonstration. "Kind of a drab place to commit treason. The stories always have these sorts of things happening in grand palaces over drinks and between sheets. I am a little disappointed at the lack of flair."

At the Keyrdegen's touch, two warriors parted to let him through. Salzum draped an arm around Grady's shoulders. "I bet you're all wondering how I knew about this little clandestine plan to undermine me. You were all so careful. Any guesses?" He patted Grady playfully. "On a lark, late one shift, I decided to try and ask Radix questions. I asked how it was enjoying its time training with Captain Dulane. Imagine my surprise when the stone thing went on and on about how kind you were. How nice it was to be seen as a person again. You were always too kind for your own good, my First. Oh, how it gushed when it told me you named a thing your tyro. And about your promise to help it."

Dulane shuddered like he was hit by a second bolt. "Come now, don't take it too hard, Dulane. I made the thing forget it even told me, just in case you got paranoid enough to ask it about me. Couldn't have it ruining the surprise."

His smile flashed bright and warm as he kicked Dulane once in his stomach and again on his wounded shoulder. The bolt shaft broke off and Dulane gritted his teeth, barely stifling his cry of pain. Salzum's kind facade faded as he spoke until a shower of fury and spittle dampened the captain's face. "Dulane, you were the first to swear your honor to me. I told you of my vision for Rockhome. I told you I would do whatever, whatever it takes to see our home safe and prosperous. You told me you believed in me. That you saw my vision and that I was the only one who could make it a reality. I trained you. Raised you up. I made you someone important! And this is how you repay my kindness? My generosity? My trust?!"

He punched the captain, opening up jagged slashes along his jaw with his large rings. Salzum, huffing air through his flared nostrils and clenched teeth, stared down at the bleeding and broken captain. His composure returned slowly. By the time Salzum turned his regard to Ludmil and her people, his mask of kindness was back in place. Having seen the beast waiting beneath it, the facade fooled no one.

"Honestly, Ludmil? You were the last person I expected to be at the center of this betrayal. You have served Rockhome longer than anyone. Under your patronage and guidance, Clan Feldspar prospers and is more productive than ever. You are a pillar of this city. I'm disappointed."

Ludmil snorted. "That makes two of us. You delve too deep, Salzum. Continue as you have and you doom us all."

"Doom? No. Imagine it, Ludmil. The Clanless gone, replaced by an indestructible army. Nothing Below, no nation Above, could threaten us again. Our conquest will be complete, our power unassailable. The wealth of the world will be ours. The ancient glories of our people will be restored. No. Surpassed!" Salzum's voice rang with zeal and unshakeable confidence. His hunger, for all the power and riches his vision promised, twisted his noble countenance into something monstrous.

"What say you?" He extended his blood-flecked hand out. "Join with me, support me, and all will be forgiven. I greatly value your counsel and your skills as a clan chief. Your loss would diminish us all."

Ludmil's ruby earrings dangled and danced as she shook her head. She laughed once through her nose. Her eyes and small smile drooped, heavy with sadness. "Salzum, you were always an overreacher. I remember when, as a young thegen, you broke your arm trying to reach the top of the Hold's entrance. I asked you what drove you to attempt something so foolhardy. Do you remember your answer?"

Salzum looked off in the distance, charmed by the cheekiness of his youth. "Think of the stories they would tell of me if I succeeded."

The old chief's lip trembled. A single tear rolled down her cheek. "You climb too high, Salzum. When you fall this time, you will break more than a bone. Please, do not take Rockhome with you."

Salzum shot the old dvergr a withering glare. "You disappoint me, Ludmil. Instead of helping me shape my great future, you will die in this place having accomplished nothing."

Dulane struggled up on his elbow. "Please, Salzum. You cannot do this," he pleaded.

"That's the great thing about being Keyrdegen. I can do whatever I want." Salzum left Ludmil standing there, trembling and defiant. The Keyrdegen took his place behind the ring of warriors wearing his face. "Let's end this. Radix, kill them all, except the captain. Be creative. Give him a good show."

Grady howled inside his head. In the geode he thrashed uselessly inside the crystal cocoon.

Be creative. A slew of memorable killing blows from his favorite books offered themselves up. Unable to close his eyes, he watched his body raise a struggling Ludmil over his head with both hands. Her composure broken, she screamed until Grady slammed her to the ground. The squished crunch of her body breaking as it hit the floor ignited panic amongst her stunned companions.

Two charged Grady, their only hope to die a good death avenging the matriarch of their clan. He put his fist through the chest of one, dragging his lungs out to flutter uselessly on his shirt. The other he slapped down. Her neck snapped the instant his palm struck her cheek. A younger dvergr, their beard nascent and patchy, shuddered in place. A wet stain darkened their pants and ran down their leg. Grady grabbed them by the arms and flung them over the heads of the warriors behind him. The youth slammed into the wall and was dead before they flopped to the ground, leaving a red, person-sized splotch on the wall.

The last two struggled to push their way past the wall of armored dvergr. They begged for mercy, pledged themselves to Salzum's cause, offered up other names as the real traitors. Grady grabbed their heads, one in each hand, and slammed them together, splattering the nearest thronger with red drops and splinters of bone. A single drop of blood trickled like a tear down Salzum's silvery visage.

The Keyrdegen's ovation included a few whistles. "Spectacular, Radix! You put on quite the show. What did you think of your protégé's display, Captain?"

Dulane didn't bother to answer. He did not even look in Grady's direction. All of his attention, all of his ire, was focused on his Keyrdegen, his master. "You... will fail. I loved... you. You are the be... betrayer."

"Poor deluded fool. You were to lead the armies out into the world. I wanted your name etched along with mine for eternity. I offered you a destiny and you threw it away for what? For that?" Salzum pointed at Grady.

"For him. Yes. 'I will sculpt a better future for my people with my might.' No good can come of such suffering."

"You were always too noble for your own good. Kreth's words poisoned your Way. I'm sorry, old friend. I want you to die with honor. Here." The warrior on the Keyrdegen's left removed the extra helmet from his belt and placed it in Salzum's outstretched hand. "You earned the right to wear the Captain's star. Seems only fitting that you die with it on." Dulane struggled weakly as Salzum put the helmet on his head.

"Radix, to me."

Grady continued to howl in his soul. Without a throat to grow raw and lungs to empty, he was able to scream indefinitely. He begged and pleaded to anyone, anything that might be listening to draw the line here. Stop this. Snuff him out and let it end. Anything but this.

Salzum leaned in to whisper in his ear. "I know you are in there, Grady of No Clan. You thought to escape me? Foil my plans? Dumb brick. You are mine. You always were. I want you looking into the eyes of your friend, your savior, your *master* as he dies by your hand." Salzum smiled, stepped back, and patted Grady's blood-streaked cheek. "Radix, headbut Dulane to death, please."

Grady's hands hooked under Dulane's armpits and lifted him like a child. Through the holes in Salzum's neutral face Dulane's eyes met Grady's, the star of his rank glinting above his brow. Dulane spoke softly, his voice crooked with pain. "It's not your fault. None of this is your fault. Find your Way. I'm sorry."

The command pulsed and Grady slammed his forehead into Dulane's. *I'm sorry.* The second hit dented the metal and washed away Dulane's eyes with a torrent of blood.

I'm so sorry.

"Obliterate him!" Salzum screamed.

Grady extended Dulane's sagging body at arm's length and arched his head backwards. The last thing Grady saw was two rivers of blood pouring from Salzum's silver molded eyes. Then his forehead connected one last time with Dulane's. There was the scream of crumpling metal. A line of pain lanced across his forehead and deep into his being.

Darkness took him.

BROKEN CHAINS

Oblivion shifted and filled. Grady hung in the dim heart of the geode, surrounded by still, smoky crystals. The sourceless illumination was gone.

Grady's chin sank down until it touched his crystalline cocoon. The recent violence played like a round in his mind, doubling up, tripling. The crescendo of repeated metal screams hit him like successive hammer blows.

"I'm sorry. I'm so sorry," Grady mumbled. A line of fire burned on his forehead. The pain flared out along the ley lines and traced his every petrified nerve. Grady hurt, but he did not suffer. He did not deny the pain. He embraced it.

It was the least of what he deserved.

The action scenes were Grady's favorite parts of the books he read. Being captured on a page reduced high-stakes situations down to consequence-free trifles. When done with a touch of skill, descriptions of gore and viscera, wounded bodies and ended lives, inspired smiles and kept him turning pages.

Dulane was gone. The second strike snuffed him. Dying in Grady's hands, his friend cared enough to absolve Grady of any wrongdoing, lying with love. He even apologized.

Salzum owned the motherlode of blame. But when Salzum asked, Grady answered. That his betrayals existed as blanks in his memory was an undeserved blessing. Had he even tried to resist? How long did he last before giving in? The guilt pushed deeper. Salzum ordered and Grady obeyed.

Disobedience was pain, after all.

If only he was stronger.

A voice intruded into Grady's misery. "Oh my poor, hm, creation. Look at you. Covered in filth. An easy problem to remedy. Yes." Then humming followed, tuneless and loving.

How could Grady have forgotten about Plenabus and his share of responsibility? Salzum wielded the weapon. Plenabus forged it. Plenabus cut into him, pushed electricity through his body, and built a cage for his soul.

A light caress on his forehead made Grady shiver. "I warned him. Yes. Made sure to demonstrate the danger of mithril. And what does he do, hm? Makes you slam your head against some! Repeatedly. Damn captain's star. Foolish and vainglorious waste of mithril." He tsked through his teeth.

Plenabus ranted as he washed away the gore covering Grady. "The gouge is nearly deep enough to spoil the rune. Who does the drunken hemorrhoid blame, hm? The genius of generations. The dvergr who single-handedly ushered in a modern age. The one artificer with the imagination and skill to make ancient legends live again. None of this would be possible without me! Me!" Plenabus furiously scrubbed at a stubborn spot on Grady's cheek. It tickled.

A cracking sound filled the geode. The crystalline cocoon shattered as his hand reached up to his cheek. The rest of it crumbled away, dissipating into dust. The crystals defining the space brightened as the sourceless illumination returned. Grady floated, free in the center of it all.

"Ow! Hm, what? Curious, yes." Plenabus's beard brushed Grady's shoulder and his breath, hot and redolent with cured meat, blew over Grady's face.

"Back off!" The avalanche rumble of his voice echoed in the space. He had spoken. The artificer's presence disappeared with a surprised squawk.

Hoping, despite himself, Grady tried to open his eyes.

The geode world winked out and Grady found himself staring up at a clockwork mass of blade-tipped, metal limbs; Plenabus's golem making machine. He let out a short scream of surprise, held up his hands to ward off any suddenly descending blades, and scooted backwards with his heels. Grady fell. His shoulders clattered against the stone floor as his feet clanked against a metal table in passing. He scrambled to his feet and backed away against the far wall.

When he touched his fingers to his forehead, the pain flared up and made him wince. *I winced.* He held his hands in front of his face. His palms were smooth stone, but his fingers flexed like fleshy appendages. They opened and closed at his whim. The silver runes and lines carved into the backs of his hands glinted in the familiar and unnatural light.

A deep breath confirmed his burgeoning hope. As air filled his chest nothing changed. All was as it should be. Grady was his own again.

Across the room, Plenabus watched on in horror. He stammered, frantically searching for answers with his eyes, as if both the why and how were hidden behind the table or off in the corner.

Pain and guilt alloyed into rage, launched Grady across the room. Through a film of red he watched his hands wrap around Plenabus's scrawny neck, tightening and tightening. The old dvergr's palsied hands, one encased in that damned bronze contraption, scraped uselessly against Grady's vice-like grip. Plenabus's face purpled and his protruding tongue swelled. It would take so little to pop the artificer's head from his neck.

Grady wrestled back control. The thoughtless, rage-inspired drive to violence was too similar to a command's forced obedience. If Plenabus was to die by Grady's hand, let it be a deliberate choice, one he fully owned.

The bronze apparatus clinked against the rune at the bend of his wrist. A jolting zap turned Grady's world white. Paresthesia coated his body, numbing him in a wash of pins and needles. The whiteness cleared, revealing the ceiling of Plenabus's lab. His body twitched of its own accord, back to ignoring Grady's silent commands.

That didn't last long.

Plenabus gulped down large breaths in between bouts of hacking coughs. Grady caught a glimpse of him crawling closer, leading with his bronze appendage. It tapped his ankle. Another zap washed the world away and redoubled the fading paresthesia. Plenabus now straddled Grady's hips.

Fury washed away any hint of dotery in the old dvergr. He plunged the shocking aperture into the rune over Grady's heart. That time the zap brought on mind-wiping pain and a large synchronized jerk from Grady's body. Plenabus shocked him again and again, until the rage faded and he panted with exertion.

When Plenabus spoke, his voice was rougher, its saw-screech cracked and abraded. "Do you like that, hm? Does it hurt in there?" He jabbed again, sending another jolt of energy through Grady. "You must think me as foolish as Salzum. I know, Grady. I have always known you were in there, yes. The scrolls were clear. To be remade as a golem was once an honor reserved for the wisest elders and the most skilled, hm, master craftsman. It was a blessing created to preserve their knowledge and wisdom." He tapped the rune on Grady's forehead. "This rune came much later."

Plenabus grew quiet as he watched the twitches overtaking Grady's body weaken. The prickling faded suddenly. Master of his own limbs again, Grady lashed out. Ready, Plenabus shocked him again, this time holding the device against his chest.

"I must make a note of that. Seems the periodic application of electricity only incapacitates you for a minute, hm, two at most." Plenabus slipped his hand free from the bronze apparatus. He fiddled with it, affixing it to Grady's chest. He cursed a few times as his hands fumbled their tasks.

A tap of Plenabus's finger on the back of the device sent a consistent stream of power into Grady. The flood of external energy filled his body and forced Grady back into the confines of his mind. Grady internally gritted his teeth and bore it. The sensation hurt less than the punishment for failing to follow a command. It did not overwhelm him like the carving.

The only way out is through.

"My child, you made the same, hm, mistake Salzum continues to make. You underestimated me. Knowledge is the true power, you see? Not military prowess." Plenabus sagged deeper into the chair, his age and the weight of all he'd done too much for a moment. "He looks at you, at your potential, and what does he see, hm? A soldier, a weapon of war and destruction. Foolish. Short-sighted, yes. Blind to history."

Plenabus leaned forward with his forearms braced on his knees. His head drooped. "Do you know what I see? I see a worker who doesn't tire. Doesn't, hm, eat. Never gets sick. One who never gets bored, yes. One impervious to the dangers of the most perilous tasks. I see freedom for countless future dvergr. A freedom from the, hm, necessary drudgery that keeps the mountain functioning. They will have time to dream, philosophize, and invent. They will see the return of the golden age our ancient ancestors experienced. We will bring that about, Grady. My genius and your, hm, sacrifice, the sacrifices of your Clanless kin." Plenabus raised his head and looked down at Grady convulsing on the floor. "I envy your agelessness. You will live to see that greatness. I must be content to be but a single droplet that will never see the stalactite it builds."

Grady heard the pop of Plenabus's knees over the clattering convulsions of his own body. He walked past Grady and opened the door to his lab. "One of you fetch the Keyrdegen. Tell him Radix is awake and off-leash." He passed Grady again on his way to a lever filled control panel. "History will roll past this moment just like all the others. Eventually, Salzum will tire of playing mercenary captain. It won't be long before he realizes that even if we transformed every Clanless on the Floor, the resulting army will not be large enough to suit his, hm, gluttonous ambition. There is no choice, yes, but to see this to the end." Two arms descended from the ceiling. Instead of blades each sported a large steel clamp. One grabbed Grady by the head, the other a leg, and lifted him back onto the table.

The arms retracted as he clanged onto the metal surface. One caught the bronze device, sending it clattering and sparking to the floor.

The corralling, full body pain ended abruptly as the current of energy surging through him ceased. Grady seeped back into his body, slowed by the unpleasant tingling.

Plenabus's back faced Grady as he annotated some piece of parchment on his desk. It took effort for Grady to leverage himself off the metal table. He leaned back onto it when his knees buckled. His body, still reeling from the electric assault, felt weak. He crossed the room in two wobbly steps, hands outstretched.

Plenabus turned at the noise and squeaked out a sharp "How?" Grady hit him with an awkward backhanded swing. The artificer bounced off the near wall and fell to the floor. The back of his head was bloody from the impact and one of his arms lay bent at an impossible angle. A red stain spread at the elbow of his pristinely white lab coat.

The room was blurry and his body felt heavy. *Almost like it's made of stone.* He tried a few breaths but his vision remained fuzzy. *I have to get out of here. He's coming.*

Grady backed up until he was pressed against one of the cabinets on the wall opposite the door. His first step faltered, growing steadier as each step added to his momentum. There wasn't enough space to build up too much speed. He lowered his shoulder and hoped this was enough.

The metal door bent around Grady's shoulder, breaking the hinges and tearing the bolts partially from the wall. Grady and the door landed unevenly on top of something bulky and armored. A gauntleted hand poked out from underneath. The impact of one metal door and one stone dvergr managed to knock the warrior out.

Grady sat next to the door and took stock of his situation. The Artificer's Spire must be filled with members of the Throng by now. If he had to fight his way out of here, so be it. His muscles failed him as he leaned down to retrieve the fallen guard's hammer. Seemed like walking was the extent of what he could do now.

I bet they'll just let me walk out if I ask really nicely, he thought. He tried to vent his frustrations by slamming his fist on the ground, but he missed and hit the downed guard's gauntlet. *Oh. That's an idea.*

Straining his ears to listen for the sound of approaching boots, he shifted the door off the unconscious warrior. "Where on the Wall are they growing dvergr this big?" He clapped a hand over his mouth. Grady hadn't meant to say that out loud. At least it came out as a whisper.

The veteran warrior was a head taller and a hand wider than Grady. Why did everything always have to be so difficult? A lesson learned long ago at the Ground Floor Orphan Asylum for the Young and Clanless calmed him. "Beggar, not chooser. Take what you can get." Working as quickly as his blurred eyes and partially numb fingers allowed, he stripped the warrior.

No matter how he tightened the straps the guard's partially empty armor rattled on his frame. He rolled up the pant legs into thick cuffs to avoid tripping. There was nothing he could do about all the excess fabric sticking out between the pieces of the thronger's overlarge armor. "I guess looking like a child playing dress-up in a parent's clothes is less conspicuous than a naked stone dvergr running the halls." Grady hesitated as his hand hung over the guard's fallen hammer.

Rattling from down the hall made the decision for him. He scooped up the hammer and ran in the opposite direction. He held the Salzum-faced helmet tight against his head with one gauntleted hand and his breastplate in place with the other to keep his rattling to a minimum.

Empty space separated Grady from the Floor below and the Hold was the only building on the Roof with walkway access to the Spire. That left only one direction for Grady's great escape: up.

The route from Plenabus's lab to the Hold's walkway was etched into his mineral brain, but the rest of the tower remained a mystery. For a bunch of innovators and scientists, the spire's interior design was unimaginative. Every hallway contained a series of numberless doors lining art free walls. In his haze, Grady struggled not to double back as he turned randomly looking for a stairwell up to the Commons.

Grady stopped in the middle of another identical hall, lifted off the helmet, and listened. No shouts. No tromping. "Think, Grady. Think."

The Hold's main stairwell climbed up the center of the building. Lesser staircases ran along its outer wall to conceal the servants' comings and goings from their betters. Nothing of the Spire leaned toward convenience, so finding a central stairwell was his best chance. Grady closed his eyes and exhaled, trying to picture the route of his haphazard flight. "It was a left, then a right, then a right." Muttering to himself helped him think.

The darkness behind his eyes dropped away and the geode returned. Floating in front of Grady was a hazy blue outline of every corridor Grady knew on this floor of the Tower. "Huh. I didn't know I could do that." Grady tracked his path to where it ended at Plenabus's lab. The cursed room was off center, closer to the Hold. Grady had run to the clear opposite side of the Tower. "That means the outer wall of the tower should be about here." As he pointed the blue wireframe spun slightly, giving him a better view of where he stood right now. The center of the building, and his only certain means of ascent, was now between him and where he imagined his pursuers were. He opened his eyes.

Back in the hallway, Grady bounced on his feet a bit and moved his arms in big circles. He still felt depleted, despite his vision being back to normal. He needed more time to recover. Grady jogged forward, more concerned with gaining time than finding immediate escape.

After a couple of turns Grady stepped out into a circular corridor that ringed the circumference of the stalactite's interior. Nothing but the same unlabeled doors and empty hallways extended in either direction until his view was cut off by the curvature of the space. One way was as good as the other and yet Grady struggled to decide which way to go. His ability to choose felt atrophied after being dormant and unused for so long. The clamor of clanking armor and raised voices came from his right. He turned to dash to his left when a similar set of sounds stopped him in his tracks.

When the doorknob in front of him turned easily, Grady counted it as a small stroke of luck. He slipped behind the door and closed it gently. He turned the knob back slowly, hoping to avoid the loud click as the latchbolt slid into place.

The room's layout reminded Grady of his cell back in the thegen barracks. Personal touches added a homey air to the small space. Comfy looking blankets and pillows were heaped on the bed. A small painting of a smiling fringe-chinned dvergr sat on the desk, angled towards the empty chair. Feeling like an intruder, Grady tiptoed away from the door until his back pressed against the windowsill.

The sound of hustling armor grew louder until it stopped in front of the door to Grady's refuge. Two voices, audible, but indistinct, conversed for a moment. An unclear affirmative started the armor clanking again. It grew fainter. The patrol's passing presented Grady with the perfect opportunity to slip inside the dragnet and be free to make a break for the stairwell that was, hopefully, where he thought it was.

He tiptoed back to the door and reached for the doorknob. It turned before he touched it and swung inward. Grady leaped back and looked up into the shocked face of a dvergr dressed in stained artificer coveralls and small ribbons woven into her beard.

"Occupied," Grady said. The dvergr stumbled back at the sound of Grady's voice. He slammed the door shut and threw the deadbolt.

"Hey! Get out of my room! What are you doing?" The door rattled. Angry fists pounded into the door.

"Uh. Sorry. Official Throng business. We thank you for your patience." Grady backed away and spun in circles looking for a way out.

The window.

Drawn by the rightfully upset tenant's protests, the clanking of armor returned. Grady breathed in just so that he could sigh. He flung the gauntlets off his hands and tore the straps holding the breast plate together. The two halves clattered to the floor as Grady kicked off the ill-fitting boots and greaves. It was a testament to what his life had become that his new, mad plan felt sane and logical.

Shards of glass twinkled out into darkness when Grady punched the window. Hoping they didn't hit anyone far below on the Floor, he stuck his head and one shoulder through the opening and levered the rest of himself out. He sat on the ledge with his back to the open air, doing his best to focus on the wall in front of him.

Once again the artificer's minimalist style bit Grady in the ass. The statues, alcoves, and pillars that abundantly decorated the Hold's exterior offered an enterprising climber handholds and ledges galore. The artificers left the exterior of their spire alone. The untouched stone flowed and rippled like melted wax. It shimmered, slick and damp.

Grady closed his eyes. "Come on Grady, you are made of stone now. There is more to be afraid of back there. A little fall can't hurt you." He resisted the urge to peer past his perch to the distant Floor below. "Maybe." Grady felt above the sill. His fingers found a promising fold in the stone. He tugged to ensure the gap's edge wasn't about to crumble.

"The only way out is through." That settled, Grady hoisted himself out of the window and began to climb.

Grady heard a loud crunch as the door was bashed in. Shouts of "Where is it? Where did it go?" overlapped one another. Grady froze as a helmeted head leaned out of the window, peering downward. "It must have jumped! Spread the word. Tell the Keyrdegen. The Floor! Get a presence on the Floor." The helmet disappeared and the shouting grew quiet again.

The Floor was indistinct in the murky distance far below him. He quickly checked in with his guts. His tank was a third full. Grady hoped it would be enough. It had to be. He began to climb, using his toes as much as his fingers.

A sad voice drifted up from the window. "Aw. My door."

PART 4

An oath, in its most basic form, is a promise. To a warrior, to any true dvergr with the mountain in their bones, oaths act as the heart of their life's saga. They serve as predictions for the future and proclaim the truths one wishes to bring to the world. The words are important, but the soul, the meaning beneath matters more.

-Vinim the Wise, Vol. 1- *The Power of Words*

CLINGING TO HOPE

Climbing the exterior of the Artificer's Spire turned out to be relatively easy. The weakness and mild disorientation caused by Plenabus's electric shocks faded during the climb. His stone muscles never cramped, his grip remained sure, and the natural exterior offered plenty of hand and foot holds.

The Wall was distant enough that he didn't need to worry about being spotted. He hoped. He realized he was doing a lot of that lately.

Grady's energy reserves were lower, but not dangerously so, as he neared the Ceiling. The top of Rockhome's interior was left in its natural state. Skinny stalactites, about as long as Grady was tall, covered the Ceiling like tightly packed bristles.

Clinging to the Tower, Grady took a moment to contemplate the wondrous pair of choices before him: try to climb horizontally across a series of stone spikes and risk falling or reenter a vertical labyrinth full of warriors out to get him and return him to Salzum.

That settled it. Falling the great distance to the Floor and shattering was the least horrible option.

Grady hung on a rounded protrusion right where the Tower met the ceiling. He had hoped to climb up amongst the stalactites and sort of wedge himself in place and shimmy through them that way. Upon closer examination, his initial plan was not, in fact, going to work. The stone spears were bunched too tightly.

He reached out a hand to grab the nearest stalactite. The play yard of the Ground Floor Orphan Asylum for the Young and Clanless forced itself to the forefront of his mind. The Flat Ladder, a series of rungs spanning over a small drop, loomed over a young Grady. Forced by the encouragement of others, Grady jumped up and grabbed the first rung. He gulped looking down at the unyielding, bare rock beneath him. His grip had given out on the second rung. The ache in his knees had hurt far less than the howling laughter of his peers.

"This is a completely different situation," Grady said to himself. "I'm so much stronger now."

And heavier. And the 'rungs' on this obstacle are vertical and taper to points. And the drop is much farther. Much, much farther.

"Shut up, me." The matter settled, his hand closed around the nearest stalactite. Tugging dislodged neither his grip nor the rock spire itself. "What's one more crazy thing?" Grady's voice rumbled softly out above the city.

With a deliberate breath Grady swung free of the ledge. His momentum carried him to the edge of his reach and he grabbed the first stalactite he saw. It snapped off in his hand and tumbled down into the city below. Grady hung by one hand, his feet dangling free. His fear, unsupported by all the little biological reactions it normally inspired, was weak. "I think I overreached."

He grabbed a nearer stalactite, half a pace in front of him. It resisted his attempts to wiggle it and it held his weight as he let go of his first hold. This method made crossing the Ceiling slow and monotonous, but it worked. A few more of the rock spikes broke away when he tested them as he went. After the first, none caught him unaware. Hand by hand he crossed the ceiling, his eyes locked forward and never down.

The Western Wall grew closer and closer. Long swathes of the higher tiers of the Wall were open balconies. The lights and the sounds of voices grew closer with each new handhold. Grady's reserves were close to empty, he needed to get his feet back on solid stone and find some kind of fuel before he collapsed. He altered his path just to the left to ensure he reached the Wall under the cover provided by a large pillar carved to look like an ancient dvergr merchant. Grady thanked the long dead artisan who took the time to carve individual hairs in the figure's beard and the complex patterns on its clothes. He clambered down the dvergr statue's front and carefully peered past it.

The Wall interior was a riot of colors. Banners covered in the brown and gold tartans of Clan Pyrite hung everywhere. Open air shops filled large, stone alcoves scooped out of the mountain. A clump of dverger filled the opening of every shop. They talked animatedly to each other as they waited their turn to be seen by the shops' proprietors. The queues on the Floor were silent affairs. This seemed more fun. Grady found the general din relaxing. Unless he jumped out and shouted, no one was going to notice him.

Perched securely at last, Grady gave in to temptation and peered downward. The impenetrable veil of fog cleared for a moment and Grady's grip tightened instinctively. The Floor proper was a full 20 levels below him. The buildings were distinct, but identical cubes. Small dvergr dots hurried along the grid of walkways about their daily business. The rumble of the carts bounced around at the edge of his hearing. Grady watched it all for a moment. Banal normality went about its way, unaware of the horrors playing out above.

The fog rolled back in and swallowed his view.

Grady clung to the statue, frozen in place by exhaustion and the reality of what he faced. The intermingled, tacky blood of the sacrificed troll, his only friend, and his would-be rescuers still covered his hands. The most powerful dvergr in Grady's world and an army of loyal warriors sought to reclaim him.

It took a moment to sink in. He did it. He had escaped! But what future was there for Grady as a stone abomination dredged up from the dark past? If there was no future, no hope, then why keep going at all? Why continue to struggle?

The only way out is through. *Besides, I can always give up later.*

A wobble in his arms set his first priority: find fuel. He climbed to the bottom of the statue and sidled his way along the divider between the two floors. Grady stopped when he heard a voice calling out above him.

"Grilled spider legs, four for three, eight for five. So fresh they're practically crawling!" Those were good prices for a basket of grilled legs. On the Floor it was generally double that and they tended to be thin and more exoskeleton than anything else.

Grady sniffed the air. The smell of arachnid meat sizzling away did nothing to hide the smoky glory of burning charcoal. His quickly emptying gut demanded to be filled. It took every ounce of willpower left in Grady to keep from vaulting up and shoving handfuls of the charcoal, burning or not, into his mouth. Grady peeked above the edge of the balcony with great care. Behind the griller's shuffling boots he spied his prize, the toppled over sack of charcoal.

Grady never stole anything in his life before. There was nothing he ever really wanted enough to surpass his fear of the potential consequences.

He licked his lips and found the sound of his dry tongue rasping across his lips unpleasant. Another wobble, this time in his knees, pushed his hesitancy to the side. Grady grabbed the bag and pulled it away in a blur and ducked back down, squatting to make himself smaller. When there was no immediate alarm, Grady propped the bag on his knees and shoveled the fuel into his face by the handful.

Compared to the nice anthracite the Keyrdegen fed him, the charcoal tasted bland, verging on bad. He could taste the impurities and inefficiencies within the charcoal. Grady felt his energy returning, but a feeling in his gut told him he would run through this latest meal quicker than he was used to. Only a few briquets remained when Grady's hunger was sated and his tank full. He hesitated as he lifted the sack to return it to the griller's side. It was a long climb down and he was not sure how long the subpar fuel would last. He tucked the sack into his belt.

It was easier going now that he was energized. His path was paved by ancestors all the way down. The Ceiling was far enough above him now that Grady was unable to make out the individual stalactites. Despite the urgency he felt to be back on the Floor and not so high up, the lives he saw playing out within the Wall, so different from anything he knew, intrigued him.

On the Floor you kept your head down and spoke to others only when necessary. The dvergr milling about in West Wall walked tall. He watched one dvergr, carrying a basket brimming with groceries, greet every person she passed by name. She stopped for a nice chat with a mushroom seller. Asked about her shift, her family, how the little one's cold was doing. In Grady's experience, trying that on a Floor-based merchant would get you punched for sticking your nose into another's business.

On the tenth level, half-way down, Grady listened in to an argument over prices.

"After what your grandma did to my aunt you are lucky I am not charging you more. You aren't getting these plates for a single coin less!"

"That's a load of dross! After the Pot Luck Incident, you are lucky I am buying from you at all! On my ancestors dead and gone, I'm not paying more than twelve."

His curiosity got the best of him and Grady risked a peek past the statue to the arguing pair. Both dvergr sported beards of white and were at least in their fourth-hundreds, if not nearing their fifths, and were enamored with the wagging of fingers in faces. How long ago did the offenses happen? Hundreds of years ago? More probably.

Truly, an excessive amount of time to bear a grudge. Was it every Clanned dvergr's duty to remember every slight done to every member of your family or your clan? The packs of Clanned dvergr making their way across the floor suddenly made more sense. There was safety in numbers and more witnesses ensured that no slight would go unnoticed.

It must be stifling to be tied so tightly to the past. The closest Grady got was the long line of dvergr who had lived in his tiny room since it was carved from the mountain's bones. They were hypothetical shadows, weightless and ephemeral. The only wrongs he had to worry about were the ones done to him. The brightness and warmth of life in the Wall was wondrous, but Grady would bet his last pieces of charcoal that more than a few Clanned Wall dwellers would envy Grady's freedom from past entanglements.

Grady climbed into the dvergr-made cloudlayer. Even his stone nose found the airborne remnants of industrial efforts and impurities foul. Grady chose not to breathe until he was free of the miasma. This layer's balcony was enclosed by large metal shutters. Effectively blinded, Grady slowed and was forced to climb by feel.

He was happy when he left the fog behind, until he looked down. The Floor, once so distant and theoretical, was much closer. The dots were now people. Grady could not make out their faces, but their clan markings, or lack thereof, were clear enough. Clinging to the wall where he could see everyone, meant that everyone could see him. Grady felt exposed. He picked his way carefully down the next couple layers, taking his time and looking for an opportunity to get some proper clothing, set on continuing his new life of crime.

Four layers up from the Floor, a storefront filled with coveralls spilled out onto the balcony. To better display their goods, the store's purveyor had a number of choice garments hanging over the railing. Grady stepped on some beloved ancestor's eyebrow and raised himself with care to see if the coast was clear. The sales-dvergr was haggling loudly with a customer over a pair of sharp red coveralls. Eyes locked on the arguing duo, Grady grabbed at a pair of dark blue coveralls and darted back below the railing to the relatively secure footing of the dvergr statue's wide boots.

Grady examined his prize in horror. Instead of the blue pair he aimed for, he had grabbed a bright orange set. In a panic he crumpled up the coveralls as small as they would go and climbed sideways away from the scene of the crime. Grady stopped when the noise of commerce grew quieter. He did a pull-up for a quick look and found himself staring down a narrow alley between the backs of two rows of shops. Grady hoisted himself over the railing and darted into the shadows.

He dressed himself in the damp of the alley while he wondered what purpose the dark narrow stretches served. The coveralls were a bit too big and billowed as he moved, but the fact they were hooded made up for the ill fit. He covered his head and face in the orange hood and shoved hands into his pockets. Grady wiggled his stone toes at a loss for how to hide them. Perhaps the bright fabric covering his body would draw the eyes up and away from his plain gray feet. Grady left the alley holding his breath, his hunching shoulders braced for screams of horror, as accusing fingers pointed at his rocky appendages.

The dvergr of West Level Four paid no attention to the smaller than average, orange-clad pedestrian. No one stopped him or called out to him. They all had shopping to do, errands to run, full lives to lead. Grady walked with the flow of foot traffic heading towards the nearest bank of elevators. If anyone thought it odd he was traveling alone and wasn't wearing his clan's colors, they didn't stop him to say so.

Advertisements for shops, restaurants, shows, and services were plastered everywhere that wasn't someone's private shop. He spotted one for a clothing store named Coveralls Are Us and one for a hat store named Top 'Em Off Haberdashery. He passed a small, steaming kiosk sporting a painted sign that read 'Chew-dles'.

"Heh. Chew-dles," Grady said under his breath. Life on the Floor required so much practicality, there was no room left for the merest hint of whimsy. The lack of a throat to burn hollowed out the raw jealousy that surged through Grady. Seeing funny-ish signs every shift didn't guarantee an easy life. *Would have cushioned the blow a little. Maybe.*

Quieter avenues branched off the long concourse. Lichens and moss softened the area and added color. Beardless children, too young to apprentice anywhere, ran about kicking an inflated bladder and crying out with excitement. A pair of adults chatted sitting on a blocky home's stoop as they watched the children play. One rose to comfort a child who fell and scraped their knee. Grady turned and hurried away from the joy and simple kindness, lest his mere presence taint it.

A casual hate for the people of the Walls untwisted from his heart as he made his way through their world. Yes, they lived the lives that Grady dreamed about. Everywhere was a riot of colors. Their existences were chock-full of relationships; friends, family, and enemies. Everyone here had a place they belonged, where they fit.

Though, this close up he was beginning to see the cracks. There was a clear hierarchy among the Clanned. If your tartan matched the proprietor of any given shop you were shown more respect and allowed to cut in line. Grady witnessed the Pyrite Clan's shopkeepers act nastily towards Feldspar Clan food vendors and the food vendors sneered right back. The Walls were not the solid igneous formation he always believed they were. The city was built on a foundation of sediment, filled with faults.

Overwhelmed by everything, arriving at the elevator banks was a relief. Without his companion armor and the status that came with it, Grady took his spot in the back of the line. He kept his head down and waited. The line was short, most people on this level only had eyes for going up. Below here were poorer levels, with cheaper shops and the homes of the less well off, then the great warehouses of Level 1, and then the Floor. An attendant waved their group forward as one of the great elevators sunk into place. He walked forward with his cohort and entered the metal box manned by the uniformed attendant.

"Destinations?"

People shouted their desired levels all at once, catching Grady off guard. "Floor!" Every head in the elevator swiveled to look at him.

Grady sunk into his hood and coughed. "Small cold." The crowd pushed back, opening up a space around him.

By the time the elevator touched down only Grady and the attendant were left. "Last stop. Floor." She pulled a lever and the accordion door retracted. As Grady passed her she said, "Feel better."

Despite himself Grady laughed, turning it into another cough halfway through. "Thanks." *If only.*

FACES OF THE LOST

Grady wandered, lost in his thoughts, trying to see what came next. If everything worked out as originally planned, Dulane and his allies would have had everything in hand. It took effort for Grady to keep their deaths from playing out in his head on a constant loop. His body never tired, but the maelstrom of physical and mental trauma wore away at his heart.

A shift in the flow of dvergr around him pulled Grady from his reverie. Identical blocks of tenements, just like the one Grady used to call home, surrounded him. A crowd was gathered in front of a wall plastered with pictures. The majority of the watching crowd wore gray, but a few brightly clad individuals hovered around the edges.

The crowd focused on a Clanless dvergr speaking with passion from atop a crate that raised her head and shoulders above the crowd. "...after shift. Nothing. Weeks have gone by. Weeks! Instead of searching for the missing, thegen prowl our streets maintaining bloody order with the ends of their batons." She held up an arm to better display the livid bruise on her bicep. The gray members of the crowd booed in agreement. The bright spots shared concerned looks.

"How many more Clanless need to disappear before something is done? What happened when little Sandry of Hematite went missing two turns ago? The search turned the whole mountain upside down. Twenty and five Clanless, citizens of Rockhome, our family and friends, are missing right now. Where's the outcry? The prayers? For Sandry, white banners were hung from every balcony, offerings were heaped to Ancestors and Founders all across the city. What has been done for the twenty and five? Nothing. You know why!"

The Clanless of the crowd shouted angry agreement in one great voice.

"To them," the speaker pointed dramatically towards the distant palaces hanging above, "we who have no clan are nothing." Angry tears spilled down the speaker's cheeks. She took a shuddering breath. "We want our people found, our friends and family returned to us." The speaker paused here and looked down reverently. "Even if it's only their bones. They deserve to be honored and known. Until they are found, I say we, the gray, Clanless masses show those above what our true worth is. Let them wear down with labor. Face the dangers of the mine. It would be hard to hold us down with their hands cramped into a claw from centuries of scribing. They can breathe the smell of their own waste and clean up after themselves. Until the twenty and five are returned, we must strike! Strike! Strike!" The speaker pumped her fist into the air with each shout.

The crowd picked up the chant, every Clanless fist punched towards the Roof in defiance. The few Clanned dvergr along the outskirts of the audience hurried away, hunched and frightened. Grady, mouth hanging open, watched the dvergr chant. Clanless from different families speaking as one. They chanted for strangers in support of one another. He forgot to breathe.

A wild impulse gripped Grady. He reached up to pull back his hood.

"Disperse!" A cadre of thegen rounded the corner and squared up in front of the crowd. Their leader, a Salzum faced member of the Throng, yelled into a cone-shaped loudhailer. The warriors menaced the Clanless with 'shroomwood clubs padded with leather. "This is an illegal gathering. The Keyrdegen has granted us leave to use violence to keep the Mountain's peace. Go back to your homes or places of employment now."

The speaker hopped down from her crate. "Run! Don't give them the pleasure of cracking your skull. Spread the word! Strike! Strike!"

Most of the Clanless scattered away from the armored bullies. A few belligerent dvergr continued to shout. "Slag the Keyrdegen! And slag you! Strike!" They held their ground as the warriors advanced.

Grady froze at the sight of the approaching silvered Salzum. As the rioters charged the armored line, as the clubs fell to their bruising work, Grady ran.

The clack of his feet on the stone pathways carried him off. The fracas's noise faded in the distance. He dipped behind a building and flattened himself against the wall, panting loudly and terrified. He pulled the orange hood down over his eyes. "You coward. Why did you run? Why?" Grady slammed the back of his head against the wall with each question.

His forehead burned. Dulane's voice, accusing and hateful in a way it never was in life, berated him. "You could have taken them. Protected those people. But you ran. You failed them. You failed to save me. Worthless. Coward. Brick. Erratic."

"Shut up." Grady growled and balled his fists. He shut his eyes tight trying to block out the voice.

Dulane's voice morphed, tightening and rising into Plenabus's vile screech. "You were such a weak, hm, specimen. Bland and alone. I gave you strength. Made you unique. Valuable. You are a wasted application of my gift, yes, a true waste."

"Shut up!" Grady punched himself in the face. The world rocked to the side and his head slammed against the wall. There was an impact, but no pain. He punched himself again. And again.

The screech warbled. When it stilled, Salzum's voice rang clear. "You are nothing more than a tool, a soulless weapon, for my hand to give purpose. My word alone empowers you. Makes you capable. A slayer of trolls. An executioner of traitors."

"No!" Grady dropped to his knees and pounded his forehead into the ground.

There was the pain. The impact of the ground against his mithril-caused wound sent fiery lances of agony to the very tips of his extremities. He did it over and over until he trembled with physical suffering.

"Grady…"

"No," he moaned in his old voice. "Not you too."

"Grady, where's the spark?" Emerlda's voice was kind and soft. It washed over him, coating his pain like oil on water.

"It's gone, 'Merlda. They took it from me. Snuffed it out. I tried to hold on to it for so long. It carried me so far."

"It remains right where it always was." The voice changed again as it spoke. It roughed into the avalanche voice of the Golem. "Dvergr are born in the dark. The dark made us what we are, it is in our bones. We love the dark because when it is blackest, the smallest light shines all the brighter."

The voice became Grady's own this time, but stronger, stripped of meekness and self-deprecation. "We love our stories, too. We let them tell us who we are, what we are worth. True power comes from realizing you are the only person who can write your story, shaped by your deeds and words. Have you made an oath you want to keep, tasks you must accomplish, Grady of No clan?"

He remembered the dead and mutilated body on top of Plenabus's table. At the time, the lunatic inventor numbered his captives at a dozen. Twenty-five, now. He'd sworn to rescue them. If not him, then who? "Yes."

"Have wrongs been done to you that need redress?" the Golem asked.

"Yes. Many."

"Are you a dvergr?" Dulane asked.

"Yes."

Dulane again. "Are you thegen?"

Grady paused. Was he? After all he'd done, could he truly be?

Dulane's voice lessened to a breathy whisper before fading away. "Swear again. Speak your oath. Walk your Way and none will question your honor or bravery. Not even yourself."

Grady grew still. The stone ground felt cool and almost soothing on his head wound.

"Uh, hey. Friend? Are you okay? I heard some sort of banging out here."

Grady looked up at a young dvergr with his first braids and the beginnings of a decent mustache. The dvergr gasped at Grady's face and brandished his straw broom like a spear. "Sinkhole below! Whatwhat's wrong with your face? Where's your beard?"

Grady stood with care, his hands palm forward. "Easy." The young dvergr yelped at the rumble of the golem's, of Grady's voice. "I'm an actor? Yes, an actor. This is all makeup. Beard was a sacrifice for the part, yeah. I was rehearsing a scene. Tada."

The broom lowered and the fear on its wielder's face shifted to confusion. "Uh, ok. Sure. Well done?"

"Thank you." Grady laid on the false bravado. "Sorry to bother you. Thanks for the use of the back of your... uh... building. Bye!" Grady turned and trotted away before the other dvergr could respond.

Once he was around the corner, Grady stopped to listen. The dvergr didn't follow. Grady moved with purpose, relying on his crystalline recall to retrace his steps. It took him longer than he thought it would to return to the wall covered in missing posters. He'd run so far.

The thegen and rowdy protesters were gone. A steady stream of pedestrians walked by. The few colorfully dressed dvergr hunched their shoulders as they passed. The Clanless pedestrians stared as they walked. A couple spared a sneer for Grady, standing in that spot of reverence in his brightly colored coveralls.

The only sign of the clash between the warriors and the protesters were some flecks of blood browning as they dried on the ground. Grady touched the droplets in silent apology. Standing solemnly, Grady looked closer at the posters. The pictures were approximations at best, drawn from descriptions of the lost. Their names were written in large, red letters beneath each face. Underneath that names, written in black identified who the lost were missed by, who reported them missing, or who should be informed when they were found.

Grady scanned each face, burning them into his memory. He worked methodically, row by row. Many of the faces seemed half familiar, shadows of people he had passed while walking to work or ones he waited in line behind at the butcher's. He stared at the last poster the longest. The image wore a familiar and patchy beard. The artist had taken pains to depict bag laden eyes and a mouth turned down as if the dvergr tasted something a bit off.

"I smiled sometimes," he said with a defensive mutter.

There was his name, Grady, written in the same red as the others. Someone noticed. Someone missed him enough to consign a poster, maybe more if there were other shrines to the missing across the floor. But who?

The phantom of Grady's heart lurched at the sight of the name underneath his. *Emerlda.* Grady placed his hand on his missing poster. He could almost feel the letters of her name.

In the alley Dulane's voice commanded Grady to swear his oath anew. But with what words? The traditional warrior's oath barely applied to Grady. He had no known ancestors to implore. No craft or clan to abandon. What good is an oath so easily twisted into blind servitude to a power-hungry monster by the addition of a mere sentence?

To walk his Way, Grady's words must be his own.

Grady closed his eyes and thought about what story he wanted his life to tell. "I will carve this oath on my soul, deed by deed. I will speak truth to power and give voice to the silent. I will protect the threatened and punish the deserving. With violence in one hand and succor in the other, I will walk my Thegen Way." Grady intended to end there, but his oath felt unfinished. *Oh, yes. What good is a warrior otherwise?* "I will heed the horn's call." The hushed words rang loud in his ears and settled into his bones. The faces of the missing bore silent witness.

"Word is he was the first."

Grady whirled around, fists half up. It was the passionate dvergr from before. He relaxed and stuffed his hands in his pockets. Despite being smaller and slighter than Grady, her inner fierceness made her seem larger and more imposing. He tugged his hood farther over his face and wracked his brain for something to say. "Huh?" He never ceased to amaze himself.

"That one, there at the end. Grady. He was the first to disappear, or the first one noticed. It's hard to say." She walked up next to Grady, to stare alongside him. She shook her head bitterly. A bite entered her voice. "All of the missing come from small families. Some were even orphans." She shuddered a little and rubbed at the tattooed family names on her upper arms like she was chilled. "It's easy to ignore gray things. They blend in with the background."

Her ire flared and she turned on Grady. She pointed an admonishing finger at him, her patience with the quiet intruder at its end. "Time to move on Clanned. Slum it somewhere else. Go home. Go back to your people. Your pity counts for less than nothing."

Grady went to shrug again and to leave without argument, but stopped mid hunch. He now walked his Way, an oath was sworn. He was done being scared. Time to tell the truth. "This is my home. They are my people." He turned to face the brave, small rabble rouser. A good look at Grady killed the question on her lips, dropped her jaw, and widened her eyes. "I am Clanless. I am gray." In his hands, his bright orange coveralls tore away from his torso. The tatters hung behind him, the legs held up by a cinch at his waist.

The stunned dvergr looked Grady up and down, unsure of what she was seeing. She backed up with her arms warding him off.

"Don't be scared-" Her scream cut Grady off and she ran away into the stream of pedestrian traffic. Her flight drew the attention of the other dvergr who, upon seeing Grady, added their own voices to the growing chorus of fearful shouts. Grady watched as the people rushed away from him. Some called out for the thegen, while others shouted for the horn to be sounded, warning of 'monsters' or 'invaders' as they ran.

Grady rubbed a hand over his smooth, bald, head listening to the screaming voices as they trailed off. "For some reason I expected that to go better." Grady spun in a circle looking for inspiration, unsure of what his next step should be. A warning pang from his gut told him the charcoal from earlier was nearly used up. "Ok. That's settled. First I find some foo- fuel." There was work to do and a fight coming. He needed the good stuff.

A refinery smokestack, standing tall above the squat buildings, caught his attention. That would do. It had to.

With his disguise destroyed and everyone running away at the mere sight of him, the walkways were no longer an option. Grady needed a better vantage point and the top of the nearby building was as good as any. He bent his knees and jumped, trying to get high enough to catch his fingers on the edge.

"Whoa!" Grady overshot the roof's edge and landed in a tumbling roll on the roof itself. He looked down at the walkway below. "I did not know I could do that." A flash of his memory from the pit reminded him that he could, in fact, do that.

From atop the roof, the Floor's buildings became a grid of platforms stretching nearly from Wall to Wall. The widest gaps were between blocks, where walkways and cart paths separated the buildings. The refinery was easier to see as its boxy shape was another story taller than the surrounding buildings.

Speed was the key. He stood at the building's edge, furthest from his destination. "If you fall it won't hurt. It won't hurt." After a steadying breath, Grady sprinted with all his might towards the building's edge and leapt mid-stride onto the next closest building. He stumbled when he landed, used his hands to right himself, and scrambled forward, maintaining as much momentum as possible.

The second crossing was easier, as was the third. As he reached the last building on the block, he planted both feet and jumped. He sailed over the walkways, the cart track, and the heads of a few dvergr going about their business. Grady made eye contact and waved to the only dvergr below who was looking up. The dvergr waved back automatically. Grady landed in a roll on the far building, whooping as he got his feet back under himself and continued on his way.

Leaping and laughing, Grady traversed the Floor in a straight line towards the foundry and his next meal. Grady gave thanks that he and his waving buddy were the only dvergr in the city who ever looked up.

The roar of the refinery devoured more of the city's soundscape with each jump forward. For the first time in he wasn't sure how long, Grady's laugh boomed freely. *This must be what a boulder rolling down a mountain feels like.*

Grady was running on remnants by the time he stumbled to a halt on the last building before the refinery's fenced in yard. Just beyond the fence, he spotted a large pile of coal near the cart docks. A team of Clanless laborers filled wheelbarrows from the deposit, wheeled full ones into the refinery, and empty ones back out. Hunger drove Grady to leap down from his perch and walk right through the fence.

The barrow drivers were the first to see Grady. The first to start yelling and the first to run. The shovelers, minds on their toil, only looked up when coal tumbled from the barrows they were filling. All it took was one to look up and warn the others. They all ran off to join their coworkers in hiding.

Grady set to his meal with a will. It was tasty enough and Grady enjoyed the flaky mouthfeel. As his feeding frenzy slowed, he looked up from his food to see a group of dvergr spilling out of a side door watching him. They whispered in a nervous bunch. An overseer in Clan Hematite colors clutched his clipboard tightly to his chest in the middle of the group.

Grady swallowed his current mouthful and sat down with his legs crossed. He reached out and picked up a large chunk of coal about the size of a good potato. He took a bite out of it. "I'm being rude," Grady said as he chewed. "Do you all want a bite?" He held the bitten coal out and smiled.

The rumble of his voice reignited their earlier panic and the Clanless laborers pushed back into the building, the overseer leading the way. The door slammed. Grady heard the distinct click of the door's bolt being thrown.

Alone, he took a moment to enjoy the feeling of a full stomach because he was free to do so.

A THREAT FROM BELOW

The horns started from the Wall nearest to where Grady revealed himself. The first peal had just ended when the others, mounted along the Walls and up high on the Roof, filled the city with their throaty calls. The great metal horns, twisted like a ram's, shook the air with their warning.

A danger from Below threatened the city.

How many of his dreams reverberated with the horns' call? Last time they sounded, Grady lost more than he could remember. The beasts that shift had rampaged through great swathes of the Floor. Before they finished, they took his family from him. They didn't even leave him their names. Only an impression of love and of being safe in warm arms remained.

Now, Grady was the monster, the danger. "At least the streets will be clear." Grady stood, licked his fingers, and dusted off his hands on his orange pants. He left the yard through the same hole he had created before.

The last horn blast took a while to fade as it reverberated in the hollow spaces of the Walls, the Floor, and the Roof. It left the empty city quiet and still. The carts on their tracks were stopped. Even the Clanless stevedores loading and unloading the goods were sheltered somewhere safe. The factories ceased their rumbling productions. The billowing plumes of smoke rising from various crucibles and furnaces slowed to a trickle.

No matter how carefully Grady stepped, the sharp tick tack of his stone feet echoed, too loud in this new, unprecedented stillness. As he walked, he planned.

A simple trip back up the Wall, across the ceiling, and back into the Artificers' Spire through a window would suffice for a mission of pure revenge. Never a wrathful dvergr, vengeance's magnetic pull unsettled Grady. Yes, he had hurt Plenabus during his escape, but the fact that he might still be alive was a wrongness that cried out for redress. The image of the ancient dvergr stomped to paste under his feet disgusted Grady only slightly more than it thrilled him.

A fitting end for Salzum needed to be more poetic. He needed to be brought low. Grady imagined breaking his arms and legs. Of hoisting the bloated ruler over his head and hurling him through the bay window of his study to watch him fall and diminish until he was no more.

"I will protect the threatened and punish the deserving." Grady mumbled the words to himself as a reminder. He chose the order deliberately. And while Plenabus and Salzum more than deserved some killing, there were twenty odd dvergr in need of help. Getting in was not enough. He needed a way out too.

That settled things and made his path forward clear.

Grady reached the North Wall's elevators without seeing a single dvergr. He expected a few peeking eyes and worried whispers, but no one dared to ignore the alarm. Ancestors forbid. Grady forced the accordion doors open to reveal an empty elevator shaft. "They must raise the elevators to keep invaders from having easy access to the Walls," Grady said with a sneer. "Of course they do. Gotta keep the denizens of the Wall safe and sound."

He sighed. Grady was in for another climb.

Rudimentary ladders, built of depressions carved into the rock, ran up either side of the elevator shaft. A larger dvergr might have struggled a bit, but Grady's delicate hands and narrow feet fit well into the shallow grooves. Grady rose into the silent gloom. The doors to each level were closed and shuttered by an additional wall of metal. He climbed until the elevator car, parked at the very top, blocked his progress. Grady ran his fingers over the smooth plate filling the space above him. The only way up was through.

He dug his toes into one rung and the fingers of one hand to another, securing himself. Grady did his best to ignore the empty shaft beneath him as he leaned out into space as far as his arm allowed. Braced in position, he punched upward with his free hand. The first punch did little but ding the metal. He fell into his body and let it work like the machine it was.

At first he only managed to fill the shaft with loud noises. It took twenty blows to put a fist-sized dent into the thick plating. The deformity grew and the metal paled as it warped under the rain of blows. When the dent swallowed his fist to the wrist, Grady decided it was time for a new tactic.

He had to wiggle his hand to free it from the bent metal. Grady straightened his fingers, splaying them slightly. With a roar, he stabbed upwards. The stressed metal screeched as his fingers pierced through. Grady gritted his teeth with the effort it took to close his fingers into a fist and grip the metal. Using his new grip as leverage, Grady dangled for a moment. He repositioned his feet on a higher rung and grabbed his trapped wrist with his free hand.

He heaved. A swath of the metal groaned in protest as Grady peeled it back, making a hole wide enough for him to climb through. He hoisted himself into the car with ease. Laying there, the long drop beneath him replaced by solid metal, Grady indulged in some panting. Despite the lack of physical exertion, it felt right to do. A bit of the tension in his mind eased.

"Now for the easy part," he said. He stood and brushed at the orange knees of his pants. He threw the lever to open the accordion doors. Nothing happened.

Grady brute forced them open to reveal the Roof's closed shutter. The shutter resembled a mini-portcullis with the crossbars laid out over more solid metal behind them. In comparison, the buildings of the floor went unprotected by their doors of flimsy mushroom wood. Old stone hatchways, easily smashed, capped the emergency shelters.

His people's defensive philosophy of putting solid metal between themselves and the danger was simple but effective. Especially when coupled with the fact that eating or killing the lower denizens slowed down the invaders and provided more time to organize defenses and protect the lives of the Clanned citizenry.

"Slag that."

Grady's fingers could not fit under the shutter's lip. He looked back over his shoulder at the work he did to the elevator's floor. Grady squatted down and, with a roar for added effect, stabbed his fingers into the metal, denting it and creating a perfect handhold for himself. He lifted from his knees, pushing down through his feet and up through his shoulders.

The shutter slid smoothly up its track as Grady straightened. It took every muscle in his body to lift it to waist height. The portcullis weighed heavily in his hands, threatening to topple him forward. There was no way he'd be able to let go and roll under before it slammed back into place. It was another feat of marvelous dvergr engineering. And Grady needed to break it.

Grady slammed his forehead into the metal, grunting with the rekindled pain of the wound on his forehead. In a purposeful imitation of his earlier breakdown, Grady struck and struck again. The pain grew too great and he slumped down to his knees, his arms held up limply by his impaled fingers. The shutter held, pinned in place by the large crease Grady beat into its middle. His pain and effort earned him a gap large enough for an adult dvergr to crawl under.

"It'll do," Grady said, admiring his handiwork. He unstuck his fingers and crawled under the ruined shutter.

Many believed the giant chains carved into the ceiling above a celebration of dvergr ingenuity. No. Grady now knew their truth. They were the chains that bound countless dvergr to hardship and toil-filled lives and crushed all beneath their immeasurable weight. *Not me,* he thought. *Never again.*

The double-wide doorway at the end of the bay gaped, empty and dark. Either it was night in the world above or the sky lights had shutters of their own.

The sight of the Commons, empty of its normal swarm of servants and functionaries, unsettled Grady. The grass, hemmed in by the dim glow of the marble pathways and entrances, rustled in the lichen illuminated gloom. The unadorned cube that marked the entrance into the Artificer's Spire squatted off to his right. Its unassuming facade gave no hint at the terrors being enacted beneath it.

Without a single thegen or member of the Throng in sight, Grady allowed himself a small smile. He'd outsmarted Salzum and his warriors. Finally, things were working out in his favor.

Grady decided to cut across the grass. It tickled his feet as he stepped onto the lush mat of greenery. He indulged himself by wiggling his toes a little. A small pang of guilt soured his enjoyment. *While you enjoy yourself, others suffer. Focus.*

He took a breath and continued forward.

"Fire!"

A loud bang drew Grady's attention an instant before an enveloping weight struck him from the side. Its grip tightened as Grady struggled, immobilizing him with his face pressed into the grass. The damp soil beneath his nose smelled alive.

The voice came from above him, furious and commanding. "Flip it over."

It took two of his captors to flip him over with a grunt. Five helmeted heads stared down on Grady, boxing in his vision. The mesh wiring, pressing against his pinned-open eye, blocked out most of the details. The blurred silver in the center closed in. It sharpened into a Throng member's Sazlum shaped faceplate. A rose gold star marked the brow.

"It's small. How did this thing kill the Captain?" Asked the head topped with a point and the knotted swirl of a blond beard beneath. Grady felt a thump on his arm and the head howled in pain.

"Idiot," said the horned head with the red whiskers. "Might as well kick an anvil. Keyrdegen meant it when he called it ugly. Really undersold it though. Why do you think Plenabus built it to look like that?"

"Enough blathering and stay sharp. You heard the horns. This thing killed a Clan Chief and her entire retinue. It murdered our Captain."

The tight net held Grady's jaw in place, forcing him to speak through his teeth. "The Keyrdegen made me do it!"

"It can talk?" Redbeard sounded more astonished than frightened.

"You have to pay better attention in the briefings." Blondy's tone was full of well-practiced recrimination. "The Keyrdegen said the thing was built to be as dvergr-like as possible. It doesn't really talk. Just mimics what it's heard before."

"I'm not a machine! My name is Gr-" The thronger slapped a thick leather gag over his mouth, garbling the rest of Grady's protest. A tug tightened the metal of the roller buckle against the back of his head. He'd been prepared to shut Grady up. The Throng knew the truth.

"To the Hold. Honor and Glory are ours this shift. For the Captain!" the leader shouted.

"The Captain!" they replied dutifully.

Under any other circumstances their struggle to lift Grady would have been humorous. It took all of them working together to raise him off the ground enough to move. Grady's body twisted in ways that made it difficult for the larger dvergr to distribute his weight. They huffed and groaned, taking a few meager steps before one of them lost their footing and Grady fell back into the grass.

"Let's try dragging it," the Salzum masked squad leader ordered. He clipped a rope to the mesh of the net over Grady's pate. Straining to look past his forehead, Grady watched the squad take places along the rope and pull. He didn't budge.

Clods of grass and dirt flung into view as they attempted one last heave. One slipped and they all tumbled out of Grady's eyeline. A brief argument about who tripped who ensued before the squad leader shouted it down. "Hoist it onto the walkway, then," the thronger snapped.

They managed to lift him and quick march to the marble walkway, where they dropped him into place. They retook their earlier positions on the rope, but with a few shoves this time. Working together they dragged Grady along the marble. Grady's elbow, trapped between his back and the ground, scraped at the softer stone producing an ear-spiking shriek.

Their bumbling provided Grady with ample time to assess his situation. Grady needed leverage to bring his strength to bear. His arms, one twisted behind him and the other wrapped across his collar bone, were useless. His legs were pinned together and the toes of one foot were curled back by the mesh's pressure. The other foot was pointed. The mesh pressed the hardest against the back of his head and the points of his extended toes, creating places to push against.

Harder you push, stronger you are. While this axiom from one of Dulane's first lessons had nothing to do with being trapped in a net, the principle remained the same.

Grady pressed outward with care lest his captors notice the growing tension. He straightened out his body and bore down through his leg, pushing against the mounting pressure centered at the top of his head and the tips of his toes. Grady inched the net closer and closer to its breaking point.

His captors continued to grunt and heave obliviously. One, it sounded like Red, griped about the ear piercing sound. "Worse than a fork and knife on a plate."

With a final thrust, Grady shoved his head and foot away from each other, rending the net at his toes. It sprung away when the tension broke. Grady flung his limbs out, expanding the tear and robbing the net of its power.

Free, he rolled as his captors started to shout. He came to his feet in the grass with the remnants of the net tied to his head by the gag. Grady tore the leather easily from his face and shooed at the net. It tumbled to the ground at his feet.

The warriors, veterans all, recovered their shock in an instant and charged as one. They trapped Grady in a ring of shields. Their briefing must have included Plenabus's notes from the first set of Grady's durability tests. Attacks lashed out at his legs from random points of the circle. Each impact messed up his footing and threatened to topple him.

Their tactic failed to take one crucial fact into consideration. This time Grady could move.

First, he needed room to think. Guided by his training at the foot of a master, Grady loosed a full-throated roar brimming with remembered pain and vestigial fear. Time slowed. One hand lashed out and grabbed a hammer right before it hit his leg. He grabbed the dvergr's wrist with the other hand and flung him into his compatriots to the side, knocking a hole into the circle.

Logic dictated he charge in while his opponents were in disarray and lash about himself with deadly force, but these dvergr were not the real enemy. They walked their Way, same as he. Only, their oath to the Keyrdegen guided them down the wrong path. Swearing the oath did not remove a warrior's ability to reason for themselves. Dulane proved that. They needed to know the truth of it and be given a chance to make the same choice.

Grady knew that this needed to end quickly before others noticed their scuffle. His attackers needed to be incapacitated.

I will speak only Truth.

Or reasoned with.

The thronger and one of the thegen advanced on Grady along the path. The others spread out into the grass to try and flank him. "I know what you were told, but I'm not a machine."

The squad leader raced ahead of the other warriors, roaring to drown Grady out. Grady blocked his attack with his forearm, grabbed him under the lip of his breastplate and twisted. The thronger flew over Grady's back and crunched to the pathway. His weapon arm sat oddly in the armor, dislocated at the shoulder and elbow. Grady gave him a light kick to his helmet to encourage him to stay down.

Then the others were upon him.

Dancing was never something Grady considered himself good at until that moment. He spun and dodged, catching attacks on his forearms and shins. "My name is Grady. I was a Clanless. The Keyrdegen and his artificer tricked me." A few blows landed on his torso and head doing little but draining his energy reserves. He ripped away one of the attackers' shields and threw it at another. "They turned me into this. I killed Dulane-" They growled and increased the intensity of their attacks. A blow caught him on the jaw, cutting him off.

Enough of this, Grady decided. *I will make them listen.*

His hands lashed out and grabbed two of the falling hammer blows. With mechanical speed and strength he crossed his arms and slammed the two warriors together with a crunch. They fell over, one groaning softly and the other unmoving. The remaining pair cut off their attack and retreated a few steps in opposite directions deeper into the grass.

Grady presented his open palms to his opponents. "I speak only the truth. I killed Captain Dulane and the others. At the Keyrdegen's orders. My will was not my own. I will bear their deaths all through this life and beyond." He hoped his sincerity was easily readable on his face. As he spoke he looked at each of the remaining thegen in turn. "I don't want to hurt you. There are others trapped below. At least twenty others. Innocent dvergr doomed to become more things like me or, if they're lucky, to die. Let me save them from my fate. Let me keep my oath. All you need to do is step aside."

The moment Grady looked away, the warrior to his right charged with a roar. "This is the Keyrdegen's will!"

Grady sighed and turned to face the charge. The warrior hit Grady's head with his hammer and gasped in pain at the impact. His weapon clattered against the pathway. Grady grabbed the dvergr by either side of his shoulders, lifted him off of his feet, and slammed his back hard into the ground. He kneeled on the warrior's chest and cocked back a crushing fist.

Grady stopped himself. *Remember Dulane. Remember who the monsters really are.* He contented himself by slapping the side of the groaning warrior's helmet. "Stay down, please," Grady said, wagging a finger in his face.

Slowly turning his head, Grady regarded the last thegen standing off in the grass. It was Blondey. "Are we done?"

The blond beard swayed as he looked from Grady, to his fallen squad mates, and back again. "I yield." He removed the helmet to reveal a soft, scar free face. He kneeled and bowed his head.

Grady positioned himself so all of the fallen dvergr were in front of him. None seemed to be in a rush to get up. "You heard the horn. They told you I was a machine, a murderous monster. Aren't you worried I'm going to kill you now?"

He looked up at Grady thoughtfully. "Not really. Can I see to my squad mates?"

Grady made a show of thinking about it. Part of him needed to know that the still dvergrs were not dead. He nodded. "What came next after you caught me?"

Blondy checked over his squad mates as he answered. "Our orders were to bring you back to the Hold. There are other squads at each of the elevators. Last report we had placed you down on the Floor. Thegen were mustering to begin searching for you down there. Volklechek," Blondy nodded towards his Throng squad leader, "was grousing about our post. About being denied a chance at earning more glory. Careful what you prospect for, eh?"

The square entrance to the Artificer's Spire pulled at him. He was wasting time. "Do I need to tie you all up or anything?"

Blondy checked Volklechek's pulse and smiled. "These lot don't look like they will be ready to go anywhere any time soon. Concussions and broken limbs are no joke." A knot in Grady's soul loosened at the news that everyone was alive, if not whole. "I think we will wait here, at our post, for help."

Grady turned to go. He paused and looked back over his shoulder. "Do you believe me?" he asked.

Blondy eased himself to the grass and massaged at his sore wrist. "All that stuff you said before? About the Keyrdegen ordering those deaths? That you are a transformed Clanless on some kind of rescue mission?"

His life sounded like an impossibility described like that. But here they were. "Yeah. That."

"Honestly?" Blondy leaned back and stared into the inky darkness of the hollowed out mountain peak. "This is insane, like living through some cracked legend." Unflinching, he looked Grady in the face. "Seems plausible enough from where I'm sitting. You fought with honor and showed my friends mercy. Monsters and machines know nothing of either."

Grady smirked. "No. I imagine not."

The blonde warrior held out his arm. "Grenson of the Thegen."

Grady clasped his forearm and the two shook. "Grady of No Clan."

"Go with honor, Grady of No Clan. Thank you for my life and the lives of my squad mates."

"You're welcome, I guess. As repayment, put more thought into who really deserves your loyalty. And what parts of your oath are truly worth following."

Grenson's smile was lopsided. He nodded and laid back on the grass amongst his stirring and groaning squad. "You better hurry. They'll be sending a runner soon for a status report. When they ask I must speak the truth."

Grady loped off across the grass without looking back. He hoped his choice to leave those warriors alive was a wise one and that Dulane watched on with pride from wherever the honored dead go.

THE RETURN TO THE ARTIFICER'S SPIRE

The entrance to the artificer's inverted tower lacked the intricate adornments and copious statuaries of other entranceways of the Commons. Grady once thought its simplicity a minimalistic design choice to set the inventor magicians of Rockhome apart from the other denizens of the Roof. Now, he knew better. They chose to not proclaim their deeds or raise up their greats to hide the horrors wrought by their single-minded pursuit of advancement.

The gate barring the stairs was just more metal for Grady to bend. The stairwell was empty and illuminated dimly by half-banked lichen lights. The upper halls looked the same as the ones below. Memories clawed at him, his earlier horrors demanding to be remembered.

At the first landing, Grady put a hand to his head and forced himself to breathe calmly. The rhythm of his breath kept him grounded in the present as the memories played out and sank back beneath the surface of his conscious mind once more.

"Steady on. Save the others first. Have a mental breakdown later."

His plan, if it could be called that, was simple. The captives could be anywhere in the Spire, but the Commons was the only reliable way out. That meant the most logical way to search was to start at the bottom and work his way up.

Grady froze on the second landing. The rattling sound of marching metal hurried him out of the main stairwell. They couldn't know he wanted to free the captured Clanless, but it made sense to protect Plenabus and his works. Revenge was a motive Salzum understood.

That meant the lower levels were, most likely, swarming with throngers. Grady patted the sack of coal at his belt, wishing it were fuller. The short tussle above cost him dearly. Not to mention the energy demanded by climbing the length of the Wall and bending every scrap of metal in his way. He took out one of the larger lumps of coal and chewed for a minute.

A part of him, confident from his victory above, argued against caution. *They'll be patrolling. In small groups I could take them. Easily.*

The computer in him warned against that sort of excess. *There is not enough fuel to power a fight with every warrior in this place.*

The temptation to listen to his newfound confidence was strong. But Grady's calculating caution was an older, more tried and true, companion. *They might have more of those net launchers. Or enough bodies to bury me in. Plenabus might have told them about the electricity too. Getting in was easy. Getting out will be much harder.*

Grady continued down a side hallway. The lack of chemical stink meant the doors hid domiciles and not labs. He was near the tower's exterior, which was odd because his flight from the patrol only took him down a couple of hallways. Why was the stairwell not the core of the tower?

He pressed his ear to the nearest identical door. Worried whispers conversed behind it. He backed away carefully and began to search for an empty room. Behind one door someone hummed a familiar lullaby. The next was silent for a long while, until a saw-on-metal snore stopped him as he went to turn the handle. More small noises warned him of a room's occupancy: the clink of a bottle, the shuffle of a shoe, a muffled sneeze. Once, a percussive fart warned him from one door over.

Grady statued up at a door with promising silence. He locked muscles with his ear pressed against the pale mushroom wood and listened. Time ticked away. The Keyrdegen would soon learn about Grady's encounter with Grenson's squad. Who knew what was happening at this moment to the dvergr Grady now risked everything to save?

He battled down his impatience. Some artificer shouting about a stone dvergr barging into their rooms would strip away the last remnants of surprise Grady had. The quieter he went about it, the less chance that others would be hurt.

No snores, or shuffles, or any of the various sounds of the living greeted Grady from the space behind the door. Being as sure as he was going to be, Grady opened the door just wide enough to slip inside. He closed it with a hand on the doorframe and turned the knob slowly back, doing his best to ensure silence during the whole procedure. The room was very much empty. The bed was a mattressless frame and the walls were free of any personal touches. It smelled musty from disuse. Grady walked across the vacant room, thanked his unknown Ancestors, and hoisted himself out of the window.

Climbing down was harder than up. Going down, he climbed by feeling alone. Grady descended the side of the tower one arm's length at a time. Going up allowed him to look for holds and the best places to step. It wasn't a fear for himself that made him cautious. Grady accepted his imperviousness at this point. No, a fall doomed the prisoners now and all of Rockhome later. This was the one chance to free them, to foil Salzum's insane schemes, and stop Plenabus from plying his nightmarish trade.

Grady picked his way down until he hung from beneath the last row of windows. The tower continued beneath him, natural seeming and whole, for another couple of stories. Grady climbed sideways, circling to the other side of the tower. Four levels above him he saw the bridge connecting the Hold to the artificers' domain, giving him a rough idea of where Plenabus's lab was situated.

The nearest window opened up into an artificer-free workshop. Great spools of wire, a variety of different thicknesses and materials, lined the walls. On the desk, a little stand held one of Plenabus's lights. A copper wire ran from the light's stand to a spool topped with a crank. Grady climbed inside, avoiding the contraption on the desk entirely. It smacked of electricity and Grady wanted none of that.

The hall beyond the room's door was empty and quiet. He reentered the confounding sameness of the hallways. He paused occasionally to point in the direction of Plenabus's lab to keep himself oriented. Echoing footsteps from around a corner told Grady the stairwell was near and occupied.

Peering around the corner, he spotted two sets of feet that disappeared as they climbed. The guard's conversation drifted down to him.

"This is stupid."

"I'm not going to argue with you about that. Orders are orders."

"It just makes no sense."

"I know."

"The horns have sounded. Why aren't we below?"

"I don't know."

"And what are we watching for, eh? 'Anything out of the ordinary'? That could be, well, anything. Especially here."

"I know."

Their voices faded as they climbed. They were patrolling. Going away meant they would be back. Grady started down the stairs, his focus upwards to keep an eye out for the ascending warriors. His foot missed a step and Grady tumbled. He clattered down the stairs and crashed at the next landing, where he lay on his back with his legs propped up against the stairwell wall. Frozen, Grady listened for cries of alarm or the sounds of rushing feet.

"Down there. Come on!" Grady recognized the complainer's voice.

Grady sprang to his feet and dashed down the next flight of stairs. They ended abruptly at a double-wide metal door. He pushed through, and twisted the doors' handles together with ease, temporarily fusing the doors together. Grady turned and cursed.

Of course.

He stood on a metal platform surrounding the shaft encasing the stairwell. The bottom of the tower was hollow. The large space's funk was a combination of biological stenches and artificial astringents. A row of cages filled the nearest wall. Metal walkways ran underneath them and descended down a few steps to a central platform hanging high over the floor. Tables covered the platform and the tools of the artificers' trade, beakers or vials filled with various liquids and odd contraptions, filled the tables. A handful of marked up chalkboards stood in between the work stations.

Monsters filled enormous cages at the bottom of the room. Two trolls chewed contentedly at large bones. An enormous, segmented something was curled into an ominous, indigo pile. A blind mole, larger than three dvergr piled on top of one another, worried at the bars of its cage, bloody foam frothing at the corner of its mouth. A couple of bright green blobs of ooze swirled slowly around their glass enclosure, one seeking pseudopod at a time. Grady marveled at the collection of horrors hanging above the city.

How had these monstrosities ended up here without every dvergr and their ancestors knowing about it? He thought of the not so central stairwell.

Hope flared. *Maybe the Commons isn't the only way out.*

A weak sob echoed in the chamber's open expanse. Metal slammed on metal and the sob cut off into a yelp of pain. "Shut it, brick. Hands off the bars or I'll come in there and give you worse." The tableau froze. On the walkway against the wall, a thegen raised a metal baton across his body threatening a cowering figure in one of the cages. More figures huddled in the cell's darkness.

The world tinted red and Grady embraced it. He and his anger were in full agreement. Heedless, he roared and charged. The guard turned, searching for the source of the cry and the percussive clanging caused by Grady's stone feet on the metal grating, and readied a fighting stance. "Halt-"

Grady leaped forward and brought his fists down together. The guard managed to adjust the angle of his shield, which dented under the weight and the force of Grady's enraged blow. The snap of the arm bones underneath and the guard's pained cry elicited a discordant response within Grady.

He reveled at laying a bully low, but the cry of pain sounded like anyone else's. Grady kicked the guard's dropped hammer off the walkway.

He raised a fist to take the guard out of the fight, but Grady paused as the fallen warrior wailed in terror and scooted away.

Squatting down, Grady met wide eyes. With contempt, he grabbed the thegen's helmet and tossed it over after the hammer. This one was young, full bearded and scar-free. "Are you alone?"

The young guard gritted his teeth, remembering his duty. His eyes betrayed him with a flick over Grady's shoulder.

Instinct drove Grady to spin down to one knee and throw up a blocking arm. The descending hammer struck his forearm on the haft just below the head. A jerk of his arm sent the hammer flying out of the guard's hand. Grady punched forward, using his back foot for leverage, sending his attacker flying backwards with a fist sized dent in her breast plate. The new attacker landed between two railing supports, her momentum carrying her towards the edge. Grady launched himself forward, belly down, and caught the guard's foot. Her helmet slipped off, then spun in the air until it plopped right onto one of the spiraling oozes.

The guard's scream was high pitched and panicked. Her flailing threatened to shake her loose from Grady's grip. "Hold still!" A desire for self preservation, aided by the commanding power of an avalanche, stilled the dangling guard. Grady hauled her up easily. Frantic panting shook her fringe cut beard.

Grady loomed over the recently saved guard with a threatening fist. "Is it just the two of you?" Both guards looked up with abject horror. *Not so fun being the powerless ones, eh?* Grady leaned in close, adding a sneer for effect. "I just saved your life. I can unsave it too. Is it just the two of you?"

"Y-yes. The rest were called away when the alarm sounded." She answered from between her raised hands. A wince told Grady she was expecting the worst now that he had his answer.

Grady stood, eyes locked on the supine guard. "Join your friend. Another sound or movement out of either of you and I will throw you at random to one of those things down there. I am particularly curious to see what that giant purple coil is all about."

She must have known because her ruddy skin paled. The guard clutched at her chest as she rose. Grady watched her limp over towards Broken-arm, her breaths hitching shallowly. He must have broken a rib or two when he hit her. *Good.* She slumped into place next to her fellow guard. Neither looked like they were raring for more of a fight.

He expected to feel more triumphant standing over them. The pain and fear evident on their faces soured it. Bereft of their helmets and weapons, the figures before him reduced to being two more young dvergr suffering because of Salzum's and Plenabus's poor decisions.

Young dvergr who Grady wanted to hurt more and more as he looked into the cells along the walkway. Each occupant pressed against the back wall as Grady walked by. They were probably wondering what fresh hell Grady was. He scanned their faces, trying to recall the portraits and names from the wall of the lost. "Finna? Is Finna here?"

"Me." A hand poked meekly from between the bars a few cells back towards the huddling guards.

Grady approached the cell, smiling. He mimicked how he used to stand and move in an attempt to make himself less threatening. "You're missed on the Floor. I've come to take you back." His palm pressed against the cell door. "All of you," he added louder for the room at large. "Let's get you out of here."

There was no visible latch or handle on the door itself. The door was designed to slide into the wall when opened. Grady grabbed the cell's grillwork and pulled with lateral force. It refused to budge. The bars bent under his grip, but the cross-hatch pattern meant it would take too long to rip the door to pieces. Time was running out. The other guards would be here soon.

"One second," Grady said calmly to Finna, "I'll be right back." He stomped over to the recumbent guards and squatted, doing his best to exude menace. Based on their reactions, he must have done a decent job. "How do I open the cages?"

Broken Ribs and Broken Arm exchanged a quick look. Broken Ribs coughed with a wince and pointed to the far end of the row of cells. "That lever," she wheezed. "Set the dial to the cell you want. Then pull."

Faces pressed against the bars of every occupied cell to watch Grady walk over to the lever and the wide number-rimmed dial next to it. A large red line separating the one and the thirty was labeled 'Emergency Release'. "Easy enough," Grady said. "Back up from the doors!" The faces and hands pulled out of sight. Satisfied, he turned the dial to the red line and pulled the lever. Down the line, the door's rattled open.

No one stepped out.

Feeling their precious time tick away, Grady's impatience peaked. He bit back calls to hurry. Few knew better than he what their ordeal must have been like. Pulling them out would be quicker, but that first step was theirs to take. Otherwise, a part of themselves would always remain, trapped in the darkness.

Finna was the first. She walked out, clasping her hands in front of her, shoulders cocked in a permanent flinch. Her eyes never left Grady. The others rushed out onto the walkway. Smudges of old sweat and blood stained their clothes. They smelled of unwashed bodies and fear. Their cheeks were hollowed by hunger, but they otherwise looked whole.

Grady did a quick tally. Twenty-five posters demanded twenty-five missing dvergr, but the numbers didn't add up. Twenty-one stood before him. Two he saw die on Plenabus's table. One was himself. That left one missing.

"There should be one more," He said. They all cringed back from the sound of his voice. "When were they taken?" They watched him, silent and lost. Grady curbed his mounting frustration. He took a deep breath and focused on generating the sound of his old voice. "Please. I just want to save as many of you as I can." The rumble remained, but his old voice tripped over top the stones in his throat.

"Grady? " One of the captives pushed his way to the front, sporting a face Grady never thought he would see again. Hoped, really.

Grady gave a nod. "Kaluk." Without his sibling, he was much diminished. All of the warriors, mad artificers, and Keyrdegens most recent in Grady's company hollowed out his bully's menace. "I've changed a bit. I'm surprised you recognized me so easily without my beard."

The snort was uncalled for. "Wasn't much of a beard, to be honest." He peered closely at Grady, taking in his petrified skin and its deeply carved channels. "What did they do to you?"

Grady felt naked for the first time in forever. He crossed his arms over his torso, covering as much as he could. "Same thing they planned to do to you. I'll explain later. How did you end up here? Thought you said the Keyrdegen's offer was a clear scam?"

He shrugged. "Came to realize the others had a point. Scam or not, there was always a chance. Turns out both sides were right. Not exactly up to my eyebrows in honors now."

Grady nodded and placed a hand on his ex-neighbors shoulder. "What about the missing dvergr?"

"They took Brenna away a while back. This shift, I think. Hard to tell time here," Kaluk said with a listless wave. The confident braggart was gone, his essence drained from him by the horrors and uncertainty of captivity.

Grady's words of comfort were cut off by a responding bang against the metal doors. "We have to get you all out of here. Now. There must be another way in and out. There is no way they marched those things down there through the Commons." The door rattled again, harder this time. "Thoughts?"

"Down there." Finna pointed to where the column encasing the stairwell met the floor. "There's a lift," she said. Others nodded.

"Alright. Let's go." Grady led the freed dvergr down two flights of metal stairs to the monster holding floor. They followed Grady past the caged things in a tight huddle, shrieking and wailing each time the things so much as twitched. The blind mole was too busy bloodying itself on its cage to take notice of them. The purple coil shifted a bit as they passed, its chitin rasping against itself.

On the back side of the central pillar, an empty cargo lift, larger and wider than any of the city's elevators, waited. It was open on all sides. Its thick chain was attached to the metal square framing the device. Here was his explanation as to why the Spire's main stairwell was off-center.

Above, the pounding on the door grew louder and more frantic. The metal complained with each impact.

Grady peered up into the darkness of the shaft. "I came in through the Common's entrance. There was no lift exit there. This must let out in the Roof, which means it's some kind of secret tunnel."

A once-fat dvergr next to Finna spat onto the floor. "I remember rising like being in an elevator. There must be a way down at the other end."

The door's screeching protests sharpened. They were starting to make their way through. Grady waved his arms, shooing the freed captives onto the platform. "Everyone on the lift. Go. I'll head them off. Get to the Floor."

They didn't need further encouragement. Kaluk held back as the others got into place. "What about you? Aren't you coming?"

"I'll hold them back. And I can't leave Brenna. I swore to save you all." Kaluk nodded. Grady gave him a crooked smile and a half shrug. "Go."

One of the prisoners pulled the lever and the lift rose into the air. Grady watched them, wishing he was on the platform too. Kaluk looked down at him and pounded his fist to his chest in respect. "Grady of No Clan!" Those with enough strength joined in. The thumping chorus continued until they rose out of sight into the dark recesses of the lift's shaft.

With a tortured roar, Grady's improvised lock gave up under the assault. The doors flung wide on their hinges and froze, too warped to swing back. Grady walked around the pillar and watched as the silvery flood of differently bearded Salzums filled the upper landing.

Enemy of my Enemy

As strong and quick as he now was, Grady knew it wouldn't be enough to overcome the mass of throngers pouring out of the stairwell. Two dozen filled the landing and seeped out onto the upper gangway. More piled in behind. Every fifth warrior wielded a long pole covered with wires that led back to a large, unwieldy backpack. They turned large cranks on the bottom of their packs, sending sparks arcing between the prongs topping each pole.

Grady's heart sank at the sight.

Beneath his mounting resignation, a deep, simmering anger demanded to be released. It urged Grady to fling himself at the armored cohort, to break their bodies faster than reinforcements could arrive. A deep breath tamped the anger down, for now.

Grady popped his last coal into his mouth. The knowledge that even with this latest morsel, his energy reserves were not sufficient for the tasks ahead robbed the lump of all flavor. Brenna needed saving. The many-limbed golem making machine needed destroying. Plenabus needed an end.

Before he attempted all the rest, the matter of the growing Throng needed to be dealt with. The fact that Grady knew in his soul that the Salzum's masked warriors were not his real enemies complicated things. Yes, a number of them before him wore Salzum's face with pride and followed their Keyrdegen with their whole being. Yes, every dvergr here would fight against Grady until their dying breath because their honor demanded it. But how many were like Dulane, trapped between their duty to their honor and their duty to themselves?

Grady backed up along the monster-filled floor, trying to keep as many of the throngers within view as possible while he thought. They quickly filed along the upper gangways, surrounding him. He was at a loss. There was no way out. *Sorry, Brenna. At least the rest are safe now. I hope.*

He bumped against the cage holding the large purple thing. Its coils rasped tighter in response. The Throng advanced down the stairs, where they held their positions, awaiting orders. Prod bearers made their way to the fore. Vastly surrounded and outnumbered, Grady found himself bereft of choices.

He raised his hands in surrender.

"On my mark, seize the abomination." Salzum's command rang from the entranceway's landing. The trappings of war encased the Keyrdegen. His armor shone resplendent in the light. The twin tails of his great braided beard disappeared over his shoulder and under the purple cape on his back. An edge of bright white fur flowed dramatically out behind him. His helmet was the same as the ones worn by his Throng, minus the silver mask.

"I'm surprised to see you here," Grady called out. "I know how much you love to delegate."

The Keyrdegen's much practiced acting skills sold his indignation. The lip curling sneer was a nice touch. "I will not bandy words with the monster who killed the best of us. Take him." The throngers surged forward at their leader's command. The pole bearers advanced, hemming him in with a fence of sparks. Grady could dodge one or two, but he'd never make it past them all.

Grady pressed against the thigh-thick bars of the cage containing the purple thing. The situation was dire, to say the least. Before him, Salzum and his minions intent on returning him to his willess existence and to a future filled with bloodshed. Behind him, a terrifying monster from Below, coiled in wait.

Safe in the walkways above, Salzum, smug and sure of victory, shouted an order. "Attack!"

Pretending he hadn't let out a tiny "Eep!" Grady forced himself between the bars of the coil's cage. Halfway through, his body wedged in place. Grady wiggled wildly. He popped through a moment before the first prods sparked against the cage. Grady's mass turned the stumble into a roll. The world spun to a halt, upside down. His feet dangled above him in the air, resting against a ridge of glossy purple carapace.

The warriors milled around the outside of the cage, unsure of what to do. Salzum yelled in the distance, "What are you doing? Get him!"

Grady had bought himself a moment, at least. In unison the prod bearers sprang back. Calls of alarm filled the room. A fluttering tickled at Grady's legs. He looked over his feet and sighed.

The nightmare thing's coils unspooled, driven by countless thin legs. Its head rose smoothly out of the undulating mass, flicking its feathered antennae about, tasting the air. Eyeless, it honed in on Grady in an instant. Regarding him hungrily, the thing clacked its giant fangs and fiddled its mouthparts. It shot forward and pinned Grady in its fanged grip, forcing him to plant his stiff arms against the beast to keep himself out of its mouth. The monster's mandibles writhed, reaching for a hold on his arms to draw Grady in. His grip slipped and the world became a dark peristaltic mass. Grady wondered if centipede stomach acid was strong enough to dissolve rock. Struggling was useless in the giving grip of the monster's throat. He resorted to biting at the soft, bitter flesh around him.

The mandibles tickled the bottoms of his feet when the swallowing waves froze. The world upended once more and Grady slid out of the centipede's maw accompanied by a hacking splorch. He sat up, wiped his face of goo, and flicked it from his hands with disgust.

The centipede hissed and began to thrash. The chitinous mass battered Grady to the floor and then flung him into the far side of the cage. He clanged harmlessly against the bars and flopped to the ground.

In the face of the giant arthropod's tantrum, no one seemed to be paying Grady any mind. The coating of centipede slime made squeezing through the bars much easier. He stumbled free and his foot caught on a protuberance just outside the cage. He looked back as he tumbled forward.

A large lever, caught by Grady's foot and dragged by his weight, clicked into a new position. The turning gears grumbled from below him.

The bars to the left of the lever disengaged from the top of the cage and sunk into the ground. The warriors on the level above shouted warnings to those below. The centipede stilled as it sensed a change in its confinement. Propelled by its multitude of legs, it spooled out of the opening. It scuttled over Grady, knocking him down. Its yellow underbelly scraped against his nose as it passed.

Then the screaming began.

Grady watched as the multi-legged horror struck into the Throng. Its sheer bulk crushed a handful into the stone. The blood leaking from bent and ruptured armor intermingled with the acidic-smelling mess oozing from a crushed battery pack. A warrior screamed as the centipede ripped him in half with its mouth talons. It settled in to masticate the soft meat so recently freed from its metal container.

"What have I done?"

A brave pole wielder jabbed at the beast. There was a zap and a small trickle of smoke. The centipede paused its meal to raise its head and scent at the air again with its antennae. It spasmed, lashing out with its heavy carapaced body, crushing warriors into the ground or battering them aside to be broken against the walls.

Salzum's commands pierced the bedlam. "The hadesi is free! Throngers back. Rangers forward."

Grady watched, enthralled and horrified, as a cadre of throngers with black bars marking their breast plates advanced. Some carried tubes that expanded into long spears with a flick of their wrists. They jabbed at the beast's face to draw its attention. Others took advantage of the distraction to cast lengths of gray spider silk rope topped with whirling hooks onto the centipedes back.

The hooks lodged into the carapace and the thrashing slowed. It bucked, but only one of the hook bearers lost his footing. The rangers flung more ropes, crossing and overlapping, pinning it down under the combined efforts of the heavily armored dvergr.

It mewled and screeched in its grating insect voice. The spears returned, rising and falling as they stabbed deep into its eyes and at the soft joint where the head met the first segment of its body. The thing shuddered and went limp.

"Wow," Grady said into the stillness that followed. Everyone who looked like Salzum refocused their attention on Grady. He slapped his forehead hard enough to reignite the burning wound there. Dulane's voice scolded Grady for his acute lack of warrior's focus and the value of his wasted opportunity. Cursing himself for a fool, Grady got to his feet and ran.

Throngers poured around the hadesi's corpse and its empty cage, the rangers leading the charge. One of the hooks tried to gain purchase on his shoulder, but Grady shrugged it off. He juked left and right, throwing off the rangers' aim. Grapples clattered around him as he ran.

One landed in front of him and was tugged back, catching Grady at the ankle and pitching him forward. Free from the fear of impacting the ground, Grady dropped his shoulder and rolled, allowing him to pop to his feet, stumble briefly, and keep running.

With a lowered shoulder, Grady sped towards the glass enclosure with the circling green blobs. Grady punched through the glass that pebbled inward, filling the air with small, blunt chunks.

Grady dared a glance over his shoulder to check on his pursuers. Gooey warmth enveloped him and Grady glided in space for a bit before coming to a stop. The cries of his pursuers sounded muffled and distant. The ooze's substance tried to push into his nostrils, ears, and other orifices. He felt it creeping behind his eyes. None of it hurt, but the experience was far from pleasant.

Two is too many things to be inside of in one shift.

Walking out was proving impossible. The slime under his feet denied him the purchase needed to move. Grady folded onto all fours in an attempt to crawl free. The slime was inside him now, squirming and searching his interior cavities for digestible materials. Grady scrambled for purchase, unable to breathe to still his growing panic. Desperation drove his fingertips into the floor. He clawed and kicked his way forward until the sucking pressure of the oozing mass peeled away from him.

Grady gasped instinctually once his head hit the air. He kicked a bit to pull his last leg free and scrambled to his feet. The bits of ooze stuck inside of him, in his ears, sinuses, behind his eyes, and elsewhere, liquidized. The draining was nearly as bad as the initial invasion.

The first slime oozed through the Grady-shaped hole. The Companions were shouting and falling back before the gelatinous approach. Pseudopods lashed out from the center mass with terrible speed, latching on to the nearest throngers. Those unlucky enough to be caught were quickly enveloped. Grady watched as one of the rangers was swallowed up. The dvergr thrashed in silent agony, floating in the green mass. Red misted out from the joints of their armor and the eye holes of their mask. The dvergr's now still form was slowly dragged back towards the thing's center mass.

Shouts of "Fire! Fire! Light torches!" filled the prison space.

Grady smashed through the opposite end of the glass enclosure and made his way towards the caged trolls. The two monsters were identical to the one Grady fought in the pit. They watched him approach at a jog, chewing idly at scraps of meat on the large bones remaining from their last meal. One lifted a gnarled, clawed finger and pointed over Grady's shoulder. It hacked up some phlegm for a moment and gestured again. Grady realized it was saying something.

Grady looked back to see the oozes being corralled by warriors wielding torches. The flames flared brightly, leaving black scorch marks behind each time they touched the green substance. Both of the oozes looked diminished. Above them all, Salzum bellowed orders Grady could not hear over the bedlam. The throngers not fending off the blob monsters disengaged and charged in Grady's and the trolls' directions.

The troll burbled some more and coughed once or twice. The other joined in. They were laughing. "Yes, I bet this is all very amusing. Probably not much in the way of entertainment down here. Right?" The trolls chewed and watched him. Over his shoulder, the warriors drew near. He was out of options.

"Do you want to have some fun?" Grady pointed at them, then up at the approaching warriors. He slammed one fist in his palm. "Sound good?" The trolls shared a bemused look. One shrugged. That was good enough for Grady.

The padlock on their cage was as thick as his wrist. He took hold of the lock and climbed his feet up the bars. He pulled with his whole body. The trolls gurgled something and coughed again. "I'm trying, okay?" Grady said through clenched teeth. In his periphery, he saw a large group of warriors getting nearer with three sparking prods rising out of the crowd. Grady roared and flexed until he thought his arms would break from his shoulders. The lock gave way with a scream and Grady's efforts launched him from the cage to barrel into the throngers' leading edge.

The trolls burst forth from their cage with throaty roars of their own. Together they stomped into the gathering warriors, swinging their arms in large arcs. Armored bodies soared through the air.

Grady disentangled from the warrior he collided with. A clear path to the stairs stretched before him. The screams of the fighting and dying dvergr jabbed at his soul. *One more to save. I'm coming, Brenna.* A sharp surge to his lower back froze him up and drained away his strength. Grady jittered internally as the electricity flowed into him and filled his world with white.

The energy's bite bothered him less than the realization that he had failed. He tried to take solace in the fact that most of the Clanless were on their way to safety. The words of his oath, to protect the weak from those who would harm them, rang in his mind, denying him any sense of satisfaction. He was no thegen after all. Just an oath-breaker. A familyless, beardless clerk. A useless erratic.

A gust of wind swept the paralyzing energy away. One of the trolls stood over him, swinging its long arms to keep the warriors at bay. Grady nodded his thanks, unsure if it understood him. When the troll saw Grady back on his feet, it charged into a small cluster of fighters, scattering them like sawdust.

Grady staggered forward. He took the stairs two at a time, using the railings to help prop himself up. The gangway was clear of opposition. Loping awkwardly towards the main stairwell, Grady could not resist a glimpse at the chaos below. The oozes, trapped in a ring of torch wielders, were much smaller and polka dotted with burn marks. The trolls fought as a pair, mauling and bashing at the warriors nearest them. They were winning, but green blood oozed from their slowly accumulating wounds. Dvergr bodies, half-dissolved, crushed, and mangled, littered the floor.

Salzum brandished a pair of axes as Grady walked towards him and the gaping entrance to the stairwell beyond. Armored, the Keyrdegen was a wall of metal. The saga of his life, etched on every inch of visible space, glinted in the light. While age had done little to diminish him, Salzum in his youth must have been a force of nature. Grady was awed by the spectacle of the ideal warrior before him. No wonder his peers raised him up to preeminence.

A raised ax stilled Grady in his tracks. Salzum spoke with a quiet intensity, clearly not wanting anyone to hear him over the din of the battle below. "That is far enough!" Salzum twirled his axes with practiced ease. "Clanless, I know you are in there. While in my company, did you listen to a single word I said? Our people wallow in the dark. Below nips at us, biding its time before it swallows us whole. It knows we are here. The deeper we mine, the more prosperous we get, the sooner It will come. Over and over our history tells us this is so. No more. I will break the cycle and you will help me. You will lead my army of golems to carve us a kingdom unlike any dvergr has ever known. Carve your legend in blood and ensure our people's place in the soft light above."

Salzum lowered his weapons and let out a tired sigh. "I don't want to hurt you, and if I destroy you now, it makes a mockery of the butcher's bill my dream has accrued. The lives of those warriors below, ultimately, lay at my feet. The Clanless filth claimed by Plenabus's experiments, died at my orders. Dulane. I miss him like a limb." The regret in his voice hardened into a violent resolve. "It was all a small price to pay for what is to come. Honor their sacrifices. Honor your teacher and help me save this city he loved so much. Submit, Radix."

Every word the Keyrdegen said stoked Grady's anger. Just when he was about to burst, his anger froze. It burned at his soul like frost. "Grady."

"What?" Salzum's eyebrows shot up beneath his helm in shock.

"I am Grady of No Clan. And you? You're full of shit." Grady stepped forward. "Yours is the only name you want written in legend. Salzum, the Savior." Grady mimed spitting. "You broke your thegen oath. You manipulated the loyal to empower yourself and your ego. You lied. To everyone. You used your might to oppress and bully. All these dvergr have died for your vanity. And your beard looks ridiculous."

Salzum roared and leaped across the space between them.

Ducking under the first swing, Grady stopped the second by catching the Keyrdegen's bracer-clad wrist. Salzum growled and kicked at Grady's knee in an attempt to unbalance him. He might as well have been kicking a statue. Grady looked down at his knee and back up with a smirk.

Grady squeezed the bracer, buckling the metal until the bones beneath crunched. Crying out in pain, Salzum chopped down with his remaining ax. It bit deeply into Grady's shoulder. His arm went numb and pain radiated from the buried blade. Grady wrenched his shoulder back, taking the ax with him. Grady held on to the Keyrdegen's crushed forearm and, with the same hand, rained down pain-fueled punches.

Salzum jerked his head around to take the blows on the helmet itself. His trapped,useless hand slapped him with each impact. He tried punching Grady with his free gauntlet, but managed only to make a bunch of noise. Grady finally managed to score a direct hit on his unarmored face. The nose guard of Salzum's helmet dented inwards and blood exploded from underneath. A couple of his teeth scattered to the ground, one of them gold. Grady let go of the demolished limb, and Salzum dropped to the floor in a limp pile.

COME DUE

The stairwell was empty. Every readily available thronger in the Spire was either dead or battling for their lives in the artificers' basement of nightmares. At each landing, Grady expected a fresh squad to arrive. Given how his luck was going, they'd be as tall as humans and wielding weapons of pure mithril.

Bereft of whatever magic or energy animated it by the Keyrdegen's strike, the upper left of his torso weighed him down. Each step drained Grady's energy and even more leaked freely from the deep gouge in his body. As he collected himself a level beneath Plenabus's lab, he dared to look. Energy, white and dim, evaporated from the wound like steam.

Even through his fog of pain and mounting exhaustion, Grady was impressed to find Plenabus's lab door replaced. Malevolence radiated from the doorway and muffled machinery whirred behind it, sending chills through the rune that served as Grady's heart.

Grady was not the only thing mithril was good at cutting. He wrenched the ax embedded in his shoulder free. It scraped against his being on its way out. The ax rose and fell, urged onward by the horrible machine sounds, pulping deep into the metal hinges like it was 'shroomwood. "No more," he said with a final chop. The door flew inward with the force of Grady's kick.

The stark glare of electric lights framed a horrible scene. Blades flashed on the ends of flailing metal arms. They carved into the still dvergr body on the metal table below. Two of the arms were working on the runes at the belly and another pair worked on the one above the heart.

He hurled the ax towards the machine's core with every working muscle in his body. The mithril edge tore through the machine's outer-plating, fouling up its guts. The arms shuddered, marring their fine line work and adding numerous shallow gouges to their victim. They twitched and curled up around their core like the legs of a dead spider.

Grady rushed to Brenna's side. The wounds caused by the machine's final spasms bled little. The fresh carvings were angry and red, but the styptic powdered over Brenna's body did its work. He pressed an ear to her chest and heard her heart beat, slow but strong. The dvergr's forehead was warm and damp under Grady's light touch. "I know you can hear me," he whispered. "It's going to be ok. I am going to get you out of here."

An enraged squeal was all the warning Grady got before something impacted into his damaged shoulder. Weakened by the wound, Grady fell to his knees. Only his good hand on the metal table kept him from going down completely.

"You are my greatest failure, my hubris given solid form." Plenabus jabbed Grady in the shoulder again with a surprising amount of force. A buzz thrummed through him. "I was a fool to think myself greater than our vaunted ancestors. Why should I succeed where they failed? Hm?" Plenabus stabbed again with each statement. Grady's body, still clamped to the table by his good hand, convulsed with each jolt. "Looking backwards instead of forwards. That was my true mistake. Yes." The artificer pressed his weapon into Grady's back, forcing him to bow into a deep arch.

Locked inside his paralyzed body, Grady cursed himself for being caught unawares again. With the energy pouring into him, Grady could do nothing but feel the remaining dregs of his strength drain away. The onslaught ceased and Grady slumped, hanging from the metal table and swaying gently.

"I had such high hopes," Plenabus said.

The unseen weapon jabbed at him again, pushing and grounding against him. But no buzz. No paralytic surge of foreign energy. Grady took an experimental breath. A space opened up inside him and filled with air. Plenabus's face, a rictus of anger, hovered over his shoulder. Spittle flecked his beard, and small collections of foam gathered in the corners of his mouth. Grady was able to count his remaining, yellowed teeth. The wire prongs poking from the new brass apparatus encasing Plenabus's hand sparked against the rune marking where his arm met his wounded shoulder. The leylines on that side of his upper body pulsed with a pale light. Grady couldn't feel a thing.

Spinning at the waist, Grady flung his dead arm up and around. It smashed into the sparking apparatus at the end of Plenabus's arm, collapsing the metal and crushing his hand. The small metal prongs at the end shattered and the wire feeding them power swung away to hang loose. Howling in agony, Plenabus clutched his ruined hand to his chest. The free wires touched his bare arm. Plenabus froze before breaking into a fit of shuddering twitches, his eyes bulging red. A metal piece deep within the crushed prosthetic popped. The bright, unnatural lights in the room went dark. Plenabus, free from the energetic flow, collapsed and started to fill the lab with the smell of gently cooked meat.

Grady mimed spitting on the smoldering corpse. He flipped it off with his working hand for good measure.

The stony numbness spread and his body grew heavier. He crawled back to the metal table holding the paralyzed, and hopefully unconscious Brenna. Bathed in the dim lichen lights from the hallway, he rested his head against the table looking at, but not seeing, the ceiling above. "I'm sorry. I failed you. I don't think I can get you out. There are too many stairs. Too many warriors. Not enough of me left."

Breathing was all Grady could do. He tried to deny his shame in the face of this ultimate failure by looking on the bright side. Twenty-one other dvergr were free now because of his efforts. Hopefully. Plenabus was dead. Salzum lay below, as broken as his machinations.

Perhaps when Grady's light went out this time, whatever part of him remained would be free to finally meet and know his ancestors, to swap stories with Dulane, and finally share those fried 'shrooms with Emerlda.

The gloom encroaching on the edges of his vision refused to finish the job and cast the world to inky oblivion. Bone deep exhaustion warred with the wedge of fire carved into his shoulder. Closing his eyes, Grady prayed to the First Ancestor for release. The moment dragged on past bearing. He opened his eyes and, with a frustrated growl, beat the back of his head against the metal table.

He did not feel as much as hear his eyelids slide open. In the darkest part of the room, the cool blue glimmer of a well-maintained lichen lamp leaked from the wall. The light was a little over head height and in the shape of a perfect right angle. *It can't be.* Maybe he wasn't done yet. Grady wobbled unsteady as he rose, hoisting himself to his feet with the aid of his working right arm.

He limped over to the light and pressed against the wall gently. The brightness widened as a door-sized panel of rock slid noiselessly backwards and away into the rest of the wall. The space beyond was a wide and empty shaft. Lichen lights hung in intervals up and down the far wall. Their meager illumination accomplished little, emphasizing the deep darkness around them.

A quick mental review of the map saved in his crystalline brain confirmed his suspicion. This was the same shaft that terminated in the prison far below. The elevator the freed Clanless rode to freedom must hang high above him. In a hollow revealed by the opened panel, a lever waited. Grady tugged it and the shaft filled with the echoing grind of working gears.

The metal-framed bottom of the lift pushed out of the darkness. Grady watched its descent, willing it to lower faster as his energy continued to ebb. It slowed to a smooth stop, its floor perfectly flush with the floor of Plenabus's lab. Grady marveled at the mechanical precision and crafts-manship his people were capable of.

"What a waste," Grady said, stepping over Plenabus's still smoking body.

With care, Grady wrapped the paralyzed Brenna in a spare lab coat. It was tricky to do one-handed, but Grady managed well enough. Even weakened as he was, Brenna felt like nothing draped over his shoulder. Grady laid her down on the lift bed, wincing when he fumbled her into a harder landing than he intended. He thumped down next to the lift's controls. The lever clicked one way and the elevator rumbled to life. Grady sighed as it descended. He reversed the lever with a shake of his head.

"Second time's the charm. Right?" Brenna, paralyzed and unconscious, didn't respond.

The world was growing hazy. The passing lichen lights blurred and sharpened in a dizzying cycle. The elevator's mechanical workings vibrated in his hollow belly as the chain pulled them inexorably up into the darkness. Grady struggled against a different, internal darkness which chose now to encroach on the edges of his vision. "Now you want me? Just a bit longer. Shift's not over yet." His good fist tapped against the rune carved over his heart. Each impact sent out little jolts of awareness, keeping his mind from drifting away.

It was satisfying to watch the chain coil perfectly back onto the massive reel bolted to the ceiling. Grady appreciated the order of it. Each loop fell into place perfectly after the other. When it reached one end, it just coiled back the other way. Grady felt a ridiculous pang of sadness when it stopped and the elevator came to a standstill.

Brenna groaned, snapping Grady back into the here and now. Grady placed a hand on her unmarked shoulder. "You'll be ok. We're almost out of here." Grady hoped he wasn't lying.

Standing up was harder than it was before, but his shoulder hurt less. That worried him a bit. Hurting meant the shoulder was still a part of him and not unfeeling, unliving stone. He apologized to Brenna as he placed her back on his shoulder like a sack of ore.

The hallway beyond the elevator was another perfect cube of space. It was a horizontal continuation of the shaft, complete with sparsely placed lights. The hallway curved into the distance. Grady struggled to look beyond his feet. One shuffling step at a time was all he could manage. Grady's own body was more of a burden than the carved-upon dvergr hanging limply on his shoulder.

His left side dragged. The arm hung useless, while his left foot grew more and more obstinate. Grady was forced to limp along, his left leg only good as a pivot allowing him to throw his right leg forward. Energy continued to dissipate from the ax carved trench in his shoulder, the cloud reduced to faint whisps. The hallway's hard lines and perfect angles softened and wobbled. His eyes were losing their focus.

The path forward remained clear. One staggering step forward after another. There was no turning back. The only way out was through.

A mechanical rattle drew Grady's eyes from the floor. The hallway ended as it began, with an emptiness filled with only a rising, taught chain. A second lift pulled to a stop. Relief splashed up against the exhausted numbness claiming Grady's body and mind, washing a bit away. A pair of dvergr, indistinct in Grady's waning vision, stepped off the platform into the hallway.

Their hands brushed against him and they called to him with garbled voices. Grady ignored them, refusing to be stopped with his impossible goal in sight. The lift's platform called to him. All he needed to do was lay Brenna down on the platform and throw a lever. They'd descend to the Floor and she'd be safe. His oath complete, Grady could finally put down the burden his body was becoming.

He could rest, regret-free and proud.

In the center of the lift Grady dropped to his knees. It took everything he had to lean low to the side and extend his arm. He felt Brenna slide from his shoulder towards the floor. Her weight disappeared from his arm before getting past his elbow. He managed only a glance to his right. Brenna, red-marked and still, was lowered gently to the floor in the hands of the blurry dvergr.

Concern blunted by exhaustion, Grady only managed a glance. Details called out to him through the general vagueness. Prisoner smocks, sunken cheeks. One arm tattooed in names. They were talking excitedly to one another, fussing over Brenna.

Good enough, Grady thought. He released his willful grip on his body and fell forward onto his face. Hands shook at his shoulder, slapped gently on his cheek. *Oath upheld.* The last dregs of energy coursed out through his runes, flashed down the ley lines carved into his skin, and winked out. Grady softened into ease, and then darkness.

A Friendly Face

A thin bright line of light expanded into a field of vision. There wasn't much to see. The cracks in the plastered ceiling made no interesting shapes. The stone revealed beneath was the same, striated gray of all the exposed stone of the Floor. The smell of antiseptic tickled his nose. The sheets were soft against his skin. All in all, it was not a bad way to wake up.

An avalanche of memories tumbled into place, crushing the peaceful ignorance of the moment. Both of his stone hands trembled as they flexed and turned before his eyes. The runes and ley lines remained, carved deep. Grady welcomed the penetrating ache that ran from his shoulder into his chest. Gingerly, he prodded at where he hurt the most and found no impressions deeper than the lines carved into him when his body was still flesh. The deep gouge was gone. It took more effort than it should have to turn his head. A wedge of pale stone marked where the ax hit him.

He marveled at his newfound wholeness. *Who knew stone could scar?*

A mug shattered on the floor, accompanied by the splash of its contents and a surprised gasp. "You're awake!" a voice called, and then repeated louder, "He's awake!" The voice fluttered his heart. A warm, soft weight pressed against him. Emerlda's body shook with relieved sobs and a sodden spot grew where her head pressed against his chest.

He reveled in the warmth and closeness. When was the last time anyone embraced him? Long before his transformation, surely. Must have been when he was a child. This was one way to break a thirty-year streak. With care, made awkward by the sudden realization that under the thin barrier of his sheets he was naked, Grady patted her hair. "There, there? I'm alright." The usual gravel grind came out as a surprisingly soft and throaty purr. He coughed, nervous in an old, familiar way. "Sorry. I don't have a lot of practice with consoling people crying on me."

Emerlda's green eyes were rimmed in red as she wiped away the flood of tears glistening over the contours of her full-toothed grin. The sight pierced Grady's heart as if it was mere flesh instead of a construct of transmogrified stone powered by runes. For a moment his mineral exterior felt skin-deep and he was himself again.

"It's a new experience for all involved." She sniffed loudly and wiped away a couple more errant tears. "Never been much of a crier, me." Her hand warmed his chest through the blanket.

The comfort and safety he felt fizzled away in the acidic surge of fear that filled him. Shadows closed in from all around. He tried to get to his feet, but his body wasn't listening. "You have to go. Now. Go. Run." He tried to push Emerlda away, but she resisted.

She shushed him some more. "It's safe. You're safe. What's the matter?"

"The Keyrdegen. Salzum. He'll send the Throng to get me. You can't be here. He'll hurt you. Use you. Go. Run. Please."

Anger creased Emerlda's face. "Salzum," she spat on the floor, "isn't Keyrdegen any longer."

Inside, Grady's confusion battled with relief, making him wish he could burp to release some of the pressure. "What? How? Is he dead?"

"It was sorta your doing. You freed the others. They came stumbling back to the Floor dragging you and Brenna and shouting their stories fit to shake the whole place down. They must have heard all the way Up Wall. Salzum was arrested the next shift. They found him in his private quarters, wounded something awful."

"All that on the word of some Clanless?" Grady couldn't believe it after witnessing the city leaders' casual disdain for the denizens of the Floor first hand.

She shrugged. "Wasn't just their words. Their captors were none too gentle. And then there was poor Brenna. It was enough to mobilize the thegen. Rumor has it they tapped a motherload of evidence. Some thegen came forward, throngers I hear. Claimed Salzum lied to them. They haven't seen fit to let the whole story out yet."

The bed groaned as Grady dropped his arms. "He's gone? Really gone?"

"Execution is in a month. No appeals. Set in stone. Ask me, a beheading is too good for him. Bury him up to the neck in some deep tunnel and leave him, I say."

Grady laughed out his agreement. His sudden freedom caused him to forget his weakness for a moment. He sat up and pulled Emerlda into an embrace. Her hair smelled of clean soap and fragrant moss.

"What a cozy scene." The figure in the doorway carried a clipboard tight to his chest under a short cropped chestnut colored beard. A hint of a smirk peeked out from under a thick mustache. He wore a stained artificer's coat.

"Behind me!" Grady untangled from their hug. The weakness returned but he continued to struggle to pull Emerlda behind him. His muscles protested, refusing to exert too much effort. A wave of lethargy swept over him, forcing him to flop back to the bed.

"It's okay, Grady. Dartuf is a friend." Emerlda stroked Grady's brow and smiled at the artificer over her shoulder. Everything in Grady told him to get up, struggle his way out, and run. The white coats were not to be trusted. Emerlda's assurances, coupled with his literal inability to sit up, settled the matter. For now.

"Friend, at least. Dartuf of the Artificers. Pleased to make your conscious acquaintance." His quick and precise steps carried him into the room and to Grady's bedside. He leaned in too closely and stared into Grady's eyes, filling his nose with the smell of astringent herbs. This close, his smirk lost its mocking edge. He was pleased with himself. "They all thought you were dead. Tongue, please?"

The tone was the same as every doctor Grady had ever visited. He obeyed automatically. "They?" Grady asked over his protruding tongue.

"Fascinating." Dartuf jotted down some more notes on the clipboard. "Everyone really. Not hard to agree. Not a dvergr born that could survive a split like that," he tapped his pen against the pale stone of Grady's scarred shoulder. "You were totally inert. There was talk of fixing you up and making you into a statue in memoriam to yourself." He snorted derisively.

Grady looked at Emerlda, who nodded, and back to the artificer fussing about him. "Thanks?"

"Can you lift your arms over your head, please? Hold them as high as they will go."

It was a struggle to get his arms to shoulder height. His right was steady, while his left shook with the effort. The artificer jotted down some more notes. "You may lower them. Thank you." From the complex array of tools and gadgets stored in his belt, Dartuf removed a small box with a dial readout. He pulled a wire out from the box by the small metal circle on its end.

Grady flinched when the artificer leaned in to attach the white piece to him. Dartuf paused. "My apologies. I am used to working on you while you are not present. This box helps me gauge how much energy there is in your system. It's how I knew you were alive in the first place. It won't hurt." His brow scrunched. "I think."

Emerlda stopped Dartuf's outstretched hand. "What do you mean 'think'? I've seen you use that thing on him dozens of times."

"This is all theoretical. It's all madness. I've been working off of Plenabus's rambling notes and correlating them with ancient scrolls. Both assumed a greater breadth of basic knowledge from their reader than I possess. It took me a week of research to understand the process that made you. The notes after your creation were less than useful. Plenabus was a ranter. Your recovery has required me to make a number of intuitive leaps that I have not been wholly comfortable to make. The only reason I have given any of them a try is that the subject, you, Grady, could not perceivably get any worse. And you haven't. Only better."

"It's okay." Grady nodded to Emerlda. He smiled gently. "There are worse things than a little pain." She released the artificer's arm.

"That's the spirit! Step back please, Emerlda. Safety first."

The metal piece clicked into the rune over Grady's heart. There was no pain, just a slight tingle where the wire met his chest. The needle on the box's readout jumped and flickered. Dartuf made some pleased sounds and wrote down the results. "Excellent. Seems you have crossed a threshold of sorts. Your body must be healed enough that some of the energy can now go to power, well, you. I'm going to double your meal portions. Some extra energy in your system will do you good. The furnace in your gut needs some priming before you are eating solids again. I find your weakness worrisome, but given all you've been through it is not surprising."

Grady sought out the artificer's face. With earnest feeling he said, "Thank you. I am in your debt."

Unable to meet Grady's gaze, Dartuf put away the meter and fiddled with his papers. "Please don't. What was done to you, and almost done to the others, was monstrous. First oath one makes when donning these robes is simple." The artificer stood straighter and placed a closed fist over his heart. "My work is for the advancement of knowledge and for the benefit of all dvergr." He sighed and shook his head. "I cannot deny that what Plenabus accomplished was miraculous, an achievement worthy of legend. Your capabilities, if applied on a larger scale, would have indeed changed everything.

"But, I've talked with Brenna. I read through Ancestor Dulane's journal where he recorded all you told him about your experience. The confinement. The pain." Dartuf took a moment, adjusted his robes and resituated his clipboard in the crook of the other arm. "Long saga short, you owe me nothing, Grady of No Clan. I, and my order, owe you every-thing. I competed with a bevy of less qualified artificers for the honor of taking care of you."

"And study me," Grady said over crossed arms.

"Yes, of course. There is so much to learn, after all." The artificer's curiosity shone through his warm smile. "Social graces may not be my speciality, but it is clear I interrupted something." He shook their hands as he took his leave. "Emerlda, keep an eye on the patient please. Grady, it was a pleasure to finally meet you. I look forward to working together."

A tension deep in Grady's shoulders lifted as the artificer closed the door behind him. This one seemed nice enough, but his robe and his toolbelt churned Grady's stomach and made his carvings ache. Emerlda shifted on the bed, placing a hand on his forearm. Grady took her hand in his and squeezed it gently. "I'm sorry I missed our dinner."

"I was pretty pissed for a few shifts, let me tell you." Her free hand reached out and traced the scarred rune on his forehead, sending a shiver through Grady's core. Another tear rolled down her cheek. "Must say though, you have a pretty decent excuse." Emerlda searched his face. She lifted his hands in hers. She turned them, examining the runes and marks roughing his skin. A gravid silence grew in the room, suppressing the gentle ease of their reunion. "I saw what they did. To the last one you saved. To Brenna. They did the same to you?"

A half spun quip and deflection unraveled. A pressure grew in Grady's soul, pressing against the back of his eyes and tightening his throat. Emerlda's eyes widened at the grief twisting Grady's face. She shifted forward on the bed and held her arms out, beckoning. Grady leaned into her embrace, resting his head on her shoulder. He sobbed, shaking the entire bed and clinging to Emerlda with careful desperation. His face remained dry with no tears to shed or snot to run. Each heave of his chest, each muffled cry was a release. Emerlda softly shushed, soothing him with rubs on his head and arm.

The torrent eased, and as it passed, Grady felt more dvergr than ever. Empty in a way he never was before, Grady struggled to sit up with some grunting help from Emerlda. "You used to be such a dainty thing," she teased.

Grady chuckled, his old smirk twisting his lips. "Used to be made of meat and bones, too."

"What happened, Grady?" Her hand was back on his shoulder.

His hesitation came from a desire to not burden her with his pain. Sure, she was taking his new statue-like appearance in stride and hadn't flinched too hard at the sound of his terrible voice. Her arms were strong and she looked sincere, but the last person who knew everything was Dulane. Salzum used Grady to kill him. Flashes of blood dripping from his hands and broken bodies lying at his feet seized his mind. There, again, were Dulane's eyes, and his whispered forgiveness as Grady crushed his skull with his forehead. The blood flowing from his eyes pooled into the shapes of the dead dvergr lying on Plenabus's table and the monster-ruined bodies of the warriors who tried to capture him.

"I'm a monster, Emerlda. A weak nobody turned into a bloody tool." The whole of his story spilled out. He avoided details and told it all to her as simply as possible. He started with being awoken by the crash of his door.

Emerlda gasped and cringed at all the right moments. She held his hand, and the power of her grip helped him get through the telling of it. Her sad smile mimicked Grady's when he talked about his early training with Dulane. Her eyes were wide as he spoke about Salzum's ultimatum to the ambassadors from the surface, the fight with the troll. He brushed over his first failed escape attempt and the lives he was forced to take. Grady tried to explain what it was like waking up in Plenabus's lab, able to move himself again, but his words failed him. It was easier to describe his descent back to the Floor. She laughed at his description of the orange jumpsuit.

Grady looked away from Emerlda then, unable to meet her eyes. "I was just going to slink off into the darkness, hide on the Floor. Forever, I guess. Then I saw the wall of missing faces."

"Phukit noticed first."

"What?"

Emerlda pushed a stray lock of hair over an ear. "That you were gone. I assumed we were just off shift, missing each other. I was ready to belt you one, honestly. Thought you had stood me up." She waved off his protests. "She stopped me one shift and said you had not reported to work for a handful of shifts. Gave me your address even. No one there had seen you either for the longest time." Red crept up her neck and stained the tops of her ears. "Then I commissioned your poster."

"I saw." Their eyes locked over their clasped hands. "It meant the world to see that you were looking for me."

"What are friends for?" She winked, causing her beard to wag. "Then what happened?"

It was easier to explain how he had gathered his guts, made an oath, and set off to free the others. He grew excited as he told her of his infiltration of the Roof and the Artificer's Spire. She cheered for him when he recounted his mad scrabble to hold off the throngers to give the others time to flee, either ignoring or not noticing his haunted air. She made him describe the centipede monster and the blobs twice. Tavern stories included such beasts. Mothers scared their children with threats about what crawled in the deeper darknesses where only thegen dare tread. Every miner knew there was danger lurking within the stone they dug. She shuddered at the idea that those same terrors were held within the city, looking past Grady's shoulder to the darkness beyond and below.

He glossed over his fight with the Keyrdegen and the climb to Plenabus's lab. Emerlda made a satisfied noise when Grady described how the mad artificer died. "Hope he suffered," she said with a hard face. Her grip tightened on Grady in a way that lightened his insides.

"The end is where it gets fuzzy. Last thing I remember was the lift coming back and seeing dvergr approaching. Then I woke up here." And with the telling of his story to its end, Grady was empty. His soul and heart were sore in places, bleeding in others. A poisoning pressure was released. The boil was excised. Healing could begin.

Emerlda nodded to herself and absentmindedly patted Grady's hand. Such a tale needed a moment to settle. Eventually, she broke the companionable silence. "The dvergr you saw were Finna and Kaluk. They won the toss."

The surprises and impossibilities never ended. "What? Kaluk? Really?"

"Mhm. They all stayed, though, waiting for you. They got tired of waiting and spent some time arguing about who would go back to check on you. They won the toss. Rode back up. Dragged you and Brenna out. He's been here a few times, checking in on you. All of them have been. Some of their families, even. They owe you their lives, yeah? That's a heavy burden. There isn't a Clanless around that doesn't know what you did. Kaluk's been swapping the story for free drinks in every tavern on the Floor. He also claims to be one of your oldest friends." They shared an eye roll.

Grady opened his mouth with a quip about how Kaluk risking his skin for someone else's benefit was the strangest part of the whole thing ready to go. A dry, hollow shifting rattled his stomach to resonate from his mouth and fill the room. He and Emerlda shared a confused look.

"Well, that's new." Grady sent his awareness down to his belly and found his tank nearly empty. He felt hungry. Not in the detached 'lacking fuel' sense that he had grown accustomed to. This sensation was far more familiar. "I'm... hungry."

"Oh! Of course, of course." Emerlda leaned over Grady and reached to a small table next to his bed. She handed him an all metal cup, closed at the top with a straw sticking out. "Try this. Dartuf's special blend. This is the stuff we've been pouring down your throat."

The cup turned out to be too heavy for him. Emerlda held the straw to his lips. Grady sucked in a mouthful of a thick sludge. Pure, wondrous delicious flavor overwhelmed his senses for a moment. He couldn't swallow it fast enough. The dominant taste was coal, earth, and age filled with the potential for fire, for energy. It was the good stuff too. Its texture and consistency were too unique for it to be likened to any of the foods he ate prior to his transformation. The drink bolstered his body and spirit. It reminded him of sipping on spiced bone broth when he was ill. The dregs slurped loudly up the straw and Grady sighed contentedly.

"You've got a little of your, uh, drink on your teeth."

Happily, Grady licked and sucked at his teeth for a moment. "Better?"

Emerlda nodded, doubt wrinkling her brow. "Let's say yes and leave it at that."

Heart light and belly full, Grady sank back into his pillow. He closed his eyes for a moment and tried to pretend everything from the time his door was kicked in to the last glimpses of the tunnel was just some creative nightmare. The reality of the warm weight on the bed next to him and the hand rubbing his arm made it impossible.

"I've been here a long time, haven't I?" Emerlda's normally open expression clouded over. "How long?"

"One-hundred and seven shifts."

Grady whistled through his teeth. Nearly half a year of oblivion. When Salzum sliced his finger at the start of all of this, it had taken a good long while to heal. The wedge carved into his shoulder was magnitudes larger. "That adds up. And how many of them did you spend at my bedside?"

Despite his airy tone, Emerlda looked away and blushed slightly. "Enough." She pushed some loose hair behind her ear again and stroked her beard. Her clothes looked slept-in.

"It'd have to be. You seem pretty used to seeing all this." He circled his hand around his face.

"I thought you were dead!" Her angry response caught him off guard. He tried to apologize, but she pushed on. "It was terrible. At first. Took me a long while to see you through all the changes." She ran a hand along his bare chin. "Your poor beard."

"Poor was the right word for it."

She hit him on the arm hard enough to make her yelp and suck at a hurt knuckle. "Be nice to my friend Grady." While she smoothed out his blankets some, Grady saw her formulating what she wanted to say. "I don't think you're a monster. No one on the Floor does. Anymore. They, we, want you to be named a Hero."

"Me? A Hero?" The idea of his name being recorded in the annals of the city's history among the likes of Samlun the Founder and Kreth the Bulwark made no sense.

Emerlda placed her hands on her hips and gave him a look that brooked no argument. "You saved twenty-two other dvergr from a terrible fate, stopped a mad artificer, and defeated a tyrant of a Keyrdegen in single combat. I'd say you meet the qualifications."

Shift change rang through the air, resonating into Grady's cubby of a recovery room. Emerlda squeezed his hand one more time and got up from the bed with a sigh. "Time for toil. I gotta be ready on the ladder in a quick hour. It will be harder to leave this time. I'll be back though."

"Bye." And she left the room. While her departure took most of the light with her, the warmth of her body and her care lingered.

Word must have gotten around that Grady was awake. A stream of visitors followed.

The dvergr he rescued stopped by, most with their immediate families in tow. They bore tokens or notes wishing him a speedy recovery. Most of them were complete strangers to him, so there wasn't much more to say beyond some version of 'thank you for saving me from being horribly cut up and transformed'. There were oaths made of undying gratitude and promises for support if it was ever needed. Grady did his best to accept the oaths with grace, but he squirmed inside as the compliments piled up. Grady truly appreciated how no one flinched at the sight of him or cringed from his voice. That more than anything made the forced socializing bearable.

Kaluk and Kulak entered his room like supplicants. They fiddled with their beards and struggled to meet Grady's eyes. Their thanks came in the form of a torrent of apologies and assurances that were only playing around back then, all friendly-like. It was a life ago, and their cruelties were petty and small. No dvergr's life on the Floor was easy. Grady's acceptance of their apologies was open and sincere.

Kulak's eyes were red rimmed and the scent of celebratory quaffing wafted from him. His smile was sloppy and his eyes grew dewy every time he looked at his brother. "Truly, can't thank you enough." He plopped down onto the bed next to Grady and patted his shoulder. "You know, you turned out to be alright. A real stand up dvergr. Especially for an erratic."

His brother's face both reddened with embarrassment and paled with rage, leaving his countenance a soft shade of pink. Kaluk grabbed his brother by the ear and, despite the other's pained protests, hoisted him from the room. The closing door thumped against Kulak's nose and muffled the surprised cry of pain. "Sorry about that. He's been celebrating. For half a year. He was a wreck when I got back. He means well. I-"

Grady waved the excuses away. If pickaxes couldn't hurt him anymore, then ignorant words shouldn't either. "It's ok. That was still probably the nicest thing he's ever said to me."

The comment eased Kaluk's feelings. He smirked. "Truth. Sorry. Again." Kaluk saluted to his chest and bowed deep enough that his beard brushed the tops of his boots. "My eternal thanks."

"I hear I owe you some thanks too." Grady's comment stopped Kaluk as he opened the door.

"Think nothing of it. Consider it a down payment on my insurmountable debt." He winked over his shoulder and let the door close behind him. "See you next shift."

Alone again, Grady leaned back into the pile of pillows he'd built behind his back to allow him to talk to his visitors more comfortably. He sipped from the second slurry cup of his dinner, savoring the flavor. High piles of small gifts and cards lined the walls of his room. All that socializing left Grady's mind abuzz. He had never spoken to so many different dvergr before.

They all knew his name. They spoke kindly to him, gave him honors and thanks. More than a few of them had their lineages tattooed up and down their arms to the point of running onto their backs. At one point, there had been a line to see him. Him—the little, bare-armed erratic who did not know his ancestors.

His arms were bare no longer. Runes and lines marked his arms and body now. Grady found it fitting that it took being turned into a singular creation to find his place among his people. Before he was taken, his life was limited. Every shift he awoke in the same small box and worked at the same small desk to accomplish the same small tasks. He'd do that for a few hundred years and die, his name forgotten. A pretty standard fate for the erratics of Rockhome.

He slurped the last of his slurry down and burped. Now, his future was an open wonder, undefined and filled with as much potential as the rolling hills and eternal sky of the world above.

◆

In the unchanging darkness of his cell, Salzum sat on the ground, his legs crossed, muttering a mantra to himself. "From devotion comes power." In the centuries following his Way, this bedrock tenet never led him astray. It had been his guide long before he knew the words.

Young Salzum owed his devotion to the idea of protecting his Clan and his City. To the simplistic vigor of youth, the path to safeguarding all he held dear stretched clearly into the future. He took up arms and earned his right to walk a Way. The thegen preached the supremacy of raw strength, military prowess, and grit. These things, they claimed, made a warrior. Salzum never thought to question these lessons, though he did find them lacking.

The old stories his grandma told him as he drifted off to sleep taught the importance of the thegen's most prized attributes but with one small addendum. All those things, they taught, were dross without nobly pursued honor. An honor built on mercy, honesty, and kindness.

What a naive fool he'd been. He'd ignored that the stories also contained monsters neutered by Grandma's soothing voice and her love for him. In tales, the monsters were things destined to be overcome again and again, reduced to mere tally marks accrued by the heroes of legend. All dvergr needed to do to win was be good enough, loved enough, and determined enough.

Patrolling the liminal edges between the familiar tunnels of home and the danger filled Wilds, Salzum witnessed true horror. For years, Salzum watched his fellow thegen, all good and strong and determined, cut down around him in ones and twos. Each a comrade or friend lost trying to stem the never ending rise of deadly things from Below.

His devotion to protect his home never wavered. A century or so into his service, he started to see his grandma's stories for the fluff they were. The great predators that stalked them knew nothing of mercy. When goblins or kobolds lay in ambush, honesty did not keep a dvergr alive. A swift death was the only form of kindness available in the tunnels they guarded.

Salzum led his fair share of thegen to their deaths in the name of protecting his home and considered the cost worthwhile. Until the whispers started.

They plagued him while he kept watch in the untamed darkness of the Wilds. *Death comes,* they promised in the chorused whispers of the honored dead. *The Below is bottomless and its perils incalculable. One shift, it will rise up and swallow your people as it has done to countless dvergr cities. Stand, try to stem its rise, and be devoured by it. Be forgotten.*

He left the tunnels behind. His devotion demanded more of him. Veteran status earned Salzum the right to request to serve in the Throng and protect the heart of the Rockhome, the Keyrdegen. From the Keyrdegen's elbow, Salzum watched the great engine of civilization transform chaos to order. Peace was kept. Digs directed. To truly protect his city, Salzum needed his hand on the wheel. Control bred order. Order protected.

When the old Keyrdegen died, Salzum put his name forward for consideration. The lessons he learned Below proved invaluable. He warned of the dangers held at bay by the thin chainmail wall of thegen. Praising progress out one side of his mouth and unbending tradition from the other, he courted the young and the old and painted himself as the moderate candidate.

Even this most lofty position possessed limits. He was forced to rely on unpredictable people, each driven by their own vainglorious and foolish desires. Salzum squeezed tighter for their own good. He changed the thegen oath and bound them to him. Used their might to bind others.

Still the attacks continued. Dvergr lives were lost. The doomsaying whispers were quiet on the Roof, but their sibilant warnings troubled his sleep.

Then Plenabus brought his mad idea to bring light under the mountain before the Assemblage. They listened to him eagerly. His last proposal to that august body led to the creation of the system that provided clean water, both hot and cold, which vastly improved the lives of every dvergr under the mountain. Surely, a mind capable of devising one marvel was capable of another. He looked so serious as he laid out his plans to carve skylights into the peak of Rockhome to allow in the rays of the sun. Salzum and the elders laughed him out of the Heart.

As he slept after that meeting, Salzum dreamt. Light filled Rockhome from the Ceiling to the Floor. Monsters and enemies stormed up from below, puffing into wisps of smoke as they touched the brightness. He awoke, a Truth burning away in his mind. To truly protect his people, they needed to be in the light.

The skylight was first. Then the gas lamps brought light to the Floor and turned the city into a marvel of stars. The youngest generation of dvergr did not know the same unending darkness as those who came before. His people were as ready as they could be to break with ancient tradition and live Above, where the dangers Below could never reach them. Where the whispers would be quieter still.

The world above was no danger-free utopia. The humans and the elves warred endlessly, monsters of a different variety haunted the unclaimed places. As proven by the stalemate with the dangers Below, thegen could only protect from so much. More needed to be done. Plenabus, again, handed him the key to it all.

He shuffled into Salzum's study late into the shift, waving around an old discolored sheaf of scrolls, ranting about ancient golems and the science-defying magic involved in their construction. The idea set his mind ablaze. If this impossibility could be made true, then before the end of the next century his people would be free to claim their place in the relative safety above.

So close. He had come so close, only to trip over some mis-placed pebble. A pebble he'd chosen because it was too small to cause an avalanche. And yet, here he sat in the darkness, diminished by one hand, muttering to himself.

"From devotion comes power." He scratched at his maimed arm with his good hand.

Dulane's betrayal cut deep. Salzum knew how the too noble dvergr would react to the truth about Radix's construction. He clung too tightly to the tenets espoused by the Bulwark. They limited him and blinded him to his true purpose. To accept the cost, Dulane first needed to see the golem's value.

It hurt so much listening to the thing recount its time with Dulane. The stories shared, the lessons taught. They reminded Salzum of simpler times, before the whispers showed him the truth. He'd cleaned Dulane's corpse himself before it was consigned to the beetles to clean his bones for burial.

In the end, Salzum himself was found wanting. Dulane taught the golem well. It showed fortitude and strength worthy of legend when it crushed his wrist and beat him near to death with his modified ax buried in its shoulder. That his plan would have worked was little comfort after the fact.

Salzum's mantra cut off as his cell door ground open and blue lichen light filled the room. Despite its softness, the light burned at the prisoner's eyes. He'd been alone in the darkness for so long with nothing but the pain in his truncated forearm and his latest failure for company.

The light bearer entered, illumination playing over his familiar ar-mor and the friendly silver face. He bowed. "My Keyrdegen, your Throng is here to rescue you. There aren't many who remained loyal, but those of us who remember our oaths stand ready. Plans are in place to retake the Hold, slay the Usurper, and return you to your rightful place."

"No."

The thronger's helmet tilted in shock. "No, my lord? I don't un-derstand-"

Salzum rose from the ground, clutching his mangled forearm to his chest. The damage caused by the golem was too severe. They took his hand to save his life. To ensure they, the city, would be the ones to claim it. He didn't blame them. What a grand display of control to execute one such as he.

The warrior fell to one knee in passionate subjugation before his shorn and ragged Keyrdegen.

From devotion comes power. Salzum's confidence in his Way never faltered, even as he suffered alone in the darkness awaiting his death.

Salzum hacked a bit when he tried to speak. From his knees, the thronger offered his warrior lord a canteen. Salzum drank the clean, cool water greedily. "Lead me from here. Take me to the others." The thronger nodded once, rose, and beckoned for Salzum to follow.

Salzum felt nothing at the sight of the dead squad of thegen posted in the guard chamber outside the cell block. Their violent deaths were inevitable. Better to die ensuring the realization of Salzum's dream than pointlessly Below. The rest of the throngers guarded the hallway beyond. Salzum's loyal warriors totaled eleven. True loyalty was rarer than mithril, it seemed.

At the sight of their Keyrdegen, the warriors saluted. "Where are we?"

The warrior who freed him from his cell answered. "This is a holding pen on the Floor, sire. They thought to punish you further by holding you like some Clanless trash."

Salzum chuckled at his enemies' ineptitude. "The utter darkness they insisted on blinded me to this greatest insult. And yet, it seems they have done me a favor."

"My lord," another thronger placed a heavy pack at Salzum's feet. "We procured you armor and arms so that you might lead us to vengeance against those who have wronged you."

"You honor me and your ancestors with your noble intentions. Your foresight does you all credit, my loyal Throng." As he spoke, his voice cast off the harshness brought about by disuse. He stepped back into the role of noble orator. "But we will not be retaking the palace. Let the Usurper keep her lofty position. She can be Keyrdegen of this doomed place." Salzum held out his arms to be dressed. A few warriors stepped forward and began to equip their leader.

Salzum let the moment build, deciding how much to tell what remained of his Throng. He settled on a handful of halftruths. "By turning their backs on me, the thegen have doomed the entire city to a slow and certain death. I will use my freedom to leave this place, head Below where death, quicker and more glorious, is a nigh certainty. But if we are strong enough and remain true to each other, we will thrive and find glory, the likes of which would make our ancestors jealous. All of you have come so far, done so much at my command. Now I humble myself to ask. Will you come with me into the Wilds Below?" Salzum looked at the silvered reflections of his face looking back at him, enraptured by his offer, and cowed by the glorious sight of Salzum, armored and defiant.

As one, the throngers cheered their ascent and pledged themselves with a chorus of "My will and the Keyrdegen's are one!"

Salzum grinned, aware but uncaring, of the gaps in his smile where his gold teeth once sat. The darkness itself had whispered a new plan into Salzum's ear as he shook with pain and railed against his failure. The whispers spoke of power beyond his ken hidden in the deepest places, for the brave to claim. Power enough to fulfill his dream, save his people, and find eternal glory.

After they were broken, of course. As his Way taught, those who refuse to follow must be driven.

A Word of Thanks

If you are reading this, then you have already consumed the 102,492 other words that make up my first novel. That you were willing to spend so much time with me, the little world I created, and the characters who live has earned you my soul-deep gratitude.

I rely solely on word of mouth- mostly my own- to find new readers. Simply tell every lover of fantasy you know about this book. Post about it on social media, if that's your thing. Leave a review on Goodreads. Earnest words from you, dear reader, will do more to sell my book than any fancy and well crafted ads could manage.

I hope to see you again at the end of my next book!

I'll just be here, meditating amongst the roots of the Kraken Tree, surrounded by its fallen, strange fruit.

M.T. Kadisin

Acknowledgements

While the writing itself was a solo experience, turning it all into a book took a whole team. I could not have done it without the help and input of everyone.

My foremost thanks go out to my wife and first reader, Jemma (Yes! The same one from the dedication). Without her support and encouragement this book never would have existed.

Next I'd like to thank my earliest readers and dear friends, Dani, Douglas, and Kadda. Their input was invaluable.

The designer of the cover, Jamie, from thenobleartist.com, gave me one of my favorite moments so far as a new author. I will never forget how he took the vague descriptions I gave him and turned it into the artistry that graces the cover. I watched him sketch it out in real time, mouth agape and jealous of his artistry. Please check out his amazing work!

Carley's editorial work on the first draft helped me see the book's initial flaws as areas of potential instead. Without the sharp eyes of Simon, Allie, and Brandon the text would be riddled with typos and missing words. They helped to polish down the book's rough edges to create a tome of which I am proud.

Last, but certainly not least, I want to thank my PR manager Sarah for helping build the machine that lets me get my books out there and for showing me how best to call out into the night.

About the author

A lifelong reader, gamer, and dreamer, M. T. Kadisin finally stopped saying he wanted to write a novel and just did it already. When he isn't sitting at his computer making the keys go click-clack, he loves cooking for his family and painting little army men. He lives in the Hudson Valley, New York, with his wife, his daughter, and his blop-tongued dog.

WHERE TO FIND MORE

Please visit our website and sign up for the newsletter for updates on the sequel, Kadisin's musings, and maybe a few dog pictures at mtkadisin.com You can also follow us on Facebook and Instagram as M. T. Kadisin and @KrakenTree on Youtube.